KALLYN JONES

KICK BACK

A LATER IN LIFE ROMANCE

OAKVILLE OBSESSIONS
BOOK TWO

KALLYN JONES

To the twice-blessed widow (and widower). You know the unquenchable pain of loss and the elation of finding love again. You stood in the gap for your family, making sure needs were met and a memory was honored. Somewhere along the way you opened your heart and found another life partner. You are my hero.

I FEEL THE EARTH MOVE

THOMAS

A perfect autumn day for Thomas Harrison involved time outside on his property, the sun illuminating leaves at their peak of color, his new lady, and a tightly formed pattern of bullet holes in a target. He would accept three of the four.

"Open. Your. Eyes." Thomas said through a tight jaw, his patience thinning with his love, Kick McKenna, though he'd never admit it. Kick's opinion regarding beginner's luck on the shooting range the other day turned out to be right. It was their third time practicing with his handguns, and he swore she made the bullets curve around a target.

It looked like more than a mental block to Thomas. He caught the flashes of panic Kick tried to hide since her coffeehouse had been attacked on Halloween. She couldn't shake her fear and soldier on when at the shooting range.

Kick set the empty Glock on the bench, the dummy sporting a few new holes—for some reason most were in the arm area. One bullet had landed in the intestinal region while the rest punished the trees behind it.

"I flinched."

And then some. "Yes."

"Why are we doing this again? I have faith in you, Banger's team, and the police." Kick muttered something else under her breath that Thomas didn't catch.

Thomas leaned against the bench, folding his arms. "I can't stay with you all the time. None of us can. It's driving me crazy. So I'm making damned sure you can hold your own if somebody comes after y'all again."

"You think there'll be an again?"

Thomas reached for Kick's hand and stroked it with his thumb. "What's going on?"

She took a step back and crossed her own arms, squeezing the biceps until her fingertips blanched.

"The first afternoon was exhilarating. New." Kick stared at the dummy. "When I look at the target now, I see Jonn Graham's face. As mad as I am, I can't kill him."

"Well, hell, baby." Thomas stepped closer to Kick. "I can change the target from a body to a bull's-eye." He drew Kick into his arms, absorbing as much strength and affection as he gave. Her tenacity still held. He should've known she'd struggle with the identity of her harasser. A part of her saw every young customer with a mother's eyes.

If Thomas was honest with himself, he'd admit he sensed the boogeyman making his neck hairs tingle. The feeling of *when* not *if* things would escalate kept his jaw clenched at night and sore during the day.

"I've missed this," he whispered into Kick's ear. A quick hug and kiss on the temple hadn't been a proper greeting, and he knew it. They'd rushed to their shooting lesson when she arrived. Banger was due in an hour with an update on his investigation. The Oakville PD stayed stuck in hands-tied mode, and Thomas required the answers that only Banger's security wizardry could provide.

"I've missed *you*," Kick returned. "I haven't slept well since… we were together." She bit her lip and looked away.

"Yeah," he said, his gaze fixed over Kick's head, watching ducks paddle in the back pond. "Same here darlin'."

"I don't want to shoot anymore. It feels too serious now, and a target change won't make a difference."

Thomas frowned. "This is *serious*, Kick. The night we met, your coffeehouse had an attempted break-in and was vandalized. Then someone threw a brick into Hugh's window. Yes, I think it's related. Later, your squawk box was damaged. All *before* the Halloween attack. There's been a media campaign against you. I don't like the online harassment of your daughter any more than y'all do." Kick shivered at his last comment, and Thomas gave her a squeeze. The Rachel issue had always bothered her the most. "Think of this as part of your self-defense lesson and another way to take care of your health."

Kick chuckled. "That was low." After a thoughtful pause, words tiptoed out. "Why are you trying to scare me?"

Thomas lowered his voice. "If you're just now frightened, you haven't been paying attention." He ran a hand through his hair and around his neck. "Want me to settle down? Prove to me you can handle yourself when I'm not around."

Kick stepped back with a stomp and wrapped her fingers around her neck. Her skin heated neither from a blush nor embarrassment. Thomas had pissed her off. Good.

"You can't be serious," she growled. "*Handle* myself when *you're* not around? Where the hell were you when I had to tell my children their daddy wouldn't watch any of them go to prom, graduate, or get married? Where were you the first time I got seriously sick after the funeral and still dragged my ass out of bed to take the little ones to school and practices, fighting a fatigue so deep I was afraid I might fall asleep at the wheel?"

Her body vibrated with fury, but Thomas didn't regret waking her up even if he'd insulted her.

"You think Jonn Graham is the first kid I've had to throw out of my store? Hell, Thomas, I'd been *handling* myself for eight long years before you came along." Kick tipped her head back and looked up at the clear sky, her hands planted on her hips. "Longer when you consider the twenty years it took me to get a fecking autoimmune diagnosis. There were times it felt like no one believed me."

Kick turned and frowned when her eyes landed on Thomas's smile. "What the hell's so funny?"

He lifted his chin. "Not laughing, baby. It's good to see your fire back."

"You tricked me?"

Thomas raised his hands and shook his head harder. "Not at all. Unfortunately, I'm an idiot, but your demeanor has had my nerves on edge as much as the idea of someone hurting y'all. So I put my size twelve in my mouth."

He dipped his knees, ducking his head to meet Kick's gaze. "Graham is more than an annoying kid. Since his father's lawyers shut down the boy's questioning, we still don't know why y'all were targeted. So, you can learn to use these"—he pointed at the guns on the table—"or you can accept the bodyguard offer." Staring at the guns, his mind went back to their first session. "The boys are eating this up. If you think I'm overprotective and pushy, how do you think *they'll* act if you stop?"

"Jaysus." Kick stared at her boots. The breeze blew several curls into her face. She finally straightened her spine and took several deep breaths while flexing her fingers. "Let's do this."

Thomas picked up the empty Sig Sauer—he had her working with his Glock, Sig, and Colt revolver until she picked one to keep—and passed it to her. "First, your stance is straight and loose, and your grip is perfect. So, keep those going. Second, practice firing the empty gun. Watch it work as you pull the trigger. Observe it from different angles as you point it forward. Then get back to targeting. Convince your brain to keep the target in your sights. Without bullets, it'll be easier."

"It'll make you feel better if I get this?" She stepped up to the bench and blew a curl off her face. "It should make *you* feel better." Thomas pressed up against Kick's back, moved her hair out of the way, and kissed her neck. "Can't deny seeing you like this turns me on though." He made sure she felt his desire against her fine ass.

"Okay then," she breathed, tossing a flirty smile over her shoulder.

He backed away as she reached for the Sig. "Work on my suggestions while I run up to the house. I have another idea."

Kick stood stock-still, staring down at the weapon, her tongue worrying her cheek.

"Kick?" he asked. He was getting familiar with her tells and guessed something else bothered her.

Her head stayed bent as she asked, "Since we're clearing the air and I want to clear my thoughts… When Banger comes… will Tess be with him?"

Thomas exhaled a weary breath. Appeasing Kick's insecurities in the past week might have been harder than handling her fears with the guns. "Doubt it. But it wouldn't matter if she was. She's like family, darlin'. Hell, when I went to Bordeaux last month, I stayed in their suite."

"You're not helping," she said through gritted teeth.

"I stay there because I've been more or less adopted by them."

"And you've never been with"—Kick pointed her finger at his chest—"or even had a crush on Tess?"

Thomas shuddered at the thought. He wasn't kidding about her being family. It had never crossed his mind, though he couldn't tell Kick why. "I swear."

Kick lifted her eyes. "Does she know this, Thomas? Because

Tess was awfully familiar and downright possessive of you when she showed up at lunch."

Again, family. To Tess, Thomas was another kid, like Banger, but he had to keep his damn mouth shut.

"Hey." Thomas pulled Kick in for another hug. Her lower lip gave the slightest wobble. "I think you're confusing protective instincts with possession. It looked to me like you surprised Tess as much as she did you. He rubbed Kick's back. "Where's this coming from?"

"Are you kidding?" Kick almost looked angry. "Tess is gorgeous, young, and happy-go-lucky. I'm a mess, old, and have all this"—she pointed to the guns on the table—"shit happening." She sighed and stepped away, digging her fingers into her scalp. "It's too much for me. If it's too much for you, I'd rather you bail now, then…"

Thomas's laughing stopped Kick in her tracks. He had never wanted to spill the whole truth so badly. *He was afraid she knew too much already.* As Kick's brow drew into a deep furrow, Thomas quieted and raised his shoulders. "You don't see what I see."

"And what is that, exactly?"

Christ, he needed to get her safe. He longed to see more smiles on her face. "Maybe you've cast a spell on me." His fingers brushed her pointy ears, currently showing between the loose curls falling out of her barrette. "You're an elven queen after all."

Kick swatted his shoulder and scowled. "I'm serious."

"Fine." Thomas schooled his features and gave serious thought to why he was drawn to Kick. "You're smart. You care deeply. You're f—"

"Don't you dare say fierce. I'm not special. I do what I need to do to make it to the next day and hopefully, the next year."

Thomas reached toward her. "*That* is the definition of a fighter. Please let this Tess thing go. She'll probably jet off to Bali as soon as some mystic invites her to his retreat." He wrapped his arm around Kick's shoulders. "I'm not going anywhere, baby. Not sure what we're doing, precisely. I damn sure want to see where it goes though. Alright?"

"Sure."

"Something needs to be done about your stress," Thomas murmured.

Kick tapped his ass. "I have an idea or two."

The smack did more than get Thomas's attention. It made his skin hum, going straight to his cock. He shifted his hips to fix the tightness while taking note of the buzz. As gorgeous as the day was, he couldn't wait for the night to begin. He'd planned the perfect evening for them. Business first though.

He took a deep breath and stepped back, picking up the Sig again. "Dry fire this while I run up to the house. The sooner we're done, the sooner you can show me those *ideas*." He waggled his brows and grinned.

"Right, handsome." She kissed his chin and took the weapon.

Thomas walked backward a few paces, rubbing his chin. Kick kept fussing over the cleft like it had magical powers. Not that he minded the attention. He'd soon get to pay attention to the parts of her he enjoyed.

He watched Kick at the bench for a beat. Her stance still looked good. *Too* good in her moto boots and dark jeans, curving in all the right places. The denim jacket with the Celtic butterfly on the back ended at her waist, highlighting her exquisite ass. Her straight spine and lowered shoulders highlighted her graceful neck. Relief washed through him, seeing the fiery woman he'd first noticed still in there.

Yeah, her courage wasn't going anywhere. Kick may need to wear the "happy armor" around her crew, but the warrior was still inside. If he ever got a chance at Jonn Graham for doing this? At least he had Banger on standby to take care of the body.

Thomas smiled and called out, "You got this, baby. Remember your breath. Be right back."

Kick let her hair sway out of the way as she adjusted her stance. She eyed the gun and said, "I'll be here."

THOMAS CLEARED THE TOP OF THE TRAIL FROM THE HOUSE, carrying an airsoft gun. He figured lightening the recoil and removing the "danger factor" would help Kick acclimate to the act of shooting. He heard Kick before he saw her.

"*What's* over, Snow?" Kick was talking to her daughter on her cell phone, pacing the worn earth in front of the firing range. "You haven't flushed four years down the toilet. ... But you're only twenty-one."

She pulled the phone away from her ear, flinching at the female sobs coming from the speaker. "Hold on a sec, Snow." Kick set the phone next to the Sig and quietly did a happy dance. Thomas rarely watched football, but he knew what a touchdown performance looked like. This rivaled the elaborate ones.

Kick took a cleansing breath and picked the phone back up, mouthing "Rachel" to Thomas. "Okay. Thomas is back. No, it's fine. ... No, I never hated Cody." She rolled her eyes. "I've watched you two grow apart for a while though."

Kick's shoulders slumped, and she squeezed the bridge of her nose. "You do?" No two words had ever held more disappointment in them. "Of course you can come home. Lee's out for the evening, so it'll be you and Macushla. She'll be thrilled for the snuggle time. ... Sweetie, I can't understand. ... That's the electrical issue. Do what I showed you."

Kick stared at Thomas, her face scrunched as if on the verge of tears. Her head dropped, her posture both exasperated and resolved. In a small voice, she said, "Be there in an hour. ... It... it's fine. ... Love you too."

Kick let the phone fall from her hand to the table. She leaned her weight against the edge as Thomas approached, wrapping his arms around her once again. He began to think his main purpose in their relationship was to make up for Kick's dearth of hugs. She responded to each one like it was a transfusion.

"I'm sorry, but I have to go."

He buried his face in Kick's neck. "What happened to Rachel?"

"She broke up with Cody, the Boy Wander."

Thomas raised an eyebrow in question. "Pardon?" He wasn't sure if he'd heard her right.

"Yes. Rach caught her boyfriend cheating. Wouldn't surprise me if he's made a habit of it."

"We'll clean this up and go."

Kick placed her hand on Thomas's chest. "It'll be better for Rachel if it's only me. Besides, Banger's coming by."

"He could meet us at your house. Then I can look at Rachel's car."

Kick reached up to his neck and pulled Thomas's mouth to hers. He liked how their kisses were becoming common. "I've already planned to take the car to our mechanic over her Thanksgiving break. If it's truly dead, I'll have it towed next week. Besides, you have enough on your plate right now. I'm sorry, handsome."

"I see." A term for the McKenna children began forming in his head, something like the *McCock-blockers*. He wouldn't take it out on their mother though. Hell, he regularly dropped everything for his family *and* the Felidae. He'd be damned if he let his libido drive his emotions all because Kick had responsibilities too. "You can't stay to talk to Banger?"

"Cody's apartment—and more importantly, his bedroom—is directly over Rachel's. She can hear them going at it." Kick laced her fingers behind her neck and stretched. "Hell. I want to hear what Banger has to say."

Tempted to ask if there weren't any coffee shops the girl could escape to, Thomas held his tongue, fearing Kick would jump on him in defense. Focusing on an understanding attitude seemed like the best route to go for both women. "Do you think she'd be alright if Bang and I brought dinner over? He could fill us in afterward, in private. Would that give Rachel enough time to settle?"

Guilt tried to wash over him for being a selfish bastard when a daughter needed her mother, but Thomas pushed it down. He couldn't shake the niggling feeling Kick's safety was on the line, as well as her family's.

Kick's eyes glistened as she raised her hand and cupped Thomas's jaw, catching him by surprise. "Where have you been all this time? Dinner would be wonderful." She stood on her toes and pressed a slow kiss to his lips. "Once she calms down, she'll probably study in her room. Still, I don't think they're ready for—"

"Me staying the night." He deepened the kiss before letting Kick go. He didn't mind so much either. A part of Thomas thought of the house as Kick's late husband Shane's. Thomas didn't know if he'd be comfortable staying there, especially with two of the children at home. He'd lived as a bachelor for too long.

Another lingering kiss and Kick ran off to rescue her daughter in distress. And she accused *him* of having a hero complex?

"LOOKING PRETTY, BROTHER." BANGER SNIFFED IN THOMAS'S direction, walking into the kitchen. "Mmm. You smell like heaven too." He teased with a Cheshire cat grin, peering around Thomas's shoulder. "Where's Kick? Is she up in the bathroom?"

"What?" Thomas started when he heard his friend's words, then walked into the kitchen to get a beer. He wore only jeans and a new button-down, his hair still damp from a shower. He flexed his hand to keep from hitting the wall. "Dammit all. I forgot to call. Knew I was forgetting something." He'd been more upset than he let on with Kick. He'd worked off his frustration with a hard weight session, losing track of time.

Banger checked his phone. "Nope. No calls. What's wrong? Where's Kick? I assumed you were"—he waved his hands in Thomas's direction—"otherwise *occupied* until the last minute."

"In my workout room, not my bedroom." Thomas sighed.

Banger lifted an eyebrow. "You dumped her already?"

"What? No. Her daughter called with an emergency."

"Ah, the little princess."

"Sure." Thomas couldn't remember the last time he'd felt so vulnerable, like he wore it underneath his shirt. It irritated him.

"Are we still meeting?" Banger asked.

"Right. Shit." Thomas opened the fridge and grabbed two IPAs, offering one to his friend. "I'm sorry, man. I meant to call and see if we could meet at Kick's house. I told her I'd get dinner while she gets Rachel settled."

Banger rubbed his lower lip. "It could work. I'm supposed to take Tess to dinner after this. Let's call her and have her meet us at Chez McKenna. I'd appreciate diffusing Tess's undivided focus for an evening."

Thomas tipped back the bottle. Would more time around Tess help Kick or make things worse? He took a long pull and decided. Tess was family and Kick spending time with her would convince her. "I like it. I'll check with Kick and make sure it'll work. Then you can call Tess. Sorry again for wasting your time. Maybe you could help me with the security update on my computer while I finish getting ready?"

Banger sighed dramatically as he fell into step on the way to Thomas's office. "I knew you were only using me for my brilliant mind." He sat in the tall desk chair. "This helps me too, brother. I want to talk to you about something."

"A Felidae something?" Thomas sat in a wingback chair across from the desk.

"Sort of."

"Well?" Thomas finished the beer and set it on the side table near his guitar stand.

"Fine. What the fuck's wrong with you?" Banger surprised Thomas with his change in attitude.

"Excuse me?"

"The last time we spoke alone, I thought you'd decided to cool it with Kick. Next thing I know, she's spending the night—not that I'd blame you. But the lessons and children and problem fixing and… and *cologne*."

"Is it too strong? I don't want to aggravate any of Kick's allergies."

"*Jeeves Crimmins*! Since when do you care about fucking allergies?"

Thomas tapped a finger on the beer bottle. "It's not a bad idea. Maybe we should pay more attention to the immune system in the lab." Research ideas popped into his head at the oddest times. He wished he'd brought his phone down from the bathroom and looked around for a piece of paper to write it down on, further distancing himself from Banger's lecture.

Since becoming a professor, he no longer tolerated dating younger women. In his rule book, they were now students or mentees, and he wouldn't cross the line.

"Are you even listening?" Banger pressed his mouth together as he waited for Thomas to signal he was. He jabbed the air with his index finger and declared, "You're hooked, brother. I told you not to let her reel you in, and you let her anyway."

Thomas shrugged. "I recall the words 'do something new.' I am."

"I suggested you buy a new fucking car. Or get a new hobby. But you won't let anything go. How old is your Camaro anyway? You look at Kick the same way you look at your car though. Don't you ever miss new-car smell?"

"Christ, you're all over the place. You'd think I was threatening *your* happiness." Thomas leaned toward his friend. "My Camaro is mint, and it's better for the planet than buying a new one would be. Now, I don't know what's going to happen with

Kick. Presently, she's good for my soul. No one's made promises, and I certainly don't have any intentions to. As for a hobby, I told you I was looking at places to board my horse Eddie. He'll keep me busy soon enough. Maybe we should find a horse for you too."

"Mmphf." Banger grunted. "I never had to get up before sunrise to water a motorcycle. I'll stick with them. Besides, *how* is an ancient muscle car good for the environment?"

"The Camaro's regularly updated. Carbon emissions from making a new one outweigh the lifetime footprint of any vehicle."

Banger rubbed his lower lip. "Is that true?"

Thomas waved his fingers. "*Hello*. Scientist." He stood, deciding he was done with Banger's counsel. "Like I said the other day, I'm tired of the usual dating scene. Kick makes me feel like myself again, but it's still casual. However, it would be *exceptionally* nice to sort out this harassment of her so she and I can see what a simple relationship looks like."

Banger nodded, then shook his head. "Fine. But I don't see how anything regarding Kick McKenna is simple." Banger cut off Thomas's response, saying, "Finish getting dressed, you bumpkin. I'll get your update going and call Tess."

"Thanks, man. I don't know why I couldn't get it to work last night." When he was halfway up the stairs, the ringtone from the house in Virginia shrilled from the bathroom. Thomas ran the rest of the way to catch it.

2

WHY WORRY?

KICK

"*H*ello handsome." I threw open the front door without checking the sidelight.

Tess smiled brightly. "I don't think I've ever received that particular compliment. I simply *love* history-making days."

I hoped my face didn't blanch along with my obvious wince. Then again, with my pasty complexion, who would know? It was no match for the olive-skin, perma-tanned beauty standing before me. "I'm sorry, Tess. I thought you were Thomas." Taking a step back, I welcomed her into my house, giving her a quick hug with air kisses.

She whispered in my ear, "It's fine, dear. I'm thrilled to see Thomas taking an interest in someone more..." She looked me up and down and shrugged. "Well, more."

Dear? Was I entering the circular stage of adulthood where young women speak to their elders like they are children? I thought I had a decade or more to prepare.

I placed Tess's jacket on Dylan's hook in the mudroom and

showed her around the first floor before putting the kettle on. Rachel padded into the kitchen, her head on her tablet. "Did I hear dinner arrive?"

She stopped short at the bar where Tess sat. "Oh, hello. I thought you were Thomas."

"That seems to be going around lately." Tess lit up as she perused Rachel and turned to me. "This must be your daughter?"

"Yes," I answered. "This is Rachel. Sweetheart, meet Tess McHenry. She's Banger's sister."

Tess violently flinched at the mention of Banger's name and said, "It's Tess Sanchez, darling."

"Oh, my apologies. You and Banger don't have the same father?"

Tess jolted again, as if Banger's name physically hurt her. I then remembered Tess had called him "Rafael" when Thomas first introduced her in his dining room. Maybe she didn't like his nickname? He clearly hated being referred to by what I assumed was his given name, not that I'd ever thought his parents had named him Banger. I felt a bit of kinship with the man, guessing we might have similar family dynamics.

"We don't." Tess abruptly changed the subject, turning to Rachel and wrapping her arms around her. "Delighted to meet you." She sat back and declared, "You're stunning."

Rachel dipped her head. The redness in her face had eased while a touch of puffiness lingered from her tears. She had been a mess when I picked her up, and she'd cried on and off the entire drive up to our house, breaking my heart into countless pieces. Her voice cracked as she said, "Thank you. So are you."

"Aren't you a doll? Tess held Rachel's chin and turned her head left and right. "You must take after your father. Though the curls could be from your mother."

I wanted to jump up and down or wave my hand in front of her face and yell, "Hello, mother in the room." *Jaysus*, was I becoming invisible too? I'd heard about how menopause made women disappear, especially to the young. Thanks to my surgery a while back, I couldn't be certain when this infamous time would descend upon me, but I guessed it was close.

Rachel answered with a light chin tip and a half smile. She'd always loved being called the "female version" of Shane, since they shared the same raven hair, ocean-blue irises, and a single dimple. Aside from the curls, she'd outwardly only received my nose, which looked like a cute button on her. On me, it disappeared. Maybe I was becoming invisible. I hoped I could use the power for good, though doing evil sounded fun too.

"Do you model?" Tess asked, still assessing.

Rachel lifted a shoulder. "Occasionally. I'm studying to be an actress and such."

"She plans to go to Broadway," I added, proud of her ambition and talent, if not also terrified for her.

"Ooh, I see it." Tess beamed. Then her lip formed a pout. "You've been crying, haven't you?"

Rachel's eyes shimmered as she nodded. Another tear slipped out, racing down her cheek.

"Oh my darling, come." Tess wrapped her in a big hug. "I can tell this is about a boy. No one knows more about messy relationships than I do."

I blew a curl off my cheek and worked on our tea. Part of me had had enough. My baby needed *me*, not this interloper. Who was Tess anyway? Something was odd about the way she and Banger never came right out and said they were siblings. If they didn't have similar strawberry hair and strong cheekbones, I would have doubted they were related or assumed one was adopted. Except they also carried themselves in an aristocratic manner, despite Tess's exuberance and Banger's sharp broodiness.

"How old are you?" Tess asked.

"Twenty-one."

"Pfft." She waved off Rachel's answer. "You're too young to settle with a boy. We *are* talking about a boy, right?"

If you asked me, Cody Dalton would always be a boy. Rachel simply dropped her head in acknowledgment.

"Do you even know what you want? What if it's not a man at all?"

My eyes flashed wide, watching Rachel blush. *There* was something I hadn't considered, though Tess had a point. My daughter had plenty of time to explore what life offered her. I hoped she had her fill before she settled down and wished like hell she never "settled" when she did.

That sent my thoughts toward my oldest, making a mental note to check on Dylan's relationship. He had informed me that my suspicions of an impending pregnancy were wrong, thank goodness. But practically every minute of my days since the Halloween attack on the Perked Cup had been focused on the investigation. I had no idea if his relationship with Suzy had improved.

I distributed the three mugs of tea and took a sip of mine, thinking of the next morning. After a long two months, which seemed like years, thanks to this crazy autumn, I'd be able to add decaffeinated coffee back into my diet. Finally the barista could partake of her product again, albeit caffeine-free. I had to survive the entire holiday season before the full moratorium was lifted. I dreaded planning the Thanksgiving menu.

The girls, as I now thought of them, lost themselves in conversation, so I headed over to the garage and dug out two containers of salted caramel cashew cream from the deep freezer. I figured we could do dessert first while we waited on the men, and girls in the movies always ate ice cream after a breakup. Since Rachel and I didn't eat dairy, this would do.

As I padded back to the kitchen, I overheard Tess ask, "You know you can live without him, right?" I bit my lip to keep from scoffing but rolled my eyes.

Did Tess think she was being wise? Rachel knew about life moving on better than most girls her age. Her dad had been our world. Shane had certainly filled mine. I shattered—Hell, we all shattered when he died. But we found a way to move on as a foursome. For the first five years, it took all my energy to put one foot in front of the other, feeling like I wore cement shoes as I did it.

Rachel's voice broke. "I do. It just… feels weird, you know? I thought life would be one way, and now it's not."

Tell me about it, kid. I placed the containers in the microwave and set it for thirty seconds so it could be scooped.

"Now darling, you're only at the starting line of life." Tess patted Rachel's hand, then rubbed her bicep to soothe my daughter. Why was the woman so touchy? She'd been the same way the afternoon she showed up at Thomas's. She'd been overly familiar with him and wouldn't have surprised me if she'd grabbed his ass.

"Would anyone like some cashew cream while we wait for dinner?" I asked.

"Salted caramel?" Rachel asked. "It's my favorite."

"Which is why I buy out the store when it goes on sale."

"Cashew?" Tess asked, scrunching her nose. "Not ice cream or gelato?"

Rachel saved me from growling. Her face lit up, and she leaned toward Tess. "Mama and I can't have dairy. But you *must* try it. It's hype. I like it better, to be honest."

Tess tipped her head to the side as if she were deciphering my daughter's slang. I watched, waiting to see if she sought any clarification. Instead, she smiled and said, "Lovely. I'll take some too, thank you, Kick." Tess's accent was the only thing I moderately liked about her so far. It didn't sound fully French, though Thomas had told me she lived at the estate in Bordeaux. Her accent sounded more Spanish to my ears, especially when she called me "Keek," the way my house manager, Carmen, did. It was a cute quirk. The revelation of her last name, Sanchez, helped seal my conclusion.

I scooped out the cashew cream and set the bowls next to the mugs.

Their conversation continued without me, so I jumped up on the kitchen counter—an old habit from when I was a kid—and ate my bowl as if I were invisible. Tess asked more detailed questions regarding Rachel's future plans. It turned out my daughter had auditioned for the Lost Colony summer theater company in the Outer Banks. That was news to me.

As the words and encouragement flowed between the two, my temperament grew surlier. The floodgates opened on my insecurities when it came to Thomas. Tess's faux wisdom had a point. If what he and I had started soured, I'd move on. I'd done it before, so I knew I could do it again. Therefore, the question mulling around presently was did I even want to take a chance again, knowing it could all be gone in a snap?

The frozen dessert had soured in my stomach, my hands had the jitters, and my chest felt squeezed, making breathing difficult. I checked to make sure no one noticed and slipped off the counter, quickly placing the bowl in the kitchen sink. I needed privacy before I made a fool of myself.

"Excuse me. I'll be..." I raced across the open space to my bedroom.

My rudeness went unnoticed though. I vaguely heard Tess ask Rachel, "Do you have supplies for a facial? They always help..."

I closed my door on girl time and paced my room. It smelled wonderful, not from the new construction—we'd used low-VOC materials besides having a whole-house HEPA filtration system. No, the suite smelled wonderful and settled me because it was finally mine. It wasn't that the ghost of Shane had been exorcised as much as he'd moved on, bringing both of us peace.

Except a current of questions flowed from me like a riptide, dragging me under. Everyone lives with the possibility of being alone. I mean, all relationships come to an end at some point. I didn't dare think of anything long-term with Thomas, so would it be better to stop before it started?

I moved into the bathroom, took a deep look in the mirror, and asked myself if I honestly thought I could keep my feelings for him in check. I suspected my near-panic attack rooted itself there. With relationships, I wasn't sure I possessed the keep-it-casual gene. Instead of a straightforward answer, my reflection stared back, clueless, sad. Scared.

I took a few more minutes in my meditation corner, sitting on the window bench, and traveled to the porch in my mind. This time it was attached to a pretty mountain home overlooking a river, the kind you wade into to fish. The solitude quieted my mind until there was certainty I could wear the robe of reality again. I figured disappointment sat at the core of my issues. My stress amped up on the gun range, then dove headfirst into mom mode to take care of Rachel. I'd been looking forward to Thomas's comforting presence all week, stuffing my stress, rolling it ahead to today. It hadn't been fair.

The past eight years had taught me to stand solidly on my own feet. The past few months even more so after my father's death. I couldn't throw that all away when a man came around offering a shoulder. I didn't want to either. I liked the woman who stood on her own power. A cleansing breath sealed the deal as I rose to those feet and left my bedroom, grateful for the time to get my shit together without the drama of dumping on Thomas.

The ladies had disappeared though. I looked around the first floor and only saw the dog sleeping in the recliner. Half a cucumber lay on the kitchen counter. A faint laugh told me Tess and Rachel were upstairs, probably in Rachel's bedroom.

The guys parked in front of my house as I was wrapping up the cucumber. I opened the front door to see Thomas approaching the steps, a large bag from Finnegan's Wake, my favorite neighborhood pub, in his hand.

"Mmm. Gimme. Gimme," I said, reaching for the bag.

Thomas grinned and held it behind his back, leaning in for a kiss. "Gimme first."

"Sure. Fine. Whatever," I returned, reaching my hand around his neck to bring his lips the rest of the way to mine.

Banger walked past us with a "Mmphf," holding a growler from Finn's.

I tipped my head in his direction and asked Thomas, "He okay?"

Thomas tracked Banger to the kitchen and turned back to me. "He's great. You heard a happy growl." Another quick kiss touched my cheek. "You'll get used to it. He's actually grateful y'all took Tess off his hands for a bit."

I blew a curl from my face and shrugged. "Wasn't me. Rachel's having a great time though."

"Really? That's fantastic."

I followed Thomas to the dining table and might have made a growling noise myself.

"Isn't it good?" He checked. "You're not still feeling weird about her, are you?"

"No," I answered, meaning it. Still, it stung to have someone else ease my daughter through her crisis, especially since I'd dropped everything to help her.

We sat around the messy dining table after finishing our meal. The fellas drank the IPA Banger picked up. The ladies opened one of my bottles of Malbec. I had club soda with lime. I sat back in my chair, content and happy to see leftovers for Liam, though he wouldn't be home until late. If I didn't know better, I'd swear Thomas bought one of each item on the menu.

My gaze moved to him and fuzzed out. *Jaysus.* I needed to tighten up, or I'd end up addicted to him. The man oozed care and competence without even trying. He made plans with Tess and Banger regarding the places she wanted to visit before she left for a retreat in Boone. The thoughtfulness in his eyes—currently bright gray—the way his cleft chin tipped as he searched his memory for unique places in the Triangle. It had me swoony, threatening to turn me into a lust ball, demanding everyone get out *now*!

Keep it together, Kick. I took a deep breath and suggested, "The art museum is currently running an exhibit of Frida Kahlo's work. Reviews of it have been quite favorable."

"Ooh, I loved her," Tess said. I found her response odd, as if she'd known the woman instead of the work, but I smiled in response.

"I do too. She's one of my faves. I've been meaning to see it."

"You have?" Thomas asked. I couldn't tell if his wheels were turning to plan a visit or if he was upset I hadn't said anything. Cyndi was my go-to museum buddy, so I hadn't thought about asking him about it until that moment.

"Yup. Well, until…" I waved my hand in the general direction of the Perked Cup. "I probably won't get over there until Christmas break now. Which reminds me, you're all invited for Thanksgiving dinner. I'm hosting and doing a big one before the kids scatter to points unknown. Deana's bringing her traditional dishes, so it won't be all my food—though I swear my stuff is tasty." I ended with a self-deprecating smirk. Years of putting up with my family's comments on my diet and cooking habits had trained me well. Thomas squeezed my hand at my words, the crinkles around his eyes giving me reassurance.

"Oh no. I don't know when I'll be back," Tess said, looking genuinely disappointed.

"I have plans as well, but thank you, Kick. It's nice to be considered," Banger added.

"Is this the only time I'll see you? It can't be," Rachel protested. "I was hoping to introduce you to my Gran." Thinking of how

Bobby would take Tess gave me the shivers. The woman could find fault with a heavenly angel.

"You'll see me again, darling." Tess reached toward Rachel and squeezed her hand. "Just maybe not for a little while." My daughter gave her a sad smile accented with a tiny pout. "We'll text and make phone dates as soon as my time at the ashram is over. It's a silent retreat."

"It sounds amazing." Rachel's sapphire irises glowed with admiration. I swear, the drama in this girl. She'd chosen her major well.

"Anyway," Thomas started. "I could come early. Joe called last night, and I plan to go up to Virginia for a late supper. He and Toni have early plans." He leaned in and murmured in my ear, "I could be your sous-chef." The idea made me want to float above the table. Naturally, I tamped it down, mentally stomping as hard as I could.

"Will you spend Christmas in Virginia or in Bordeaux this year?" Tess asked him. She knew his family then.

"I'll split my break between here and Virginia. I have a project I'm working on."

"Other than the research?" I asked.

"Yes."

I wondered if he'd have time for me but didn't want to bring it up in front of the others. Banger still gave me the feeling he didn't approve. I'd accepted he'd finally warmed to me, but I didn't think he liked the idea of *us*.

DREAM A LITTLE DREAM

KICK

I wiped down the dining room table, stretching my shoulders as I set everything to rights. They were sore from the combination of target practice and worry. Thomas and I finally found our alone time, more or less. Banger and Tess had left for a movie, and Rachel retreated to her room to finish a paper.

Banger, Thomas, and I had met in my office after dinner to go over updates on the Halloween attack while Tess hung out with Rachel a while longer. Avenging Angel Security—Banger's firm (now that I knew his given name was Rafael, it made me chuckle) —was still working on it. His best people hunted down strong leads. One of the security team members had "persuaded" a tattoo artist to admit he had recently done multiple insignia like it.

They were sure the person wearing the sapphire earring had been Jonn Graham, leaving me crestfallen. I accepted it in my heart too, but I hated the confirmation, hated the idea of someone I knew scaring so many children. Next to injuring one of my own children, it had to be the worst way possible to get to me. We all figured that was why he'd done it.

After that, I checked out. My chest grew tight again, making it painful to breathe. For a minute, I wondered if my food was cross-contaminated, but Thomas had assured me he'd let the staff know my order was specific for me. Stress caused me to struggle again.

In the end, I had let Banger's resolve and Thomas's reassuring tone lull me into a sense of security and forced the rest to roll off my back.

I snapped my cleaning rag, dropped the sponge on it, and wiped my brow with my sleeve. Thomas stared at me from across the space, coming from the guest bath. He dipped his chin and stalked directly to me. My half smile sped him up. He moved on me until my back hit the island counter.

I gasped. "Do you want more food?"

"No. I'm stuffed from supper."

Holy hell, his eyes had turned to navy and his brows drew together. I didn't know his lust face well yet—it was too dark when we were together—but we'd done enough for me to guess this was it.

My words came out breathy. "Then why are you looking at me like I'm a grass-fed, medium-rare filet with sautéed mushrooms on top?"

"Am I?" His mouth hovered over my ear. "You *are* rare."

My breath strangled delightfully. Then he stepped into me, pressing our bodies together. I rested my head against his chest and let myself relax.

"I've been wanting to do this all evening. I'd hoped Banger's update would ease your mind. Rachel seems better. So why do you look like someone kicked your dog?"

"Oh." I waved off the question. "It's stupid. Let's go find a movie." I moved to take a step toward the living area. His hands locked around my biceps, keeping me in place. "Would you like a whiskey?" Another round of deflection.

"No, Kick. Tell me what's going on. I won't think it's stupid."

I took two ragged breaths and steadied my temper on the third. If Thomas hadn't been around, I might have lost it. "I dropped our plans to rescue Rachel, but it was Tess she needed. Hell, once they got to talking, I was invisible. I put her before you for nothing."

Thomas set me on the counter and stepped between my knees, allowing him to hold me close and meet my gaze. "Is there more?"

"As I drove to Snow's place, I had flashes of girl time, giving her motherly wisdom, being needed. Tess bogarted it all—nice as she was—and there was the problem."

Thomas blinked and shifted his head left and right, letting me know he didn't comprehend.

I blurted on a deep exhale, "I thought I was ready for an empty nest, okay? Hell, I have all kinds of plans for when Liam goes to school. I figure I'll finally have the time required to truly feel better, you know."

"Among other things."

"Right? Lately I don't know. Every day leads to a series of lasts I'm not sure I'm ready for after all. In September, Liam had his last Homecoming, but it was mine too." I paused a beat, letting my words sink in. "Like I said, it's silly."

Thomas pressed me to him this time. My legs squeezed his waist, clinging like a koala. It felt... too good. Not for the lust factor but for the way his whole body and soul settled mine.

"Christ," he muttered and stepped back, running his hands through his hair. "Here I wanted to thank you for sharing your daughter today."

"You did?"

He nodded. "Yep. Tess is a natural nurturer. She thrives on it.

Kind of like you." He chuckled. "She drives Banger nuts with it, but I think she's lonely."

"Then why doesn't she have her own kid?" I grumbled.

"It's… complicated."

Aw, hell. I'd lived long enough to learn to not judge someone's parental status. Looking fit and fertile didn't mean everything was copacetic on the inside. For all my health issues, I'd managed to make three healthy babies, but assuming others could was a huge mistake.

He pressed a long kiss to my forehead. "Maybe you could rest easier now? No one will ever replace you as Rachel's mother."

"No, but you and I still didn't get our day."

"I'm here now. We'll have more too. Soon."

I agreed, smiling with new resolve. He'd said some things I already knew and all the things I needed to hear.

WE TOOK A WALK TO STRETCH OUR LEGS AND ALLOW MACUSHLA TO burn up some energy before bed. Liam was supposed to have run with her earlier, but he'd had a band emergency. Already filled to the brim with drama, I didn't fuss at him. When we returned, I changed into lounge pants, a tank, and a waterfall cardigan as a reward for making it through the day. I made popcorn, drizzling it with melted ghee and nutritional yeast to make it "cheesy." We settled on the living room sectional with the bowl and drinks, watching *Tombstone*. We'd discovered we both loved the version with Kurt Russell and Val Kilmer, et al., while strolling the neighborhood.

During the opening credits, I turned to Thomas. "There are a couple more events I'd like to talk to you about."

"What's up?"

"Well, Liam's birthday is next weekend. We're having a party at the Perked Cup so his band can play. I was hoping you might like to go?"

"I'd love to." He flashed me a shy grin. "Are you sure he wants me there? Who else is coming?"

"Lee does." I tapped my chin. "As far as grown-ups go, the regulars will be there. The café will be about half his friends and half adults."

"Sounds great. What else?"

"Well… do you usually attend the Winter Gala at Lord University?"

Thomas wrinkled his nose. "The stuffy dinner where faculty is supposed to mingle with the old-money blowhard donors, then they give speeches about the amazing things they've done together?"

I swallowed a suddenly dry lump in my throat. "That's the one."

"What about it? Are you going?"

I gave him a sheepish grin and wiggled my fingers. "I fall into the blowhard donor category of your scenario. Though I'm not old-money."

"You?" Thomas's brow furrowed, incredulous. I almost laughed.

"Remember when I told you about the McKenna Family Foundation?"

"Oh shit. Right."

Reluctant and nervous, I sighed and said, "I'm giving our speech this year. I could use a friend in the audience if you wouldn't mind."

"Mind? I'd be honored. I'm sorry I sounded like a spoilsport." The hand wrapped around my shoulder rubbed my arm. "Have you done this before? I've only been once, but I don't remember you being there." Thomas's fingers traveled to the tip of my ear, and he smiled. "I would've noticed."

I shivered from the contact, not knowing what to make of his appreciation of a feature of mine I'd always associated with yet another genetic failure. "It's been a while. Even in good years,

December tends to be a hard month for me, so Dad and Dylan were probably there when you attended. They've always been the speakers too. Dad could charm the room by simply standing at the podium and smiling. And don't get me started on my son. Women trip over themselves to talk to Dylan. He inherited the art of speaking from his father and grandfather. Anyhoo, Dylan has an event the same night, and Dad… well. It's up to me now."

"I'd love to escort you. Thanks for asking. You don't want me to speak, do you? As a faculty member, I'm not sure it's protocol."

"No, no. My foundation manager and I are working on a speech. Thanks, sweets. I'll get comfortable with it after some practice. Having a handsome face to find in the audience will help more than you know."

"Happy to oblige." He squeezed my shoulders. "Any more upcoming command performances for me?"

I smiled at his snark. Teasing Thomas was a hell of a lot of fun. He also had a brilliant smile—often reminding me of a middle school boy with a dirty secret. "Nope." I set the empty bowl of popcorn on the coffee table, and Thomas grabbed me before I could settle back in my previous spot. "What are—"

He arranged us spooning on the sofa with me in the front. He pulled the quilt off the back and spread it over us. "Your arm candy wants a better snuggle."

I chuckled at his joke and happily settled in. We stayed that way for a long while, saying our favorite lines from the movie while his hand absently explored my belly. The simple gesture would be the highlight of my day, relaxing with a brilliant, devilishly handsome man who mysteriously found me interesting enough to hang out with too. It was fun, natural, and terrifying.

Eventually his hand worked its way under my tank, grazing my breast. "Mmm. Way better. Thought I caught the telltale signs of bralessness."

I looked over my shoulder and smirked. "You make it sound illegal."

"Never." He deliciously rumbled into my ear, "It should be required." His hand alternated between massage and rolling my nipple between his fingers, setting off my arousal meter.

"Thomas, you know we can't—"

"Shh," he whispered in my ear before lightly touching the tip with his tongue. "Don't worry. Promise we won't put on a show. Relax, baby." His strokes slowed down and lengthened until I followed his command. As my breathing synced with his, my eyes nearly rolled back into my head, lost to the bliss of Thomas's touch. "Your body drives me crazy."

Chuckling at the sentiment, I almost reminded Thomas he hadn't really seen anything yet, between the dark and currently being under the blanket. Words scrambled in my lust-fuzzed out brain though, dissolving them into a mix of moans and hisses.

Thomas rolled me toward him, his hand thus drifting under the waistband of my pants. His irises flashed a midnight blue now, and he made his own buttery gasp at his discovery. "No underwear, Kick?"

I managed a throaty, "I take lounging seriously," eliciting a toe-curling, rumbly laugh from the man rocking against me.

Taking advantage of my new position, my hand meandered into Thomas's sweatpants, finding him equally commando. When I'd declared my desire to get cozy on our walk, he told me he kept a gym bag in his trunk, then joined me in the comfy-fest with Adidas sweats and an LU T-shirt. "Great minds think alike?" I asked, running my hand along his length from tip to base and back.

Thomas did his best to pull away. "No. Not me. Not now."

"But—"

"I have to wear these home. Don't want a mess."

"Don't you have shorts in your bag?"

"Kick," he warned. The middle school boy spark on his face died for a moment, and I almost apologized. For what, I didn't know. I just wanted the moment back.

"Please. Let me..." He finished his thought with a deep kiss, his tongue diving in for a taste, a dance, hell, a swim. My brain officially scrambled. His mouth traveled down my neck and settled at my collarbone. All thoughts and words surrendered to wonderfully electric sensations. His fingers resumed their pursuit of my pleasure, making the current grow until I vibrated with my release.

Each breath puffed through my nose and gritted teeth as I fought a fierce battle between the need to let go and the impending scream I feared would accompany it. Thomas fixed my dilemma by kissing me again, capturing my moans with his mouth.

I was trying to remember how to inhale and exhale when the front door flew open.

"Yo doggo." Liam greeted Macushla, whose nails did a tap dance on the tiles in the foyer.

My eyes flashed to Thomas as my heart took a roller-coaster dive. The handsome bastard winked, mouthed a shushing noise, then grinned at me like he'd won the biggest prize in the world. I narrowed my gaze and scowled. This wasn't funny. I didn't want to act like a teenager hiding from her parents—I paid the bills, after all—but it felt like it had done back then.

Thomas bit his lip to keep from laughing and snorted anyway, leading to a low chuckle.

"Fam?" Liam walked straight to us, though I knew he couldn't see us. Then again, the television was still on, airing the late news. "Oh, hey." He dropped into the recliner perpendicular to our position on the sofa. Fortunately, I'd already sat back up, facing the screen, and propped my head in my hand on the armrest.

"Hi, Wee Man. Aren't you early?" He had a midnight curfew and always texted if plans changed, especially if he wanted to stay out longer. Not that I knew where my phone lay at the moment. I chastised myself for dropping yet another parenting ball.

"Mr. Moore made Jax come home early when he found out she was the only girl at practice. Apparently, the guys and I planned to jump her instead of working through the harmony on our last song for my party."

"Liam," I scolded even though I mostly agreed with him.

"Come on, fam. Why would we go to the trouble of making a band and do something so horrible? Plus why would I wait until eleven p.m. to do it? We'd hung out most of the day. It makes no sense."

"Calvin doesn't see your band the way you do, sweetheart. To him, it's a hobby."

Liam dropped his cheek into his hand, making him difficult to understand. "He also assumes we males can't control ourselves."

"Mm-hmm." He'd tapped into one of my major pet peeves. The man had always been weird about our kids' friendship. He initially tolerated it because it got him close to a famous football player. I made a note to ask him what had been going on between his best friend and her parents. His frustration sounded like it had been brewing for a while.

Thomas rubbed small, soothing circles on my hip under the quilt. I appreciated the show of support.

"What do you think, Prof?" Liam had begun using Thomas's title as a nickname instead of an honorific. It was kind of cute.

"How old is Jax?" Thomas asked.

"Seventeen."

"When's her birthday?"

"March fifteenth."

"Well"—Thomas exhaled—"there's your answer, pal. Don't get between a girl and her father, especially when she's a minor. Trust me."

"Tragic." Liam slogged over to the fridge, warmed up leftovers, and sat with us, eating while we watched the rest of the movie. It didn't take long since my boy inhaled food like a starved puppy. He set his dish in the sink and stretched while bellowing a yawn that sounded somewhat like a moose call.

"I'm whipped and heading up. Will I see you in the morning, Prof?"

Thomas shook his head, but I answered, "We're waiting to catch the *Saturday Night Live* cold open, then calling it a night."

"Okay." Liam bobbed his head. "Night, kids."

"Good night, sweetheart."

"Night, Liam." Thomas stretched his arm around my shoulder and squeezed me into his side, like we were when we started the movie. He leaned into my hair and chuckled.

I swatted his abs and huffed.

"Hey." Thomas turned to face me. "Are you upset with me? Do you regret—" The look on his face was so pained he couldn't finish the thought.

"No." I let my forehead fall to his. "It's… I regret nothing. You're… amazing. It's not like I'm going to ask the kids' permission to see you. But if they were little, I'd keep you from them until we knew for sure what we're doing. Having you sleep over with them in the house feels more… well, more than what I think we are. Am I being silly?"

Liam asking if Thomas planned to stay the night stuck with me though. He obviously didn't mind, but I needed to make sure. I saw it as a respect issue. Unfortunately, I hadn't found any more alone time with Liam than I had with Thomas since Halloween. All our lives were pretty hectic.

Thomas took a while to answer my question, his voice thick and thoughtful when he finally said, "No. You're not silly. You're a mother." Thomas spoke quietly into the space between us. "You know I only wanted to make the troubles of the day disappear, right? It's hard to see you upset over so many things. I'm going to make damn sure the pressure on you eases. Promise."

I sat back and cupped his cheek. "You really are the sweetest man." I kissed Thomas's lips, holding mine to his for a long moment, wishing they were a conduit to my thoughts and I could let him truly see what he did to me.

Yes, people had my back. Also true that some didn't. It had been a long time since someone wanted to put me first. I smiled, unbelieving. I didn't want to become addicted to Thomas's heart any more than I wanted to be reliant on his help.

Thomas must have sensed my mood shift and changed the subject. "Can we spoon a little more? No hanky-panky. Just want to hold you longer before we call it a night."

We stretched back out and arranged the quilt over us, catching the weather report. "Besides, this couch is so big and comfortable it's easy to get lost in."

"You can thank Shane there. He insisted most furniture was too small for him. When we saw this piece, he declared it man-sized." I chuckled at the pleasant memory. "Truth is, I agree with you on the comfort factor. I love stretching out on it too."

Thomas grunted and his body stiffened.

I looked over my shoulder. "You okay?"

He answered, "Mm-hmm," but his warm, attentive gaze had shut down.

"You sure? Did I say something wrong?"

He pecked a kiss on my head. "Everything's fine."

I knew he wasn't, though I wasn't comfortable enough with him to push the subject. I feared the possibility of making him angry and let it drop.

Thomas stayed quiet the rest of the night. Even during the cold-open sketch. His bottom arm stayed under me, but he moved his top hand from my hip to his own.

MY STUFFY NOSE WOKE ME IN THE MIDDLE OF THE NIGHT. AN obnoxious voice on the TV preached nonsense to insomniacs and had infiltrated my dream. I turned off the television and fluffed the throw pillows, stealthily maneuvering into a more upright sleeping position. I could've moved into my bedroom, but Thomas still snuggled beside me. I didn't want to disturb him. Okay, I also wanted every minute with him I could get. Until the preacher—which I turned off—invaded my head, my sleep had been pleasantly dark and empty.

Once resettled, my breath evened out as I absorbed the peace of the night. Faded light from the streetlamp illuminated the ceiling through the clerestory windows at the fireplace and in the kitchen at the other end of the open space. Staring up at the faded light hovering above us, I embraced the sensation of sinking into the dark bottom of the room. It was a warm, cozy retreat from my worries and other things that might go bump in the night.

As the drift began, Thomas shifted, laying his head on my chest. He made a soft, agonized sound, which broke my heart and left me to wonder who chased him in his sleep.

I brushed his hair off his forehead, my nails lightly massaging his scalp, my fingertips barely touching the sad furrow between his brows. His face relaxed, and my breath caught on his beauty. Full lashes lay against angular cheeks, softening them. His sculpted lips lost their tension, barely parting.

Thomas's arms wound around my waist and tightened as he snuggled deeper. I continued to barely stroke his hair as I whispered, "Shhh. You're okay." His body stilled, and it occurred to me he might require more.

I continued whispering, "Let's walk down the stairs to my favorite spot." I shared the secret porch from recent meditations, wondering if any part of him heard me. I believed words spoken into the dead of night were said to the soul without the judgment or influence of a conscious mind.

I hoped sharing my special place would scare off whatever affected Thomas. I also hoped it would encourage his subconscious to open up and know his secrets were safe with me. In my heart, I pledged to hold on to them like the treasures they were. His breathing evened as he clung to me for support.

When finished, I couldn't stop thinking about what might haunt him. My struggles seemed to either tattoo themselves to my face or they blew up into a flare—lately, literally. This man rationed out his private thoughts like they were needed for a war effort. Then again, maybe they were. The one-sided nature of our evening hadn't set well with me. Perhaps with this, right here, his heart showed me what he needed most. Maybe there was a way I could ease his burden too and could be useful to him after all. It might also mean I could become his essential person—like he was becoming mine.

Though I didn't dare whisper my desire into the night. Instead, I turned my lips toward his ear, whispering, "Dream a little dream of me." I drifted off to the lyrics swimming in my head.

The next time my eyes opened, I was wedged between the sofa and the coffee table. I slowly stood, extracting one limb at a time, noting how the suspect in my couch-ousting had snuggled into Thomas's side. Macushla had already resumed dreaming—running and growling in her sleep—but I was sure it was a ruse. I knew the second I entered the kitchen, she'd practically apparate at my feet, asking for breakfast.

The clock read six in the morning, and I didn't feel like dozing. Once Thomas had relaxed and I conked out, I'd slept better than I had in days. The couch was comfortable, but I knew the reason had more to do with my company. I padded into my bathroom to take my thyroid medicine and go through a quick get-ready routine.

True to my suspicion, Koosh appeared in front of me as soon as I started filling the water kettle in the kitchen. The smart little shit threatened a bark, like she knew I was trying to be quiet and let Thomas sleep. I fed the blackmailer before taking a moment to open my brand-new bag of decaffeinated coffee. The time had finally arrived to give coffee another go. We called it a "challenge" in the autoimmune world. I fought the urge to rip the bag open, choosing to savor each moment, smelling the fresh grounds. Nutty, rich, with a hint of vanilla and spices. I couldn't wait. Catching the kettle before it boiled, I let the water drip through my brand-new pour-over carafe, opting for simplicity from my first cup.

I poured the finished liquid gold into a thermos and filled my favorite mug with the rest. My eyes drifted shut on the inhale, and my mouth watered from anticipation.

4

TIMELESS

THOMAS

Countless years of waking up in strange places kept Thomas from freaking out when consciousness came back to him. He opened an eye and checked his surroundings. Kick's living room. He'd spent the night on her sofa—no, on *his* sofa. Thomas hated how much the thought irritated him, but he couldn't deny it either.

He sat up and spotted Kick in the kitchen area, her hands wrapped around a mug. She took a sip and tilted her face to the ceiling, her eyes closed. She appeared to be right on this side of orgasmic. He cleared his throat, partly to keep from scaring her but mostly to distract himself from the amorous lust she inspired.

Kick started and set the mug down, a guarded smile on her face. "Hey handsome. I didn't wake you, did I? Sorry if I did."

Thomas answered with a gruff morning rasp. "No. But who were you talking to?"

A warm blush spread across Kick's face as she lifted her mug with both hands like it was the Holy Grail. "My coffee. Again, I'm sorry. I was trying to be quiet, but the excitement over my first sip got the best of me."

Thomas studied her bashful demeanor. He had meant what he said to Liam the night before about planning to go home. He also couldn't deny how good it felt to sleep with Kick in his arms again. Once his frustration with himself passed from being pissy over Shane picking out the furniture, he had to admit how nice it was to be in her space. Her late husband might haunt it here and there, but no one could deny how she inhabited every square inch of this home. He didn't mind waking up to the sound of her voice at all even if her words were kooky.

He pushed away any further thought of going down that trail, unsure how far he could get while under the Felidae's radar. From their first interactions, Thomas had envisioned them maintaining their own homes no matter what happened. He'd learned to love his space and his projects. Since the morning he saw Kick fixing breakfast in his kitchen, he wasn't so sure anymore.

He rubbed his face and shook his head, smiling. He could honestly get used to this. "Don't worry about it, baby." He padded around the living room furniture and into the kitchen, gave Kick a kiss on her cheek, mindful of his morning breath. He said a slightly foggy, "Morning."

A wide grin spread across Kick's face. "Good morning, handsome." She ran her hands through his hair. "You look like you're about to go on stage with the Cure."

"Who? And why?"

"Oh, come on." She giggled. "You're not that young. *Surely* you know who the Cure is. Anyway, your sleepy head and face are cute."

Thomas lifted a shoulder. "I'll take your word for it." He tipped his head to the side. "Mind if I use your guest bath?"

"Help yourself."

"Can I have one of those when I get back?"

"Like you have to ask at the barista's house?" Kick raised her mug. "This is decaf though. Would you rather have an Americano?"

"If it's no trouble."

"None at all."

"Thanks darlin'." Thomas entered the bathroom and took care of his morning routine. After a quick shower, he dug out fresh underwear and a T-shirt from his gym bag. He paired it with the jeans from the day before and headed back into the kitchen, eager for his espresso.

Kick had everything waiting and put the cup together as he walked over, handing it to him with a twinkle in her eye. "You know"—she ran her hands through his wet hair—"your hair is about as straight as mine is curly. It fascinates me."

Thomas took a sip, savoring the smell as the cup neared his nose, the bitter, nutty flavor mixed with the crema as it slid down his throat. "Fascinates? Isn't it boring compared to yours?"

"Uh-uh," Kick said. "There isn't any sign of porosity. I bet your hair never frizzes on you."

"Can't say it has."

"Absolutely incredible," she remarked, as if awed, carefully sifting a piece away from his forehead.

Thomas took another pull and grinned. "Don't you mean apoplectic?"

"What?" Kick's eyes flashed with mirth and annoyance when she realized what he referenced. Ever since their acquaintance became a friendship, Thomas had occasionally teased her about the note he'd found attached to the smoke shop door on the day they met—how the staff at Mick & Hugh's was apoplectic about being closed. It was so Kick and made Thomas chuckle inside any time he thought of it.

She swatted him on the bicep. "Smart-ass. I might put you to work for that."

"It'd be my pleasure either way, baby."

Since there were four for breakfast, Kick made a full meal. She asked Thomas to sauté loose sausage while she chopped up mushrooms, bell peppers, and spinach. She planned to put them all in a frittata. As soon as Thomas had the sausage done and drained, she put him to work on two packs of bacon. Apparently, Liam could down a pack by himself.

Kick had just placed the frittata in the oven when Rachel came downstairs. "Hey guys," she said with a jaw-cracking yawn.

"Good morning, Snow," Kick said in a perky, motherly tone. "Feeling any better?"

Like her Disney Princess namesake, Rachel floated to her mother with a dancer's grace and bent to kiss her cheek. "Much. Thank you. Good morning, Thomas. I didn't realize you were spending the night."

"It wasn't planned," he sheepishly said over his shoulder.

"We both fell asleep on the sofa watching *Saturday Night Live*," Kick explained.

"Aw"—Rachel snuck a piece of bacon—"how cute. It's like you're teens or something."

"Um, thanks. I think." Kick chuckled. "Which do you want to do, sweets—make your own latte or finish this guacamole I'm making?"

"Ooh, are we having breakfast burritos?"

"Frittata."

"Even better. I'll make a latte. Thanks, Mama."

"Snow, when you're done, would you mind waking your brother? This pan's about ready to come out of the oven."

"Lee's up. He's in the bathroom— Welp, never mind. Here he comes."

Macushla ran up the stairs, barking and chasing her favorite person down the steps to the living room. Liam picked her up and placed her around his neck while walking into the kitchen. "Mmm. It smells great down here. You should stay over more often."

"Liam," Kick scolded, looking embarrassed.

Rachel handed her latte to her brother. "Here, squirt. You can have mine. I'll make another even though you should make both since I had to put up with your face pubes in the bathroom."

"Rachel," Kick warned again. "We're about to eat."

"No kidding. I almost lost my appetite. They're stuck in dried-on shaving cream droplets." Rachel shuttered dramatically. "Disgusting."

Thomas finished the last of the bacon and turned off the burner. He took the stool next to Liam and watched the McKennas in action.

"Do you know how spicy it is to be an only child now?" Liam retorted.

Rachel answered, "No, Lee. As a matter of fact, I absolutely do *not*. How spicy is it?"

Liam pressed his elbows into the quartz counter and leaned forward for emphasis. "It's big. Heaven."

Thomas bit the inside of his lip to keep from laughing out loud. The boy had his mother's sense of snark.

Kick finished preparing the bowl of guac and placed it on the island counter. "Here I thought it would be nice to have two of my children home for breakfast. Silly me." Thomas let his head hang and laughed.

"Some things don't change," Rachel said.

"Nope," Kick agreed. "Do you think you two will still argue like this in front of your future children?"

"Yep," Liam answered. "I'll make sure to have the most kids so we can gang up on their aunt and uncle, and I'll finally win."

Thomas broke into a belly laugh while Kick and Rachel rolled their eyes. Kick looked at Rachel and said, "A clown to my left"—

she turned her head toward Liam and sighed—"and a joker on my right." Then she gave Thomas a huge, gorgeous grin. *There* was something he could eat up every day.

An hour later, breakfast was finished, the kitchen was cleaned, the pleasant sound of the kids playing *Smash Bros* floated down from the loft, and Kick ran around the house like her pretty ass was on fire. Thomas had repacked his gym bag, set it on the bench in the mudroom, and presently stood watching her fret from the hallway in front of her office. Kick carried a loaded basket of what he assumed to be dirty clothes into the laundry room.

"What's wrong, darlin'?" He followed her down the hall.

Kick shook her head as she sorted the clothes, loading the darks into the washing machine. She unsuccessfully flipped her hair out of her face before sighing and tucking it behind her ear. "Rach wants to go home sooner rather than later, but Lee can't drive her because he has a test tomorrow. So I'm cramming as much work in as I can before I chauffeur again." She paused her work. "I'm sorry I'm such a poor host."

"The last thing I want to do is pile on your to-do list, baby. What if I took Rachel home?"

Over her shoulder, she said, "You're heading out to the gym."

"I'm not teaching. Sundays are informal, so I can arrive any time. Plus it would give me a chance to peek under the hood of her car."

Kick stopped again, turning around. "Why would..." She sighed, tucking the hair back again. "You really want to do that? You know it's unnecessary, right? I don't expect you to take us all on. The kids act like children sometimes, but they're mostly out of the nest. Hell, they've been practicing their flying skills for years now."

"It doesn't mean an older bird can't show them a thing or two, does it?" Sure, he had a family, but Thomas had missed this part of it, the care, the imparting of wisdom, even learning from a bright, young mind. His students were never close enough to count. Not like this. He practically champed at the bit to help.

Her eyes narrowed and she huffed a breath, murmuring, "It feels like a big ask."

Thomas stepped into Kick's space, gently pushing her hair back yet again. "I have the time. It's a simple favor, and it would ease my mind to know what's going on with Rachel's car."

Kick's eyebrows raised. "It would ease *your* mind, huh? So I'd be doing *you* a favor by having you relieve my impossible day?"

Thomas answered with a big smile. To be completely useful, even to a few? She had no idea.

"You're slick."

"Thank you. You can pay me in kisses."

"Um, okay. As if I wasn't going to. Which reminds me, let me give you the name of the towing company I use. If you think it needs it, call them and put it on my account."

Thomas cleared his throat. "Give me the name of your mechanic again. If I can't get Rachel's car working, *I'll* have it towed there. My dime."

"Thomas…"

"Kick." He raised his voice in a squeak to imitate hers.

Her lips pursed to keep from laughing. It didn't work, and she giggled. "Okay fine. Thank you." She let out a sigh of relief. "I do have a lot on the list today."

Thomas tapped his lips. Kick was still smiling when she pulled his head down to meet hers. He took advantage of her open mouth and their privacy, deepening the kiss. His fingertips adjusted her jaw to fit the angle he sought, and he let his tongue dance and linger with hers. She still tasted like coffee. The comforting, spicy flavor of it fit her.

One hand drifted down to her ass, pressing her into his erection. Her sweet moan traveled from his cock up to his heart, and he broke their connection. "*Now* you're welcome."

Kick's hazy gaze took a moment to clear. Her smirk returned when it did. "I swear you're twelve."

He tapped her button nose. "Which means I keep you young. A kiss from you will sustain me for the rest of the day."

"That's all it took?"

Thomas patted her fine ass and left a relaxed Kick to her chores as he called for Rachel.

RACHEL SAT IN SILENCE FOR THE FIRST QUARTER OF THEIR DRIVE into Raleigh, and Thomas let her, giving her some space to ruminate. Every so often, his eyes sliced to the passenger seat, and he saw her face morph through the five stages of grief. He thought he also caught worry for family and possibly—probably—something to do with school. The girl seemed to let all her emotions show on her face, like her mother.

Thomas considered tuning the radio to an easy jazz station, thinking it would keep his brain engaged without disturbing Rachel. Before his hand reached out, Rachel spoke, her head turned toward the passenger window. "Do you think it's strange how you and Mama have the same car… the make, I mean?"

"Strange?"

Rachel shifted her body to look at Thomas. "Do you think it's fate or something? Like kismet or serendipity?"

"Ah. I see." They came to a red light, so Thomas took a moment to look at Rachel and found her returning his gaze. "Like attracts like, so it makes sense your mom and I would be drawn to the same model car. Nothing more went into it."

"Like attracts like, huh?"

"Not the woo-woo stuff about money and intentions, in case it was confusing. Socially, people of like minds have migrated together since the beginning of our species. It's mutually beneficial for survival and helps make the days more pleasant if each party has a mix of similar interests. Does that make sense?"

Rachel turned back to her window. "So she's safe with you?"

Now he understood. Thomas's back straightened as he immediately answered, "Yes, Rachel. As much as it's in my power, Kick is safe with me. Do you worry about her?"

"A bit. Since Granddad died, it's… difficult again."

Thomas's professor instincts kicked in. He'd learned the hard way how a struggling student could look like they lacked motivation when, in reality, they were drowning with worries. "You can rest your mind about your mother. From what she's told me, it's been a rough year, but remember her progress too. Hell, she had her first coffee this morning. Make sure you celebrate her victories, alright?"

"Okay. Sure."

Now fully in professor mode, he figured he'd press on. It was another way to help Kick out and get to know her little clan. "It won't be long before we reach your place. Are you ready for it?"

Rachel's quiver reached her chin. Still, her voice stayed steady. "Tess and Mama helped me see that what's bothering me isn't the loss of Cody so much. We weren't ever a 'together forever' kind of couple. I think he hurt me because he didn't know how to say goodbye. I didn't either, to be honest."

"I'd love to give him a piece of my mind. Maybe accidentally pop his nose in the process."

Rachel laughed, which meant Thomas had achieved one of his goals. "If it were necessary, my brothers are totally qualified. Shit, I wouldn't be surprised if Dylan shows up when he finds out. Did you know he ruined my first kiss?"

"No. But I can imagine."

"It happened during the Homecoming dance after Daddy died. My crush before Cody had asked me. Dylan saw him kiss me in the courtyard outside our school gym and rushed him. He gave the boy a black eye. It was my brother's first of several suspensions after the accident. I think Dylan blamed himself for it and decided he'd fill Daddy's shoes to make up for it. He thought he was defending my honor." She stared straight ahead for a few blocks, then quietly murmured, "It was a sweet kiss too."

Christ. Thomas knew all about people in intense pain tripping over each other despite their mutual love. He mulled over what to say next when she said, "The thing is, Mom was engaged to Dad by the time she was my age. She planned their wedding during her last semester of college. Her last semester. Then she immediately moved across the country to settle in before Dad started training camp in San Francisco."

Thomas shook his head at the thought. "That's nuts."

"No. It's romantic."

Thomas turned to her and sighed. To him, it showed Kick's lifelong struggle with boundaries, as if her eventual health issues were nature's way of getting her attention and teaching her to put herself first once in a while. He knew better than to talk so intimately about Kick to her daughter though. "I know, she's badass."

"She had her shit together, okay? She knew what she wanted and went for it." Rachel hung her head. "I've been too scared to let Cody loose. Fuck all, half the time I can't decide what to eat for dinner, especially since my teacher wants me to lose weight."

What the hell? Currently, Rachel wore a large, plaid, flannel shirt over leggings. Her shirt seemed to swallow her, but he'd seen her in fitted clothes before. She had the expected dancer's body. Lean, toned, and flexible. She'd demonstrated the last after breakfast when she lifted her leg to the kitchen counter and folded her body over her knee, then switched to the other side. Kick responded like it was a common practice. She'd huffed, swatted her daughter on the leg, and told her to use her barre upstairs in the workout room.

An odd feeling stirred in Thomas's gut—a fatherly one he didn't want to acknowledge. Some fierce desire to chase down this so-called instructor and chew his or her ass out traveled from the growling pit in his stomach up to his heart. Damn if it didn't scare the shit out of him.

Rachel sighed, stretching in her seat. "Anyway, my point is, this Cody thing is a big reminder that it's taking me too long to grow the hell up."

"Well, it's not a good idea to compare yourself to your mother, darlin'," Thomas drawled, tipping his head to consider. "I mean not only because of different times and different generations. Your life circumstances are different too." They waited in a left-turn lane, so Thomas let his gaze linger, making his next point. "It's not a big extrapolation to guess why your mom took on so much pressure in her senior year. It might have been a crushing amount of work, but it got her away from her mother in the end. Hell, she put half a country between them." Thomas's mouth tipped at the corner at the thought. "It's a wonder she stayed on the same continent."

"She loved Daddy."

Thomas winced. He didn't understand why he'd suddenly become so sensitive to the topic of Shane McKenna. He'd been serious when he'd told Kick it pleased him to know she'd been loved. "She did. They also could've eloped, had a small wedding, settled in California before getting married, or several other things. My point is y'all should grow up the way that works for *y'all.*"

He was about to ask Rachel about plans for the summer when they pulled into her parking lot. Thomas spotted her car near the fence and frowned. He parked as close as he could and jogged straight over to investigate.

"Dammit all." All four tires had been slashed.

"What the hell?"

"Were your tires fine yesterday?"

As she opened her mouth to answer, her head turned, her eyes narrowed, and she tracked a male leaving the apartment building.

Thomas guessed who it was by the low growling sound she made. "Is that Cody?"

Rachel nodded.

Thomas stalked over to him, intercepting the young man before he reached his Dodge Durango. "You do this?" He pointed to Rachel's car.

"Do what, and who the hell are you?"

"Rachel's friend." Thomas stepped into Cody's space. The boy's face flashed with fear. Through gritted teeth, Thomas slowly snarled, "Did you slash her tires?"

"What? Fuck no."

Rachel caught up to them, keeping a distance. Cody lifted his chin in her direction. "Didn't take you long, did it? I *knew* you had others."

"He's seeing my mom! But of course you'd go there. Makes you feel better, doesn't—"

"Look at me, asshat," Thomas warned. "You swear you didn't touch her car? We already know you don't mind hurting Rachel personally."

Cody tried to move away, but Thomas pinned him to the truck.

"I didn't do shit. She ain't no innocent bitch neither," Cody squeaked.

Thomas's nostrils flared, his hand clenching into a fist.

Rachel placed her hand on his arm. "Please, Thomas, let it go." She turned her glare toward her ex, who was panting from the fear-fueled adrenaline rush. "The twat-waffle isn't worth shit."

"Cute—" Cody started but was cut off by Thomas.

"Not another word to her, do you hear? If you see Rachel, you politely smile, but you never say another word to her again. And the next time you fuck a girl, do it in silence. Better yet, do it at her place. Got it?"

Cody's face busted into a wide grin, and Thomas's stomach

dropped. He'd said too much and let the little fucker know Cody had gotten under Rachel's skin. "Sure." Cody waggled his eyebrows at Rachel, and Thomas almost hit the kid then. He held back, knowing an assault charge wouldn't bode well with the university. Thomas almost didn't care since he had a crack lawyer. *Kick might care though.*

"I never stepped out on you."

"Not what I heard."

Thomas growled, wondering if there was more to the social media shit going on with the girl.

Rachel stepped between the men and pushed Thomas back with the poise of a young lady who'd done this before. She turned around and asked Cody, "Can you just tell me if you saw or heard anything from the parking lot last night? You and Kierra must have come up for air sometime, not that she got off, I'm sure. Maybe I should text her. I bet she needed something to keep her distracted."

"I'm not supposed to talk to you."

Rachel folded her arms over her chest. "You can nod for yes or shake your head for no."

Cody shook his head, turned around, and climbed into his truck. It roared to life, and he revved the engine. He lowered the window before putting it in gear. "Are you wearing my shirt? Give it back!"

Rachel shouted back as he pulled out, "Hell no! It's the least you owe me."

Thomas reached into his pocket and pulled out his phone. He couldn't believe he'd almost punched his girlfriend's daughter's ex-boyfriend. He thought back to Rachel's story of Dylan running rough-shod over her crush. *Christ*, he was devolving into a boy. He had to rein in the protective, fatherly instinct ASAP.

After yelling, Rachel turned around. "Who are you calling?"

"I'm texting Banger. He needs to check this out." Thomas met her gaze. "You should call the police."

"I was going to call Mama."

Thomas sighed and looked at the sky. "Absolutely do *not* call her. She has enough going on. We'll fill her in when we have answers." He pegged Rachel with his professor's stare. "You want to grow up? Now's a good time to start. Filing a police report is simple."

His phone rang, and Thomas answered it, walking back toward Rachel's Honda Accord. "Hey, man..."

5

TIGHTROPE

Tess bounded through the doors to Thomas's lab with more energy than she should have. She'd always had this annoying joie de vivre, as long as she kept herself away from her dark spaces. He thought time spent with her gurus and daily yoga practice had done Tess a world of good. For now, Thomas appreciated it. He hoped some of it would rub off on him.

Her attitude hadn't transmitted to Banger though. Thomas's friend pulled up the rear of their trio. Banger usually checked on the lab a few times a year, after hours to run security sweeps. The university did their own, but Banger trusted no one's authority or talent more than his own. Regardless, Thomas's team knew his friend, and they'd all passed another thorough analysis into their backgrounds after the near miss with Presley. Thomas still couldn't believe his talented protégé had almost blackmailed him.

When Thomas mentioned a new lead showing a link between mitochondrial performance and an area of "junk DNA," Banger asked if he could check it out. They'd made it a group visit when

Tess began citing recent studies from universities around the world having nothing to do with Thomas's or Nigel's facilities. She'd shocked the men with her interest and questions regarding where the science was leading.

"Well, friends, meet the gang," Thomas said, sweeping his arm across the space. They greeted Spencer, the day's lead; Jules and Charon, two of his undergrad assistants; and his new right hand, Bethany. Thomas turned to Tess. "My other team members aren't on today's schedule." The trio turned a corner. "Ah, here's Gautam."

After they all exchanged greetings, Thomas explained to Tess, "G is probably the most important person in the lab. He's our data collector and helps us interpret our shenanigans."

Tess made a namaste bow, greeting Gautam while Banger dipped his head, looking embarrassed. Thomas dipped his chin in a tight smile. He understood Banger's irritation with Tess, but she'd always made Thomas laugh. "How delightful. Have you had any interesting recent finds?"

Gautam gave her a shy, thoughtful smile. "As a matter of fact, many." He turned toward his computer monitor and clicked through a few folders. "I'm not sure how much Professor H wants to share."

Tess tipped her head up at Thomas, a proud grin across her face. "Professor H. I'm still not used to hearing it."

Thomas shoved his hands in his pockets. This was the closest he'd probably get to showing his family his work in action. Presentations in Bordeaux didn't really count. He turned his attention back to Gautam before he lost his cool points—at least that's what his students had called them. "Don't worry about it, G. I plan to introduce them to our current stars." He couldn't believe how much he wanted—no, needed—Tess's approval of his work. Most of the Felidae cared about results, not the details on how they'd been achieved.

Thomas led them around the corner to a work area with a

rodent rack. He figured plates with smears wouldn't matter much to Tess. The cage he had in mind was already on the counter, as Charon had just removed the top and was taking notes. "Come see our new mice."

Tess oohed and aahed over the mouse pups while Thomas explained, "We'll check them soon to see if any were born with the genetic variance my assistant, Bethany, recently discovered in their parents." He hoped at least a few from the litter had what he was looking for. So far, following this route proved more fun than trying to track Toni's progress. He believed the two tactics would meet and merge soon.

"Are you certain you don't want to retest Rafa and me?" Tess asked. Stalwart in her refusal to use Banger's preferred nickname, Thomas stayed equally stubborn in his desire to stay out of their standoff while his friend walked away.

Thomas studied Tess while she added, "We have much in common with these babies, don't we?"

He nodded. "You may be right. I'll let y'all know if I need it. I still have a sample from you and two from—"

"Who's with Gautam?" Banger asked in a low-voiced huff, jabbing his thumb over his shoulder. "I haven't met him."

Thomas peeked around the corner and turned back to the group. "That's Drew. He works at the lab next door. Gautam's probably running a sequence for him." When Banger's scowl wouldn't ease up, he added, "We do it all the time when G is slow here. The professor Drew works for is studying genetic variances in colon cancer, and they don't have the resources I do." Thinking some food and a dram might lighten his friend's mood, Thomas said, "Why don't we go eat?"

As the trio passed Gautam's station, he and Drew looked up from their work. Thomas put a hand on Drew's shoulder. "How are you holding up?"

"Taking it a day at a time, Professor. You?"

"The same." Thomas hoped the young student was telling the truth. "If you need anything, let me know."

Drew nodded slightly. "Thank you."

"What was that about?" Banger asked as Thomas reached him and Tess, who were waiting at the door.

Thomas sighed and said, "Drew was Presley's boyfriend. They'd met while studying in the lounge at the end of the hall. I don't mind letting him borrow Gautam on occasion, and it probably helps him to deal with his grief. One of my students told me Drew had already bought Pres a ring."

Banger stared down the hall toward said room, his jaw flexing. "Shit."

THE TRIO SETTLED INTO A DARK WOODEN BOOTH AT THE BACK OF Thomas's favorite pub near campus. He knew Tess would've preferred Garam Masala at a local Indian place, but the interior architecture here lent itself to more private conversations. Not only did the booth they shared come with high-backs, the entire pub was divided into small, themed rooms. It kept the noise down and allowed for quiet conversation. Plus Banger's mood lightened when he discovered the pub offered the largest selection of whiskeys in the Carolinas. He ordered a flight of rare Highland scotches.

Tess let a soft smile brighten her eyes. "This is nice, Michael—I mean Thomas. Thank you."

Thomas dipped his chin to acknowledge her mistake, then lifted a questioning eyebrow. "I haven't been Michael for a while."

She patted his hand. "I see you so rarely that I still forget. *Pardon.*"

"If you didn't jet-set so much, you might see me during the meetings in Bordeaux."

She scrunched her face and took a sip of water. Then Tess

stilled and seemed to consider his words. "You're right. It's been hard there lately. I can visit here more often. You and Rafa are family, no? I can trust you."

Thomas wondered if the same suspicions he had were on Tess's mind, while Banger mmphf'd at the inference to his given name, as usual. Tess leveled Banger with what Thomas thought of as a European growl. It was part Spanish, part French, and fully continental. "I will *never* refer to you by that vulgar name."

He muttered, "It's never been about what you think it is."

Tess flicked her wrist, dismissing him. "No matter. I must speak with you two. I have your sworn secrecy, yes?"

Thomas shifted his gaze between his tablemates. "You know you do," he said. Banger huffed and nodded.

Tess leaned into the middle of the table. "Well, the definition of *loyalty* as we know it may be changing."

The waitress arrived right then, setting down a sampler of boxty, Scotch eggs, and a selection of potato-and-cheese croquettes. Banger reached for the first glass in his flight, a settling smile stretching across his face as the first sip went down. Thomas kept with a local bourbon called Mystic and savored the smooth finish. Tess picked up a glass from her own flight of Highland whiskies—the same one as Banger's—and sniffed it.

"What?" she asked after taking a drink. "Some aspects of life in those mountains weren't so bad."

To distract him and keep his mood easy, Thomas said, "You go first, Banger. Tell the server what else you want."

"Is your name actually Banger?" the waitress asked. Thomas cringed, wishing the topic of his friend's name would drop already. After the man himself affirmed her question, the girl continued. "Is it possible it's in reference to a legend? My grandmother used to tell me old stories when I was little."

Tess scoffed, and her demeanor soured.

The corner of Banger's mouth lifted in a defiant smirk after he finished the first glass. "Which one? There are many legends in the Highlands."

"Right?" the server asked, for no reason Thomas could figure. "My grandmother grew up there. She told me one about a laird from a long time ago who loved to hurt girls." She blushed and didn't continue.

"It's not my favorite of the stories, but I've heard it," Banger said grumpily, nearly growling.

"Oh, no matter." The waitress waved her hand. "I'm sure it was only my gran's way of warning me about troublesome boys, like the Laird Mackendrick or something."

"Did it work?" Banger asked while Tess turned shades of red Thomas didn't know she could achieve.

The young woman laughed. "I've always had a soft spot for bad boys, so I guess not."

"Your gran had sight then." Banger leaned toward her. "Bad boys need someone to believe in them anyway. And remember… folks say the *men* of the village started that harsh tale. I think they were jealous of the laird." He winked at the server and gave her his order.

"Tess, Banger and I have picked up on the weird stuff happening with the Felidae too." Thomas wanted to take advantage of the quiet time before their meal arrived. He hoped Tess might have actually seen or heard something that could help him get to the source of the discord.

"That's because you're both smart."

"Well, the old man shut down communication between Thomas and Oxford," Banger grunted.

"No?" Tess asked, her eyes pinned to Thomas.

"Yes, he did. The atmosphere at last month's meeting was

tense at best. The only person from the other team who acted relaxed around me was Ellie."

"I bet she did," Tess muttered.

"What's wrong?" Thomas downed the last of his bourbon, wishing he'd ordered a second.

"She's been sneaking… secret calls, texts… meeting with staff in the barns."

"Sounds like she's helping to run the vineyard and the Felidae," Thomas said.

"The vineyard is Alaric's." Tess bit her lip, leaned into the middle of the table, and continued in a low voice. "She runs the estate, not the wine. No, boys, something isn't right."

"I picked up as much from *Grand-père*," Thomas said, his throat dry. He'd never known Tess to be so keyed up.

Tess pointed at him and wagged her finger. "Get those mice strong. Find your answers fast."

Thomas ran his hand through his hair. "That's pretty much what *Grand-père* said too, but the mice are secondary. My real hunt is with the DNA. We won't know much about the mice for a few generations."

Tess nodded vigorously. "I can relate."

Thomas reached across the table and grabbed Tess's hand. "I wish I could change what happened to you." He turned his head to Banger. "To both of you."

Tess's face darkened a moment before shaking it off.

"Is your lab secure?" Banger growled.

"Why?" Thomas looked back at Banger.

"I don't like Drew having access to your equipment. My team needs to run him," Banger added.

"Because of Presley?"

"Who is Presley?" Tess asked.

"My former right hand at the lab."

"She was killed in a hit-and-run in September," Banger told Tess. He pointed his third snifter glass Thomas's way. "She was planning to blackmail Thomas. She knew about *us*. We found it all when we went through her stuff. Brother-man, here, should've thought about this before now." Banger turned a hard glare on Thomas.

Banger was right. Kick had already softened him. If she hadn't distracted him, Thomas would've kept his focus on the research. He probably wouldn't have been blindsided by Presley either. He hung his head guiltily.

Tess's brows drew together in a furious V. "I have money. Let me fund the rest of your research."

"Tess—" Money wasn't Thomas's hurdle. Legality and credibility were.

She raised her hands. "What? Then you can control all the facets of your work. This is good, no?"

"For once, I agree," Banger added.

Damn it all. Thomas enjoyed teaching now. He couldn't say that though. The research had to come first. Before anything. Or anyone. Why did he desperately wish he could let Kick in on this? She didn't need more on her plate, but he sure could use her instincts.

"I have wine. It's vast, and some important cases are going bad. Wine doesn't age like my whiskies or cognac. The cases are suited for collectors who simply want old things. It's rare, see, worth millions—hundreds of millions."

Of course it was. *Christ*, Thomas wasn't an unbalanced nut case who jumped at every anxious scare. He'd worked too hard to fall prey to someone else's emotional whims. Until Kick, he couldn't remember the last time he'd found himself out of sorts. Kick was nothing compared to this though. He had to understand the discord within the Felidae before he made such a big decision. Deep in his heart, Thomas figured it would probably happen soon. He made a mental note to call his lawyer just in case.

Thomas turned to Banger. "Go ahead and run any check you

may or may not need. Just... please don't tell me about it." Dammit, this had to be as illegal as hell. Not that he worked completely aboveboard either. "Not unless y'all find something I must know."

Between the McKennas and the lab, he wondered if the intrigue would ever end. What the hell might happen next?

6

I HOPE YOU DANCE

KICK

Cyndi Sendaydiego, my dearest friend, paused her work, hanging the decorations for Liam's birthday party. She snapped her fingers in front of my face. "Are you breathing, Kicky?" She had me imitate her deep inhale and exhale. "Why are you so stressed? More than usual, I mean." She looked around the room. Lee and his band were setting up while Thomas oversaw the sound check. My other two kids had arrived early and were setting up the finger foods Carmen's daughters had delivered.

Carmen was my house manager and had developed some of those typical health issues many women contend with in their middle years. Earlier in the year, she'd begun experimenting with her favorite Puerto Rican recipes, adapting them for my autoimmune issues, and they accidentally helped her. It wasn't long before she'd finagled her whole family into eating this way. Her girls had taken up the mantle and were developing a catering business.

"The morning's gone smoothly, chica. You did good." Cyndi's voice was soothing.

My gut told me this would end up being one of the easiest of the kids' birthdays I'd thrown except for the wild card that terrified me.

"What you see on my face is dread. The day's been too smooth. I'm waiting for the 'Bobby shoe' to drop."

Cyndi's face lit with recognition. "Why'd you invite her anyway?"

"She's technically Liam's grandmother"—even if she didn't want to be—"and she won't stop reminding me how she missed my birthday."

"Didn't you plan for her to be gone?"

"I didn't set the ship's schedule. It was a beautiful coincidence though. I took it as a birthday present from above." I chuckled.

"There's my pretty bestie." She pointed at my face. "Stay like this the rest of day. No matter what."

My laugh deepened, then fizzled out like a balloon with a pinprick. "Whatever. What if… Maybe I'm too much like my dad… or Charlie Brown? I keep hoping she'll let the mountain of shit go, but the most I've ever gotten from her are crocodile tears. Still, Dad asked me to keep trying. I can't stop now."

Cyndi set down her tape and gave me a quick, tight squeeze. "Can't say I can relate. My 'rents are fabulous and across the country. You've done a great job with this though. And a shit ton of us love you. Count me at the top of the list."

"Thanks, sweets."

She helped me finish the decorations, and as we carried the step stool and supplies to the back closet, she nudged my shoulder. "Thomas fits in well over there."

"You think so?"

"Dylan's hard to read, but the rapport is there with Snow and Lee."

"He's spent some quality time with them. No complaints came

in from any side, not to me anyway. Also, Thomas is not the type of man to give me a piece of his mind about what's wrong with my kids. They speak well of each other though."

We returned to the front and stopped to watch Liam and Thomas finish up with the rented soundboard. I turned to ask her about work and discovered Cyndi had been staring at me, a smarmy grin on her face. I did a double take and furrowed my brow to ask *What?*

"You're gone for him."

"I'm… No." I waved her off and walked behind the counter, my safe spot. I felt an urgent need to make certain the regular restaurant napkins had been swapped out for the birthday ones. Cyndi settled across from me and stared until I insisted, "We're casual. We're doing *casual.*" I emphasized the point with a curt nod.

"Bull," she scoffed. "Make me an ice tea please. Caffeine's in order if I'm to believe you."

Her snark tempted me to tell her to do it herself. It wasn't like we were open to customers. In this case, I welcomed the distraction. Even while talking about Thomas, I kept looking over my shoulder for Bobby, wondering what kind of mood she'd be in, whether the quiet mouse or the worked-up snake would show up. Whether she'd allow the party to be fun.

I made us both iced teas—mine decaf, of course—and passed Cyndi's across the counter. "Who's the giant piece of candy hanging out by the door? I'd love to lick his stick," she said, working her straw like she was the lead in an eighties teen film.

I hissed when she made googly eyes and tapped the solid wood surface to get her attention. "His name is Zach. He's a friend of Jake's, and he's our security guard for the party. So leave him alone, missy. He can't be distracted. Not that he would be. Zach's a professional. He's thinking about going into law enforcement."

Cyndi sat taller and shimmied, sending Zach a wink. "I do love a man in uniform."

"He could be your nephew," I snapped. "Besides, what about Manu?"

She finally turned to me and set her cup down. "I know how to 'do casual,' Kicky dear. Which is why I know you and Professor Dad Jeans are fooling yourselves." She turned and watched Thomas walk over to us. Before he rounded the corner, she leaned in and muttered, "I thought you were dressing him now. What happened?"

I whisper-snapped back, "I only bought a few things. For all we know, he needs to do laundry. You better zip it though. I've already been to a party where the guests had fun at Thomas's expense. Let him be, please. It's Liam's day, not ours."

"You're no fun." She pouted. "Can't flirt with the young ones, and yours went and covered his cute ass with baggy denim. How am I supposed to get my entertainment?"

"Oh, I don't know, the band maybe? They'll play soon."

Thomas scrubbed his hands and stepped up to us while Cyndi continued, "But who can I dance with? You won't let me have any fun." She turned her attention to Thomas. "Will you save a dance for me, Professor? Or does Kick have all your slots?"

I sighed in defeat. How could I deny Cyn a little fun at my expense? She had held my lonely hand for so long. This was new for the both of us. Thomas's mouth lifted at the corner, giving me the impression he knew what we'd been discussing. "I'll check my card, Cynthia."

"Cyn," she said. She loved being able to pick up men and greet them as 'Sin.'

Thomas's smirk grew. "I noticed."

I wanted the subject changed ASAP, so I asked Thomas, "What would you like?"

"I've got it. I came over here to relieve you. Why don't you go greet the guests and make sure Liam's ready. Settle any nerves he has with your magic."

Who was I kidding? I was a goner. My brain fritzed on the sweetness overload, but friends did amazingly sweet stuff for each other. Even friends who might be more than friends, though not sure how much more. I caught myself grinning and sighing when Thomas leaned down and kissed my forehead. It didn't matter if his jeans were a little baggy. I liked how he chose function over fashion. His striped button-down hugged his strong shoulders and made my mouth water if I thought about it too long. Plus I'd picked out the shirt.

Regardless, I couldn't be hot and bothered on my son's eighteenth birthday. I had to be the responsible mom and hostess and keep my cool.

It didn't help that my favorite nightstand toy was currently recharging from a sudden overuse. Frustration masturbation was no fun. Between an important research lead and a goodbye dinner for Tess on Thomas's part, and sick employees on both our parts, we'd spent the week infrequently texting or talking on the phone. I'd taken to sending him "gifts" via the *Pokémon Go* app, if only to annoy him while letting him know I thought about him too. It beat sitting by the phone.

"Go on," he encouraged. "If it gets crazy back here, I'll call you over."

I caught Cyndi grinning like she'd discovered the world's largest stash of Lick-A-Sticks.

"Thanks," I said, poking his solid six-pack and feeling like an awkward idiot. But Cyn had rattled me. I moved around the counter as she tracked me, mouthing "Casual" and lifting her eyebrow.

I shook my head as she belly-laughed. Maybe we were kidding ourselves, but I couldn't afford complete honesty. Not yet. Like I'd told Thomas after our first fight, self-delusion was highly underrated. There were times it was the only thing keeping me going.

"Mama." Rachel intercepted me as I was about to pass Cyndi, preventing me from swatting her arm. "Gran texted me."

"Oh?"

"Yep. She's not coming. She said she couldn't reach you."

I fished my phone out of my back pocket and swiped it awake. No missed calls, texts, or emails. "What did she do, send up smoke signals?"

Rachel threw me her disappointed-parent glare. "Gran said she doesn't feel well. It *is* November after all." When it came to the dysfunction between Bobby and me, Rachel grew more impatient with me by the year. She didn't know the complete story though. Hell, she didn't even know as much as Thomas knew about what had gone down between us. So I couldn't fault her. Plus Bobby worked overtime to make sure my daughter had all the details on her side of things. It was easier to be the occasional bad guy in their scenario.

Still. I rolled my eyes. "It's November in North Carolina, not the Midwest. The temperature's going to the upper sixties today, but whatever." I knew Bobby wasn't sick. *I* knew *she* knew I knew she wasn't sick. I also knew she used Rachel as a messenger to keep from having to tell me. Well, Bobby's games worked in my favor today. She hated not being the center of attention, so fine, stay home. No way in hell would I call her and beg. For the first time since I'd unlocked the café in the morning, I took a lung-filling inhale and completely relaxed on the exhale. Now this could be the best birthday party I'd ever thrown.

My gaze met Cyndi's and knew she was thinking the same thing.

"Thanks for telling me, Snow. Want to come with me and greet guests?"

Rachel bumped my shoulder. "I've already welcomed most of them, but let's go anyway."

. . .

LIAM'S BAND PLAYED A FORTY-MINUTE SET, THEN BROKE FOR refreshments and adoration from the teen side of the Perked Cup's dining room. I sat at a table with Thomas, Cyndi, Deana and Gordon Douglas (who'd stopped by between grandkid events), Hugh and Maggie Reynolds, and my friend Charley Rodriguez.

After doing a stellar job on the construction of the Perked Cup, my dad and Hugh had hired Charley to remodel their store. Along the way, she'd become my friend and my go-to for any carpentry needs. Her company had recently redone my master bedroom.

Liam tapped the mic to get everyone's silence. He cleared his throat. "Thanks for coming to my party. Y'all are the best."

He turned to the kids at his table. "To the band, thanks for your support and trust in my crazy ideas. We've come together and are finding our flow. We're more than Metaphorical Chemistry. We've got the real thing, and it's big."

My eye roll over their name was an automatic reflex, and I hoped it went unnoticed. I'd made a case for Second-time Toddlers when the kids were naming the band. For some reason, it didn't fly.

Lee raised his cup in a toast, then addressed the crowd again. "We can't wait to play another set, and if you need a live band in the future…" He held out his hands and grinned while the room laughed. "You know my mom's number."

He continued, "Speaking of Mom… you get to be last." I narrowed my eyes at him with a warning glare.

"Settle down." He chuckled. "You know you get your own shout-out. Things have been tough lately, but I honestly can't remember the last time our life was easy. Thank you for all the shit… oops, I mean stuff"—the room laughed at his gaff, more at him recognizing it than him correcting it—"you do behind the scenes. It may look like we kids think the world revolves around us... since, you know, it does." He flashed his darn dimples. "But we see what you do and how hard it can be. Or at least *I* see it. Rachel and Dylan are probably oblivious."

"Shut it, dimp," boomed a recognizable baritone from the middle of the crowd. They laughed again while I shuttered at my oldest son's new nickname for his little brother.

Liam raised his mug. "Thanks for this party. More importantly, thank you for being our mom and dad wrapped in one squeezable package. We love you."

Not once, when planning this day, did I think he'd do something so special for me. The tears dropped steadily as my baby recognized my often futile efforts to make sure my kids turned out okay, despite the loss of our family's glue.

I dabbed some tears with my sweater cuffs and met Liam in the middle of the dining room. We hugged for a long time or until he lifted me off my feet and made the room laugh again at my protests. He set me down and kissed the top of my head.

When he was born, I immediately bonded with him over the brown curls like mine. Bobby noticed them too, and I think that solidified her dislike for my youngest on sight. Then Liam sleep-smiled while I held him, and his daddy's dimples showed up. I was a goner and knew he'd always be my special little buddy.

What no one ever acknowledged as my body fell apart in his first few years was how my little buddy lightened the dark moments with goofy grins and precious cuddles. Liam had never been the reason for my autoimmune disease, despite Bobby's claims otherwise. Hell, the symptoms raised their heads *years* before my son was born, even though doctors told me they were in my head. No, Liam wasn't the reason I was sick; he was the reason I didn't give up. More than once, I'd convinced myself my family would be better off with a different mother, a better mother.

Back then, I couldn't imagine how this tiny human would eventually kiss the top of my head. Presently, he seemed to love doing it to make a point—like he'd achieved a life goal. He still made me laugh on a daily basis. Knowing he was currently one inch taller than his father had been and would never share the experience of exchanging that first, knowing glance over it, I let Liam gloat as much as he wanted.

"Thank you, my Wee Man," I said when I squeezed him back. "You still have several months before you head down your path, but always remember: 'whistle, I'll be there.' No matter what." I kissed his cheek and watched him walk away.

Liam moved through the crowd, chatting and back-patting his way to the stage. The band played their version of "Somebody That I Used to Know," with Lee and his best friend, Jax, singing leads. It was the first time I heard it in full and I was captivated, standing still in the middle of the crowd. It's a sacred gift to see your child become the person they're supposed to be. I had no clue what Liam wanted to study in school and suspected he didn't know either. It didn't matter. He was showing me who he was right on the stage.

To my surprise, when the members of Metaphorical Chemistry put their instruments down—everyone but Liam—Thomas jumped up on stage with my son. He picked up a guitar that rested in a corner and placed the strap around his neck. Then he and Liam played a duet of Stevie Ray Vaughan songs. They continued for two more songs before calling it an afternoon. Both men—it was hard to think of my baby as a man, but it's what he'd been since 8:33 a.m.—received a standing ovation as they high-fived.

"Jesus, your man is in the wrong profession," Cyndi said, leaning into me while we clapped.

My sentiments exactly. I stood gobsmacked next to my friend, unable to do anything but clap. Thomas played like he'd been a member of Double Trouble himself.

How was it possible? Moreover… "How did I not know about this?" I asked Thomas as he stopped in front of me for a proper postperformance hug.

We sat in our seats, and Thomas took a long pull from his waiting ice tea. Then he turned his middle school smirk on me. "You saw my guitar in the first-floor office."

Did this imply there was a second-floor office? Or was it where the third-floor stairs led to? What else didn't I know?

He leaned into me and kissed my cheek. "You know the important stuff." A buzzing energy radiated from Thomas, and I was a heel for not amplifying it. On the other hand, I'd let everything out of the box—Every. Thing.—stuff my *kids* didn't even know. Thomas, obviously, still held back. My face slid into a scowl despite my attempt to mask it, or it must have given Thomas's reaction.

"Hey, now"—he slid his hands along my back—"we're busy people. It'll flesh out in time."

I couldn't rectify how an ability like that didn't ooze from him. I'd known plenty of people with talent outside their professions, and the discovery of their other expertise always came up right away. We'd also been distracted by so much—too much—since we'd met.

"I suppose. You promise you weren't hiding it from me?"

A sexy chuckle rumbled from Thomas into me as he drew me tight and kissed my head. "If I wanted to hide it, I wouldn't have played in public now, would I?"

His answer, though true, did nothing to reassure me. My instincts yelled he hid something, and it often felt like multiple things.

"Fantastic job with the party, darlin'." He held his gaze on Liam's group. Seeing him command his table, having the time of his life, lifted my spirits. I had done a fantastic job. One day at a time was what mattered in my world.

However, despite my hatred of ultimatums, it seemed like Thomas and I were heading for one soon. While I enjoyed his interest in my mind and my life, an ache sparked into being in my heart.

7

GIRLS JUST WANT TO HAVE FUN

KICK

"Whatcha doing tomorrow night?"

I jumped, almost dropping a gallon of milk. No one ever snuck up on me while I rearranged items in the cooler.

"What the—" My adrenaline still ran high after the Halloween incident, sending an overwhelming urge to strike out until my mind registered who had spoken. "Rachel… what're you doing here in the middle of the morning?"

"My professor canceled class, and I wanted to see you. I'll get a latte and study for a while here too."

Right. Rachel went to a small college, so I could see where getting away to Oakville for a couple of hours could be a fun break from reminders of her recent ex-boyfriend.

I set the jug of milk in its place, then kissed my daughter on the cheek. "It's always lovely to see you. Go ahead, make yourself a cup. You don't need Deana or me, sweetheart."

"Mom." When I didn't respond appropriately, Rachel rolled her eyes. "I asked you what you're doing this weekend?"

"Oh." I'd missed it thanks to my blood pressure spike. "Ah, making and freezing pies for Thanksgiving. Why? You want to spend the night? How's the rental holding up?" Thomas had arranged a tow to the mechanic for Rachel's Accord and rented her a car. I didn't know what to think of that, to be honest.

"What if you and Aunt Cyn went to the eighties club with Bella and me? I have the week of Thanksgiving off. I can help with the food then."

I crossed my arms. "Why do you want to take two old ladies to the club? Is this a trick? Because Cyndi still knows how to party. She might dance even you under the table, Miss Snow."

Rachel nudged my shoulder. "No. Geesh. After Lee's party, I realized I miss you. Bella and I are planning to blow off the stress of school and the Cody stuff. I thought you might want to do the same. It's been crazy around here though."

"No kidding."

She leaned her head down to mine. "What do you think?"

I tapped my lip. "I'll see what Cyn's up to."

"You can invite Thomas too, if you want."

"He's busy, but thanks. He's my ride to and from my IV appointment on Friday. We'll have breakfast."

She bounced lightly on the balls of her feet, an easy smile spreading. "He's a good guy, Mama. I'm glad you're finally moving on."

"Thanks, sweetie," I said. It felt more like we were stuck, but it also seemed like I'd been challenged to be patient in every area of my life. It wore thin. A night out would do me some good. Since Rachel had turned twenty-one, we'd hung out at the pub to catch a live band, but I'd never considered going to a club with her. Why not? It probably helped her to use me as an excuse to not hook up. My motherly instincts told me she wanted time before taking a new direction.

I smiled up at her. "Sounds fun."

"You two look adorable," Rachel said, fingering the lace hem of my tunic. "Love the hippie dress."

As if I'd ever wear this as a dress. The slightest wind and "hello cellulite."

"When you're forty-seven, it's a tunic, sweetheart."

She giggled at me, but could I blame her? Rachel didn't have a single dimple or jiggle where it shouldn't be. "Your girly combat boots go great with the moto leggings." She stepped to the side to greet Cyndi and compliment her black leather ensemble, complete with platform boots. For my tiny friend, all her shoes came with platforms. The best part of her outfit, though, were the beaded earrings resembling a peacock's tail she'd made. Cyndi fed her creativity with a successful side hustle making jewelry.

We had met Rachel and her roommate, Isabella, out front of Ducky's, an eighties-nineties-themed nightclub in downtown Raleigh.

Cyndi squeezed both girls. "You're so considerate for arranging this." She grasped both girls' hands and pulled them out of the long queue. "We're blowing this line though."

"But—"

She walked us to the bouncer and looked back. "Consider it an early holiday present from Aunt Cyn." She scanned the bouncer like she was picking out a dessert. Her head tipped back, index finger pinching her bottom lip in approval. "My, my, aren't you a prime one?"

"That's why he's a bouncer," I murmured. "What are you doing?"

She shooed me away and popped her caboose. "Cynthia Sendaydiego. I reserved the Spyder."

The bouncer skimmed his tablet. "Yes, you did. Show me those IDs, ladies, then you're all set."

Before it registered, the four of us were lounging in the best spot in the house, like we owned the place. A low-banked booth, it resembled the Ferrari from *Ferris Bueller's Day Off*. It took up prime real estate on an upper level and overlooked the dance floor.

Ducky's interior design was based on John Hughes's films. Whoever came up with the concept possessed an eye for detail. Other half-moon booths filled out our level in a plush material the color of Molly Ringwald's hair. They filled quickly as the same hostess who escorted us dropped off each group.

The bar on our level occupied a long wall. One bartender looked exactly like John Bender from *The Breakfast Club*, including the same ripped plaid shirt and fingerless gloves. His partner looked like Iona from *Pretty in Pink*, with a platinum wig and a fantastic cat eye. I danced in my seat, like a giddy toddler on her birthday.

I turned to Cyndi. "This place is fabulous. I hope there's a Molly Ringwald doppelgänger around here."

"She's the manager," Cyndi answered, reminding me she'd been here plenty of times. Despite having each other's back, our lives had been very different. Sometimes we were more like siblings than friends.

A server, dressed as Ferris himself, arrived. "What can I get y'all?" He flirted shamelessly with the girls. Seeing Rachel slowly come out of herself boosted my mood more. We both knew she'd done the right thing in letting Cody go, but it was good to see her posture return to its default of dancer-perfect again.

"You're getting *crunk* tonight, right? You promised. You deserve it," Cyndi said, pulling my attention from the girls.

There was the hard part. The hard work never took a day off. The bruises still covering my arm and the time away from my business all flashed before me. I couldn't live in fear of setbacks either. I laughed, pointing to my heart. "*Crunk* in here? I promise. With *my* liver? Two drinks max."

"Oh, my liver!" she bellowed, bumping my shoulder.

Had I forgotten how Cyndi made the joke whenever she over-imbibed in college? Wow, it had been too long since we let loose.

I turned to Ferris. "Do you serve Herradura?" No matter the progress, I was keeping to the six-month experiment with naturally gluten-free liquor. Fortunately, there were plenty.

"Yes. Do you want a round of shots?"

"No." I'd made good progress but not shot-drinking progress. "How about a Horseshoe Margarita? Just a splash of agave."

"Can do." Ferris turned to Cyndi.

"Sex on the Beach, honeybuns," she said with a wink.

"Schnapps? Cranberry juice? I thought you were working on a low-glycemic index plan. That's a lot of sugar," I asked by her ear for privacy after the server moved to the girls.

She tapped my arm. "No mothering on Girl's Night Out. You're not supposed to bug me about a cheat day."

I jolted, embarrassed for calling her out. Normal people had cheat days even if I couldn't. I still wasn't completely convinced my indulgence was a good idea. "Sorry, chica."

Cyndi stretched out her arm and pulled me into her. "It's all good. Promise you'll loosen up even if you can't get plastered, okay?"

I gave her a big smile. "Promise."

Rachel ordered the same drink as I did, and Bella chose a local IPA. This was the first time my daughter ordered something other than beer when with me. "Branching out, Snow?" I asked after Ferris moved on.

She shrugged off the question. "I'm staying away from gluten." Since when? I hadn't noticed her plate at Liam's birthday party.

I studied my daughter, hoping the low light would keep her from catching my scrutiny. Rachel seemed a little pale, more like me than her father's golden tone that she usually had. She shivered and rubbed her hands over her arms. She wore a dancer's shrug over a plaid, sleeveless skater dress. I didn't like this. She'd never been easily chilled before, like me.

"Are you cold, Snow?"

"It's fine." She sent me a small, fading smile, which failed to reassure me. "I'll warm up as soon as the drinks come."

Cyndi elbowed me and pointed to one of the half-moon booths across the balcony from us. It was filled with men who looked to be in their twenties. They were put together, like new professionals. "Two of those cuties are eyeing our girls."

Boy, was I out of practice. I didn't know what to do. "Should we leave them alone or something?"

"What's wrong?" Rachel asked after laughing at something Bella had said. With the music pounding, it was hard to hear across our little table.

I tipped my head toward the men. "You've caught someone's eye. Do you want us to go?"

Her laugh came at my expense now. "Why would I want that? It was my idea to bring you here. I thought you'd like the atmosphere."

"I do; it's fantastic. Won't I cramp your style though?"

The laughter grew. "You speak appropriately for this place. No, Mama, I came here to dance and make sure you get lit. For as much as you can." She winked at me. Even though it was a sarcastic comment, it set me at ease. "Strangers never believe you're my mother anyway. I don't think it'll keep anyone from coming by." She paused and waved her fingers at the table. A cute blond fella waved back, and it was my turn to laugh.

Our drinks arrived, and I raised my glass. "To the McKenna women and the sisters of our hearts."

They all returned the toast, and we let ourselves sink into the booth for a bit, absorbing the vibe of the crowd and enjoying the music. We each ordered a refill during our catch-up fest while flirting continued across the balcony.

Hanging out with Rachel and Bella came naturally—a pleasant surprise. I'd never, ever have considered partying with my parents. Here, we were simply grown women of varying experiences, enjoying a luxurious night out. Admittedly, it helped to not be squished into the general population downstairs. I could lose myself in the music on the dance floor, but squishing around tall tables with a young crowd? It would have been uncomfortable, to say the least. Once again, Cyndi had my back.

Eventually the pull of my favorite songs grew too great. Slightly tipsy and ready to let loose, I stood, adjusting my blouse and shaking out my hair.

Cyndi and I made our way down the steps to the dance floor while the girls said something about the bathroom. The center-piece of the enormous dance floor was a black-and-white mural of the namesake, Ducky from *Pretty in Pink*, hanging behind the DJ's area. It was backlit, so the white areas changed colors. As we descended toward it, the music changed to a Prince tribute and Ducky glowed purple. The light shining from it bounced off a big disco ball, turning everything the singer's signature color.

We entered the fray as "Delirious" finished, transitioning into "I Would Die 4 U." The dance Cyndi and I did included the requisite hand gestures as we pointed at each other for "U" and dissolved into laughter. "Little Red Corvette" finished the set without Rachel or Bella joining us. I wondered out loud what kept them when Cyndi pointed up toward our level. The young men from the half-moon had left their group and sat with our girls.

"Looks like tonight was good for both of us."

Cyndi nodded, rubbing my arm.

"Is it weird I'm glad for her?"

"Why would it be weird?"

I didn't personally know any mothers who wanted to meddle in their children's love lives, but I knew there were plenty who did. Not wanting to go into it, I pulled Cyndi back to the music and kept dancing.

When the tribute finished, we poured waters from the stand near the dance floor. I downed my little cup and finally said, "I've always felt like I had to hide my male interests from Bobby." I chuckled. "Even after I was married."

Cyndi shook her head. "Bobby's never been a normal mother, Kicky. Sometimes I forget how much you've had to figure out on your own." She took our cups and threw them in the trash. "Miss Thing has a brilliant head on her shoulders, thanks to you. The girls will come down when they're ready. Let's shake what our maker gave us."

The floor pulsed to La Bouche's "Be My Lover" as a black light shone from Ducky again. It made my skin glow purple, courtesy of my ghostlike quality. The beat fit the vibe of the crowd, who spent most of their time jumping up and down.

Cyndi and I managed more than that and worked up a sweat. The girls joined us then, bringing the entire group of guys with them. After swaying and rocking to the songs and briefly showing the youngsters variations on the Running Man, the music slowed to give us a break.

I recognized the live version of the song from the audience's cheers alone. The sultry opening bars to one of my all-time favorites made my heart leap as my skin embraced the cooling sensation of mellowing out. I closed my eyes and shifted my shoulders as the lone guitar was joined by other instruments. My hips hit the two beats of the drum and the story of the "Hotel California" began for me. As I moved with the crowd, I let the song consume me as it had so many times over the years. It simultaneously haunted and healed my soul.

I spun to Cyndi, who wore a conspiratorial smirk. My gaze

tracked the group, counting, wondering why it felt bigger. Or was I so in my head I didn't notice the crowd move?

"Need a partner, darlin'?" A leg melded behind mine when I stepped forward, my body recognizing the owner and automatically following when his hips shifted back. A huge smile spread across my face as I glanced over my shoulder. "You didn't jump." Thomas's Southern baritone warmed my ear.

"Nope. What do you think it means?"

"Maybe you sensed me watching."

"You were?"

He leaned over my shoulder and purred, "Sexiest sight in the room."

Holy hell, he smelled good. The crisp notes of a peaty Highland scotch on his breath touched my nose as his lips grazed my cheek. A hint of his sandalwood and citrus stayed with me when he pulled away.

It had only been a day, but I'd missed him. As expected, I'd passed out on the way home from the doctor's office. Thomas had settled me in my room for a nap and left. His presence currently made my knees weak. And my sex stir. My head fell back in a giddy laugh as he took hold of my fingers and spun me, then held me tight before I recognized the direction change. He lowered his head and raised his eyebrow, seeking permission the way he'd done when we danced at my birthday dinner. Cool, navy eyes bore into mine as passing light from the disco ball flashed a speck of silver, revealing the mischief there.

Still trust me?

A thrill slowly traveled up my spine. A corner of my mouth lifted as I winked. *Bring it, handsome.*

He began a slow-paced Salsa, matching the sexy tempo of the song. The achingly easy pace of the dance differed from any I'd ever performed when competing. The steps committed to my muscle memory, Thomas only needed to shift a hip for me to know what came next. As he changed our hold, he had me duck and sway with him in an arm loop. It felt as if we'd been dancing together for years and like we could do this forever.

Thomas pulled me in, and his dark button-down shirt brushed where my billowy sleeve had bared my arm. The silkiness caressed my skin, sending a shiver that had nothing to do with the room's temperature. Butter-soft jeans barely shielded strong thighs, brushing against and between my legs as we moved. The surrounding space opened as our group stopped to watch, then a larger crowd paused to give us more room. Thomas refrained from adding in flashier moves, yet something about us drew attention. For me though, the crowd disappeared. His shoulder shifted, and I was seduced by another cross-body lead.

"Thomas," I pleaded, but for what, I wasn't sure. To be alone? To melt back into the crowd?

"Shh. Don't think. Feel." He rasped quick breaths across my cheek. He pulled me back in, perhaps taken by the moment as much as me.

It all became a drug unto itself while the keening guitar vibrated through my bones. Here was the part of the song which always threatened tears and a longing for what my life could've been, as it reminded me of the trap of chronic illness. How there was no hope for a cure, no breaking free. This, though, felt like a celebration, a desire fulfilled or one promising more.

I didn't want the intoxication to end, and the chase of notes to the finish brought a slight panic. I wanted to dance forever. When the song concluded, we fell into each other's arms in shock, but the sound of clapping broke us from our trance.

I threw my arms around his neck and jumped as Thomas finished the work, bending his back and planting a hard kiss to my lips. A piercing whistle burst our bubble.

"I only told you Rachel and I were hanging out. How did you know we were here?"

"By accident, really. Rachel mentioned it to Banger's assistant when they called her with some follow-up on the cyber harassment."

I cringed at the mention, not wanting reality to taint my beautiful reprieve.

"Sorry, baby. I didn't mean to dampen your fire."

Thomas pulled me off the dance floor, resting his back against a column, pulling me against his body. "Y'alright?"

I gave him my best smile. "I'm fantastic. You didn't dampen anything." I went on my tiptoe and teased him. "Well, nothing you don't want dampened."

Thomas growled and kissed my jaw. With the bubble gone, we were both painfully aware of the crowd. "Can we get out of here?"

My voice caught in my throat, boiling with need. "I'd love nothing more. But—"

Thomas tucked some hair behind my ear, stroking the tip. "The elf queen can't leave her people, can she?"

I cleared my throat. "It was Rachel's idea to come here. To cheer up both of us." It would've been different if Thomas and I had made a commitment, but abandoning the group, my family? I was never the girl to ditch her friends for a quick lay, even one that could be more.

My hesitance proved how much was still unsaid between Thomas and me. We had feelings so hot they scorched, but the constant cancellations on both our parts, the dropping of everything for someone else, it showed where we really stood.

"How about a drink instead?"

"I've had my tequila quota for the night, but I'll take a club soda and lime."

"Look at you"—he grinned—"behaving while being bad at the same time."

In a snap, our heat lowered back to friends-who-might-be-more. I bit my lip and shrugged. The boundaries were helpful when they were reasonable. They helped me have energy for a night like this. I hoped there'd be more. Many more nights out with great friends, a grown child, and a deliciously sexy man. This glimpse into how the next phase of life could work turned out to be a gift I'd never expected.

"Meet you at the bar? The ladies' room is calling." A minute away would also help to clear my head.

MODERN LOVE

THOMAS

A bartender with fake platinum hair made time to dance around her space but couldn't manage to get it in gear enough to shoot up a Jack and Coke and a club soda. *Maybe her wig is on too tight?* Thomas turned his back to the bar. It kept him from glaring at the woman.

He didn't see the appeal of the garish club. It celebrated a time when people had terrible taste. It made Kick smile though, so he liked it. He never paid attention to the movies the place supposedly enshrined. Thomas could tell how much she adored them by the way her face lit over each additional detail she discovered. For that, too, he gave kudos to the management. Not so much for an efficient staff.

A too-young woman slinked down the length of the bar toward him. Normally, this would've been the beginning of a game to distract him. Lure her in, play the pursued, set the terms for the night. Women who approached first rarely looked for long-term relationships.

"Hey handsome, what're you doing alone?" In a skimpy top revealing nothing, tight ripped jeans, and hooker shoes. The visual enhanced her "playing grown-up" vibe.

She insisted on touching his arm, making his skin crawl. When Kick had stroked his shirt, it made Thomas's skin hum. "I'm not."

Where the hell was the damn bartender?

"Get a girl a drink and I'll listen to anything you want to say."

She stepped into Thomas's space, stroking his chest. He caught her wrist as he shifted back and hit the bar's edge. A wild-haired brunette caught the corner of his eye. *His* wild-haired brunette.

"My name's Lili." The girl ran her tongue over her teeth.

She should never do that again. Christ, he'd bet she was no older than Rachel. The problem with being the pursued? The pursuer discouraged no as an answer. "Help a guy out here?" Thomas called over his shoulder.

Kick stepped closer, a smirk on her face. "You looked like you had everything under control."

"We were talking," Lee-whoever snarled at Kick.

"The conversation's over, sweetheart," Kick answered with the familiar disciplinary tone and stony stare he remembered from the first time he'd laid eyes on her. Like then, it stoked his fire.

"Tried to tell you… was waiting for my lady," Thomas added.

"Her?" The girl's face contorted. "She's *ancient.*"

Kick slid her arm across the back of Thomas's shoulders, and he finally took a deep breath. He liked bars with history. And regulars. He couldn't relax here at all.

"The word you're looking for is *grown,*" Kick said with a devilish glint in her eye. She waved her fingers. "Shoo now, little one."

Thomas happily shrugged.

"Fuck off." The co-ed wobbled away on her too-high heels, scanning the room for another sucker.

"Guess we're even now?" Kick asked.

"How do you figure?"

"You bailed me out. Now I've rescued your pretty face." She kissed his cheek for emphasis.

"I had to ask for your help."

Kick's brow raised as a corner of her mouth ticked up.

"Touché." Thomas surrendered. He pulled her in close and kissed her quick. "Made your point."

Kick scanned the bar top. "Where are the drinks?"

"We've been abandoned." Thomas raised his hand once more, snapping his fingers to get Platinum's attention.

"Hey Iona!" Kick bellowed. Platinum's gaze shot their way, an apologetic pout on her face.

"I'm sorry, guys."

"No worries. Can you have Ferris send our drinks over to the car?"

The bartender nodded. "Can do. Sorry again."

"Isn't this place great?" Kick asked as she swayed toward a booth resembling a Ferrari Spyder. "She looks just like Annie Potts from the movie. They've thought of all the things."

"What movie?" Thomas stared at the booth while Kick slid in first.

"*Pretty in Pink*, Professor. Didn't you pick up on the club's theme?"

"I heard about it. Don't know any of those films by name though."

Kick clicked her tongue. "What rock have you been sleeping under? Do you even know why we're sitting in this car? It's one of the signature features here."

After Thomas settled next to her, shaking his head, Kick explained *Ferris Bueller* to him, along with some vital aspects of eighties pop culture he'd missed.

"I'm sorry we couldn't duck out earlier," Kick said, absently teasing the drink straw with her tongue.

Thomas swallowed hard. He still craved getting her alone. The heat they'd created on the dance floor hovered on the edges of his control, waiting for permission to blaze. He took her hand into his lap, rubbing Kick's palm with his thumb, tracing her lifeline.

"Do you ever do something just for yourself?"

She chuckled. "Do you?"

"You're my *just for me*," he answered, feeling the grin spread, hoping every muscle contraction would tell her the truth he had sworn to hold in.

"And you're sweet." Kick turned in to him, draping her free arm across the back of the booth. Her thumb mimicked Thomas's as it stroked his neck. "Rachel picked this place for me, knowing how much I love eighties music. Then Cyndi pulled her magical strings and reserved the VIP spot. She mentioned another group has the second time slot or something."

"So, y'all don't plan on closing the place down?"

"Are you kidding?" Kick let a sexy chuckle roll through her body into Thomas's. "I don't know about you, Professor, but it already feels like two a.m."

He finished his drink with his free hand. "Would you want to come back to my house after?"

Kick's eyes lit up as a smile spread across her face. "Liam is spending the night at a friend's house." She scooted closer, enough for Thomas to peek at her purple satin bra and how well it embraced her perfect breasts. He bit his lip. Could they finally get their much-needed alone time?

She kissed his jaw and purred, "Your wish can be granted."

Thomas picked up the tumbler to distract his shifting in the seat. Whether she gave him an eye twinkle or growling frown, each minute with Kick was doing the impossible. She cracked the safe he'd locked his heart away in, one slow tumbler tick at a time.

"Thank you, Genie."

"No problem, sweets. Let me text Lee." She let out a deep sigh, chuckling. "The kid thinks he's my guardian now."

Thomas couldn't say he blamed the boy.

"There you two are," Cyndi called out, moving toward the Ferrari.

A fit, middle-aged man hung out on the edge of Thomas's vision. He stole quick glances over there to see if he recognized the guy and make sure he meant no harm.

"Where else would we be?" Kick chuckled. Cyndi leaned in and whispered something, causing a loud gasp from Kick. "That's how you roll, not me."

"Only saying…" Cyndi tucked a few strands of hair behind her ear. "I would bless it."

Kick bumped her friend's shoulder, and they fell into each other, laughing. It didn't take a rocket scientist—or a geneticist—to figure out that Cyndi had half expected to find them banging in a dark corner. As much as he would've accepted the offer, he was proud of Kick for rejecting the idea. He didn't want any part of their relationship to be cheap.

Cyndi swayed too much in her seat, as if the room spun for her.

Rachel and her roommate dumped themselves into the other side of the booth. The server Kick called Ferris brought out a platter of wings she had ordered for the group, guessing everyone would return soon. As the kids dug in, Kick pulled something out of her purse, then unwrapped it.

"What do you have there?"

She bit off a piece of what looked like a Slim Jim. "A Paleo meat stick. I keep them around for emergencies, like needing extra protein to soak up any remaining alcohol." She managed a sassy smile while chewing.

Thomas couldn't resist the pull of the words. "A meat stick?"

He waggled his eyebrows. "Save room for my meat stick when I get you home."

Kick blushed and ducked her head. "Another reason for some extra energy." She tapped his thigh. "Nice middle school joke, by the way."

"Always." Thomas winked and took a sip from his glass. The guy he'd kept his eye on stepped out of the shadows.

The man bent over the booth to speak to Cyndi. "Hi, I'm Randy. I loved watching you dance."

"Ooh, I bet you *are randy*." She batted her lashes, extending her hand for a flirty shake. "Muscled as well. I'm Cyn."

Thomas chuckled as Kick turned toward him, rolling her eyes, mouthing, *She loves being able to say that.*

Randy grinned like he'd hit the Powerball jackpot. "No way. You look too much like an angel. Can I buy you a drink?"

"Mind if I disappear for a little while?" she asked after scooching out of the booth.

"If you must." Kick feigned annoyance, but she squeezed Thomas's hand under the table. Not for the first time, Cyndi reminded Thomas of Banger, who was conspicuously absent at the moment. It also didn't take a PhD to figure out where he'd wandered off to. All those young ones downstairs? Hell, maybe the high-heeled princess had preyed on the man. Thomas laughed to himself at the thought.

"She'll eat him up," Kick muttered in Thomas's ear. His brows shot up until he clued in that Kick was speaking of her friend and not his.

"I bet." He took some wings for himself.

"Aren't you having any, Mama?" Rachel took advantage of the empty space and slid next to Kick, who shook her head.

"The sauce isn't safe. No worries for you though. They're grilled, not fried." Kick glanced over her shoulder. "I thought the fellas you found might like some."

"They went back to their booth." Rachel dropped a bone and wiped her fingers.

"We could take what we don't finish over there," Kick offered.

"Relax, please. You don't have to be a mama all the time."

"Wait until you're one."

Rachel shivered briskly and wiped her forehead. "The guys went their own way when Bella made it clear we didn't want to do anything more than dance." She placed her head on Kick's shoulder. "We came here for a girl's night." She leaned around her mother and addressed Thomas. "No offense. It's cute you hunted her down, actually."

"It wasn't hard," he said. "You told us where y'all were."

"I did, didn't I? Yay me." She beamed and Thomas melted yet again, his memories flashing to another similar young smile. Why did they all seem to fit each other seamlessly? He reminded himself this wasn't like back then. Times had changed and so had he.

"...tell me you were in love?" Thomas overheard Rachel whispering to her mother.

"What?" The alarm in Kick's voice set Thomas into action. He wanted no part of their tête-à-tête.

"Excuse me, ladies." He leaned into Kick, who was studying the dance floor and seemed as eager to get away from Rachel's misinterpretation. "My turn for the men's."

She nodded at Thomas, then grabbed his hand to keep him in place. "Snow, ready to hit the floor again?"

"Sure. This place is so fun. I haven't danced like this in ages."

Kick did a double take. "The school bills I pay claim otherwise, you know." She tipped her chin up to Thomas. "Meet us downstairs when you're done?"

He leaned down and kissed her cheek. "It's a date."

While he walked away, Rachel told her mother, "This dancing is for me."

In the men's room, Thomas bumped into Banger. "Find yourself a *bic?*" Not long ago, he'd found his friend's code word for a hookup—a disposable woman—appropriately funny. Most of the women had the same attitude toward them anyway.

Banger adjusted his shirt and rerolled his sleeves while checking himself in the mirror. "You know it." He sighed. "It's all about the carburetor, brother." Thomas waited at the door, knowing Banger itched to say more as he washed his hands. The man could never resist. "Surprised you let your woman out of your sight after practically nailing her on the dance floor."

"Don't," Thomas muttered.

He raised his hands. "Civilized fucking is still fucking. That's all I'm saying. Speaking of, when are you taking your little show to its natural ending?"

Thomas opened the door. "Later. At my place. Civilized, you know? Besides, you're the one who suggested we come here."

Big hands clamped down on Thomas's shoulders. "If my stud buddy's given up bics, I should facilitate his own carburetor maintenance when I can."

Thomas looked at the ceiling, chuckling. "There's no hope for you, but thanks, man. Where're you headed?"

"To the bar to wet my other whistle." Banger smacked his lips. "Seems my throat's dry. You?"

"Meeting the ladies back on the dance floor. Listen, they reserved the Spyder booth upstairs. No one will mind if you relax there a spell. We left some wings on a platter if the staff hasn't bused them."

"Naw, I'm good. I'll get a drink and find you. Then again, you'll probably have another audience soon."

"Don't worry. No more big scenes tonight."

NEW SENSATION

KICK

The girls and I bumped into Cyndi on the stairs.

"Are you going to dance?" she asked.

My voice never carried in loud places, so I answered with a nod and a smile.

"Good. I'll come."

As we reached the bottom, the music changed to something slow. "Well, hell." Cyndi grabbed my bicep and gestured toward the bar. "Let's get a drink."

I told Rachel and Bella we'd catch up and pivoted with my friend. "Where did your dance partner go?" I asked Cyndi.

She scrunched her face like she'd tasted something rotten. "He kissed like a plecostomus. I cut him loose."

I shuffled to keep up with her swift little feet. Cyndi must have been very thirsty. "You kissed him already?"

She slipped her arm through mine as we reached the bar line. "My sweet, amateur Kicky... I test drove the important stuff first. I'm too old to waste time getting to know someone first."

Okay then.

We were next in line, so Cyndi asked, "What do you want?"

"A club soda and lime."

"Perfect. I should dilute my blood alcohol level too. Pace myself, you know?"

"Exactly." We both stepped up to the bartender, but Cyndi ordered for both of us. I moved over to make room for those behind us and watched the floor. Rachel and Bella were easy to spot, dancing with a mixed crowd of people their age. A couple of kids looked familiar.

"Here you go." Cyndi handed me a tumbler with the lime wedge already floating.

"Thank you, chica." I took a big drink and had to keep myself from doing a spit take. I made the same face Cyndi had done a few minutes earlier. "This is tonic, not soda. I can't have it." Cyn took it when I pivoted to take it back to the bar. "Give to me. I'm parched," she said.

"Fine by me." It didn't solve my dry mouth though. "I'll go get some water from the station."

"I'll be right here."

It took several minutes to make my way through another line, but I filled two of the tiny cups and slammed them down. As I squeezed through the milling bodies to find the trash can, the smell of all the cologne ever made threatened to knock me off my feet. Unfortunately, it masked nothing. I caught a glimpse of the gray receptacle when the paper cups went flying out of my hand. A big monster had grabbed me from behind, smelling like ten packs of cigarettes. I felt his sweat soak into the back of my tunic.

My fight-or-flight response hadn't abated since the attack, and it jumped into action immediately with the added thought of *Where the hell is Thomas?*

·   ·   ·

"Here he is! Here he is!" Cyndi waved wildly with one arm at Thomas while the other stayed around my shoulders. A small crowd had gathered, thanks to the show my bestie made when she found me fighting off Mr. Big and Hairy.

Thomas rushed to us. "What's wrong?"

"Kicky beat up a guy."

"What?" His gaze rapidly swung around the group.

"Cyn…" I gave her a warning look and turned to Thomas. "Some big guy grabbed me from behind. The asshole said he'd watched us dancing and wanted his turn. Before I could tell him to buzz off, he tried to take me toward the door. I think he meant for us to leave here."

"Dammit." Thomas jammed his hand through his hair, then pulled me in.

"I'm fine." At least I was now. I couldn't stop the post event shaking, but it made all the difference being in his arms.

"Fine? You were awesome," Cyndi added, smacking her lips. "I came up at the end, thinking our girl needed an assist, but she put those platform boots to good use. On the Sasquatch's foot and balls."

Thomas growled, now looking farther out. "Sasquatch?"

Cyndi shrugged. "He was huge and furry. Not in a fun way, either."

"And smelly." I added.

"I see." He lifted my chin with his thumbs. "Where is this guy now?"

Cyndi tapped his pecs. "Sorry, Professor, the Sasquatch got away. He took off when I shouted and security came over."

He sighed and growled again. "Y'all want to leave?"

My flattened palm traveled up Thomas's chest, stopping at each plane change until it reached his neck. I needed to feel him to stay calm. Plus something else was happening to me. My body felt like it was waking up, like each cell wanted to touch and experience as much as it could. "No. We came here to dance and relieve stress. Let's do it."

Cyndi took a step and stumbled forward. Both Thomas and I grabbed an arm.

"Alright there?" he asked.

Cyndi giggled. "I'm just still *intoxth-icated*. I need more water. Or dancing."

Our group moved back to the edge of the dance floor. Back in the shelter of my people, my body relaxed and became inspired. Cyndi and I showed the kids more dance moves from high school and college. I could swear the crowd cheered us on until I stumbled into Thomas. He deftly righted me, but I couldn't stay on my feet.

"The room's spinning," I complained, my nose scrunching in confusion.

With his arms holding me up, protecting me from the crowd, Thomas guided us to the downstairs lounge area.

"I'm okay. Swear." I protested his movements, thinking they were a show of power or disappointment in my behavior. But the room wouldn't stop swirling, and I couldn't figure out where I'd screwed up. Clearly I'd become a complete lightweight this fall, thanks to the detoxing.

Thomas turned to me with concern on his face when I'd been expecting judgment. "Tell me exactly what happened while I went to the restroom."

I smiled, happy he wasn't mad at me. At the moment, I would've told him anything. I filled him in on meeting Cyndi on the steps and the tonic water mix-up.

"What's wrong with tonic? Don't you like it?"

"Uh-uh." I leaned into the railing surrounding the dance floor. "I can't have the high fructose corn syrup."

"Ah. I see."

I continued, "So I went to the water station and downed two of those smallish cups." My hand swept through my hair. It didn't occur to me how crazy it might make my curls look. I didn't like my hair sticking to my head and had to make it stop. "The guy came up behind me—like you do sometimes—only, I hated it immediately. He was slimy and smelly and all over me. He didn't want to dance."

"Doesn't sound like it," Thomas said in a rough, angry tone.

"My boots came in handy." I smiled, then frowned when the man's face flashed through my memory.

"Kick?"

I stared at the floor, suddenly fascinated by the mix of black and purple swirling into a pattern—anything to take away the image of his face. I wanted to force it away, rub it out of my synapses.

"I probably need more protein. Some carbs too."

Thomas gave me a gentle shake. "Let's go since there's nothing you can eat here."

"What's going on kids?" Banger asked, appearing out of nowhere.

"Hey, hiya, security guru." I didn't know why I said something so dumb. Thomas had mentioned arriving with his friend, but this was the first I'd seen him.

"We need to leave," Thomas answered.

My head tipped up fast, and I took a step to compensate. "But the girls—"

"Should go home too." Thomas said soothingly. He bent his knees to meet my eyes. "Please. I have to get Banger going on this guy."

"What guy?" Banger asked.

"Someone tried to take Kick against her will. Obviously."

"The hell? Why didn't you come get me?"

"Sorry man. Was making sure she and Cyndi were good. At first I thought the guy had made a free grab. It doesn't sound like it now."

Thomas repeated what I'd told him to Banger, making me

cringe with embarrassment. The girls arrived before we could retrieve everyone.

"Mama, we need you to do more of your kick-ass old-school moves," Rachel half begged, half whined.

Thomas raised an eyebrow to let me speak. I didn't want to think about how good it felt to not have him step in. Cyndi had Bella's hands and did a sloppy jive in the background, ignoring our conversation.

"You two are so funny!" I called out while fanning the hem of my tunic, suddenly scorching hot. Not the best place for my first hot flash, but what did I know? I turned back to Rachel. "What did you say, sweet girl?" I brushed some wisps of hair behind her ear. "Such a good girl."

"Well fuck. Yeah, we're out of here," Banger said for me.

Rachel's face fell, but she didn't look surprised, only resigned. "Are you still driving us home?" she asked me.

"Of course—"

"No." Thomas interrupted.

"I'll take the girls," Banger said.

By now, Isabella and Cyndi had joined us properly.

"Another thirty minutes of dancing and I'll be sober enough to drive Mama," Rachel insisted.

"No. Let's go, princess." Banger said, his arm extended toward the coat check. Bella frowned at both of them.

Thank you, I mouthed to him.

He passed me a tiny grin and said to Thomas, "I'll speak to the manager on our way out."

"Because of the guy? Isn't it common in places like this?" I protested.

"Let me check," Banger insisted, and I snapped my jaw shut. He walked away with his hands around the necks of Rachel and Bella. I frowned but just as quickly couldn't remember why.

I turned to Cyndi for help, but she was studying the light

from the disco ball, her hands up as if she were trying to catch the rays coming off of it.

We followed behind Banger and the girls to the front of the club. Rachel and Isabella retrieved their coats while Thomas and Banger spoke with people at the desk. One of them was the security guy who let us in.

I tapped Cyndi on the shoulder. "You okay, chica?"

She'd been swaying next to me with her eyes closed. While still moving to the music, she said, "I'm f-faba... aw-thum, mamacita. I swear I can *feel* the music inside me." She shimmied in a circle and fell into my side.

Thomas returned. "Did you get your coats?"

I looked at Cyndi. Did we have coats? I couldn't remember. Rachel and Bella had disappeared from the coatroom window.

"Can y'all stay here while I check?" he asked.

"I have to pay the bill," Cyndi and I said at the same time.

"I invited you," I told her.

Before Cyndi could make her case, Thomas butted in. "It's taken care of."

"What? The tab?"

"The whole bill."

"Again?"

I was about to pout when Cyndi elbowed me in the side. I came this close to falling over. My amazing platform boots saved me again. "Thank him properly," she ordered.

Thomas dipped his head. "It's my pleasure. The four of y'all were... a fun diversion."

"Yeah right."

"He likes you...," Cyndi stage whispered, getting some spit on my cheek. I wiped it off with the neck of my top.

Thomas dropped his head between us. "Promise me y'all will wait here while I get your things."

I held up three fingers but couldn't remember where the gesture came from and shrugged. "Someone's honor."

Thomas laughed lightly. "Be right back."

Another wave of heat swept through me, making it hard to breathe. I slid my arm through Cyndi's. "I think I'm getting hot flashes of all things. Let's get some air."

The current bouncer bid us farewell as he held the door for us, the cold air relieving my unbearable heat.

"We're waiting for your fel-le-la," Cyndi sang for no reason other than a lack of sobriety.

Jaysus, she needed to stop swaying. Or was it me? I said to no one, "I need my re-remedy." My tongue started failing me.

"How're you ladies doing?" Two of Raleigh's finest approached. They looked way too young to be cops. "You don't plan on driving tonight, do you?"

"Well…" I looked at Cyndi and back at them. "I s'pose we can walk, oci-ociffer," I answered while swaying. "Is that the right word?" I asked Cyndi's nose, after missing my aim for her ear.

He grabbed my arm. "Easy there. Do you need help? Why don't you come with us?"

I yanked my arm out of the policeman's grip, anger arriving from nowhere and at the wrong time. "Listen here, lad. You look no older than my son. So, scram!" I flapped my hands in his direction and almost fell over. "Fly away and leave us old ladies alone."

"No." He took my arm again. "Let's not cause a disturbance."

"If there's a disturbance, you made it. Who says we *need* taken care of? Because we're women and you… you're… men? Is that why?" My tone rose with each word. I draped my arm over Cyndi's shoulder and bellowed, "We don't need no damn men!"

"Yeah." My feisty friend jumped in. "S'right. We don't need any goddamn men! Even ones with badges and… and… guns and… shit." She paused, pivoted to me, and whisper-yelled, "They have guns, Kicky."

The two cops stood back with folded arms like they were watching a street performance, which they more or less were. In the back of my mind, a tiny person tapped on my shoulder and tried to tell me something wasn't right. I'd sensed it for a while, but a disconnect kept the voice mute.

I flung my free hand, almost making us fall again. "Stay strong, s-sister." I shooed at the officers again. "We pay our bills, we get ourselves off, we don't *want* to pick up your shit around the house *and*… We. Can. Get. Ourselves. Home."

"Now there's a visual." An amused Southern drawl filled my ears, and I remembered why we were freezing our asses off in the first place. "There a problem, officers?"

"Are you with these two… ladies?"

"I am." He bent to us. "Sorry, it took a while. My phone went missing, but I found it in the Ferrari."

"Have you been drinking?"

Thomas put his hand to his heart. "I promise, I'm sober as a saint."

My eyes popped wide at him. "You are? How wonderful."

Thomas's warm smile buckled my knees. He wrapped an arm around my waist and kept me steady.

"We could stay at the Sher-Shery— the hotel," I told the air.

Thomas slid my jacket around my shoulders as he answered, "No. You're staying at my place after we drop off Cyndi."

I popped up on my toes. "How wonderful. You were so fun last time."

Thomas's warm chuckle melted the parts of me that were frosting, literally.

"Good fun," Cyndi agreed, as if she'd been there. "You two deserve your time. I won't even bother you about the threesome."

Thomas froze, his brows raised almost to his hairline.

I leaned toward the young officers and sweetly said, "Thank you, *ociffers*. We're fine now."

The front one raised his hand to his hat and said, "Have a good night, Mrs. Mack."

I flinched, nearly falling over. "I knew he looked familiar."

"Friend of Dylan's?" Cyndi asked.

"In his grade," I whined.

"Sucks to get old," she moaned.

Thomas put his arm around us both to steer. He checked me over and frowned. "Don't understand why you're acting so sauced."

I stood up straight. "I'm not pithed."

"You're slurring your words."

"Ith's not slurring. Ith's schpeaking in curthive. Ith's an ancient art." I leaned around him and fist-bumped Cyndi.

"We can prove it. Say the magic drunk word," she said.

"Oh yeah." For some reason, the code word we'd used to check on each other in college easily popped into my memory. "Sup... super... oh shlit." I giggled.

"What's this magic drunk word?" Thomas asked with a smile in his tone.

Cyndi answered, "Sup-floos. Shit. I can't do it either."

"Super... are y'all trying to say *superfluous*?"

"Yay! You can drive us home." I clapped in relief. Until then, I had no proper way of knowing if Thomas truly was sober. Plus I could feel my body fading as fast as my mind.

Thomas stepped forward, a tighter grip on our shoulders. "Right. Any chance either of y'all can tell me where the car's parked?"

I pointed to the deck catty-corner from us. "Fourth floor." My eyes raised to his. "Hey, I remembered."

"I'm so proud," he mused.

"You spoke sarcasm. That's so cute." I tucked my head into his shoulder. "I knew there was a reason I liked you."

WHERE DIRT AND WATER COLLIDE

THOMAS

The women confirmed their lack of sobriety when halfway across the street. They began singing the Irish drinking song "Whiskey in the Jar"—with clapping included, but not necessarily at the correct times. With an amused headshake and wondering what he'd gotten himself into, Thomas coaxed them forward.

Kick urged, "Sing, Thomas. I'll teach you the words."

"Everyone knows the words, darlin'."

"Come on then."

"No." At least she sounded nice. He couldn't carry a tune if it meant his life. Still, by the time they stepped off the elevator, Thomas's ears rang. He steered them through the garage, wasting five minutes before Cyndi remembered they were parked to the right of the elevator and not the left side. He opened the driver's side door, pulled the seat forward, and helped Kick's friend out of her platform boots. As soon as Cyndi hit the leather seat, she curled into a circle, reminding him of Kick's dog.

He let the seat fall back, stood and found himself alone. Kick had disappeared. He ducked back into the car to turn on the engine and heat, then went to find her.

Kick sat on the garage floor against a column with her head on her knees. Thomas crouched down to better check on her and rubbed her calf. "You okay in there?"

She groaned, and her breath hitched.

He shifted his body to search her eyes. "Is there something you need?" He hadn't looked for water in the car, but they'd passed a vending machine on the first floor.

"Huh?"

"Do you need anything?"

Lifting her head, Kick's mouth pressed into a line as she stared off. In a faraway sound, she said, "What do I *need*? I need to let myself jump off the cliff and dive deep in love." Her finger made a circle over her heart. "I need a hole right here because desire burns so hot it leaves scorch marks, but s'okay since love fills in."

She stroked the butterfly charm around her neck. "I need to stop being transformed by disasters and have love transform me instead. I need to be forever chased even though I'm fiercely faithful. I need chemistry, so alive it's sentient."

She crossed her arms and rubbed her biceps. "I need to drift off to sleep and awake to skin on skin, with no need for an extra blanket. I need no doubts I'm the most important person on the planet." She lifted her head and met his gaze, point-blank. "I need extraordinary, and I won't settle." Then she exhaled a shaking breath and laid her head back on her knees.

Thomas fell on his ass as if pushed. *I'll be damned.* He ran a hand through his hair and took a couple of deep breaths to slow his racing heart.

Shit. Fuck. Hell. "She's right."

She deserved all of it. *Christ,* she'd earned it. Could he be this person though? She'd laid out the stakes in detail. All his other shit was simply that. A slow exhale whistled painfully from his chest.

When Thomas lifted his head, Kick hadn't moved. He shifted to his knees and jostled her lightly. She either slept or had passed out. A couple of harder squeezes and she jolted, lifting her head to see who'd done it.

"Everything's spinning," she complained.

He moved some curls out of her face. "Can you make it to the car? It's getting cold. Or do you feel sick?"

She smiled and brushed an errant piece of hair out of Thomas's eye, mimicking him. "It's getting long." She let her fingers run through it. "Like silk." Thomas sighed, wanting nothing more than to let her continue the simple caress. Still in a distant voice, she declared, "Ever since the curls tightened, you can't do this with my hair. It's the only thing I miss about not straightening it."

Throat dry and mind clouded, he croaked, "Why can't you?"

With a quiet chuckle, she said, "I told you. I end up with a head of fuzz, silly."

Entranced, he couldn't stop himself from demanding, "T-tell me again—how to do it."

A sleepy smile stretched across her face. Her eyes remained closed, making her face angelic. Her hand lifted to the back of his neck to demonstrate. "You come from underneath. It's okay to grab and scrunch or gently tug, but don't pull through. As soon as there's resistance, stop. Or it's Janice Joplin time."

Thomas dropped his forehead to right above hers. Irresistible. He craved to see what happened next, like he needed his next breath.

He reached toward her nape and slid his hand to cup the base of her skull.

"Mmm." She purred and nuzzled his hand, kitten-like.

He moved his fingers slowly back until reaching the resistance she mentioned. His hand returned to her neck, fingers curling, turning it into a light massage.

"Yeah. Perfect." The ethereal tone remained and her eyes never opened. His angel if he allowed it. "I miss this."

A bitter breeze ruffled her curls, snapping Thomas out of his trance. He reluctantly stood and pulled Kick up with him.

Thomas moved her closer to the light fixture and lifted her chin, checking her pupils. The improved illumination from their new height confirmed his suspicions. If he hadn't thought so before, Kick's "true confessions" session settled it. Brown flecks in her irises were completely absorbed by enlarged pupils, and they didn't respond to the brightening. "Can't believe I'm saying this, but I think y'all were drugged, baby."

"What? Why?" Her head lobbed slightly.

"You're certain you had no more alcohol tonight? No vodka in your soda?"

"Uh-uh." Kick shook her head and tilted, falling into the cold cement column. She stuck out her tongue. "Only yucky tonic water. Then real tap water. I filled the cup."

"You were slipped something somewhere." He drew her in tight and growled.

"'S impossible." She mumbled as if she were only half-awake. She nestled into Thomas, melding her body to his, unconsciously swaying, rubbing on him.

"Can we go to your house now?"

Damn. Now she was horny? Thomas welcomed the crisp wind gusting at his back.

He pried himself away and opened the car door. It wasn't hard to shut himself down. He'd never do anything with her in this state. Thomas buckled Kick in. "We're going somewhere alright."

When he found out who'd drugged her—he guessed both women too—there'd be hell to pay. Thomas texted Banger his suspicions and asked his friend to double-check Rachel and her roommate. He stretched into the back seat and checked on Cyndi. Out cold but breathing. Her pulse seemed fine, but he wasn't a doctor. He put the car in gear, livid at how something like this happened under his nose.

"Cyn's address is on my phone," Kick mumbled, her hands unsuccessfully trying to work the zipper on her purse.

"She's coming with us to the Emergency Department."

Both women were out when they pulled up to the emergency department's entrance. Kick ended up walking in with his assistance. The staff brought out a gurney for Cyndi.

BANGER CALLED WHILE THOMAS FILLED OUT PAPERWORK FOR THE women. He considered it an absolute joke since he knew so little about them, but he didn't want to upset Kick's kids. They'd been through enough in the past few months. They were all probably sound asleep anyway.

"The girls showed no signs of drugs, just drunk and pissed at me for waking them," Banger reported.

"Kick will be happy to hear it."

"Are you sure you don't want me to bring them in?"

"No," Thomas answered. "Let them sleep. Are you going back to the club?"

"Almost there. That bartender better still be on duty."

"What about the guy who grabbed Kick?"

"From what you told me, it doesn't fit the timeline. I haven't forgotten him though."

"Thanks, man. Sorry to make you stay out so late."

Banger chuckled. "Your woman's a menace—a good one, but still a menace."

THOMAS SAT IN THE CHAIR NEXT TO KICK'S BED, WATCHING HER sleep like a peaceful Sleeping Beauty with an IV and a heart monitor quietly announcing each beat. What the hell would he do? Both women had been drugged, so the bar staff was suspect. No one had manhandled Cyndi though, and she'd clearly felt the effects first. He remembered the Randy guy she'd disappeared with for a time and texted the info to Banger.

Regardless, at least two had been involved, which probably meant another planned attack. Thomas craved breaking someone with his bare hands. He wanted to join Banger and help his friend find the answers to his questions, but he couldn't leave Kick. Thomas couldn't even let his phone or the lab distract him. He kept going over the way she'd spoken with her heart in the garage. He wondered if she'd be mortified by what she'd said even though they were the prettiest words he'd ever heard. More than anything, he wanted to give her everything she wanted—no, deserved.

Kick finally stirred, and she sat up with a start, her hair hanging down like a veil shielding her face.

"Hey there." Thomas shifted to the bedside, but she didn't look up. "How are you feeling?"

With the same out-of-it voice, Kick said, "I have to take my detox pills so I don't get sick."

"It's alright—"

"Will you get it from the car? The stuff called... you know... when you want to cook a steak outside? You use... oh, what's the stuff...?"

"A grill? Propane?"

She shook her head so hard the monitor beeps increased.

His own memory of older remedies clicked in. "Are you thinking of charcoal?" Thomas asked.

Kick's shoulders sagged in relief, and she finally looked at him. "Yes. Activated charcoal. Thank you. If you hurry, it should still work."

Thomas pointed to the IV in her arm. "You've had medicine for about a while, darlin'. It'll be enough for what happened tonight."

Kick's head shifted from the line to the half-full fluid bag, then around the bay they were in. Her brows furrowed in confusion. "What did happen?"

Thomas took her free hand in both of his and rubbed Kick's knuckles. "What do you remember?"

She leaned back into the pillows as she ran her IV hand over her hair, getting it caught. "Jaysus, I'm a fright. Can you get a scrunchie from my purse?"

She already sounded more like herself. Relieved, Thomas reached for Kick's purse, unzipped it, and set it on her lap. He found himself impressed with how she could pull it all into a bun while attached to an IV and not fully sober.

"I remember seeing Banger."

Thomas didn't expect this. "What about him?"

"He took the girls home."

"He did."

"Banger put his hands around their necks like he was steering them. He was disrespectful."

Thomas snickered. Of all the things her currently beleaguered brain could remember, she took the mama bear route. "True. Do you remember waiting for me outside?"

"No. Wait... cops?" She reached for her forehead. "Oh hell. The kid knew Dylan. We yelled at him."

His laugh grew. "That's right, occifer."

"Where the hell were you?"

Between laughs, Thomas said, "Getting our coats and finding my phone, remember?"

"Nope."

"Do you remember the parking deck?"

"Uh-uh. Should I?"

He held his tongue and looked down at his shoes. Thomas longed to talk to Kick about what she'd said, but he figured she'd feared the feelings in those words as much as he did. It was a good thing she didn't remember them. Her lack of memory also fit with the information he'd read about the drug's effects. "No. Just curious. You sang pub songs."

"Oh *jayz*. Were we loud?" She shifted against the pillows. "Par for the course, I guess. Songs and booze go together like bangers and mash when you're from an Irish family."

Thomas flinched at the mention of liquor. "Kick..." *Christ*, he didn't want to dump more bad news on her, but the nurse would be in soon and catch her up, regardless. He decided then. Nothing would come before keeping her safe anymore. He didn't care if the Felidae objected. He couldn't ignore this feeling pulling him in. She wouldn't be his last priority, his emotional retreat from everything about his life he hated. She needed him, and he'd be there.

"You're not in the emergency department because of two cocktails from hours ago."

FLY ME TO THE MOON

KICK

My face scrunched up when Liam walked into my medical bay with Thomas. It had nothing to do with the night's events either. I should've been happy that my son had someone to rely on besides me, but I felt my forehead crease deepen. The fecking damsel-in-distress situation—yet again—made me prickly. I'd grown used to being ghosted when I needed people and accepted the reality of taking care of business alone. Thomas's helpfulness messed with my head even if I *had* asked him to call Liam for me.

Adding to the matter, the two of them didn't look like friends or a teacher with a student. They looked like a father and son—granted, a young father. I should've overflowed with appreciation. Instead, I found myself in a torrent of confusion. On the rare occasion I had let myself envision finding another life partner, I'd pictured it as something personal. I'd never thought a new relationship could help my family.

Oh, who was I kidding? There wasn't a family for Thomas

and me. We were special-friends-who-might-be-more at an indeterminate time. Boy, did I miss the days where a girl would get a varsity jacket or class ring to let her know precisely where she stood. Maybe our timing simply stank.

I held my arms out to my son, and he rushed me for a hug. "I'm okay, Wee Man."

Liam sat on the bed and dropped the duffel bag of clothes and things for me and Cyndi as Thomas took the chair. I brushed a curl out of Liam's eyes, and a hint of doing something similar flashed through my memory, only I couldn't see the face. "You don't mind me having Thomas wake you at Collin's?"

"Naw, we were up." Liam answered with the enviable energy of an eighteen-year-old. "I'd have been mad if you walked through the door in the afternoon like nothing had happened."

Oh. Right. I was supposed to spend the night at Thomas's house. I caught his gaze, and Thomas passed me a slight, knowing grin. Yup, bad timing.

My nurse slid the door open. "Only one family member at a time allowed in here." She held up a tablet. "I also need to do a run-through on you."

"Again?"

Thomas and Liam stood. My son moved to the door, but Thomas leaned down and kissed my cheek. "How about I take the boy to get a coffee? Promise it won't hold a candle to yours."

"Flatterer," I grumbled, though a smile pulled at my lips. "Will you check on Cyndi too?"

"Of course."

I turned to my nurse. "Do I have to pee in a cup again? I'm sure I can get you a quart now."

She smiled and shook her head. Her face filled with the kind of empathy that made a nurse great. "We're done with specimens. If you can stand, I'll help you to the restroom. After I get your vitals, a detective would like to speak with you."

As the reality of another attempt to hurt me settled in, I started shaking.

Alone in my room again, my mind raced through the night's events, desperate to remember anything. It stubbornly remained a kaleidoscope of fuzzy images and happiness. The contrast to what Thomas told me about what happened made the shakes worse.

Tony Bennett's "Fly Me to the Moon" tiptoed gently from the speaker in my patient bay. It soothed the restlessness as I leaned back, closed my eyes, and sang along. No invisible monster would beat me. There was a moon to see after all.

"You sound nice, Kick," Detective Nick Ross said, quietly sliding open the glass door, Thomas following closely behind.

"Only one visitor allowed," I warned.

Thomas put his finger to his lips and winked. "Shift change."

Okay then.

Thomas settled on the foot of my bed while Nick took the chair. "Can I get your statement?"

"Why you? We were in Raleigh last night."

The detective flushed, fuming with anger. At least that's what I assumed. "It's not illegal to drug a drink and the grabbing you experienced is common behavior, given the setting. So there's nothing for the RPD to do. I'm here as a follow-up to your previous events."

Events?

Thomas grunted, and I reached for his hand.

I adjusted my ponytail and let the detective's words sink in. "This wasn't illegal?"

Nick shook his head. "It would be special circumstances if you were hurt or… worse. There's a bill in the general assembly to fix this loophole. From what Mr. Harrison told me, you're only here because of your medical history and his insistence. Odds are, you would've slept it off and assumed you'd had too much to drink."

Jaysus. "What about Cyndi?"

Thomas cleared his throat and answered, "She's getting IV fluids with some extra medicine in the bag. She took it harder, but she'll be fine."

"We were drugged then?"

"The preliminary assessment suggests so," Detective Ross replied. "I'll go over the tapes with your security team soon," he added.

My… Oh, Banger again. I blew out a shaky breath.

Thomas jumped in. "From what I gather, Cyndi took the brunt of it."

"Given her high blood pressure, it's a good thing your boyfriend brought you two in," the detective added. "She could've been in big trouble if left at home."

I flinched at the knowledge someone might have really harmed my best friend. The ridiculousness of the entire situation seemed to slap me in the face.

"And you think this is related to the other harassment?"

"I don't believe in coincidences." The detective's voice dropped. "Honestly, people don't have this much bad luck, Ms. McKenna. First I need your account of events. Then we wait—for the final toxicology reports and for the footage to show us anything."

"Where's Liam?" I didn't want to risk him overhearing anything even though I couldn't remember much.

"Sitting with Cyndi," Thomas answered. He brushed loose wisps of hair from my forehead.

Again, my boy was witness to the fallout from an attack on me. "How is he, Thomas? Is he scared shitless? Lee might never let me out of the house again." My breath hitched.

A corner of Thomas's mouth lifted. He continued to play with my curls. Maybe he was scared too. I sure didn't know what to make of it all. I only knew I didn't plan to go away quietly.

"He'll be alright. I talked him down. Made some promises." Thomas glanced at Nick and back at me. "Stop stalling and tell

Detective Ross what you can even if your memories are still fuzzy."

What promises?

"Fine." I shifted in the bed. My hips hurt for some reason. "I remember the inside of the club, the Spyder, the bartenders—"

Detective Ross lifted a finger. "Tell me about them."

I closed my eyes to picture them better. "One dressed like John Bender from *The Breakfast Club* and the other like the woman from my favorite Molly Ringwald movie. Shit, I can't remember the name." I squeezed Thomas's hand. "You surprised us... our dance. Chicken wings on our table. A meat stick."

Thomas affirmed my memory with a broad smile. An image of a girl clinging to him came to mind, and I frowned. "A child playing grown-up called me old."

"That was all before. What do you remember after Cyndi bought the sodas?" Thomas asked.

"Iona..."

"What?" both Thomas and the detective asked.

"The other bartender cos-played as Iona from..." I snapped my fingers a few times. *Pretty in Pink.* I sank back into my pillow, relieved to have the words off the tip of my tongue.

Detective Ross tilted his head like a dog hearing a weird whistle. "Which means...?"

I stretched my neck. Why did IVs always seem to tighten my muscles? "Let's see... Platinum wig, cat eye makeup, black-and-white dress. She had a button nose."

He typed away even though I only remembered the superficial things about her appearance.

I turned to Thomas, remembering what he'd asked me. "Cyndi bought tonics, not sodas." I bit my lip as a confusing image came to mind. "Why do I see a werewolf attacking me? I kicked him. He howled. I think he tried to bite me. He was mad."

"Cyndi said he was large and hairy and called him Sasquatch," Thomas reminded me.

"Good. So this suspect looks wolfish. Do you remember anything else about his appearance?" Nick typed on his pad.

I continued my trip through my foggy memory as it appeared. "I couldn't find my way back to the dance floor or to Cyndi. It's like a labyrinth formed around me out of nowhere. There were bodies and flashing lights."

I continued for several more minutes, trying to bring up any image from the night, but they grew murkier with each successive word. The images contrasted with an overwhelming feeling of joy and love I remembered. To keep from crying over the contrast of my feelings and reality, I bit my lip and held it together. I wouldn't let my head travel to the place where my night almost ended up.

Detective Ross sighed. "You might not think it's much, but you helped, Kick. I'll let you rest and call you when I have an update. If you remember anything else—especially any new, distinctive features of the man who grabbed you—call me." He gave me his business card, though I already had two at home. "It's fine to leave a message."

The nurse entered with release papers. All necessary samples were squared away, and since I could move around on my own, there was nothing else for them to do for me. I dressed and stepped out into the hall.

Detective Ross turned to Thomas. "Thanks for your help, Mr. Harrison. I'll call you if anything needs clarifying."

"Please do."

To me, he added, "I'll check in to see if your missing pieces come back."

I shook his hand and watched him leave. As my nurse passed by, I tapped her arm. "May I see Cyndi Sendaydiego?"

"Sure." She pointed to a treatment bay two doors to the left. "In there."

I scanned Thomas for a hint of his plans. "Right behind you," he answered my unasked question.

I slid the door open and stepped around the curtain. Cyndi looked up and smiled through tears. "Hey, chica."

"Jaysus." A few steps more and I scooped her into a squishy hug. "Oh, sweetie."

She pulled back, slightly annoyed. "We were drugged."

I scrunched my nose. "So they say."

"Kick—" Cyndi's chin quivered.

"You won't blame yourself."

"They said it was the tonic and—"

"Shh." I hugged her again. "It doesn't mean *you* spiked them. Besides, you ended up with the worst of it." I leaned back and studied her warm brown eyes. "Feeling any better? Can I bring you home with me?"

She shook her head so hard a tear flew off her cheek. "No, chica. Lee's so freaked. He'd probably spend the day watching me breathe. That's no way to get my beauty rest."

"But—"

She tapped my knee. "I texted Manu when my fingers started working again. He'll be here soon with a change of clothes. He agreed to play nurse too." She waggled her brows and gave me a Cheshire cat grin.

I sighed and tried not to smile. "Leave it to you."

"Me? Look at you. *The Unsinkable Molly Brown.*"

"So you think I was the target?"

Cyndi gave me a pity nod. Her face turned serious, contemplative. "Did I go off with a man?"

I swung my head to Thomas. I didn't remember a man.

He cleared his throat. "He said his name was Randy. If the cameras were working, he'll show up by the booth at least."

Cyndi ran her hand through her hair, and I watched it fall back into shape perfectly. "The staff pressed me hard to do the whole rape kit enchilada. But I said no." She shivered. "I would know about that. And I would *remember*. I do remember a man grabbing my ass and pulling me up against him, but I think it was this guy. He was harmless." Something like recognition crossed her expression, and her hand flew to her mouth. "Shit. I didn't mean like your grab. It was—"

I pulled her hand away from her face and squeezed it with my own. "I know." I chuckled to push down a threatening tear. "Hell, I remember so little. It's like Thomas told me a story about a woman who sounds like me."

"I hear you. After the drinks, all I have are feelings instead of memories." Cyndi closed her eyes and sighed. "They're amazing though." A smile spread across her face. "I *felt* music. Did you know Prince feels incredible?"

"I wouldn't expect any less from him."

My knee hiked up on the edge of the bed, and I moved my hand to Cyn's forehead, running my fingers through the silky bangs of her perfect bob. Another flicker of a memory flashed, then disappeared. "You look better. I think."

She lifted her arm with the IV. "It's a magic potion. Thomas said you only needed the basic fluids. I told you, you're unsinkable."

She turned her head to Thomas, who was texting in the visitor's chair. "With your handsome entourage to boot."

Cyndi dropped her head, and her breath hitched.

"Hey now." Careful of the IV line, I wrapped her in a hug and said into her ear, "We're okay."

She cried into my shoulder. "Take my mind off this, Kicky." She sat back, dabbed at her face with a tissue, and rearranged her blanket. "Tell me something embarrassing about you to make me feel better."

"Why? No."

She faked a frown face. "You owe me for taking the hit."

I flinched at the word *hit*. I dropped my gaze. If this was about hurting me, Cyndi had been collateral damage. Her high blood pressure could've turned the night into a tragedy. I caved in to the guilt. "Fine. I can't seem to grasp anything today. It took me forever to get dressed because my hands wouldn't work."

Cyndi waved a hand in dismissal. "That's expected. You can do better."

I peeked over my shoulder at Thomas, who had his nose buried in his phone. *What the hell.*

"Okay. You know those nipple hairs that pop up out of nowhere—like an inch long overnight?" I checked back. His head stayed down, but his brows had raised high.

"Sure. Everyone gets those. You pluck them, you move on. So?"

"One grew out of my neck," I murmured and plopped my head in my hand, wishing I could sew my lips shut.

She clapped her hands together like a goofy seal. "Oh, fabulous. It sucks getting old."

"You suck."

Cyndi waved a casual hand. "That's nothing, chica. Is your pudendum balding yet?"

"Excuse me? No."

"Just wait."

Thomas jumped in his chair and sounded like he choked.

I tapped Cyndi on the shoulder. "Stop messing with him. As if you have this problem."

"Who says I don't?"

I rolled my eyes, feeling like my daughter. "Knowing you as I do, you'd convince someone from the Hair Club for Men to bend the rules and do a transplant down there. You wouldn't give in to aging so easily."

She pressed a finger to her chin. "You may have an idea for a new business… Genital Hair Transplanting. We could call it the Pussy Club."

"Sounds like a place I know of in Tampa." Thomas snickered.

I snapped my fingers in his direction. "Please. You're encouraging her."

He grinned and returned to his reading. I knew they both messed with me while I sought to be a comfort.

I turned back to Cyndi and found her staring at Thomas, her head tilted to the side like she was evaluating him. "He makes a pretty picture. The accent though? In the deep timbre? I don't think I'd ever want him to stop speaking. It's like butter."

"I know, right?"

"Right here, ladies." Thomas exhaled. "Besides, y'all are the ones with the accents."

Cyndi fanned herself.

"Oh, for Christ's sake. You feel better." I laughed. "Stop screwing around."

"I guess I am." Then she tsked me. "Humility is good for you though, Miss Unsinkable."

As if I had no experience being publicly humiliated. *Firecrackers in a café, anyone? How about graffiti with impossibly poor grammar? Or a lying newspaper article?*

"Did you get the magnifying mirror I told you about?" Cyndi continued, snapping me out of my mini pity party. "They are a godsend for your neck situation."

Thomas snorted behind me. I turned and glared, though he dared not look up. "Keep looking at your phone." He coughed another laugh. I knew he remembered the whole Dorian Gray fiasco in Target last month. I returned my attention to Cyndi, who watched our interaction with curiosity.

"I found one. Thanks for not telling me how bad my brows were, by the way. You're supposed to have my back..."

Her chin quivered again.

"No, no, no. That's not what I meant."

"I didn't have your back, Kick. We could've done the water cups like you wanted."

I hugged her again. "Who's paying dearly for it, eh?" Tipping her chin up, I added, "It's not on you."

"Okay." She turned away as the tears dropped.

"You want us to go?"

She wiped her eyes while nodding vigorously. I kissed her on the head and touched Thomas's shoulder. "Are you taking me home, or is Liam?"

He stood and lifted an eyebrow. "Are you joking?"

"Right." Of course Thomas would see me home safe. I welcomed this protective side now. I didn't know what had come over me.

"We're getting food first. I heard there's a burger joint near here that serves gluten-free bison burgers and fries. They have a dedicated fryer."

He knew about dedicated fryers. I almost swooned.

Liam had been napping in the waiting room while we visited with Cyndi. "Can Liam join us?"

Thomas looked confused as he answered, "I assumed he would."

There was my problem with the man: I didn't feel like I had the right to assume anything. Should I though? Did it matter?

For the first time that day, I noticed him. Without definitions. Not a protector or even a friend. With no qualms about age differences. I *saw* Thomas Harrison. The man with a sexy cleft in his chin, a Cary Grant stare, and a giant heart. Some of the bliss I had experienced the night before came back.

Just him. Just me.

I grabbed Thomas's bicep and let my head fall on his shoulder. "Thanks, sweets. For everything." I looked up into his reassuring silver irises. "You think life will get quiet now?"

1 2

THANK YOU

KICK

My doorbell rang twice before it registered in my brain. The roasted-till-golden Thanksgiving turkeys rested on a rack. The dressing, sweet potatoes, and gluten-free Hawaiian rolls were currently baking. And I was in gravy mode.

Of all the items on the menu, the fecking gravy put me on edge. To me, making gluten-free gravy was tricky at best. I had two boxes of store-bought sitting in the pantry in case it back-fired. Since they had garlic and onion on the ingredient list, going that route would mean no gravy for me.

"I'll get it," Deana called out.

I mentally retraced the previous arrivals and remembered Cyndi had yet to show. The last we'd spoken, she was still recovering from what we called "our night out" in order to avoid the word *drugging*.

I glanced at Thomas, who vigorously mashed a giant pot of potatoes. He laughed and said, "Looks like the clan is complete."

Clan? Oh, this man. He'd lightened everyone's mood since walking through the door. I really liked this version of him.

The house was pleasantly full—a rarity lately. It pleased me as much as the sweet and savory aromas filling the space. Deana's daughter and son were at their respective in-laws, so she and Gordon had arrived with multiple desserts and what smelled like an amazing mac-and-cheese side.

Cyndi sauntered in, looking well and gave cheek kisses to each of us. She set up a charcuterie board, featuring a mix of German sausages her mother had made, on the sideboard in the dining area. A tray of lumpia with multiple sauces sat next to it for our appetizers.

"Can I do anything?" Cyndi asked as she washed her hands in the kitchen sink.

"Nope. Pour yourself some wine and join the others for some football. We won't be long."

She practically swayed at the word *wine*, and I immediately apologized.

"No worries, chica." Cyndi waved off the apology. "I'm just not ready yet. What else do you have?"

"I'm trying out a lychee-flavored sparkling water if you'd like. I've only had one, but I liked it. It's in the cooler on the screened porch."

Cyndi's eyes lit up. "Now we're talking. Thanks, Kicky."

She passed by my friend, Charley, my son Dylan and the Douglases, who were watching the game in the great room, on her way to the cooler. Like a second hostess, she gave out hugs and kisses as she went by. It was a surprising coincidence so many had accepted my invites, but I buzzed with the joy of hosting a crowd like in the old days.

Back then, Shane would insist on hiring a caterer or renting a room in a restaurant to keep me from wearing out, but the kids were also little and required all my energy. Now they'd become a tremendous help. Each took a turn either cooking or zhushing up the house in the past week. Plus I didn't know any chef who wanted to handle my diet issues on Thanksgiving.

Along with the game downstairs, an epic *Smash Bros* tournament could be heard with occasional roars from the loft upstairs. My other two and Dylan's roommate, Henry—he insisted we call him Dummy—kept trying to lure Dylan up to join them.

My gaze landed on Bobby's sour visage as she sat by herself at the kitchen island. She had been at the center of activity when Rachel and the boys were chopping and setting up, but their services weren't needed anymore.

I didn't know if the crowd bothered Bobby, the noise did, or both. There wasn't much I could do about it, so I kept her vodka tonics weak but flowing. She finished her current one and set it down. "Are any more *strays* showing up?"

I gave the gravy another stir. It was almost ready. "No. We're all here."

With a snide tone, she said, "Good, 'cause you're making me eat with some damn rude people today."

Apparently, her first comment had been a rebuke I'd missed. I set the spoon on the stovetop and turned around. "What's wrong?"

Bobby tipped her head toward the great room. "These people can't even say hello."

I'd sworn everyone had. As I slowly scanned the room, Cyndi caught my eye and piped up—Bobby had spoken loud enough to be heard over the TV. "There you are!" Cyndi strolled over to my mother and forced a kiss on her cheek. "Between my trays and these giants, I didn't see you sitting here. We petite girls need to stick together, don't we?"

Cyndi stood in Bobby's blind spot and mouthed *battle axe* while Bobby shot full-tilt laser beams out of her eyes at me. My mother hadn't wanted a kiss or a hug from my best friend. They hated each other. Bobby had simply been back to pushing random buttons to see if one would upset me. Well, I wouldn't let her. It was a day of thanks after all.

I fixed Bobby another vodka tonic. Mostly tonic—the corn syrup didn't bother her. "Here. Why don't you have some appetizers? Cyndi's mother made the sausages."

"Pfft." She waved me off. "I won't spoil my dinner. You're almost ready, right? Or will we have to eat cold turkey?"

I'll give you cold turkey.

Thomas jumped in. "Speaking of… my potatoes are finished, and I can carve the bird now. I'll grab a beer first though." He walked toward the door to the screened porch. "Can I get anyone something? Gordon?"

"Please." Gordon jumped up and joined Thomas. I figured both of them required a break from the tension, and I couldn't blame them. It took a lot of energy to deal with Bobby Allen. I'd taken a couple of days off after the girl's night out, but my energy wasn't all the way back.

"Since you're heading that way, can you turn on the heater too? It'll be easier to set up the summer table out there instead of trying to finagle another one inside."

"Yes, milady." Thomas flashed me his cheesy grin, and the stress melted away.

"You're not seriously making a kids' table, are you?" Dylan asked from the sofa, his love for football still overruling his need to dominate his friend and siblings in all things Nintendo. Football connected Dylan to his father. He was my only child with genuine memories of the years Shane had played on Thanksgiving Day.

"You'll be more comfortable as a foursome out there than crammed around the one in here," I answered.

Dylan waggled his beer can. "This disqualifies me from kid table status." He tipped his head toward the porch. "I say *that's* the adult table and in here is the geriatric one." His challenging smirk reminded me of his preteen years when the hormones showed up, bringing the cocky grin along for the ride.

I shook my head, laughing. "Whatever gets you through the day, lad."

No matter what happened with Bobby, it would be a good day. Hell, it would probably be the last big feast for a while. My heart ate up the buzz, the intergenerational camaraderie, the extended family. I'd worked hard for this.

Deana and Cyndi collected the things needed to set the second table. "Thank you," I said to them as they passed. Bobby groaned loudly.

"What's got your underwear in a twist?" I leaned down and quietly asked. I'd thought the weak VTs would've set her at ease by now. Instead, they turned up her volume. One of her brows lowered, and her face fell into a maniacal smirk, like she was about to impart a terrible truth I'd been too stupid to realize for myself. "You're living the life of Riley now, aren't you? Your world will fall apart next year when your boy toy finds someone his own age. You'll have run the kids off too. Next year, it'll just be you. And me."

"Aww, thanks for caring, Mother," I said, tapping her hand, my words laced with sarcasm.

"I promise you, Ms. Allen, this boy toy has no intention of going anywhere," Thomas said from behind us. His voice held a clear warning in it. My heart sank and jumped at the same time. *Shit, shit, shit* ran through my head. Talk about rude guests. Bobby held the honors there.

He handed me a cold LaCroix. "Thought you might need this."

"Much appreciated." I mouthed the words, *I'm so sorry.*

Thomas's phone buzzed, and he pulled it from his pocket. "Can I take this in your office?"

"Of course." I watched him hustle to my study, wondering who it could be, pretty sure his grimace at the screen matched the one I gave Bobby. As I stared at the closed door, a scorched smell reached my nose.

"No, no, no!" The gravy. I only tolerated arrowroot for a thickener, but it was tricky. It didn't take much to end up with a gelatinous goo.

Our dinner started off with quiet niceties. Sitting Bobby at the opposite end from me—the place of honor—served mostly to keep her as far away as possible while allowing me to monitor her from under my lashes. More than once, I wished she had stayed home, like she had for Liam's birthday.

I cleared my throat, determined to be the proper host, directing the conversation when called for.

"Charley's brother lives in Spain, Thomas."

"Did y'all grow up there?" he asked Charley.

She shook her head. "We were raised in New Mexico."

"No kidding?"

"Yes. Teo normally visits this time of year, but he's on assignment."

"And Charley is the first woman to head a premier construction firm in the Triangle."

"I remember," Thomas graciously said, pausing to study me. "The work you did for Kick is fantastic. I've made extensive renovations in my house and would love some woodworking tips."

Their conversation took off after that, and Deana leaned into me. She, too, had begged to stay as far away from my mother as possible. "You don't have to work the conversation so hard. Relax, shug." I gave her a smile to let her know I'd heard.

The gravy boat passed to me, and I raised it, not being able to partake myself. Having burned my attempt, I'd heated up the store-bought. "Anyone need more?"

"Wonderful job, Kicky," Cyndi cheered from her end of the

table. Everyone chimed in as I added butter to my cornbread dressing. It wasn't the same without gravy, but I'd be darned if I'd eat it dry.

Thomas clinked his wineglass, getting our attention. "A toast to the hostess. Thank you for opening your warm home and serving us this magnificent feast. I still don't know how you pulled it off with the substitutions." He waited as my friends laughed. "What did you call it?"

"Well…" It took a moment before his question registered. "Oh, it's gluten-free, dairy-free, low-FODMAP and soy-free for Rachel and Liam."

"Amazing." His bright face turned to the rest of the table. "I thank the rest of y'all for bringing side dishes, desserts, and drinks. Mostly, thank you, Kick, for showing us your enormous heart and beautiful smile. You're the embodiment of what today is about."

The volume rose with a chorus of "here, here's," "cheers," and a loud "damn straight." Thomas's *slainte* rose above the rest and made me smile. He even pronounced it correctly. It was the toast my father and Shane had always used. Though I'd long become used to holidays without Shane, this was the first Thanksgiving without my father. Is this why Bobby misbehaved?

"That's what my family says," I told him.

"I figured."

Everyone took part in the toast except for Bobby. She scrunched up her face like she'd tasted something rotten and mouthed a mocking *y'all* to everyone and no one. My brows pulled down, and I opened my mouth to tell her off, but Thomas patted my hand and murmured, "Let it go."

The table returned to a buzzed grouping of conversations of twos and threes. All except for Bobby, but by that time, I didn't care. There could be no way she was missing my father when she had treated him so terribly while he lived.

My gaze instead drifted to the table on the porch. Fortunately, the day was warm enough for alfresco dining with the addition of the warming lamp. But Dylan looked as quiet and out of place as his grandmother did at our table. I hoped it didn't have to do with being out on the screen porch.

He entered the dining area and asked, "Mind if we start one of the pumpkin pies?"

"Where's your gorgeous fiancée, dear?" Bobby called out. She turned to Gordon and announced, "He's about to start a computer company, and his wife will be a doctor. Isn't it fantastic?"

"Yeah, well… RIP," Dylan muttered. As he cut the pie and reached for a server, he added, "We're not getting engaged after all. I'll get your ring back to you, Gran."

"Don't worry about it boy-o. It's probably a simple quarrel." Bobby turned a heated glare on me. "What did you do? You've never liked his girl."

Nothing. And there was the problem. I'd let my troubles take over my thoughts and forgot about the possibility of being a… nope. The G-word wasn't welcome inside my head. I also noticed Bobby couldn't remember Suzy's name. *Ha.*

"Not a thing. I agree. Suzy's lovely." And she would make a fine wife for someone else.

"It's not like that, Gran," Dylan warned, crossing the room. "Drop it please."

"Crap," I murmured under my breath.

Thomas, Charley, Deana, and Gordon all stared me down with questioning gazes. I shrugged and shook my head. Dylan had left the door open and the table outside erupted in laughter, with Liam at the center of attention.

Bobby tsked a response. "That boy's a troublemaker and a show-off. Like his father and this one." She nodded toward Thomas. "No wonder you gravitated to him." My jaw dropped as she stunned me speechless. She added, "Just wait. That's all I'm saying. Just. You. Wait."

"Mother—"

"Enough," Thomas said, deep enough to make everybody stop eating. "Ms. Allen, I've heard enough."

I covered his hand. "It's okay, Thomas."

He gentled his voice for me. "Let me. Please." He turned back to Bobby. "You don't like me. Fine. There's one thing I've learned over the years and that is that family is a treasure. No matter how short or long y'all's time together, taking it for granted is a travesty. To stomp on it the way you do is criminal. No matter how you feel about me, you will not speak to me with disrespect. Moreover, I won't listen to you put down your daughter or any of your grandchildren."

"Are you going to allow this?" Bobby pushed hard against the table, her chair scraping the floor, looking at me. "Well, I *never*." She stormed out of the room and slammed the door to the guest bath.

Deana and Cyndi beamed as they watched us. Gordon wore a smirk too.

Thomas raised my hand and kissed the back of it. "This is bad timing, but I'm afraid I've got to head up to Virginia now. I don't want to take my family for granted either." He rose, and I followed. "It was nice seeing everyone."

As Thomas sorted out his jacket from the others sharing the same hook, I asked, "Can I give you anything to take?"

He shook his head. "Joe and Toni have it covered. It's more about having a few days to spend with them anyway."

"Right." My heart wouldn't stop racing after the confrontation with Bobby, knowing round two was imminent. "What do I do? About you know who?"

He gently lifted my chin. "Boundaries, Kick. Tell me"—he tipped his head toward the dining room—"would your father have intercepted the scene back there?"

I nodded, adding, "Shane too."

"Darlin', despite your promise to a dying man, your father

wouldn't want her speaking to y'all like this. It's high time your mother learned about boundaries." He leaned in and kissed my cheek, whispering, "It has to come from you."

I thought of the Psalm I'd gone to pieces over in front of him. I couldn't imagine a scenario where Bobby would ever consider a boundary to be pleasant.

"Was it Joe who called earlier?"

"Huh? Oh yeah. They were running late. Now I am." He pressed a kiss to my lips like he was transferring courage and confidence. "Hold on to the good parts of today. You've got this."

At that moment, I knew I did. "I'm fine. Don't worry. Thank you for being my sous-chef."

"Had fun being your sous-chef." His thumb stroked my cheek. "I loved watching your face light up as the meal came together. Simply gorgeous."

Lord almighty, his eyes were smiling for me, making those little creases that weakened my knees.

Thomas called goodbyes to the house and left me wanting more. Missing him already.

As soon as the door shut behind him, the one to the guest bath opened.

"Well, good thing he's gone," Bobby declared with a sweet smile. "I don't understand what's so wrong with our family that you had to invite them. It's your deep-seated desire for attention, isn't it? Your father and I worked long hours and you've never gotten over it." Bobby sighed in disgust and took a step to move past me and back to the dining table.

My hand around her bicep stopped her, my tone unusually calm, a small smile on my face. This wasn't a ploy for attention or an emotional outburst. It was what we both needed me to say.

"Oh, hell no. I'll send a kid over with leftovers, but you're leaving now."

13

WHAT ABOUT YOUR FRIENDS

KICK

A plate slid through my hands, crashing into two on the floor. My fingers weren't the only part of me that wouldn't stop shaking. Yes, I'd stayed cool-headed while I told Bobby she had to leave. I was proud of myself for holding my ground without blowing up.

Since she'd left, memories flashed through my mind as my friends—my true family—helped me clear the table. The first scene coming to mind was my wedding reception. Bobby had flirted shamelessly with Shane's Uncle Billy, the McKenna patriarch. My mind's eye watched one of the sweetest men I would ever know wearing a tuxedo covered in chocolate sauce. Bobby had scooped some into a glass from the fountain she'd insisted on and dumped it on Uncle Billy after he'd put her in her place. Considering her usual reaction to being told no, I'd gotten off easy with a house-shaking door slam earlier. Who knew a tiny woman in her late sixties could manage such force.

I'd nearly tripped with a pile of dishes when a memory from

Dad's funeral appeared. Roberta Allen, "devoted widow" wearing bright yellow, huffing from boredom and loudly smacking gum while the rest of us were blubbering messes.

"Go sit down, sugar," Dee soothed, taking the next dish as it dangled from my hand.

"How about a coffee?" Cyndi asked.

I shook my obedient yet reluctant head as I slid onto a barstool. "Remember? It's not allowed right now. It would be too late for me anyway."

"Not even for special circumstances?" Cyn persisted.

"No sweets. I'll take an herbal tea though. Can you put the kettle on?"

She filled it and took my place in front of the dishwasher.

"You may be upset, but I'm proud of you," Deana encouraged.

"Me too," Gordon said, sliding an arm around my shoulders. "It wasn't easy, but you did it."

I smiled up at him. I was proud of myself too. It irritated me how much doing the right thing didn't stop me from physically reacting to the confrontation. I tapped my collarbone to calm down, making sure I didn't hyperventilate.

"Any chance the hot water's for coffee? It would be the perfect accompaniment to Dee's sweet potato pie," Gordon asked, rubbing his hands together.

"Shoot. You're right." I jumped up to make a big pot, but two enormous hands on my shoulders pressed down, settling my ass back where it belonged.

A deep chuckle came from above me. "Stay. I'll get it."

"I'm the barista, remember? You're the drug developer," I said, accompanied by a grin. Gordon worked in testing for a local pharmaceutical company.

Gordon was already at the french press, chuckling and checking with Deana to make sure he had the right number of scoops. "I've learned a thing or two from you ladies"—he kissed Dee on the cheek—"especially mine."

"You sure you don't want an espresso? Or foam?"

Dee laughed. "Wrong man, shug."

"Okay, fine." I settled in my spot, taking in the smells of pies in the warming drawer and newly brewed coffee. It didn't matter that I couldn't have any. The comforting aroma was enough. The prohibition was temporary, and my full belly wanted nothing more. My heart filled with my friends' encouragement. This was the purpose of family. It didn't matter whether we shared DNA.

Rachel sat on the stool next to mine and spread open the newspaper. "Lee and I plan to do Black Friday tomorrow. Want to come? We asked Dyl, but he's not vibing."

"At four thirty in the morning?" Rachel nodded vigorously. "Absolutely not." I kissed her cheek. "Thank you though. What are you buying?" I leaned over to see what she had circled.

"This blender's a great deal."

The grown-ups in the room all cooed like we were watching a toddler try to walk in heels. Over the years, we'd all had our fill at battling the predawn cold and the cranky, grabby crowd.

"Why would you do this when you don't have to? The world's changed, Snow. Order the blender online. I bet you can get this exact one."

Liam slid onto the third stool. "We want to say we did it once."

My gaze stopped at each of my friends. They each rolled their eyes, smirking. I knew, like me, they were thinking, *Oh, to have their kind of time and energy.* Me? After two days of chopping, brining, spicing, and stirring, I planned to sleep in and rest my body—especially my right arm. I hoped for a dreamless night and didn't know what I'd do if Bobby haunted me there.

"Holy shit." Rachel gasped and slapped the paper closed.

She and Liam both looked like they'd been caught being naughty.

My brows drew together. "What now?"

"Nothing," they said in unison.

I held my hand out, wiggling my fingers. In an instant, they were both six and three again, caught putting my makeup on Rachel's dolls. Mouths gaping in surprise, as if the dolls had wrecked their own faces. "What's in the paper?"

"Trust me, Mom, don't look," Liam pleaded.

Rachel knew better and slid it over.

On the opinion page was a piece about my coffeehouse: A Visit to the Perked Cup: A Lesson in Lies. All the warm fuzzies left the room. This person claimed to have been a regular who was disappointed in our "irresponsibility on Halloween." My defenses went up. At the same time, I recognized my disappointment, but how could I have expected something so public? Graham had been allegedly messing with *me*. I didn't think he'd take his anger out on random children. But if he wanted to make my life difficult, he'd succeeded. My fingers were crossed that the holiday shopping season could turn the business around.

True to its word, the opinion piece was a lesson in lies. It started out reaming my former employee, Madison, for being rude. I'd give the writer that one. Maddie's parents wanted her to quit after the attack. She'd fought with them over it without my knowing. Then she became hell on wheels for it. I let her go, telling her she could come back if her parents changed their mind or when she turned eighteen.

The next item involved complaints about the new camera installation. It claimed, in a vague, "sources say" way, that the cameras invaded privacy by listening to every conversation in the café, which wasn't true. Video coverage had improved along with clarity, but the mics were by the counter where any dangerous encounter would happen. The thought still gave me chills.

The last two claims made me laugh out loud. It said someone on the inside "verified" cameras in the bathrooms. It wasn't only a lie, it was illegal. As much as I'd have loved to know the identity of the weasels who regularly made a disaster area of my restrooms, I'd never.

Then it declared Jonn Graham innocent, saying he ran from the scene because he was frightened, like the rest of the crowd. It argued he hadn't been in the café, though my cameras caught otherwise.

I folded the paper back up and set it as far away as my reach allowed. "Nope. If Herself can't ruin my day, this sure won't."

"What's up?" Deana asked, holding out her hand.

"A piece in the paper telling readers to boycott the café. It also claims we're picking on poor Jonn-Jonn Graham. It's not worth your thoughts."

Ever the protector, Gordon picked it up and read it. His gaze passed between Deana and me. "It's lying, right?"

"Most of it. Maddie let her argument with her parents bubble up on the customers before I let her go."

Dee clicked her tongue. "Poor thing."

"Are you going to sue?" Gordon asked.

"I might threaten it, but opinions are free speech. Plus the editor doesn't like me." I tapped my chin, landing on an idea. "The business section reporter loves his free Friday coffee though. I wonder if Banger's team can help me with a rebuttal. It should help if someone at Angel can send reassurance that we don't invade our customer's privacy. I might be able to get the paper to advertise a new sales campaign too—for free—to make up for this mess." My eyebrows popped as a sneaky grin spread across my face. War could be fun when I wasn't battling my mother.

"You mean the study-hour plan?" Liam asked.

I nodded, loving the idea of making the paper eat its words.

"What's this?" Deana asked.

I pointed toward my office. "Marketing flyers I'm working on. Half-off drinks between three and five with a school ID. Like happy hour for a coffeehouse."

"Great idea, Kicky." Cyndi beamed.

"Thank you." I motioned toward Liam. "Wee Man helped."

"I've got a box of beaded bookmarks ready for holiday sales if you want them."

"Fantastic." I said, grateful for the help and hopeful my ideas could counteract this smear campaign. My energy hadn't returned, but I'd be ready when it did. Active support from my friends went a long way too.

I'D GIVEN THE COUNTERS A FINAL WIPE AND STARTED THE dishwasher for the third time. Our guests had rolled themselves out the door about half an hour earlier, stuffed like the birds they'd eaten.

Thomas had texted that he'd arrived safely at his family home. I dimmed the kitchen lights and rolled down the new shade over the kitchen window.

Dylan sat alone on the sectional, watching the evening football game. The other kids had resumed their Nintendo marathon with *Mario Kart*.

I plopped down next to my son, passing him two fingers of Defiant. I sipped herbal tea with a pink hue, reminding me of a warm flower. "Okay, lad. I've been a shit mom, but I'm here now. Fill me in. I was obviously wrong about a possible baby."

He scoffed and tasted his drink. "No, you weren't."

The tea caught in my throat. "She's pregnant?" I sputtered and checked my tone, whispering, "Suzy's having a baby?"

A sad squeak came from his usually deep voice. "She was."

I set the tea down and wrapped my arms around my son. "I'm so sorry, lad. Miscarriages are rough, but you can get through it. Stay close to her."

He shrugged me off, bending over and grunting. "Suzy didn't lose the baby, Mom. She aborted it and told me after the fact when I asked her if she'd missed a period." A sad keening escaped from his chest, punching straight through mine. How could I have missed that?

"How did I miss it?" He whimpered. "You keyed in to the clues as soon as I told you."

I rubbed his back, my tears matching his. The light from changing commercials reflected off falling tears, shining diamonds dropping for a life never known. "Oh, sweet boy. Any idea why she didn't come to you first?"

"She said she didn't want me ever to know." His throat caught. "I would've taken care of it, Mom."

"We all would've helped you. Gladly." I pulled him back and started rocking him while patting his shoulders. "It'll happen in due time."

"But I still love this one."

I grabbed his chin with a firm hand. "Listen to me. He or she would've adored you, but it does you no good to think of it as alive. It was a potential life. Did Suzy tell you how far along she'd been?"

Dylan shook his head, his eyes wide as he tried to absorb my words. I hated the bluntness, but motherly instincts told me it would help him move on. "You have no way of knowing whether the fetus would've made it to the end. It's the tragic truth of every pregnancy. What happened after she confessed?"

Wiping his cheek with the sleeve of his flannel, he said, "She left. We're done. Not because of the ba—procedure, but because her doing it without a word to me says everything I needed to know about us as a couple. Suze is staying on her best friend's couch. When Mai's roommate graduates next month, Suzy will officially move out of the condo." Dylan's tears resumed their descent down his rugged face. A shadow of his toddler-self sat before me, softening the masculine edges so much like my father's. I pulled him back into an embrace, wishing I could do anything more. I would trade my health gains in order to take away his pain.

He spoke in a scratchy rasp into my shoulder. "I don't know what's more painful." He sat back, running the sleeve over his face again. "That's not true. I was so numb when Suzy left. It seemed like the next step, like we'd been heading there since the summer. The dreams about a little boy or girl wake me up in the night, not her."

My hand cupped his jaw, thumb stroking his cheek to soothe. "Your dad would have been thrilled to know how much you want to be a father yourself."

"I didn't realize it until it was too late. Maybe if I'd said something?"

"I can't believe she wouldn't give you a reason she did it."

"She did." Dylan lifted a shoulder. "Medical school. Even if I took responsibility for it after, Suzy would have to take leave to deliver and recover. She never asked her adviser about it though." He shrugged. "Add in the terror of having to tell her parents, I can almost see things from her perspective. It's still no excuse in my opinion."

"They placed the weight of the world on her shoulders."

"I'm mad as hell over her doing it without talking to me."

"You should be." I took a sip of tea, trying to settle my nerves. I envisioned the situation from Suzy's perspective. "She probably felt so alone."

"Alone? She had me."

Shit. I hadn't meant to say it out loud. I took another sip. "Says a lot about where you fit in her world, doesn't it?"

"That's what I mean," he scoffed. "Her parents' wishes came before mine. I can't believe I almost asked her to marry me."

I squeezed his knee. "Don't beat yourself up over a first love. Learn from it and take small steps forward. It's a good thing finals are coming up. You can focus on them and rest over the holidays."

"God, finals." Dylan ran his hand through his hair. "I can't focus on school. I feel stuck."

"Maybe I can help. Go pour a couple more fingers of the

whiskey and meet me on the back patio. Leave a tiny sip for me. We're going to need it."

"What are you doing?"

"You'll see."

After tearing apart my closet until I remembered I had stored it in the office, I located an old Chinese lantern, grabbed my jacket and fire stick, and set it up. A few minutes more and Dylan lifted the lantern until it warmed enough to take off on its own. I held his hand as we tipped our heads back, watching it catch an updraft and float toward the stars. We both sniffled as we said goodbye in our hearts to the one who wouldn't be.

Watch over him or her, Shane, I silently prayed. Then I took a small taste of Dylan's Defiant, observing my family's tradition of toasting their dead. Some things overrode doctor's orders. Dylan knocked back the rest of the amber liquid when I handed the tumbler to him.

The sliding door rumbled as it opened. "Whatcha doing out here?" Rachel asked, wrapping her plaid blanket around her.

"Saying goodbye," I answered in a hushed tone. The golden blaze grew smaller by the second.

"To Suzy?"

"Sort of," Dylan answered, clearing his throat.

"It's beautiful. Can I say goodbye too?"

"Sure, sweetie." I opened my other arm and wrapped it around her middle. I didn't tell her about the little soul we wouldn't meet. Dylan could share when he was ready.

A light breeze stirred our hair as we watched the fire drift from sight.

A MUG OF WARM WATER AND LEMON STARED AT ME FROM ITS PERCH on my desk. It was a poor substitute for the black gold from the Perked Cup, but it kind of worked. Dr. Chaddha, my physician at the functional medicine clinic at Lord University, had recently given me some encouragement to hang in there with her detox program. Thanks to Thomas's quick thinking, the setback from my night at Ducky's could be managed quickly. I might not even need to extend this strict regimen beyond what we'd planned. It motivated me to see the protocol through.

I should have followed her protocol and meditated to clear my mind of the previous day's "mama drama." Instead, I stared out the window in my home office, rehashing everything Bobby had said and done. She would still be livid, and she'd find a way for me to pay. Lemon water couldn't stop the growing anger, but one thing could. If the stress Bobby loved to cause could lift, I knew my head would clear, and I wouldn't drop the ball with my kids again.

My hand jittered while dialing my brother.

"Kick?" His voice was raspy, and I scolded myself for calling him so early.

"Hey Hubert—" My joke of a nickname.

My little brother's actual name was Robert—as in named after our mother, Roberta, not our father, like other boys. You could say he was named after our Grandpa Sullivan, who was a Robert and never forgave Grandma for only birthing girls. But we knew better. Bobby either didn't notice or didn't care how it looked. Only those who knew my middle name knew she'd named both her children after herself.

"Cute. What'd she do?"

"Sorry to wake you." Bert had started out "Robby" until the neighbor kids noticed how much it sounded like "Bobby" and started calling him a mama's boy. He'd made sure "Bert" stuck instead.

"No, we're up. I have the boys today. I haven't spoken much yet, is all." It sounded like he took a pull of coffee. Lucky dog. "Spill. We were about to start the season off with a *Die Hard* marathon. Since you're distracting me, the guys went back to their *Switch.*"

"*Die Hard* isn't a Christmas movie," I protested on behalf of the true classics.

"The hell it isn't. And quit stalling."

My quiet laugh filled my office. As much as she'd tried to pit Bert and me against each other, we eventually admitted we were the only members of an elite club of crazy. Our support for each other overtook the initial resentments until it ran deep. At least I hoped it did.

"Where to begin?" I filled him in on Bobby's antics since she'd come back from her cruise.

"She threw out the Curse of Cromwell shit on Lee? God, I haven't heard that one in decades."

"It was my fault. I thought a vodka tonic would calm her down. I forgot that booze makes mean people meaner, not nicer."

"Geez. What did Liam do?"

"He's so amazing, Bert. He brushed it off, went upstairs, and started a *Nintendo* tournament. I've never understood how a grandmother doesn't like her own grandson. Wasn't my big crime not being a boy? I gave her two."

"No," he replied. "Your crime was being first. Girls come second in her world."

My breath hitched from being so keyed up. With everything else, I'd forgotten about what a shit she'd been to Liam when she'd first arrived.

"What can I do?" I could almost hear his fingers rub his temple as he hesitantly asked the question.

"I may have kicked her out of the house, but I need Bobby out of the state. Please take her early. I need a break."

"Won't it cost you extra to change her ticket?"

"Don't worry about the fecking ticket," I snapped, then took a deep breath. "In fact, tell her you received a bonus and asked about changing it. If she thinks I want her out of town early, she might turn us down out of spite."

"Uh... you *do* want her to leave early."

"You don't have to tell her, Bert. Please." I was so desperate, I resorted to whining. "For your big sister."

"The same one who poured hot sauce in my cocoa? It was spring by the time I figured out Swiss Miss wasn't supposed to make me cry. *That* big sister?"

"I paid for it too. Bobby used the Shillelagh on me. The bruises lasted into summer."

"I'll pay for this."

"Are you kidding? The golden boy does no wrong. She'll clean and cook and spoil your kids rotten."

"They don't need her mind games when their parents are in the middle of a divorce?"

I sighed, defeated, and admonished my selfishness. "You're right. Never mind. I'm sorry."

"No." He stopped me. A long sigh followed. "You're right. She's coming down anyway, and you need to get better. I still feel bad about having to cut the funeral trip short." Bert's ex had planned to take the boys on a trip to the Grand Canyon when Dad passed. She pitched a fit over the inconvenience. "What's a few days early?" he added.

"For real?" I squealed and tapped my toes.

"When should I expect her?"

"The tenth?"

"A few days before the original date? How about next weekend?"

"For real?"

"Of course. It'll be my Christmas present for you. Don't expect a package in the mail."

"I'm paying for her ticket." I laughed.

"The best presents are from the heart, right?"

"Yes, they are. Thank you, little bro."

"Yeah, yeah. Make the flight for Sunday, okay? I have a date Saturday and plan on having her stay over."

"Ooh. Keep Bobby far away. She'll demand proof of fertility."

"No kidding." He laughed this time. "I'm not looking forward to her annual 'when are you having a girl' pester either."

"Wait, you're getting a divorce. How are you supposed to get a daughter from the woman she hates more than me?"

"Kick," Bert groaned. "She doesn't hate you."

"Bobby had to marry Dad because of me. Plus I was born with curly brown hair, while she has perfect blonde hair. It's practically the same thing. You have no idea how much it helped you to favor her."

"What does your hair have to do with it?"

"That's what you took from my spiel? Today's products weren't around when we were little. To her, the stubborn, frizzy mess growing out of my head was proof of my obstinance."

"Damn. You two deserve a permanent separation."

Don't tempt me.

"Text me the flight info when you have it," he added softly.

My voice hitched, making me unable to speak.

"I know. Promise me you'll have a great December."

"Mm-hmm," was all I could manage.

"Love you too, sis."

As the Proverb said, my brother was born for adversity. We didn't come by it naturally, but I could breathe again with this burden about to be lifted. I could deal with the *momster* for a week.

I padded into my bedroom and sat in my new meditation corner. Instead of settling onto what I'd thought of as "my mind porch," my mind continued to race. Twenty minutes later, with my Christmas shopping list worked out in my head, attention drifted to Thomas, hoping he was having a pleasant visit.

Rachel tapped on my doorframe. She held up my phone. "Sorry about interrupting, but it's Thomas. I thought you might want to take it."

14

SHE'S ALWAYS IN MY HAIR

THOMAS

*T*homas reluctantly entered the coffee shop in downtown Raleigh. He ordered a pour-over black and took in the Día de Los Muertos decor. The place had atmosphere. He'd give it that. Young professionals bustled about, giving it the opposite vibe of the Perked Cup. All the lower-level tables were filled by people with laptops. Thomas saw the staircase and guessed Banger was upstairs. He'd already sent a text stating he'd arrived. His friend sat at a corner table, and they spotted each other immediately.

"Hey man," Thomas said, feigning indifference. He pulled out the chair on the opposite side of the table with his foot and sat. A significantly smaller, albeit quieter, crowd hung out here. "Okay Lucy, 'splain."

"What? The location? The last-minute summons?" Banger inquired, looking ragged and gaunt.

"All of it. Is everything alright? How's Tess?"

Banger took a sip of coffee and blew out a slow breath. "She's safely settled at her retreat outside Boone. I don't want anyone knowing I'm back, which is why we're not meeting at Kick's. I'm trying to stay away from the north end of the county—officially anyway."

What the hell? "What's going on? Is this about Kick's attack?" It's what he had assumed when Banger left the urgent voice mail. Thomas's foot tapped double-time to the Latin music filling the space.

Banger nodded once. "Partly. I'll hold the details until she arrives. I have a question for you though. It's a completely different topic."

Thomas's foot paused. "Shoot."

"I've been going over the footage from Kick's. Liam's birthday —this Charley Rodriguez—"

Thomas tapped the table lightly. "Yes. She was at Thanksgiving. What about her?"

Banger lifted a shoulder as his eye narrowed. "I've known of her since some of our work overlaps. Anyway, something struck me as familiar and I didn't know why. So, I did some digging."

Thomas rolled his wrist to get Banger to move on.

"Her background checks out the way ours do."

"What's wrong with our background checks?"

"Not a thing, unless you know what to look for."

"And you think this woman is…"

"Not who she claims to be. Possibly one of us," Banger finished.

"Impossible," Thomas mused, rubbing his chin. "We'd know, wouldn't we?"

Banger shook his head. "Not necessarily. Look how long it took to find you."

"That was decades ago. Completely different times. There's no proof. Right?"

Banger raised his eyebrows, letting Thomas know he'd keep at it.

"Do you want me to do anything? Arrange a meeting? The lab is on the verge of—"

Banger raised his hand, cutting Thomas off. "I've got it. Just keep your girl close, okay?"

"Planning to." Thomas knew all of Banger's reservations about Kick, still he couldn't hide his grin. It almost sounded like his friend was giving a blessing, despite them.

"Good. I don't like the weird coincidences happening around her."

Thomas thought he heard his friend mutter "menace," but Kick approached before he could say anything else. It didn't matter since Thomas's priorities shifted the night they went to the club.

"Mr. McHenry, are you trying to send a message about my coffee?" she asked as she sat between the men. The glint in her eyes told Thomas she was teasing his friend.

Banger actually gave her a little smile. "No. I have my reasons for meeting in a neutral place."

She took a sip of something Thomas assumed was decaf coffee. "I'll save you my 'don't you know how busy I am' rant since we all are. I assume this is life-and-death important."

Banger let out a cleansing breath. "There's news about who drugged you and your friend."

Kick's shoulders dropped. "I was kidding." She took another pull from her cup and leaned in. "Okay, let's hear it."

Thomas braced. Cameras were notoriously unclear and often turned off. If they didn't have answers soon, he might lose it.

"The main camera at the upstairs bar had been mysteriously turned off."

Kick tilted her chin. "Cyndi bought our drinks downstairs."

Banger tapped the side of his temple and pointed at her. "And there's footage of him adding something to those glasses. Both drinks were tainted, which is why your friend had it worse than you. Plus she drank more alcohol before it happened."

Kick scrunched her nose and Thomas couldn't tell if it was from anger or guilt. He reached under the table and squeezed her hand.

"There's more," Banger added.

"Lovely."

Banger slid a still photo in front of Kick.

"Here's the John Bender look-alike." Thomas leaned over her shoulder and agreed, not that he knew the character. He recognized the bartender.

"Right. Do you know the other guy?"

She shook her head, but her back stiffened. Her gaze whipped to Thomas as her brows drew together.

He rubbed her arm. "You're safe now."

Banger continued. "This was before Cyndi bought the drinks." He slid the photo to the middle of their four-top and laid two new ones in its place. "We think this is him with you, Kick."

She gasped and looked away. "It looks a lot like my messy hair." She inhaled deep and turned back. "The last photo showed the same man near the front door. It fit with Cyndi's description of him storming out of the place when Kick didn't cooperate."

"His grungy beard and effect is quite lycanesque. Looks like Detective Ross correctly interpreted my odd memory of fighting off a werewolf."

Without thinking, Thomas leaned forward and growled. "Dammit! Who is this guy?"

Banger whipped his head around and shushed him. "The management at Ducky's has fully cooperated. They're pissed. Your detective questioned the bartender. Turns out he's young Graham's cousin, but—"

Thomas interrupted. "Daddy Graham's lawyer is his lawyer now."

"Ding, ding, ding." Banger finished his coffee and leaned back in his chair. "It ties him to Halloween, so he's a person of interest, but he's not in custody. He admitted knowing your wolf-man."

Kick shivered. "Please don't call him mine."

"Right. Sorry." Banger tapped the table while Thomas gave Kick's hand another squeeze. "Anyway, my people dug more and found out where Wolfy works. Any guesses?"

Thomas ran his hand over his face. Could it be this easy? "Graham Construction?"

"Give the man a prize."

"No." Kick gasped, her eyes wide. "Does Big Jonn know about this?"

"Working on it. The guy's in the wind though. Since the bartender is family, how could he not know? Oh, I almost forgot the best part—"

Kick's hand went to her forehead. "How can there be a best to any of this?" Banger stared at her for a minute, so she rolled her hand. "Lay it on us."

"The cousin has the same tattoo as young Graham."

Kick's brow furrowed. "Does that mean he beat up my squawk box?"

Banger and Thomas shrugged. Thomas knew the answer before he heard it. "He's still a person of interest. Thanks to counsel, he's not saying anything."

"JaysusMaryandJoseph." She tucked some hair behind both ears, then grasped her hands behind her neck, letting her elbows fall to the table.

Banger lifted a shoulder. "My sentiments exactly." He tapped the table again, getting Kick's attention. "My team's on it. *I'm* on it. In fact, I'm leaving after this to chase down a lead."

Thomas brushed a curl off Kick's cheek. "You're my priority now too."

She frowned at him. "You don't have to choose."

"Kids," Banger said. "Deal with this later. I have a request before I go."

"Anything," Kick said, her face determined.

Banger turned to Thomas. "This is for you, brother. Will you feed my fish? I ran out of those vacation feeding tablets. If you pick up some and stop by once, my assistant, Siobhan, can do the rest when she gets back from her own mission."

Kick pursed her lips. "How long will you be gone?"

Banger collected the photos and answered, "I don't know." He looked back at Thomas. "I'll probably fly directly to France for the holidays. But I only need this week."

Wherever this lead came from, it must have been moving quickly. Banger rarely ended up hanging like this.

Thomas nodded his support, but Kick said, "Could Rachel help you?" She lifted her hands as the men's mouths opened. "She's coming up on finals and could use time away from—"

"The breakup drama," Banger guessed.

The corner of her mouth ticked up as she agreed with him.

Banger pinched his lower lip. "If the princess wants, she could stay at my condo. I'll give you the code."

Thomas tried to study his friend without him or Kick noticing. Where was this coming from? It took years for Banger to take on Siobhan as a right hand. "Bang—"

The man made a swiping motion as if he knew Thomas's concerns. "She's a good kid and could use the peace. Besides, I don't like how often the brats in her building prop open the exterior doors. They have no sense of responsibility."

Kick winced and frowned at Banger's words. She didn't ask for clarification, and Thomas chalked it up to her motherly worries. He didn't think she already knew Banger had cameras of questionable legality pointed at Rachel's building. Then again, she also didn't know they'd been on her street for weeks too.

"Aren't you taking the kids to the mountains for Christmas?" Thomas asked her.

Before she could answer, Banger said, "Have your daughter call my assistant when she doesn't need the place anymore."

Kick gave him a grateful, slightly adoring smile. Thomas knew it well. He wanted to know it better.

Banger's chair scraped the floor as he stood. "Well, guys, I'm off. If you need anything, you know to call Siobhan. She's me while I'm gone. I'll check in with her when I can."

Thomas grabbed the sleeve of his friend's jacket. "Thanks, man. I don't have to tell you to stay safe."

"I'm always careful." Banger shrugged. "No guarantees on safe." He took a step and turned back. "See you in Bordeaux?"

Thomas shook his head. "Just Virginia this year." He patted Kick's hand. "I have other plans for the break."

He adored Kick's pretty pink blush.

Banger dropped his chin, pivoted on his heel, and took off down the stairs.

Thomas moved to stand, and Kick cleared her throat. "Wait a minute."

He scooted back in and waited for her.

"Why do you act like you have to choose between me and your career—like it's one or the other?"

Thanks to the Felidae, it was. He sighed.

"Thomas," she soothed, "this isn't an either/or. We don't have normal dates, unless you call greenway walks, shooting lessons, and rides home from IV appointments dates." They both chuckled. "You've been good for me and my family. Why can't I be good for your career?"

She rubbed his forearm, which made her sweater run up and expose her bruises. The added IV from the emergency department meant her usual arm hadn't had time to recover. He hated how she looked like she'd been beaten. Had he been good for her? It didn't feel like it. At least Banger's team had made progress.

Thomas made himself focus on her words. "You are doing better with the airsoft gun. I want you to move back to the Sig the next time we practice."

She clicked her tongue. "That's what you took from my speech?"

They both laughed as Kick swatted his bicep. She made a

sweet, swooning noise he'd noticed she did when his rumbly laughs stayed low in his chest. How he liked the sound *she* made.

Thomas rubbed his neck and said, "Alright, darlin'. I'll think about your speech."

"Good. I want to see you succeed, Thomas."

"You do, don't you?"

Kick blinked at him a few times. "Of course. I hope one day you'll be able to tell me all the details, because it sounds like you're working on something huge."

He hoped like hell he could tell Kick everything too. The real question was, how would she take it?

15

I MELT WITH YOU

KICK

Thomas parked his Camaro in front of Mick & Hugh's, walked around the passenger side, and opened the door. I growled as he bent down, like he intended to pick me up. Then I almost laughed as he jumped back, leaving me room to step out of the car.

His concern touched me. Deeply. But having had the "stiff upper lip" drilled into me from an early age, I couldn't get past the visual of being carried into the smoke shop. Once again, Bobby's admonition about how nobody wanted to hear (or see) my sob story came to mind. As I had already told Thomas, as cruel as her words had been, they were also right. Add the harassment of me, my family, and my business, and it also felt like eyes were following me wherever I went. Someone on the community social media page had already posted a photo of my bruised forearm, implying it was proof I used drugs. I uninstalled the app from my phone right after seeing it.

"I'm sore and stupid tired, but I'm not an invalid, Thomas." *Jaysus*, how I wished I could curl into my sweater and take a nap in his front seat. I stuck a foot onto the asphalt and pushed up. "Thank you, though." When I took a step, I swear my foot refused to work, forcing me to reach for the roof of the car. I sighed in frustration. Maybe I should've brought a cane with me. "I suppose a girl might use an arm."

Thomas smiled at me in the same way I used to smile at my toddlers, who didn't enjoy asking for help. Without a word, he wrapped an arm around my waist and propped me up against his side as if we were simply walking into the smoke shop like a devoted couple.

"Katie, you came," Hugh called out after Thomas opened the door. "Dylan told me you had one of your appointments this morning. I was about to call and make sure you still planned on decorating today."

No surprise to anyone I'd overbooked. The IV treatments had been easing up when it came to knocking me out, until I'd been drugged—yeah, it was time I stopped dancing around our girl's-night-out fiasco and called it what it was. My doctor had added something to the medicine bag to help my liver recover, and my body felt like it was back at square one. I hoped it would go by quickly.

There were also multiple reasons I wanted to stop by the smoke shop. After kissing Uncle Hugh's cheek, I told him, "I'll decorate for you after I take a nap in Dad's recliner. I have some samples for you too. Remember?"

"Oh right." He followed Thomas and me to the office as the three of us passed Dylan behind the counter. I smiled at my son, both from gratitude that he hadn't left Hugh hanging in order to finish his thesis and to reassure him I was fine. Dylan had cut his hours significantly, but it still helped Hugh. I was sure he would have sold the shop outright if my son had left him all alone.

Before dropping into my father's raggedy yet comfy chair in the back office, I pulled some CBD ointments and lotions out of my tote bag and spread them out on his old desk, gesturing for Hugh to look them over.

Thomas took the blanket from the back of the chair and opened it. He tipped his head, silently commanding me to sit. I gladly obeyed this time.

He tucked the blanket around me. "Why are you recovering in this ratty thing?" he asked with a chuckle, sounding both confused and sexy.

My jaw cracked on a yawn. "Carmen brought in extra help today so they can deep clean. If I tried to sleep, they would tiptoe around the house and struggle to get it done right while I worried about making them mess up their big job." I smacked my lips together, hating the cottonmouth the treatments caused. "And I promised Hugh I'd decorate the shop for him."

Uncle Hugh looked down at me sheepishly and quietly said, "You have a better eye for it than I do."

I reached for and squeezed his hand. I'd done the holiday decorating since the store opened and had a system. "I know. After my nap, I'll be good to go." My tongue practically stuck to my cheek, and I turned my focus to Thomas. "Would you mind getting me a water bottle from the fridge? It's in an alcove in the back hallway. Hard to miss."

He kissed my forehead, and my sore body relaxed. "You got it. Be right back."

"Okay, Hugh, check out this stuff." I pointed at the jars and tube on his desk. "I think you should stock these, but try them out first. You know, like you do with cigars."

"You don't want me to smoke these though."

I ignored the bad joke and opened one of the jars of the salve instead. I held it up and demonstrated. "Scoop out a small bit and rub it into your hands. Pay special attention to your arthritis spots." Hugh did as told with an open curiosity.

"It's a little warm." He sniffed his hand. "Smells nice too, Katie. Not girly."

I nodded as I finished rubbing mine into my elbow. "You could sell it now since there's no THC in it. Your notes suggested an interest in focusing your expansion on using cannabis for health issues over recreation."

Hugh's eyes lit up. "That's the idea."

"Around here, it's a good tack. You'll want recreation products, but you could still emphasize aspects like relaxation, energy, and such." I held up the jar. "I've been using this for years—ever since my doctor told me to stop taking acetaminophen. I use it on sore muscles too. Mostly my back."

He smiled widely. "I knew you would be the perfect partner for this."

Hugh asked about the other products, and I filled him in on terms like full-spectrum CBD and CBG, among other things. I thought the lotion would be perfect for his wife, Maggie.

"You think this will help us get the license?"

"Absolutely." I screwed the lid on the jar and put it back with the others. "Take them home and try them. Hell, you and Maggie should take notes. I'll email you some websites you can study for more information. The board will appreciate it. Knowing them, though, you'll go far if you have a ready-made clientele who love these and might be curious about trying stronger things."

As I wondered where Thomas had disappeared to, he returned with three bottles. I opened one and chugged half of it. I set it on the desk with an audible sigh of relief. "You're my hero."

Hugh tapped my foot. "Are you sure you're set to decorate later?"

I did my best to give him a confident smile, hoping he couldn't see through to the truth. "It'll be ready tomorrow."

"It'll be perfect." Hugh placed the jars and tube in his briefcase on the opposite side of the office. He zipped it and took it with him. "Thank you, dear." He strutted out of the room with more pep than I'd seen him have in a while.

Thomas's gaze followed him out. "What did you give Hugh?"

I lifted a shoulder. The little movement hurt, and I wished I had more of the salve in my bag. "A CBD-CBG salve for his arthritis."

"It must've been a miracle."

"Naw." I laughed. "The hope did that." I switched to a whisper. "I think Dad's death scared him about leaving Maggie alone. He's betting on setting her up with the cannabis profits."

"Can it work?"

I shrugged. "Possibly. Other than a medical issue, Hugh and Maggie have little overhead. Not like someone raising kids."

"Like you," Thomas suggested.

I closed my eyes and leaned back, thinking of how many more years of college tuition payments I had ahead of me. Then I wondered if Liam would ever get around to applying anywhere. "Don't remind me." At least my family had the buffer of our inheritance. My mind drifted to the families the McKenna Foundation helped. I hoped we helped them enough to ease their worries.

My aching feet finally yelled at me loud enough to get my attention, and I shifted in the chair.

"What's the matter, baby?"

I shifted the blanket, hoping it would help. I scrunched my nose. "Would you mind helping me with my feet?"

"Are your shoes too tight?"

I shook my head and ended up stretching my neck. "No. The more the medicine works, the sorer my muscles get."

"Sure." Thomas wheeled an office chair over by the footrest. His hand traveled along my calf, gently squeezing, resulting in one of those sensations of pain that feels so good.

I opened my eyes when his massage stopped and saw the grin spread across his face.

"What?"

Thomas's face filled with warmth, showing me the real him. "You and your boots."

"They're moccasins, not boots." As comfortable as crocs without the hideous style. "They're usually comfortable." I shifted farther as he removed them. "Nothing's comfortable at the moment."

"How's this?" Thomas rubbed small circles along my Achilles tendon and over the top of my foot.

"It's heaven." I smiled at my weirdly dreamy voice, barely recognizing it as my own. Thomas's touch transformed something in me, especially since the attack. When we found common time to be together, he seemed to make sure he touched me as much as possible even if it only meant holding hands.

To distract myself from an entirely inappropriate arousal—why hadn't I rescheduled the deep clean? I asked him, "What took so long getting the water?" I finished the first bottle and dabbed at my mouth with my sweater cuff.

Thomas sighed as if he had to steady himself. "Dylan cornered me about us—I'm a bit shocked because I thought it was obvious we were together."

"Well—" I could relate to my son. I guess we both wanted formal declarations. The lad probably thought more about his own pain, though, and wanted to make sure I was settled. He'd taken on too much after his father died—of his own accord, but I could see where he would need reassurances.

Thomas kept his focus on a troubling spot on my instep. "You know you're my priority now, right?"

"Sure, sweets—" He hit a potent spot, making me groan. The pleasure raced through me, almost as intense as an orgasm. It took my breath away.

I looked up, and Thomas's eyes had glazed over. *Jaysus-MaryandJoseph*, why hadn't I had the foresight to be doing this in my bedroom or his? Because I was a distracted, overthinking idiot, that's why.

Thomas's thumb stuck on a spot I'd swore felt like a rock under my skin. I gasped and might have done more, but my brain fuzzed.

"Seriously?" Dylan stuck his head through the doorway and scolded us. "I can hear you. You're creeping out the customers. Me too."

Thomas's hands sprang away from me as if he'd been shocked. His eyes dropped to the floor as he panted, like he was struggling to catch his breath.

Hell. Would I ever get "me time" that didn't involve a nap? I bit my lip. "Sorry, son. The medicine is wreaking havoc on my body. Thomas's foot rub helps the pain, but I'll be good. I promise."

Dylan squinted but nodded and shut the door.

"I should stop," Thomas said, though he had resumed stroking my shins.

I shook my head. "I should've known the spot would be tender. My hands don't have your strength, so I've never had such an intense reaction to it."

He switched back to small circles with light pressure. "What do you mean you should've known?"

"It's been a while since I dabbled in acupressure, so my memory of the foot map is a bit faded, but I think you hit the spot for the liver. The liver area is always tender." I sat back and let out a cleansing breath. "I promise to behave."

"Christ, darlin', you kill me," he said with a slight laugh and exhale of his own.

"How so?"

Thomas rubbed my foot over his jeans, letting me feel his entire erection. He closed his eyes and shifted in the chair while I flexed my toes, wishing I could do more. So much more.

"Damn, baby."

"That's my line," he rasped with a smile in his tone. "I wish I could take you right to my bed right now, but I'm going straight back to the lab from here."

Despite our desires, it sounded like neither of us had figured out how to work the other into our lives yet.

"If you took me anywhere in your car, I would fall sound asleep before we arrived anyway."

"Then I should probably go." He rolled his chair closer to me and kissed me long and gently. It made the desire worse, but it helped to be on a similar page. "Is the pain better?"

Was he kidding? I might have been floating above the chair. "Much. Thank you." My jaw popped again on a long yawn. "I swear it isn't you."

I reached for Thomas's neck to give him a hug, and the gauze bandage I'd forgotten to remove pulled on my sweater sleeve. I rolled it up to unpeel everything. "Can't wait until these are through."

"What the hell happened now?" Thomas exclaimed. He grabbed my wrist and examined my entire forearm while I wished hard to be invisible. The embarrassing paparazzi-like photos came to mind. This was worse than those had been.

I dropped my arm and my shoulders. "A new tech worked in the treatment room today." When he simply stared at me like my explanation said nothing, I continued, "In some ways, starting a line is like an art. My vein blew out with half the bag left. She had to"—I didn't know why this embarrassed me so, but I hated it and took a deep breath to continue—"thump my arm to make another vein surface. My regular arm is still healing."

"Goddammit." Thomas pulled my hand to his lips and kissed along the bruises, reminding me of Gomez Addams. Only I wished I had Morticia's badass confidence.

"I didn't mean to whine," I said. "I might only need four more."

"Is it helping?"

I nodded and thought ahead to when I could have all-day energy again.

"Good. Let me tuck you in."

I sat back and drank down the second water bottle as Thomas made quick work of my other foot. I made a break for the restroom, then let him wrap me back up in the blanket, ready for an hour of peace.

He gave me another panty-melting kiss. When Thomas pulled away, he was flushed as he dropped his forehead to mine.

"I feel like a tease," I confessed.

"Whatever for? I initiated the kiss and the foot rubs. I like it when you let me take care of you."

"Well, I don't like leaving you frustrated."

"I'm not."

Right. I could see the bulge. Hell, it looked Photoshopped, even though I knew it wasn't.

I let my gaze travel from Thomas's face to below his waist and back, then raised my brows to let him know I didn't believe him.

"I'm a grown man, not a boy, darlin'. I'll be fine when I walk out of here. In fact, I'll float, thanks to you."

I'd almost run out of my last bit of energy and needed to get on with the napping. I lifted my hand to Thomas's chin and gently stroked the cleft in his chin. If I dreamed about anything, I hoped it would be about his kisses. I smiled against his mouth as we kissed one last time. "You're like an early Christmas present."

"Then I'll wear a bow the next time I see you."

Please let that be code for we'll have sex again soon.

I sat on the meditation porch in my mind, clearing away the naptime cobwebs. In real life, I was sitting in my father's recliner, legs crossed under me, hoping I did meditation correctly. It relaxed me. Energized me too. I considered both a victory. One of these days, I'd look into finding an actual meditation coach. Or a guru. In the meantime, whatever this place could be called, it worked. At least it did until the noise level on the other side of the door disturbed my peace.

I opened my eyes to find the glow had returned. However, multiple colors shifted around me instead of the light blue color it had been. I didn't have time to ponder what it meant since a commotion had clearly been growing outside. I flapped my hands and shimmied my body, willing it to fade. It had long stopped frightening me, probably because I always felt better after it appeared. As long as I was alone when it happened, I usually let it flow because it also reminded me of a warm, friendly hug.

Someday soon I planned to get an energy reading. Someone in that line of work should help me understand it all. At the moment, it stayed another item on an unending to-do list.

I stepped into the salesroom, ready to complain about the noise in a mom voice but discovered a literal crowd staring me down. A half dozen customers—then again, reading their frowns, probably not—stood in the center of the space, holding signs and chanting, "Don't buy from immoral businesses." Someone else threw in "Jesus is the reason for the season," which seemed oddly random.

I wanted to reply that axial tilt was the actual reason for the season but thought better of it when I saw my clearly exasperated son. Dylan had his hands in front of him, trying to push the crowd back outside without touching anyone. Thank goodness he'd kept his head. My son had a history of fighting and winning. He was a big man, which sometimes meant hotheads tried to provoke him to prove their own manliness. Given our present circumstances, I didn't want him dragged into the fray.

I moved to the area behind the counter, seeking some distance. I whistled, then called out, "Let me guess: this has something to do with the opinion piece in the paper? If you have questions, I'm willing to—"

A familiar woman with a pin-straight, bleached, stacked bob pointed at me and declared, "Look at her arms. I told you she shoots up."

My gaze dropped to my forearms. Sure enough, I had pushed up the sleeves, probably from warming up while sleeping. Well, hell. I hastily pulled my sweater sleeves down and bunched the cuffs into my fists. I wanted to tell her an actual addict is better at hiding the track marks, but I wasn't sure if it was true. It wouldn't have mattered anyway.

I stared at the countertop, wishing I could clean it. *Inhale for four. Hold for four. Exhale for five... Again.*

In my periphery, I saw someone outside edge onto the side-walk, carrying a long gun. *Oh, hell no.* I really should have rescheduled Carmen and her crew. I might've been able to convince Thomas to stay with me for the afternoon. Murphy's Law struck again.

Moving to the end of the counter, I planted my feet and crossed my arms, my jaw set. "Lock the door Dylan." The last thing we needed was someone bringing a rifle into Hugh's store.

"You can't hold us against our will!" Blonde bob yelled. I thought I recognized her from Liam's track meets.

"No one's keeping you here. You folks refused to leave when Dylan asked you to leave. Now, *that* is illegal, plus you're turning my friend's store into a fire hazard." I pointed to a sign over the door. "The shop also has a no-gun policy. I'm not about to let you risk a good man's livelihood over lies in a newspaper."

The man next to the blonde said, "I told you this place was immoral too. I heard the big guy's her son. Bet he does drugs too."

I rolled my eyes and took a cleansing breath, afraid to move anything else. Dylan's high school football record was still spoken of around town. I wondered if these people lived in Oakville, aside from blonde bob woman. *Jayz,* I wanted to hit someone. I wiggled my fingers to make them relax.

This group definitely didn't want to hear my sob story. Without letting my gaze leave the crowd, I ignored the accusations and said, "Anyone who wants to leave can go out the back with Dylan." I tipped my head toward the front. "This door stays locked for now."

The noise volume ticked back up with the theme of me infringing on their rights, not the other way around.

I pulled my phone out and texted Jake at the Perked Cup.

ME

A hyped-up crowd won't leave Hugh's. Can you spare anyone to help? By anyone, I mean you.

I loved having a strapping young veteran in my corner. This kind of situation didn't faze him. He texted back quickly.

JAKE

Sorry, Mrs. Mack. The same group sent people in here first. I pressed the emergency button when someone broke a coffeepot. You should do the same. OPD will be here soon.

More hell. I jumped up to see over the crowd. Sure enough, a mob actually picketed in front of my coffeehouse. My blood boiled at the thought of someone marching behind the service area and scaring my staff—again. Plus why the hell did people consider breaking my stuff a viable option?

I texted back.

ME

Will do. However, if Liam's there, don't let him explode. Lock him in your office if you have to.

Jake texted back a thumbs-up. I worried about Lee more than I did Dylan.

After pocketing my phone, I pressed the button under the counter, then stood on a nearby chair and yelled, "The police are on their way, so I suggest you get the hell out now." I pointed at a camera. "We already have evidence of who's done what this afternoon."

Instead of scaring them off, the people resumed chanting, "Don't buy from immoral businesses."

Like clockwork, I heard the police sirens. The added honking told me they were at the intersection near our shopping center. All but three in the crowd rushed toward the back, and Dylan urged them to stay calm while he opened the door.

The remaining people faced me while the crowd outside stopped pounding on the windows and turned around, holding up their signs as the police cruisers arrived.

My hands dropped to my waist as I took in another long breath.

"Stay strong," an older, portly man said to the other two. "We'll shut her down soon. Cara, you'll have the coffee shop by the New Year."

My head snapped up. "Excuse me? On what grounds? You clearly don't understand the concept of a lease agreement." Or how good my lawyer was.

Old portly held up a hand and counted off. "We know you broke the agreement. You dealt drugs there. They were found in your diner."

"I called the police myself when I found them. And it's not a diner."

"Exactly. Y'all serve weird food, not American stuff. What's a scone? My granddaughter said it's European."

I threw my hands in the air. "It's coffee, pastries, and sand-wiches. If you don't like excellent coffee, go somewhere else. No one's forcing anybody to use my café… or Hugh's shop."

"There's my point." He held up a second and third finger. "You lure our children into unholy thinking. It's bad enough you put them in danger on Halloween. You teach them your wrong ways every afternoon."

"The kids do their homework in a safe, monitored environment... if they want to."

"We have issues with their homework too." The man moved his index in a circular motion. "You're all swirled together. In cahoots."

For feck's sake. A thought sparked, cluing me into what might've been the source of their rage. "Are you upset over me caring about kids who aren't my own? Or is it the diversity tutoring after school?"

An exceptional children's teacher at the high school had started the group in September. It had something to do with the school not being able to sanction a program that would only benefit a minority of students. An off-campus group could zero in on disadvantaged kids who would benefit from time with a peer tutor. It had to do with economics more than race, but there was an overlap of both. Of course I'd jumped all over sponsoring it. It had the added benefit of helping kids from different backgrounds get to know each other better than they would have while surrounded by their normal peers.

"It's not natural."

I inhaled sharply as the man hit my last nerve, but a team of officers knocked on the door and saved me from chewing him out.

Grateful for the reprieve, I stepped over to the door and flipped the lock. I hoped this wouldn't affect Hugh's ability to secure the cannabis license. I wondered if it was why he'd been dragged into my harassment. The crowd wouldn't object to selling cigars. Hell, we lived in tobacco country. Our neighborhood was built on former tobacco fields, and yet drive five minutes in any direction, and you'd pass land still growing it. Cannabis, however, was a different story.

What I wouldn't give for Thomas to show up and save the day like he'd done with Jonn Graham. I wouldn't yell at him. I'd kiss him in front of anyone. Well, what do you know? In the middle of the chaos, I realized Thomas had become my safe place. His new declarations about priorities had done the trick.

At least I had the upcoming Christmas gala to keep me hopeful. Spending time with the McKenna Foundation families and Thomas together would fill my spirit bucket that this crowd threatened to drain. Add in my plans for some sexy times at my house after the presentation—Liam was spending the night at a friend's—and I could forget all about this afternoon.

16

KING OF PAIN

THOMAS

Thomas collapsed into his bed, eager for the serenity of sleep. He'd spent many nights sleeping cramped up on the love seat in his office, pulling his weight with round-the-clock shifts in the lab. The only time he took for himself was the hours spent with Kick, making sure she made progress with her health, getting to know her and her family better.

The anger over her drugging, right under his nose, hadn't lessened. Thomas hoped Banger's silence equaled good news. His friend had a way of disappearing only to return right before a major story broke around the world. The last time he'd done it, a prominent drug lord turned up dead. Then Banger pulled into town with a smile and light step. It's why Thomas trusted him to get Kick out of danger, and he allowed himself to be the one comforting her when a riled-up crowd caused more trouble like they'd done the day before.

He fell asleep to the memory of her laughing after dinner. Knowing he could lift her spirit—and Liam's—did the same to his own. The next thing he knew, Thomas found himself back in the trenches and smelling the noxious gas. Instead of trying to breathe it in like he usually did, he pinched his nose and ran to get away from it. He didn't care about the angel he used to wait for anymore. He ran to find Kick, realizing she'd become his safety. As dreams often do, in the next instance, Thomas sat on a veranda in the desert, his Uncle Theo next to him, pride in his eyes.

Thomas dropped his head, unable to keep looking at another person he hadn't protected. As if Theo knew Thomas's thoughts, the man gave his shoulder a good shove.

"Get over yourself, boy. I'm not here to yell." Theo dropped his voice to a soothing, fatherly tone. "I want to tell you I'm proud."

Thomas had respected his father, but Uncle Theo had been the father of his heart. When he'd searched Thomas out during a very dark time, their bond had become unbreakable, even when Theo would take off for years at a time. But did he forgive Thomas for what had happened?

Before Thomas could ask, Theo said, "It's my fault a cannon ball killed me, not yours." The old man chuckled. "If anything, I blame myself for stepping in front of the damn thing."

Thomas blew out a deep breath in relief. "Thank you." So much weight lifted with those two words. Thomas had spent enough years with the Felidae to know some of the members carried enough energy to travel between the physical and the metaphysical world. He'd always hoped Uncle Theo possessed that freedom, but this was the first time they'd spoken since the horrible night he'd died.

"I needed this, Theo."

As if reading his mind again, the old man said, "I know. That's not why I'm here though."

Thomas wondered if someone was in trouble, his breath catching on the intake as Kick flashed through his mind.

Theo shook his head and reached for Thomas's shoulder. "Untwist your britches, son. Your work… your cousins can help."

Thomas's brow furrowed. "Cousins? You mean you…"

Theo smiled and tilted his head. "Yes, boy." He looked out over the expanse. "I believe we're on my old balcony—well, my wife's family's veranda—the way the house was built into a hill. It's a bit of both."

"Y-you had more children… after—"

"Yes." Theo dipped his chin. "They're like *us* too."

How was that possible? He had never mentioned children back then.

Uncle Theo lifted a shoulder. "I didn't feel worthy of raising them. I couldn't handle seeing another family age without me."

So, there were more subjects to study? Thomas rubbed his forehead, both excited and perplexed. *Where would he find these people? Did they have families?*

Theo spread his arms wide. "Start with this estate, I guess. Sorry, son. I'm new at this."

If Thomas did his math right, Theo had been gone for years. How many were there?

"Two."

Christ. He jumped at the words. So Uncle Theo could read thoughts. The last thing Thomas wanted to do was yell at the father of his heart. He missed the man dearly.

Theo's big hand raised up and dropped onto Thomas's knee, squeezing. "I agree. Let's say we sit quietly and rock for a spell."

At the moment, Thomas wanted nothing more.

The next morning, Thomas rang up the house in Virginia. This wasn't a call to make from the road. He wanted to keep his head in case he didn't get the answer he hoped for.

"Hey, Joe, how are y'all holding up? Are we doing the holiday open house or going low key this year?" The Harrison estate was part family home and part historical landmark. He and Joe used to cater brunches for the locals during the holidays. Between his progress at the lab and with Kick, then seeing his uncle—he'd been surprised to discover he remembered it all—Thomas felt like he was walking on a cloud.

"Let's go low key. Toni's not ready for the hoopla. She found out she can spend Christmas Day with Ken. It lifted her mood tenfold when his caretakers passed on the news."

Thomas shared the joy. Watching Toni deal with her husband's battle with Alzheimer's felt like witnessing a slow-motion crash. His heart perpetually broke for them and soared for their small victories, like this one. "Wonderful news."

Some silence passed before he found his courage. Joe had become quite the homebody. "Hey, I called to ask what y'all would think of coming down with me for a few days after Christmas. There's someone I'd like you to meet."

"What kind of someone?"

Thomas didn't blame Joe for making him spell it out. He hadn't even introduced Vivienne to the family.

"It's a woman, Joe. Someone I've grown fond of. She's—"

"What has your precious Alaric said about her?"

Thomas's eyes squeezed tight. This was why he'd made the call before heading out. "He said to pursue other interests and—"

"There's no way he'll allow this, Thomas."

"As long as I keep my vow, it's none of his business." Thomas walked out onto the back deck to cool off. He watched the sunrise through barren trees. The warm, vibrant colors mixing with the foreground reminded him of Kick's hair. He had to find a way to make his worlds exist in peace.

In a clipped, gruff voice, Joe warned, "I won't run interference this time."

"What are you talking about? What interference?"

"Can you honestly tell me you didn't know they watched her

the whole time? Alaric was obsessed with it." Joe cleared his throat. Thomas sensed his emotion growing, like he wanted to yell, but reined it in. "Why do you think I left the Felidae anyway?"

"I don't know, Joey. You won't tell me."

"The Felidae made orders to kill Vivienne if anyone found proof you'd broken your vow of secrecy. They protect the Society above all else."

Thomas fell back into an Adirondack chair. *Did it matter? What did they think would happen if my research was successful?* He thought back to the early days in the Felidae. No one ever asked him about his personal life, and he didn't see the need to volunteer anything. "You can't tell me they expect me to live like a monk." *Of course not. Grand-père practically told him to go find a girlfriend.*

Instead of answering his question, Joe laid it all out. "They ordered me to spy on Vivienne and kill her if I found evidence she knew about the Society. Or about you. So I left. I made sure she was safe. Then I told the old man to fuck off."

Thomas pressed a hand to his chest in a sad attempt to stop his heart from pounding so hard. He wondered out loud, "What do they think will happen with my research? If it works, everything will come out."

"I don't know, and I don't care," Joe snapped back. "As long as y'all leave me and Toni alone. The horses and the estate are all I want from the world now. If everything goes public, leave us out of it. At least until Toni is stable enough to make her own decisions."

"Hang on." Thomas redirected. "Do you think the Felidae will harm Kick—that's the name of the woman I wanted y'all to meet." Apparently, he had already changed his mind. "I mean, without confronting me first?"

An exasperated exhale came through the phone. Thomas's hands started shaking, so he pulled his Bluetooth out of his pocket and activated it, hoping to finish the call without dropping his phone. He had enough to worry about.

"I love you, man," Joe began. "You've had my back for as long as I can remember. You know I begin and end with family. I don't give a shit about changing the world. But you've always had an arrogant cluelessness about you. I just didn't know how deep it went. I figured you *knew* about the surveillance and that was why you stayed away from Viv so much."

Thomas scoffed. "We weren't a close couple. Not sure if you could call us a couple at all."

His voice much softer now, Joe said, "To answer your original question, I would like to meet this woman who seems to have miraculously found a way into your heart. It'd be nice to meet someone normal for a change. It'll be better for everyone if y'all come up to the estate though."

"She's taking her kids to the mountains for Christmas and can't get away after either. She runs her own business."

"Kids?" Joe barked a laugh. "Now I know you've gone off the deep end. Tell me something. Does Banger know about this woman?"

"He does. His company is in charge of her security." Thomas hadn't explained it right, but he was too frazzled to fix his meaning or to explain further. "Why?"

"Who do you think took the Vivienne assignment after me? It didn't end with me. It never ended."

Dammit all.

Suddenly chilled to the bone, Thomas went inside his house and poured himself two fingers of bourbon. With as few words as he could manage, he ended the call after assuring Joe he'd be there for Christmas dinner.

He watched the backyard descend into blackness along with his mood. His cluelessness about Vivienne was arrogance, as Joe had said. He hadn't loved Viv enough to protect her at all costs. There was the indictment.

Was all this effort to protect Kick and her family a waste? Was his frustration with how long it took to get intel on the drugging simply folly? The harassment played out like a stupid, public frenzy with Kick as a scapegoat. If needed, she could move. She'd done it before. He knew, without a doubt, Banger would make the bartender and his accomplice pay even if the police couldn't.

But did Thomas put Kick in more danger? He obsessed over the possibility he might be the downfall of the woman he'd fallen for. Yeah, he knew he loved her already. What would he do about it though?

DIAMONDS AND PEARLS?

KICK

"Settle down so I can finish this updo." Rachel clucked her tongue at me. "I don't remember you ever being this fidgety." She worked an asymmetrical french braid around the right side of my head and rolled pieces of lower curls into a loose bun at the nape. The result made small bits of curly fringe edging the look. I loved the romantic style.

"It's her hawt daaate," her roommate, Isabella, sang with a cute, throaty flutter.

"Right," I protested. "It has nothing to do with giving a ginormous, super important fundraising presentation for the first time in years." I sighed to release the stress and smirked. The talk wasn't the source of my nerves. Sharing about our foundation families came easily, and I wished I could take the floor longer to highlight all of them. If I had to deal with a handsy director to help them, it was worth it, especially with Thomas at my side.

No, I itched for alone time with Thomas. At this point, our

first night together seemed like a dream, given the circumstances of throwing us together after the attack. Tonight would be different. We were different. I'd been planning our own after-party for days, and I wanted it to be perfect.

Rachel secured the last bit of hair to the bun and spun me around to face my mirror as I grabbed my glasses to survey her work. For the first time since I'd picked up the progressive frames, I wished I'd ordered contacts. I silently cursed my eyes for getting older. The blurriness was harder to accept than cracking knees and thinning eyebrows. I thought about Thomas's perfect vision and deflated some.

"Are you listening, Mama?"

I shook my head, embarrassed at being self-focused when Rachel had given up her last Saturday of the semester to help me get ready. "I'm sorry, Snow. What'd you say?"

She tilted her head as if trying to decipher my thoughts. *Let it go, sweetie. You're too young to understand.* "I said it's time for makeup. Are you sure you don't want to get into your dress first?"

"No. My dress is a wrap, like my robe. I'd feel better leaving it to the end."

"But I can't remember where to have the makeup stop."

I looked down. "I'd say do the whole décolletage. The neckline is open." Very open.

"Okay, then." She turned to my kit and pulled out products, then set to work, gooping me up. "What's this stuff?" she asked, a tiny vial held between her fingers.

"Dab a little on the under eye, and it deflates the bags while lightening dark spots."

"Huh." She squinted to read the ingredients. Maybe it wasn't only me. "Can't wait to see how it works."

I settled back into the chair and closed my eyes. "Remember, this isn't a swanky awards show."

"Shush. Photographers will be there. They always are." Her voice dropped in the way it did when someone focused on two things at once. "You and Thomas will be in all the area newspapers, along with Lord University materials, I'm sure."

"Good point," I whined, already imagining how bad my photos would look. Add in Thomas next to me, and I wanted to cancel the whole thing. *Humble yourself for the families*, I reminded myself. "Come to think of it, you should go for me next year."

The product smearing and dabbing ceased, so I opened my eyes to find Rachel staring at me with a rebuke on her face, looking a lot like Deana's. "You do perfectly well with the presentations. Hell, if Dylan's wasn't on the same night, you'd join him too."

"I like the presentations fine," I agreed, settling back in the chair. "It's the media. I take the worst pictures."

She laughed. "True. I can teach you how to pose though. It's easy when you understand the mechanics."

I sighed again. "I'll always be more comfortable behind the lens. You, sweetheart, take a beautiful photo with your tongue sticking out and your face screwed up."

Bella barked a laugh. "She's right. You do."

Rachel returned to the makeup and picked up blush and a brush. "Hush, both of you, and let me finish."

Not long after, I stood in my closet, wearing sexy undies with the loose bits caged in. Literally. To me, modern shapewear felt like trying to go to the bathroom in a wet, one-piece bathing suit, then pulling it back up. Panic attacks in those situations might have ensued multiple times.

I'd chosen a full-coverage garter with boning to hold my stomach in. Despite my best efforts, my tummy pooch stubbornly refused to be tamed.

The dress was amazing. I stared at it a moment, letting the soft velvet sleeve slip through my fingers.

The shopkeeper of Cyndi's favorite boutique scored a vintage

DVF velvet dress for me. I had seen it a few years prior and saved the picture as a "maybe one day I'll splurge" kind of thing. In my wildest dreams, I didn't think Debra would locate the actual dress.

A forest-green velvet, the dress matched my eyes and complemented my hair, after I'd pumped up the auburn highlights with red rinse. It flowed like liquid to my ankles, with the designer's signature wrap style, a high slit, and deep bell sleeves. The belt and sleeve lining were done in silver, which I matched to my shoes.

Debra "happened to have" a pair of 1920s reproduction dance shoes perfectly matching the dress. Knowing Cyndi, she had mentioned to her friend how much I hated stilettos. When I had met her at the boutique, these curvy little beauties were the only chunky-heeled Mary Jane's in the shop. They offered plenty of comfort for walking and dancing. When I spun in the dress, the sides opened, showcasing the silver beauties.

After dressing, I sat on my new bed and soaked in the moment. This night was so different from the stressful NFL parties requiring my presence.

My thoughts brought me back to the worst one. Overweight with no explanations for why and crushingly tired all the time, I dreaded each minute getting ready.

Some of my friends had pretended to support me, but their actions told a different story. I could tell they were caught between judging me for my inability to lose what everyone called "baby weight" and rebuking themselves for thinking that way.

The NFL wives didn't pretend though. They flat-out ignored me. Some also had kids and paid beaucoup money for their gorgeous bodies, either with a personal trainer or plastic surgeon. I guess, to them, I needed to "get with their program."

I didn't blame them anymore. Many had been under their own pressures as they ignored the common-knowledge philandering of their husbands. Many times I asked the universe how

I'd found a husband who stayed faithful to a woman in my messed-up circumstances while other players strayed so easily. We were a rather medieval group of noblewomen with our happiness levels dependent upon whether we had hit the relationship lottery.

Presently, I ran my hands over the plush velvet again, sending out a thank-you for having friends who supported me. I looked around my room and smiled at the space I had recently remade into mine alone. We were both ready for a future with new memories. I thought of the man who was on his way to escort me for the night. We'd come a long way in a short time, and it lifted my heart to have someone who would walk by my side again. Thomas took my weird lifestyle in stride—actually seemed to find it fascinating. The rumor mill surrounding my family didn't scare him off either. If the upcoming articles in our town paper didn't fix my PR problem, Thomas promised to bring in a team to turn it around. I believed he'd do it too.

I stood and moved to my new, full-length mirror, turning from side to side, checking for lint or wrinkles. Rachel knocked on my door and peeked her head in.

She gasped. "You look beautiful, Mama. It's like I'm little again and you're going to one of those swanky parties of Daddy's." The best part of those evenings had been Rachel sitting on her own stool, pretending to get ready next to me. She would chatter nonstop about the colors I used and how to do my hair. I guess not much had changed there. It was nice to hear she had sweet memories of those times too.

In my new shoes, Rachel and I stood eye to eye—such a contrast to those old, insecure days. She approached quickly. "Let me do one thing…" She gently coaxed a couple more curls down onto my neck and one tiny loose wave from in front of my ear. This act felt familiar too.

I snapped my fingers. "The jewelry!" Cyndi had surprised me with an early Christmas present when she dropped off the dress after picking it up from the tailor's. She'd made me a beaded necklace and matching earrings. The neck piece was more like a neck sculpture. A butterfly rested on budded branches moving from my collarbone down to the top of my cleavage. The colors were maroon, silver, and black, with splashes of green. Drop earrings with the same beads and tiny buds hung in a delicate thread down to my shoulders. I adored everything about the set. I set it in place and turned around.

"His jaw's going to drop."

"Thanks, sweetie. Speaking of... I need to fix my purse before Thomas arrives. And Snow?"

She looked up from cleaning the makeup.

"Thanks so much for helping me." I touched my heart. "Especially since it's the last Saturday of the semester."

Rachel pinched her brows and waved it off. "Don't worry about it. Since you hooked me up with the fish-sitting for Banger, life has been nice and quiet. I made major gains in finishing up." She squeezed me as tight as she used to when she was a toddler and whispered in my ear, "I'm happy for you."

After arranging my purse with the necessities and placing just-in-case medicines in my cape pockets, I paced my room, singing along to pop Christmas songs. Rachel insisted she answer the door when Thomas arrived so I could make an entrance. *Love my girl.*

At five on the dot—late for Thomas, but he probably didn't want to rush me—the doorbell rang. Rachel knocked on my door to make it official. I handed off my cape to her and entered the living room, walking around the staircase to meet him. As I turned the corner and he came into view, I don't know who was more stunned. My jaw dropped, making it feel the way Thomas's looked.

He stood in the entry in a three-piece navy suit by Tom Ford. I recognized the cut and fabric since I was contemplating purchasing the same one for Dylan's upcoming angel funding meetings. Tapering slightly from the shoulders to hips, it fit Thomas like a dream. My dream. My scorching-hot dream. This was so unexpected.

His midcentury look had grown on me to the point I liked the quirky sophistication. But this? The man was fire wrapped in fine fabric, threatening to burn me while I begged for more.

In the years I had attended this event, I had only witnessed a few faculty members looking this put together. All of them were independently wealthy. *Oh boy.*

"You went all out," I said to him, but he didn't hear me.

Instead, a low wolf-whistle floated past Thomas's lips. "Wow! Is this for me?"

I nodded slowly, aware it was the first time I'd ever heard the sound without my hackles raising.

Thomas moved with purpose across the entry to me. His eyes picked up the suit color, showing a deep navy as he approached. He gently lifted my hand, making me feel like a treasure. He held it high over my head as he slowly spun me.

"I love your hair up," he said near my ear. Before I could say anything, he added, "Christ, Kick, you're stunning," letting me know the dress and Rachel's work had done its job. He kissed me on the temple, which I took as a sign he didn't want to mess up my face. "I'll be the envy of the men at this thing. Ready?"

I smiled as my answer since my tongue momentarily glued itself to the roof of my mouth. He reached for the cape in Rachel's arms.

"No, you don't," she called out, handing it off to Bella. She pulled her phone from her pocket and raised it. "You don't leave looking that amazing without a photo."

"You're kidding?"

She planted her feet in front of us. "After enduring all the pictures for Homecoming, prom, and yada, yada *I* had to pose for? Bet your ass you're taking a picture. Hell, you made hors d'oeuvres and invited the neighbors over one year. You're getting off lucky."

I lifted my eyebrow in acquiescence. "Touché. But no posting it to Insta, okay?"

"Oh, it's getting posted," she retorted. "I don't have to tag you though. Now skooch together. Good. Remember what I said about posing? Take a step back and pop your knee out… There." I thought she pressed the photo button a dozen times. "Now have fun and behave. No, wait… you used to tell me that. Be bad and don't behave."

I noticed Thomas's tie was slightly askew and straightened it. Really I needed an excuse to put my hands on him. I blew out a long breath to steady myself. His chin caught my eye like a magpie with anything shiny. Unable to help myself, I ran my thumb in it and noted the contrast between his soft, freshly shaved skin and the solidity of his jaw.

He chuckled as he approached Bella. He took the cape from her and laid it over my shoulders. The left side of his mouth lifted into his sarcastic smirk. "You have an opera cape."

I fastened the buttons and pulled the satin-lined hood over my head. "Problem?"

He shook his head once. "Not at all. It's real. I mean, the cape doesn't look like a reproduction."

"Nice catch, Professor." I shrugged like it was nothing. It had been a big deal for me to buy something so extravagant. As the wife of a professional athlete, it had been expected and was another thing I'd been failing at. "I have a thing for art deco and picked this up at an auction in the midnineties." I slowly turned in it and tried Rachel's pose again. "It does something to the soul to walk in one. The satin won't frizz my hair either."

I held it out at the sides, admiring the soft silver velvet and the butterfly appliqué wrapping both sides. The design caught my eye when I'd first seen it, but the hand of the fabric had sold me and had motivated me to engage in a bidding war over it.

He dropped his head slightly and checked me out from the top of his midnight-blue eyes. "Let's go darlin'. My chariot awaits."

Rachel waved and giggled. "Have fun! We'll finish cleaning and get the hell out before you return."

For the first time that night, Thomas frowned.

QUANDO, QUANDO, QUANDO

THOMAS

Thomas wished like hell they had enough time to stop at the hotel bar for a drink before heading into the gala proper. But a head-on accident on a two-lane road made them run late. They arrived just in time for Kick to meet with the event coordinator. She sent off a text of their arrival as they walked past the doorman. The sound of the band warming up drifted into the lush lobby. A new presence in downtown Durham, the hotel boasted a modern look with a two-story waterfall quietly flowing over crackled glass, greeting guests as they entered.

He watched Kick glide up the staircase with a dancer's grace to the central hub and gathering area of the hotel. The sight irritated him as much as it fed his desire. A tiny honey blonde with a bright smile strode over to her.

"My goodness, Kick, how lovely you look." The two women enthusiastically embraced, and the newcomer held Kick at arm's length. "It's been a while since I've seen you." She bobbed her finger in her face and feigned a disciplining scowl. "Too long, missy."

"Good to see you too, Anna Leigh. You never age. And I love your dress."

"This old thing?" The woman Thomas pegged as the coordinator laughed. "I'm on duty tonight. But look at you. Go check your gorgeous cape so we can go over the details one last time. Someone called out sick, so you're bumped up."

Kick sighed as she unbuttoned the cape. "Of course."

Thomas felt his phone buzz inside his jacket pocket.

When she made introductions, Thomas said, "Why don't y'all get up to speed? I need to make a call and can find you after." He turned to Anna Leigh. "Will y'all be in the ballroom the whole time?"

"For as long as I need her," she answered in her perky, Southern accent. "Afterward, I make no promises."

He kissed Kick quickly and took a step toward the desk. He felt her pull his hand and turned back.

"Everything okay?"

Thomas's life had been a distracted blur since his talk with Joe. He wanted to close her up in a tower like a treasure, but what did it matter if he ended up being her biggest danger? He wasn't about to blow her night with his stupidity though. "Sure. See you in a few." Thomas presented his best grin and kissed her temple.

As he moved to the check-in desk, he heard Anna Leigh ask, "What's your dreamy Dylan up to these days?"

Kick gave her a hesitant laugh and moved out of earshot before he caught her response. Another perky voice asked, "Good evening. May I help you?"

He looked up, realizing he reached the desk clerk. Before he could answer, the sound of a stampede stole his words. A large group of teenage girls, each carrying equipment bags and dressed in warm-ups, jogged past him with a handful of women taking up the rear. They passed, and his reason for being at the desk came back to him.

"Right. Is it too late to book a room? I'm attending the gala." If he couldn't keep Kick—and he'd concluded he needed to let her go for her safety—he'd give himself and her one beautiful night.

The clerk's mouth drew down. "I'm so sorry, sir. We're booked solid." She pointed in the direction the mob had passed. "Lord U is hosting a girl's travel Lacrosse tournament this weekend. We don't have any rooms available. All the hotels around here are booked. We can schedule a cab if you'll need one."

He shrugged and sent her a half smile. "Won't be necessary. Thank you." His phone buzzed again. "Where's the bar?"

She pointed to her right. "Around the desk and down the hall a few steps. You won't miss it."

He tipped his head. "Thanks again." Finding the lounge was easy. A handful of what looked like exhausted parents had already pulled together bistro tables and settled around them. He took a stool at the bar and ordered a double Laphroaig. The text was from his assistant, Bethany.

BETHANY

> Third time running this protocol and it's a success again. Congratulations, Professor! We have our breakthrough. Do you want me to run it one more time?

THOMAS

> No. That'll do. Thanks.

BETHANY

> You should be excited. This is huge!

THOMAS

> You're right. I am. Excellent work! Y'all have been invaluable. Thanks again.

Thomas tucked his phone back in his pocket and took a

swallow of the whisky. He lifted his eyes and noticed the bartender studying him.

"Bad news?" the young man asked.

He shook his head. "No. Great news, actually. My team made a historical breakthrough." *One giant leap for humanity. One disaster for me.*

The bartender tilted his head. "Then why do you look like your aunt died, man?"

Thomas let out a ragged breath and answered, "Good question." He fired off two texts, then finished the rest of his drink. He set the glass down on top of his payment and a hefty tip. Thomas nodded at the bartender and stood. "Thanks, man. Have a good evening."

"You too. Congratulations."

C*ROSSING THE OPEN LOBBY, THE NOISE GREW LOUDER AS GUESTS* arrived. Thomas sent a text to Alaric, keeping his promise to be a good Felidae soldier. *Christ,* the old man will probably want him flying out to Bordeaux. He hoped they wouldn't try to keep him from his family for the holidays. How did he end up regretting success with his life's work? The phone buzzed back almost immediately, but Thomas couldn't bring himself to read it.

He checked his coat and finally stepped into the ballroom. Designed with the typical modern tricks, it used mirrors and lighting to make the room appear larger and airier than it was. He spotted Kick at a curving bar in the far corner.

Thomas kept his eyes on her while he traversed the room. The man next to Kick was too friendly. Her body language roared discomfort yet with an air of politeness. She'd once mentioned not liking a sleazy department head, and Thomas guessed this was the guy, based on his overindulgent demeanor.

Time to put the big-boy pants on and let the worries go... the research too. She needs you now.

Weaving his way around the dining tables, he stepped right up behind her, pulled her into a tight, one-arm squeeze, and kissed her temple. "There's my lady. Who's this gentleman keeping you company for me?"

Kick relaxed into Thomas's arms, and he swore she let out a tiny "Thank God" under her breath. With a crisp smile, she said, "Professor Thomas Harrison, this is Dr. Ted Drummond. He's the head of the Center for Integrative Medicine, and his office is the first point of contact for the McKenna Foundation."

"Pleasure to meet you." Thomas offered his hand to the man, who looked ready for retirement.

Dr. Drummond studied Thomas closely, then turned back to Kick. "I see you've hooked a young one. Didn't know you were one of those feminists." He stared directly at her cleavage and cleared his throat before adding in his drawl, "Well, *Mrs.* McKenna, wonderful as always. Looking forward to your presentation. Lord knows I adore those women you find for us, considering the exposure brings in more private pay clients. My favorite kind of woman." He raised his eyebrow and cackled like Yosemite Sam. He lifted Kick's hand and kissed the top of it as she stood board stiff. Drummond walked away, calling out to another colleague near the dance floor.

"*Jaysus*, that man," she exhaled. In a cartoon falsetto, she said, "You're my hero."

"A guy can try." He kissed her properly. "Have I told you how beautiful you look?"

Kick tapped her finger on her lower lip. "Hmm. Maybe. It never grows old though." She giggled. "Can you believe Dr. Drummond? I swear, in one breath, he ogles me like I'm his future mistress. Then he basically accuses me of cougaring and acts like he's disgusted by it." She shivered. "It makes my skin crawl. Did you know he's older than my father if he were still alive?"

"No surprise, he looks it," Thomas growled. "Tell me you don't have to speak to him anymore."

"I will on stage. He behaves when a spotlight's on him. Don't worry."

"He better, or there's going to be an added feature to your presentation."

"Are you cave-manning?" She ran her fingers up the side of his sleeve, across his shoulder, and down the lapel.

"Am I imposing on your feminist sensibilities?"

A smirk escaped, and she peered up at him through lowered lashes. "I'm torn because I find it nice." Her hand slipped inside his jacket and around his waist. "And it might turn me on."

"This tears you up because…"

"Because I want to do the same. If a woman waltzed over to us and catted all over you, I think I'd lay her out."

"You're right." He pulled her against him. "It's a turn-on."

Kick raised her hands and wiggled her fingers. "Don't make me ruin my nails, okay?"

Thomas chuckled while shaking his head. "Can't always hold in this magnetism." As usual, he thoroughly enjoyed focusing on Kick and letting the rest of the world go to hell.

"Have y'all decided on an order?" a kind-faced, middle-aged woman asked.

"Jaysus. I'm sorry we've taken up the bar."

The bartender laughed softly. "No problem, miss. Glad y'all chased off the doctor before he grew more hands. I've worked at events he's attended before. There's always one or two ladies he zeros in on."

"I'm glad too." Kick blew out a breath, making a few curls bounce on her forehead. "I'll take a club soda with lime. The soda though. Not tonic water."

"Sure. Are you the designated driver tonight?" the bartender asked.

"No. Maybe?" Kick's nose scrunched in the cute way Thomas

liked, but he could tell she wasn't over the shock of their night at the club. "I don't want alcohol tonight."

"What if I made you a cocktail without spirits… mix some juices with club soda? It's what I rely on when I'm working."

Kick's face lit up. Thomas took a moment to commit it to memory. "As long as it isn't tonic water, it sounds fabulous. Thank you."

The bartender turned to him. "What about you, sir?"

"Do y'all have a local bourbon?"

"Mystic?"

Thomas hummed. "A double with a big rock."

"My pleasure." The bartender turned away to fill their orders.

By this time, the ballroom had filled, and Anna Leigh announced it was time for the guests to take a seat.

Thomas accepted his glass and led Kick by the hand to their table. They were in front of the stage since she was speaking. He pulled out the seat for her and heard a woman call out, "There you are, Mrs. McKenna. I've been looking everywhere for you." The stranger hugged Kick and was introduced to Thomas as Eveline Boggs, the patient whose story was featured in her presentation. "Honey, the photographer wants our picture for the paper. Can you believe it?"

"No," Kick whined. "I hate being in front of the camera and had planned to hide from them."

Eveline's body posture deflated. "He said he needed both of us for the story. I told the reporter about all you did for me and my family. I swear, Mrs. Mack, he only wants the photo. They can get the rest when you're on stage."

Kick inhaled and turned to Thomas.

"Go." He shooed her on with his hands and gave her a tight smile.

"You can come too," Eveline added. "We'd love some man candy in our picture."

Kick giggled and lifted her eyebrow. "Magnetism. Can you join us, Mr. Candy?"

He stood and followed the women to a fireplace in the lobby. The photographer and Eveline's son were waiting in chairs. The little group was arranged with the men behind the women. While the photographer checked the light, Kick chuckled some more and turned her head toward him. "Definitely chocolate."

He leaned over and asked by her ear, "What's that?"

"If you're my man candy, you're a fine chocolate."

He snickered at her side. "Thought you can't have chocolate."

"It's not a loss if you're the substitute. While I'm standing on stage later, I'm going to contemplate finally getting to have my chocolate later tonight." She covertly ran her tongue over the edge of her top teeth. Thomas shivered with desire. He could play. For a night.

"Only if you do a good job," he purred and discreetly patted her bottom, getting a hop and a squeak from her.

They smiled for a half dozen shots, shook hands, hugged, and set off for their salad courses.

Toward the end of their dinner, Thomas leaned into Kick and asked, "Everything alright, baby? You've only eaten the vegetable, and you didn't touch the salad or soup."

She lifted a shoulder and smiled apologetically. "Croutons were in the salad. Bisque soups are made with flour and the same with the gravy. But it's okay. I ate a large, late lunch and snacked while the girls primped me. The steamed broccoli is fine." She patted his thigh to reassure him. "I'm used to it. Don't worry."

"There's nothing I can do?"

"Don't bother the staff. The kitchen isn't set up for someone like me. Cross-contamination is a real risk back there."

He grimaced, and she tapped his leg again. "Happens all the time. Call it motivation to leave early." She flashed him a flirty grin and batted her lashes. "There's a protein bar in my cape."

Of course there was. "Alright, I'll leave you alone." He tapped her knee in return and finished his dinner, feeling bad for pressing her and frustrated at not being able to fix it. It made his irritation come back too. If anything happened to her, he already knew he'd lose his mind.

Kick finished the vegetables and turned her attention to the woman sitting on her right. She was the wife of a doctor at the clinic. She fussed about how long it had been since Kick attended a gala, which had been a common theme for the night. He overheard the older woman tell her, "It's wonderful to see you've finally moved on, dear." Thomas turned his focus to the man on his left, a friend of his boss.

The time finally arrived for Kick to speak. Dr. Drummond introduced the segment and a short film featuring Eveline, her family, and how the McKenna Foundation helped her move from a patient without hope of living a vibrant life. In the nine years since she'd met Shane in a waiting room—inspiring his idea for the foundation—Eveline had thrived as a single mother and had become an entrepreneur who offered a service to other foundation clients.

Dr. Drummond introduced Kick, and she rose to a polite applause. She moved with her dancer's grace, long neck held high, a serene smile on her face as she stepped on the stage and crossed to the podium. She maintained her dignity as Drummond grabbed her in an inappropriate hug, his hand resting on the top of her ass. Kick's eyes barely flashed as she kept her brave mask in place while Thomas's hands fisted as he rolled his shoulders.

"There's a saying about chronic disease I can attest to," she started. "A healthy person has a thousand dreams while a sick person has one. The McKenna Family Foundation has been honored to work with the Center for Integrative Medicine at Lord University Medical Center for the past nine years. Each year, new names are added to our roster of beneficiaries, and we know those names are more than medical files. They are ten women and one man, seven spouses, twenty-three children, and five grandchildren. When a person is sick with an autoimmune disease, every relationship is affected, every activity must be considered…" She leaned into the mic. "*Every* aspect of life was radically changed."

"Work shifts are shortened because there isn't enough energy for a forty-hour week, 401Ks get cashed out, beautiful houses are sold to pay for medical treatments, vacations vanish because there isn't enough money left over once the bills are paid. Insurance won't cover many treatments, so a patient who barely meets rent and food will often go without medical intervention and watch their health deteriorate for a lack of options. Such was the life of Eveline and our other foundation friends."

Kick tucked a curl behind her ear. "To be blunt, the rate of suicide among the autoimmune community is astounding. The blood-brain barrier is often crossed with the diseases, radically affecting mental health. Moreover, the pain of having family, friends, and dreams ghost your life as an illness takes it over can be too much to bear."

"You know this already though." Kick looked out at the audience and paused. "My apologies for beginning on a downer. I only wanted you, our beloved research teams, to remember how high the stakes are in our community. Mostly, you know about the difficulties surrounding the quest for the elusive diagnosis and the 'oh shit factor' that sets in once a patient receives it." The audience laughed while Kick lifted her gaze to wink at Eveline.

"It makes my heart soar to see our clients and their families improving in all areas of their lives. Because of their progress, the whole family dreams again. You'll hear about some of these life changes in a moment, changes you help bring to fruition."

Kick checked her notes and sighed. "What continues to keep me up at night is knowing how many more families out there need your help. So tonight I've gussied up and squeezed my hiney into a fancy dress to stand before you and share about the changes coming next year—the tenth anniversary of the McKenna Family Foundation.

"Thanks to the efforts of the Annual Fund Campaign, we will take on five new clients next year and for each of the following five years." A robust applause filled the room.

Thomas's jaw dropped. He sat in awe of her poise, her command of the crowd and the way she charmed every attendant. Kick shared about partnering with a cab company to give clients vouchers for rides to and/or from treatments, which often left a patient unable to drive afterward—something he knew well.

Eveline went back on stage to share how her daughter opened a drop-in daycare center around the corner from the clinic. It was another partner, using vouchers so clients didn't have to cancel appointments for lack of childcare. She spoke of help with food—partnering with local markets, and vouchers were a common theme—and job placement once a client had improved their energy.

Pride filled his heart, along with a sense of unworthiness. Thomas saw how far Kick and the others had come. He was moved by her determination to pull up as many others as possible. He knew he had to keep her safe at all costs. Hers wasn't the only life on the line. He wished he hadn't made his last call home. A drop of sweat fell down the center of his spine.

The segment finished with Kick bringing up the foundation's executive staff and Eveline's family, who handed each grant to the researcher receiving it. She stepped back while the rest of the group received a standing ovation, but it was Kick who received the applause.

Thomas stood with the audience and beamed. His phone buzzed with the fifth text since the speeches began. One side of his heart burst for the woman who received more of his adoration by the minute. The other side hardened with a sense of dread.

The last presentation was half-finished by the time Kick made her way through the crowd of well-wishers and she returned to his side. He hugged her tight, not wanting to let go. Adrenaline boosted the lavender and exotic floral scent at her neck, making it smell like passion. He could coat himself in it if they weren't in public.

"I'm so proud of you," he whispered. "How did I not know the extent of this?"

"We're still getting to know each other, remember?" She smiled demurely, placing her arms around his waist and tipping her head back. "It only *feels* like we're old friends."

Kick was right. Despite their natural rapport, they were totally, painfully, new. He reached over and rubbed her back, afraid his hand might be too sweaty to hold hers as emotions ran wild.

The band eagerly played upon completion of the dog-and-pony shows. Kick leaned into Thomas and asked, "Please dance a couple of songs with me. I need to release this nervous energy."

"You didn't get it all out on stage?"

"No. Mine let go after the fact." She pouted as a thought crossed her mind. "I should've thought to reserve us a room."

Dammit all.

19

DON'T LET GO (LOVE)

KICK

The band played a holiday song by Dean Martin as the guests stepped away from their tables. The university always hired a full-sized jazz band, and I practically buzzed as Thomas and I made our way to the dance floor. I longed to be in his arms. Since we had to wait a bit to be alone, dancing would serve for a nice appetizer.

Several people stopped us on the way to the dance floor to congratulate me and the work of the foundation, which meant we missed Dean. The brief time the band took between songs gave us a chance to find a spot on the floor and get into hold. They began a sultry version of the song "Quando, Quando, Quando." It fit my mood and the mood of our time together so far.

Thomas opted for a Latin-like sway with subtle steps and occasional turns instead of a formal ballroom-type display. As much as I loved the fun we'd had before, I appreciated his instinct to stay low key this time. He basically took us around the floor in what I'd call a lover's hold, with near, full-body contact. Caught up in the evening's success, the beauty of the song, and the feel of this man, I sang the words into his ear.

Then I felt his phone buzz.

"Do you need to answer it?"

He set his chin and sliced the air briskly. "Later."

The band moved immediately into "A Kiss to Build a Dream On," and I continued to sing. Since the song was slower than the last, Thomas kept me in a tight hold for the entire song even as he lazily spun us. At the end of the song, he kissed me deeply. A small group near us quietly clapped when we came up for air, and I blushed. Thomas was waking something in me, and I longed to celebrate it.

I was proud to be with him and proud of him. I might've felt the spark of L-word feelings for him and savored the revelation without the pull to rush anything. It was a treat to enjoy each moment with Thomas as they came.

His phone buzzed again.

"Sounds important," I said.

He nodded, and we exited the floor. He swiped his phone and frowned.

I brushed his shoulder. "Tell me what's wrong."

He looked at me with a confused expression, so I explained, "Your smile hasn't reached your eyes all night."

"I'm sorry, baby." He sighed and glanced down again, then back to me. "I need to return this."

I reached behind his neck and rubbed the newly clipped hairs there. "Feel what you feel, Thomas. I only want to help and support you." Taking mysterious calls out of the blue had already become a routine for the man anyway. I didn't mind.

He flexed his jaw and gave me a grin that still didn't reach his eyes. "It won't be long."

"Take as long as you need. I'll head to the restroom and fish my protein bar out of my cape."

His brows drew together in a way I recognized in myself. It always equaled my resting bitch face. Despite my attempts to lighten the mood, it wasn't working. "Any chance we could leave after I make this call?"

I smiled and ran my thumb across his chin. "If you hadn't asked, I might have begged."

We left the ballroom for the lobby, traveling in opposite directions.

I guess I took a wrong turn. When I found a bathroom, it was blissfully empty and stayed so the entire time I used the facilities. It gave me a chance to process the evening so far—how happy Eveline looked, how much it filled my soul to make a difference in someone's life, how far the medical treatments had come since I first fell sick. I also imagined what the rest of the evening would hold. I wasn't ashamed to admit what I saw excited me even more.

After retrieving my cape, I found a nearby love seat to perch on and fished out the protein bar. I asked the universe to let me snack in peace. As fun as peopling had been, I'd had my fill. I was needy for my alone time with Thomas, hoping we could finally take the next step to "something more."

I finished the last bite and stuffed the wrapper back into my pocket, wondering where the hell Thomas had gone. He still hadn't returned. I worried something had gone awry at the lab. He'd told me about some crazy mishaps already this semester. Then there was the tragic accident of his first assistant.

When we danced though, he'd been the attentive man I knew and desired. Then I realized what was wrong—his sexual tension was probably worse than mine. I'd been distracted by the stress of recovering from the drugging and preparing for my speech. I hadn't had time to give in to lust. Add in our opulent surroundings, the attention, our gorgeous clothes, he probably yearned for alone time more than me. Poor guy.

Why hadn't I thought to book a room? I'd overheard someone earlier say the rooms were filled.

I stretched my spine from side to side and looked up to see Thomas finally returning, his face blank. Well, he was simply steeling himself for the crowd. I didn't think he liked the spotlight-like attention either.

I stood as he approached and asked him, "Is everything good?"

He gave me a tight nod for an answer, so I reached up on my tiptoes and purred into his ear, "I can't wait to be alone." I hoped it would lift his mood.

Half his mouth lifted. Again, it didn't reach his eyes.

"Quando, quando, quando," I sang.

Thomas's jaw flexed, and his nose twitched.

I gave up and placed my head on his shoulder. "Tell me about it in the car?"

"Sure."

THINKING IT MIGHT CHEER HIM UP, I PRACTICALLY ATTACKED Thomas when he shut the door to his Camaro. Leaning over the shifter, I kissed along his jaw, slid my hand under his jacket and began unbuttoning his shirt.

It didn't matter if the parking garage was cold or that we hadn't ordered a limo. I didn't want to wait.

His eyes hazed with lust, but his hands stayed at his sides. "What are you doing?"

"I'm still keyed up. I need you."

Thomas growled, wrapped his arm around my waist and pulled me on to him as the split in my dress exposed my legs and garter.

"Ah, damn." He groaned. "Black satin."

"Hate lace," I said for no reason other than the loss of my mind to lust. My lips worked the other side of his jaw, but I couldn't kiss the flex away. He wouldn't relax. Still, his fingers stroked the material, hugging my ass. Working his way under the material, he slid it aside and trailed his fingers through my folds.

"Dammit all. You're soaked."

"Please, Thomas." I fisted my hands in his shirt, took a moment to stroke his abs, then worked on his belt, my body pulsing along his erection.

His free hand found my jaw and angled it for a deep kiss. I lost myself in his aggressive tongue, the taste of a peaty scotch there, and his sandalwood scent in my nose. Amped up on adrenaline, I didn't notice his tongue was dueling, not dancing.

"Yes." I slid my hand into his pants, wrapping my fingers around his length, coaxing the heated gasp I wanted. Thomas went stock-still. He pulled away—his mouth, his hands. I even felt his body try to sink into the seat.

His no came out gruff and firm.

Out of breath and still not in my mind, I whined, "What the hell is wrong?"

"I spot at least two cameras with perfect views inside the front seat..." He looked around frantically. "Need to keep you safe."

Safe? There wasn't a soul around besides us.

"I'm sorry." My core ached from need and continued a slow pulsing along his thigh. "How did you know?"

His hands moved up to my shoulders and flexed. "You hang out with Banger, you learn things. We're getting out of here."

I hoped the drive home would settle Thomas and help him open up, but the tension continued to emanate from him. Every minute or so, he inhaled a long, sharp breath and released it violently.

"You're angry."

"Yes."

"Is it the phone call?"

"Let me get you home."

"Did I do something?"

"Christ, no." He exhaled again. "You're perfect. It's..." He never finished his thought, and I didn't know how to help. We sat in a keyed-up silence the rest of the drive, the air in the car so electric with words longing to be said and need dying to be filled it could've propelled us the rest of the way if the Camaro needed it. I opened my mouth to speak several times, but words caught in my throat. The tip of my nose tingled and my chin quivered.

WE ENTERED MY HOUSE WITH THOMAS STILL WOEFULLY TIGHT-lipped. I removed my cape, strode to the liquor cabinet, and retrieved the Redbreast for him. I poured it neat and offered him the drink. He accepted it on an exhale, deflating his warrior's posture. Then I turned on my sound system, hoping music would help ease whatever caused this mood.

"I'm sorry, Kick."

"The phone call," I acknowledged while walking back to Thomas.

He shook his head. "Yes. And no. It's me." He downed his whiskey in a swallow, ran a hand through his hair, and barked an angry "Shit!"

I reached for him. "Please let me help. Is there a problem at the lab?" As a mother, I'd learned early on about twenty questions and pulling answers from the reluctant.

His shoulders bounced as he heaved a cynical scoff. "Not at all. We hit it huge today. Made a repeatable breakthrough, which makes it official. This might be the beginning of a fundamental shift for… people."

"Oh, fantastic." I wrapped my arms around him, genuinely thrilled for his accomplishment. A hesitant pause preceded his reciprocation, then he held me so tight he wouldn't let go.

The air in the room took on an ominous feeling. A knot formed in my gut. I thought, for the first time, the night might end differently than how I'd planned. "You're not happy about this? Or did I actually do something wrong?"

Thomas sighed while clinging to me. "I've been summoned to Bordeaux. Immediately. It means I'll be gone for the rest of the month. I had planned to turn the work over to someone else once I hit this milestone. I didn't expect it all to happen so quickly. It was supposed to be my trigger to leave."

Leave? I leaned back to catch his eye. "You're shitting me, right? Thomas, if you knew you were out the door in a few months, why'd you start with me? Or have you changed your plans?" My breath caught, and I inhaled deeply to dampen my temper.

"I thought there'd be a couple of years before I had viable results. And… and I don't know what I want," he admitted gruffly while stepping out of my space, leaving me aware of his absence. And scared.

I held on to the island counter and let my head drop, taking my eyes off him so I could think this through. "Have we had an expiration date all along? I thought you wanted to see where we could go. You're the one who said we would have more. We're set for it tonight too. Rachel's back at Banger's, fish-sitting and studying. Liam took the dog with him to a friend's house. I was more excited about this than I was about the gala. That was mostly an excuse to splurge on a dress"—I lifted an eyebrow—"and buy sexy underthings."

He iced me out and stared at me with his shitty mask in place. So I tried harder. I took a step toward him and purred, "*Quando,* Thomas?" Another step. I ducked my chin. "*Quando?*" I pressed against him and ran my hand around his neck and put my lips up to his ear. "We're finally free. If not tonight, *quando?*"

He made a low, frustrated rumble in his throat but only moved when he flexed his jaw.

I stepped back and leaned into the island countertop. My brow furrowed. I was still processing the signals, not believing what I saw or heard.

"I don't get it. You're going to sit at my table, so to speak—one

I've worked hard to set—and tell me you have no appetite?" I untied my dress, letting it fall open, and swung my arms out to my sides. "It's an all-you-can-eat buffet, Thomas. What am I missing?"

"We'll never work," he murmured.

I jolted as if struck by his words. I reached for his hand to reassure him, but the contact zapped me. "What the hell?" I curled my hand into my stomach. The pain sparked more anger, and I hissed. "Maybe you're right. The commitments you made to me a couple of weeks ago meant the world to me. But I don't know about this hot and cold with you."

Thomas's masked face gave me nothing. He looked at me like I was a stranger, and I couldn't figure out why.

"You know it, don't you? You know I don't throw my heart or my body to just anyone. You know exactly how important you've become." I silently begged for a quiet resolve to stomp out my panic and temper. I wrapped my hands around my neck and whispered, "You *know* me."

He scanned the living area, refusing to look at me. Several times his face lifted toward the den space upstairs. Yet he stayed silent, stewing like the hours before a hurricane arrives, when the clouds quietly swirl together, their spin deceptively slow and beautiful.

I repeated, "Everything is set. We can finally let go."

He kept quiet except for an exaggerated exhale. Why wouldn't he speak? He'd already become the one I confided in. *Jaysus*, I told him everything. Why didn't he feel the same?

I couldn't wait out the silence. I had to open my mouth, had to say something. My temper woke up with a low rasp. "I wasn't looking for you." My eyes narrowed as my composure crumbled. "I stayed away from the bar scene and… and those swipe apps. I didn't need this." I pointed my finger in his direction. "But you needled. With your charming smile and hypnotic accent. You convinced me you cared. You made me care. You offered your security connections and defense lessons. *You* made me feel like I was important."

The energy unleashed, and I stomped around the island in my underwear and heels. I stopped and squared off with him, my hands on my hips. "I'm not disposable, Thomas. If that's what you wanted, you could've found a 'bic' like Banger does." His gaze snapped to me while mine narrowed again—confirming my guess. "That's right. I figured out your icky bro code term. I told you, I puzzle things out. You made me think we'd be important." My last-ditch effort expressed, I slumped against the counter, confused. Beat.

Finally words rumbled and rambled from Thomas. The ones I picked up were, "I can't have you in another man's house. It's *his* home."

A relieved giggled burst past my lips. "Seriously? Sweetheart, I'll pack a bag. We can go anywhere. I adore your house. We can talk about your issues with my home later."

Thomas shook his head. "My plane leaves in a few hours. I have to pack."

I folded my arms and assessed the truth between the lines. "There's more to this. If this were about a plane to catch, we'd waste no time with a silly fight. We'd enjoy each other and celebrate the time we had."

His nostrils flared, and his gaze struck me full-on. "Silly? You jerk me around for weeks, pour yourself out to everyone but me, then bing! You decide you're ready now. I'm supposed to just hup to, and *I'm* ridiculous?"

My head spun with his false interpretation. "That's not how it happened, and you know it. What's really wrong? I've told you feelings are neither right nor wrong, they simply are. Something else must be going on here because it's all very wrong right now."

"Want to know what I feel?"

"Yes. Please."

"I *feel* like I'm out of here." He stormed over to the hook where he'd left his coat and jacket.

"Fine. Get *ye awa*! But you walk out my door, you don't come back." The heat from my face told me it was blood red. My chest heaved, only not in the way I had hoped.

"You were going to leave me eventually. I might as well make it easy." He punched his arms into his beautiful suit jacket as it hit me how upside down the night had become.

"*Me* leave *you*. It looks like the other way around from where I stand. You're the man-child running from something good. At least it's done before we took it too far."

Thomas threw his coat over his arm and yanked on the front door. "Small favors." He stormed out, icy mask in place. I heard the Camaro thrum to life, then roar down the street as if the car were furious too.

I paced in circles, pulling out the pins in my hair, letting them lay wherever they fell. My breath puffed like a bull with no one to charge. With an ironic timing, En Vogue's "Don't Let Go (Love)" began pounding from the speakers. Perfect. The house now seemed to mirror my angst. I moped back to the island and collapsed onto a barstool. My head dropped onto my folded arms. Fecking hell, his earthy scent lingered on my arms like I'd been marked. My heart sure had, but why? It didn't feel like Thomas had purposefully duped me.

Too stunned and exhausted from the day, my body trembled as I sobbed. I only had the energy for a single tear though. It stealthily slid along the bridge of my nose and onto my forearm as I failed to comprehend what had happened. My heart felt like it shouted through the Bose speakers about how I had a right to lose control... *bet your ass I did*. Then the ladies urged me to not let go... *Oh hell*. It was too late. Thomas had gone. Now what?

2 0

SOLITARY MAN

THOMAS

$\mathcal{E}$ ver since Thomas had landed in Paris at noon on Sunday, he'd been physically and emotionally inoperable. He played the dutiful protégé for Alaric. At times, he even let himself feel proud of his work, but moving through the days reminded him of slogging through a cold bog. He gave himself credit just for functioning in the meetings at all.

Finally free for an afternoon, Thomas escaped to Tess and Banger's quarters for a nap. He hoped his near exhaustion would help keep away any dreams of Kick and her destroyed visage as he walked out on her. He sank into a comfortable winged-back chair and stretched his feet out onto the hassock. Thomas spotted a cashmere throw nearby and pulled it over himself.

As he waited for sleep to set in, he watched the river flow by outside the window and thought about drowning. He didn't want to do anything so drastic though. Not anymore. Part of his problem was he couldn't be sure what he wanted. Thomas considered the possibility he might drown in his own heartbreak.

The one he'd caused. Once again, he'd have to get used to being alone. Only this time fate hadn't changed his course. Thomas had done it all by himself. He powered off his phone and placed it on the side table after deciding to own his cowardice and let the wound fester. He deserved it. One thing he knew, he didn't deserve the McKennas. He sure as hell wouldn't put any of them in danger.

Dammit all. His head was fucked, and he ached for it all to stop.

ELLIE WOKE THOMAS UP FROM HIS NAP WITH AN ASSERTIVE CALL OF his name from the main hallway. Then he heard a round of fast raps on the door to the suite. *So that's where the noise came from.* He'd heard it in his dream. Kick had been calling for him, locked in her bedroom, and he couldn't open the door.

"One second, *Grand-mère.*" Thomas rubbed his face to wake up and caught sight of his azure-blue aura glowing full tilt. Funny how his dreams of Kick brought it out. He inhaled deep into his diaphragm and squeezed his fists, making the energy draw back inside him.

Ellie's exasperated sigh on the other side of the door made him wince. He took another breath to steel himself for whatever bothered her, and something did trouble Ellie. She wasn't a woman to hunt someone down personally. She'd lived too long with staff.

He eased the door open. "What's wrong?"

Ellie clicked her tongue. "You are, my dear."

Thomas gestured for her to enter, then saw his little mess in the sitting area. He cleared off Tess's prized Bergère. "I'm sorry, *Grand-mère,* I haven't been feeling well." He folded the blanket and placed it on the back of the divan. When he resettled in the winged-back and regarded Ellie properly, she looked like a disappointed mother.

"How old am I, Thomas?"

He chuckled. "Surely you don't want me to answer your question. Not sure I know anyway."

She leaned forward while keeping her back posture perfect. "We both know we don't succumb to viruses beyond a small sniffle. I might not know our origins..." She tipped her head in Thomas's direction. "That's your job—yours and Nigel's. This much, I do know."

How could Thomas tell her he was heartsick? Second-guessing his actions had been keeping him up most nights.

Ellie reached over and squeezed his hand. "I'm proud of you. I've been trying to catch you to tell you in private, but you spend most of your days closed off in here. You missed breakfast this morning too. So now I'm concerned. This is not you. Focusing on Europe doesn't mean I don't care about the other teams."

Thomas rubbed his brow. He wasn't comfortable talking about Kick with Alaric, so there was no way he'd want to seek advice from Ellie. Not with the mysterious warnings from the past few months. He had to get his shit together and fake it till he made it at least.

"You should be floating off the floor—dancing and playing music like you usually do." She raised her hands in the air. "You won! Celebrate it."

"It's not a race, *Grand-mère*." He put on a smile and hoped it looked real. "I am happy about the work." His thoughts traveled back to where the idea came from—his former assistant and a conversation about Paleo cookie recipes. "You know, we found these genetic variances thanks to Presley's suggestion back in September. I know there are more too."

Ellie's face lit up. "How is Presley? She's a lovely young woman."

"Oh no." Thomas's shoulders fell. "I'm sorry. I thought Nigel would tell you. Presley died in October. She was hit by a car. She..." He almost mentioned the suspicion it wasn't an accident, but he'd promised Banger he'd keep the information secret. Damn the Felidae and their vows.

Ellie's hands flew to her face. *"Quelle horreur!"*

Thomas nodded. "It was awful. I'll make sure her name stays with the work though. Presley was a brilliant scientist." *Even if she was a blackmailer.*

"You've had a terrible season. No wonder you're out of sorts. When someone becomes used to disappointment, they rarely know how to respond to achieving their heart's desire."

If only Ellie knew he'd let go of his "heart's desire" to save her. Because of them. He didn't think Ellie would understand. Or, really, she understood too well. Thomas had heard rumors about her past and knew Ellie could be more ruthless than any in the Felidae, despite her elegant, gentile appearance.

"I know you and Nigel are working on separate aspects of our secrets, but can you explain how your variances differ from his work? In the meeting with Alaric, the barrage of science terms lost me."

Thomas rubbed his chin. He wondered if the actual rift lay between her and Alaric. Surely *Grand-père* would have kept her up to speed on all the projects. "You know Nigel studies telomere length… why ours stay long without the health risks associated with artificial enhancements, right?"

"Of course."

"You could say my work goes back farther. To live as long as we do, there have to be variances in our DNA. I think the genetic differences affect several systems in our bodies. It's also why some of us have special… talents, as you call them, and others don't." At some point, he hoped to study the reappearance of his aural energy.

Ellie dipped her chin to let him know she followed his logic.

"My team and I found some anomalies that keep our mitochondria from atrophying over time, the way most people's do," Thomas continued.

"This is from your granddaughter's samples?"

"Twice-great… yes."

"How do you know it isn't isolated to your bloodline?" She gave him a knowing smirk and raised an eyebrow. Ellie had been following along the whole time. He wondered why she hadn't asked the question during the team meeting. "Wonderful instincts keeping tabs on your extended family, by the way. I wish the rest of us had your foresight."

Thomas patted her hand. "Making sure everyone prospered and lived happily kept me from feeling so lonely. By the time I met y'all here, the system was in place. It's nothing special"—he shrugged—"other than being lonely."

Ellie gave him a curt nod. "This is a nice way of saying you didn't abandon your family once they turned on you, like the rest of us did. I appreciate how you understand, and you are special." She closed her eyes and sighed—a peaceful, hopeful sound. "Another female Felidae would be… a dream come true."

Before Thomas could say anything, Ellie tapped his hand and stood, ending their tête-à-tête. He mirrored her, following her to the door as Ellie spoke. "Cook is preparing beef bourguignon for supper. It's your favorite, no?"

This smile came easily. Thomas appreciated family in whatever way it came to him. As the matriarch of the Château Longévité, Ellie knew when to slip out of her business role and into a mothering one. Since most Felidae members were much younger, she embraced the intention.

"Sounds wonderful. Thank you." The bright sky drew his attention outside. The sun had cleared away a drizzly day while they'd been talking. "I think I'll go for a run. Promise to be back in time for dinner."

Ellie kissed both his cheeks and pinched one for good measure, making them both laugh. "You better."

. . .

AFTER DINNER, THOMAS SAT IN THE FIRE ROOM, THE OLDEST room in the château. The cozy atmosphere reminded him of the oldest rooms in his homestead. It was also where Alaric kept the instruments for evening gatherings. The old man had been dispatched to the distillery for an emergency though. Despite Thomas's appreciation for his favorite of the cook's meals and his earlier run, his dark mood returned easily. Sitting alone sipping cognac didn't help even if it was from one of the vineyard's prized bottles. He took Ellie's pseudo-advice and picked up his favorite guitar. Playing his emotions would be a better solution than drinking them. Besides, it took too much liquor for him to get drunk enough to forget.

Halfway through his song, Banger entered the room, surprising him. The man wore a huge grin. "You're the man of the month around here. Congratulations, brother."

"Thanks, man." For a minute, Thomas absorbed the praise. Ellie had been right about getting too used to disappointment.

Banger poured a dram of Ardbeg whisky, picked up a bodhran that he kept by the fireplace, and sat across from Thomas. "What should we play?"

Thomas lifted a shoulder and chuckled. "Don't ask me. I don't even know what I was working on."

Banger frowned. "It was a Prince song." He tipped his head from side to side. "Something else going on with Kick? Siobhan filled me in on the mob at the coffeehouse and the smoke shop. I thought it had been handled. Did Kick tell you anything else?"

Thomas's blood ran cold. His heart might have skipped. He slammed half his cognac. "What mob?"

"What..." Banger rubbed his lip. "Is something wrong with you two? Is this why you look like a lost puppy when you should be sitting here with your chest puffed out?"

"Why does everyone keep telling me how I should feel?" Thomas snarled, then finished the liquor. "I left her, alright? The night of the gala—when the test results came back too—I walked out. Then I flew here."

"What about protecting her? After the drugging, I thought Kick became your priority over everything else."

Thomas rolled his neck, then rose to pour another drink. "She still is. Kick's in more danger from *me* than whatever the hell her neighbors are up to." Once the glass filled, he turned and glared at Banger. "Isn't she?"

"What—?"

Thomas looked around to make sure they were alone. "Joe told me about Vivienne. All of it. Finally."

"I see." Banger rubbed his brow and took another sip of scotch. "What do you need me to admit?"

"Joe said he was assigned to watch Viv and kill her if I told her about the Society. It's why he retracted the vows so quickly." If Thomas hadn't been staring at Banger, he would have missed the head tip.

"That's Joe's story. What do you want from me?"

Thomas set the glass on the bar and folded his arms. "He said you took the assignment after Joe told Alaric to shove it."

Again, Banger confirmed with a nod. Thomas's head fell, but his friend jumped in before he could express his disappointment.

"I knew it was too much for Joe and volunteered to take over as soon as he stalked out of the old man's office." He raised his hands. "Before you work yourself up more, sit and listen."

Thomas shuffled back to his chair and sat, studying the way the spirit clung to the sides of the glass.

"I was tasked with taking her out if necessary, but I wouldn't have done it."

Thomas's head snapped up, confused.

"Need I remind you? My wonderful sire killed my one true love to teach me a lesson. I did it to another Felidae not long after, believing the lie." Banger sighed as he dropped his gaze to his own tumbler. "Time has a way of smoothing us out, like this liquor. It distills us until we're transformed." He turned his eyes on the dancing fire, and Thomas watched them darken. "If she had put anyone in danger, I would have followed the order, but I volunteered to make sure Viv survived. I thought the paranoia was idiocy. Still do." He swirled his glass, took one last swallow, then pointed at Thomas. "I did it for both of you. There are others who would've finished her immediately. It's the easy way."

"To teach me a lesson."

"Precisely. You weren't fully vetted when you made your vows. The old man changed the rules after you."

Thomas's hands rose to his neck and squeezed. "Here I thought your father was just a diabolical asshole."

"No arguments from me there."

"I feel like an idiot for not noticing. What else have I missed?"

Banger waved the glass in front of him and sent Thomas a sad smile. "When I found you, I was so happy to have a potential friend in this crazy existence I left some things out. You were too happy to see the dark side or to even consider one. You see it now though, don't you?"

Considering everything that had happened these past few months? He saw a lot now. Thomas stopped swirling the cognac and took a sip. It settled on his tongue before he swallowed it, similar to how reality was settling in his head, but it refused to travel to his heart.

Banger refilled his tumbler, walked over to the door, and closed it. He was halfway back to his seat when he said, "On to Kick. I understand you being over the bics, and you can't take off to get away from her, thanks to your job. So, is there a way you and she could work out an arrangement? Like you had before?"

"Not if y'all plan to kill her." He raised his hands to hold off Banger's comeback. "Besides, I didn't want an arrangement this time. I wanted it all with Kick—her friendship, her family, her friends—not just her body." Thomas ran his hands over his face, coming to grips with the truth. "She inspired me at the gala,

Bang. A nurse from the clinic took a chance and asked Kick to help with an injustice going on at the clinic regarding pediatric patients. You know Kick. She had to help even though this was outside the focus of her foundation. So I volunteered—"

"Fuck." Banger gasped and squeezed his eyes shut.

"I don't mean me personally. It's a real estate and legal issue. The people who handle my assets can look into it. It's mostly a matter of money and contacts. I have plenty of both."

"Okay. Good." Banger sat back and took a sip, settling himself.

"But don't you see? The actual results of my research are far into the future. I can do good now with my resources. That's how Kick lives her life. She does as much as she can with each minute she's given. It's—"

"Well, fuck. You're gone for her after all." Banger blew out a slow breath, and Thomas sat up, ready to take the blow. "You did the right thing. Don't look back. If I were you, I'd spend as much time away as possible. Since you still have the university commitments, consider renting a place near campus. Mostly, stay away from Oakville. Don't read the paper. Stay off social media. Let me handle the McKennas. I promise I'll make sure they're okay. You have my word."

Thomas sank back in the chair as if Banger's words had hit him.

His friend continued, but Thomas barely registered the words. "As soon as you can, find another position, or let me set you up with a private lab in another state. Whatever you do, don't look back."

Thomas let Banger's words sink in. They made sense, but what did logic have to do with any of this? His mind kept going back to the phrase "like attracts like."

WAY DOWN WE GO?

KICK

Darlene Love serenaded the café with holiday classics while I filled coffee orders. I had opened for Deana, and the rush gave me a bit of an energy lift. Thanks to stress and the lack of sunlight, sleep had more or less taken its own vacation since Thomas had walked out on me. I took a second to sip from my decaf almond-milk latte. The americanos would have to wait until I could reintroduce them after the new year. Until then, I drank the decaf while inhaling the rich aromas surrounding me and pretended.

When Ms. Love pleaded with her baby to "please come home" for the holiday, my energy nose-dived. *Stupid Christmas songs.* This particular song hadn't bothered me for years. Then again, it wasn't Shane I pined for presently.

I told myself I was perfectly fine. He-who-must-be-forgotten and I had dodged the bullet, not going any further. Still, I missed his touch, his fine ass filling out a pair of jeans, his arrogant saunter, his gentle kiss. I wanted the rough, demanding kisses he'd given me too.

I missed our conversations most of all, the way his accent had sounded like home in such a short time and the way he made me feel like the only person in a room. Then there was the dancing… *Jayz*, I loved dancing with someone again.

After Darlene Love made a run of "pleases" and a last beg to come back, I set a filled cup of coffee down on the counter a bit too hard. Actually, I slammed it down and splashed it over one of my regulars.

"Ack! Mrs. Salmaan, I'm so sorry." Grabbing a rag, I dabbed at her ruined sleeve. "This is so embarrassing. I-I never—"

She leaned in to catch my wild gaze. "It's alright, dear. I'm fine."

I filled a fresh cup and gingerly passed it to her, then took a twenty-dollar bill from the register. "Here, no charge today. This is to clean your pretty blouse."

"No, Mrs. Mack. Keep your money. I can fix it myself, no problem."

I tried to check on her skin under the cuff. "Are you sure you're not hurt?"

"I'm fine. Truly. We all have man troubles from time to time." Mrs. Salmaan lifted her cup and blew into the opening.

"Excuse me? You don't think my jitters have to do with"—I lowered my voice and leaned in—"those articles about me?"

"Pfft." She waved her free hand. "No one I know believes such nonsense." She gave me a wise, gentle smile. "In my experience, a woman in your state has a man on her mind. Whatever it is, you should fix it. That's all I'll say." She dipped her chin at me. "I hope your day improves, and don't worry about the spill."

Mrs. Salmaan shuffled out the door before I could explain there was no fixing my situation, which was a good thing. I didn't want to argue with her, and I didn't know if I could hold my tongue either.

But hey, I didn't go from Professor Jekyll to Mr. Hyde at the gala. I didn't give up and walk out without a decent explanation. I hadn't gone radio silent either. Okay, maybe I did, but in my mind, it was up to Thomas to make the extra effort. I deserved one fecking great apology. No... a grovel. I'd take an amazing grovel. Hell, I gave him all my cards when I had come clean about Shane's accident. Yet Thomas had the nerve to still keep his tight to his chest.

There was one positive thing to take from the experience. I was pretty sure... No, I was certain my desire to love again had been stirred. *Stirred?* More like an outboard motor dipped itself into my lake of desire and let her rip. So if Thomas wasn't the right man for me, *universe, show me the honey.*

Such was the mantra running on a loop in my head. Still, my heart had a new hole—a roughly six-foot-tall hole, with a fabulous ass and sexy cleft chin.

My next customer stepped up to the counter. Before I could ask for her order, she gestured toward the door with her thumb. "Mrs. Salmaan was right, you know. No one believes those ridiculous rumors. In fact, I think some protesters were paid."

"Sure." I chuckled and tucked a curl behind my ear. When I looked up, the rest of the line was nodding their heads along with my customer. "Thank you, Mrs. Tan."

Come to think of it, business had picked up since my rebuttal interview and afternoon promotion had been printed. The editor had done everything but retract the opinion articles. According to my contact at the paper, my lawyer had done a great job threatening them with a libel lawsuit. I hadn't contacted a lawyer, however. I'd bet money on who did though. Blast that man. I hated him for thinking he could dump me and take care of me at the same time. "For my safety," my ass.

"You should know I come by here every time I go out so those bastards won't shut you down. Our neighborhood needs you. Shoot, our whole town does."

I bit my lip to keep from crying. When I looked at the line again, their heads kept bowing. Some added in an "I do the same thing," along with other words of encouragement. I think I inhaled deeply for the first time in several days.

I called out, "You people are the best. As my thank-you to this town, I declare today a free coffee day. It's all on me."

I checked with Crystal in the drive-thru. "Make sure drive-thru orders receive our gratitude too."

"Absolutely. You're fantastic, Mrs. Mack."

I laughed at Crystal's enthusiasm. The girl didn't need caffeine in the morning. She made her own energy.

Shortly after the rush, Deana sauntered into the café, singing a gospelly carol. As much as my customers had lifted my spirits, I couldn't believe someone who had just had her girls smashed until they were practically see-through could be gospel-Christmas-song cheery. I did a double take as she walked up to me after taking a minute in her office.

"You look dead. Still not sleeping?"

I answered, "Nope" as I wiped down the counter.

"Why don't you spend some time in the back? Get a little rest. You're not supposed to come back full time for another two weeks."

I rubbed at a spill on the bar as if I could also make the pain go away by scrubbing the cloth hard enough. "Okay, Mahalia. But I'm off tomorrow for my last IV treatment. I'll be fine."

"Kick, sugar, don't wear yourself out and get sick before your trip. You'll be mad at yourself if you can't enjoy those kids."

"No worries." Even I could tell my soldiering-on smile didn't reach past my upper lip. "It's all good."

"Who you convincing?" She clicked her tongue. "The professor hasn't reached out, has he?"

"Not since the voice mail about the protesters. I guess

someone at Angel Security told him about it. I don't think he'll call again."

"Heyyy"—she drawled until it was a six-syllable word—"stop this pride."

Pride? Was she kidding? I shrugged as I continued wiping. "Thomas had a point, Dee. Granted, I'm not sure what his point was, but he did both of us a favor."

Deana carefully took the rag from me and placed it over a towel bar to dry. "You don't need this added stress. It's been a challenging enough fall."

I laughed at her last words. "I should've known though. It's been so long since I had a man in my life. I thought it'd be butterflies and rainbows if I ever jumped back in. I had forgotten how a relationship is mostly stress."

She reached for my shoulder and squeezed it. "Have a little faith. I believe in you two. There's magic in the air when you're together."

I growled, not wanting to think about our *magic*. "The only thing I know for sure is it takes both parties to be in a relationship. Only one has to leave for it to be over."

"A fight isn't necessarily the end, Kick. Even a big one."

My hands needed something to do, so I adjusted my ponytail, then folded my arms, hoping it made me look stronger than I felt. She was right about the nap. "It wasn't a fight, Dee. It was a blindside." I vigorously shook my head, trying to make the memory of his cruel words go away. A hard shell had erected around my heart since you-know-who had walked out. Unfortunately, it numbed me out to everything, but it beat crying. Besides, he walked out, not me. Feck all if I would get on my knees.

"Call Thomas tonight if you don't hear from him first. Do it for me. Gordon thinks you should too."

I laughed. Deana knew the depths of my fondness for her husband. "Well, if Gordon says so…," I drawled. "I'll think about it after the nap."

"Promise?"

I rolled my eyes and sighed my acquiescence. Anything to get her to stop talking. "Pinky swear." I probably wouldn't have any energy anyway—

"Not good enough. You need to Oprah swear."

"Seriously?" I leaned against the counter. Only ten minutes in the café and the woman exhausted me. The nap didn't whisper to me. It screamed in my head like a cranky toddler in a department store.

Deana answered with an evil side-eye that I was sure still terrified her children. For a moment I was afraid she'd fire me if I didn't obey.

"The man was adamant about his desire to break up."

"Pfft." Her hand plopped on her hip like it had its own mind. "Men are emotional creatures."

I barked a laugh at her turn of a usually misogynistic phrase.

"Truly." A customer came in, saving me from the grilling. "Go," she ordered. "We'll finish later."

I couldn't wait.

DEANA DID PICK IT UP LATER. AFTER A POWER NAP, WE BUZZED through the lunch rush, keeping the free coffee going. Word must have traveled fast because we worked almost right up until the high school let out. We had about fifteen minutes for a lunch break and ate in our favorite corner of the dining room to monitor things.

In between bites of a chicken wrap, Deana picked up the conversation as if it wasn't hours later. "You know, you freaked out on him because you had unresolved feelings for Shane. I'll tell you, Thomas hung in there. He knew something was wrong with you, and when you called to explain, he practically came running."

I sighed, fearing she'd finally found the one argument that could work.

"Gordon thinks his voice mail was a 'man's apology'."

"Does he?" I sipped on my iced cardamom tea. "Dee, I begged him to tell me what was wrong. It's obvious something ate at him. But he wouldn't budge. What about my self-respect?"

"Granted, it sounds immature." She took a long pull on her drink and snapped her fingers. "Is this about your age differences again? I swear, you may not feel like it now, but you look as young as he does."

"No," I snapped. *Jaysus*, would anybody listen? "Since you brought it up—sort of—what about my illness? Maybe the days apart got me thinking—"

"Lord Jesus—"

"Stop. I'm serious." After wiping my hands, I brushed back a curl. I didn't want to admit it, but truth was truth. "Maybe it's better to not tie him down with my illness. I didn't know I had an autoimmune disease lurking when I dated Shane."

"But you're doing fine. You've made so much progress this fall." She pointed a finger at me. "How do you know it isn't on account of meeting the professor? At least a little."

I nodded my head, considering the merit of her argument. "I'm doing better—now and hopefully for a long time—but I can't stop the clock. Healthy or not, aging has its own problems. I don't want to take away Thomas's best years with him saddled as a caregiver."

"You think Thomas won't age? What if you get better and end up having to take care of him? Hmm? Plenty of young men get sick."

"You're not helping."

"Because all I hear are excuses."

Aw, hell. Was she right? Thoroughly confused, I didn't know whether to cut a latte or pour a piece of cake. I craved peace. I thought it would come from Thomas, but...

"Give me time to think. If I don't hear from him before the holiday, I'll call Thomas in the New Year. Something preoccupied his mind during the gala, and his emergency trip had to be part of it. At the very least, we both need time to cool off." I lifted a hopeful shoulder. "Maybe we can salvage something when he gets back."

I knew I couldn't handle hearing the coldness in Thomas's voice again, and I hoped the downtime would help me grow a pair of ovaries by the time he returned.

I WISH I WAS THE MOON

THOMAS

"Do you have free time soon?" Banger asked Thomas. "I have news about Kick."

Thomas sat in the solarium off the kitchen, finishing a café au lait, a croissant, and sausage. He had been enjoying spending time with the chef and sous-chef—the only kitchen staff who worked at the château this time of year. Lately he'd kept his visits to the big gatherings, keeping interactions with the servants short and formal. He missed the times spent chatting and helping around the property. Now that he saw those memories through a different lens, Thomas wondered if he'd ever have the moments back.

He checked his phone and rubbed his forehead to finish waking up. He couldn't get the dueling thoughts of Kick and his research out of his head.

"I have time now," Thomas answered Banger. "About to get some air. Want to join me? Otherwise, I could cut it short. Are you working in the suite today?"

"I am, but I'll join you. We'll need the privacy."

Christ, now what? "If you're trying to upset me further, it's working." Thomas spent a few minutes staring at his research notes while Banger ate a quick breakfast staring out the wall of windows. His brain refused to focus as he worried about what Banger might have to say.

He set his tablet and phone to the side and told his friend, "I'll be in the garden when you finish."

As Thomas stepped outside, clouds drifted away from the sun, warming his face. He peered up and wondered if it would shine for Kick today. It wouldn't rise in Oakville for a few more hours. The distant fields had a beautiful, sleepy quality, like an army of plant soldiers at rest. Voices traveled across the quiet fields from in front of the winery. A small crew unloaded a delivery of barrels for the new wine.

It hadn't snowed yet, but frost lay thick on the land. Small spurts of breath steam puffed from Banger's mouth and nose as he approached.

Anticipation got the best of Thomas. "Spit it out, man."

He waved off Thomas's impatience. "Need to pick these words carefully. You know my freelance work is a secret."

"You know I'd leak nothing you tell me."

"True. The thing is my two jobs for you have accidentally overlapped. Only, I'm not sure how closely they're tied."

Thomas's brow furrowed. He gestured for Banger to lead the way onto the lane running up field two. It would take them to the highest part of the property. He yanked down on his knit cap, though he wasn't cold. It was nervous energy. "Go ahead. I'm listening." He couldn't imagine anything making him feel worse about what he'd done to Kick. Then again, when didn't Thomas feel guilty?

Banger cleared his throat. "Brace yourself, brother. I have more questions than answers right now."

"Sounds ominous." Right then, a loud crash floated up the hill, followed by yelling down at the winery. The commotion assured Thomas they couldn't be overheard. "Let me have it."

"First. The bartender's in the wind. Law enforcement had nothing more than grainy camera footage of a legal gray area, and the guy's lawyer wouldn't allow questions. So, his passport hadn't been confiscated."

"Where did he go?"

Banger sniffed and shrugged. "Whoever sponsored his trip is good. The kid played charter plane hopscotch. He added in a couple of boats for good measure. We're working on it."

Thomas hoped the boy stayed as far away for as long as possible. He figured Kick was safer that way.

"We do think we have Kick's werewolf—one Taylor Johnson."

"Where is he? Why aren't you with him?"

The men watched an owl take off from a nearby tree. It circled the field, hunting for mice and other vineyard pests. Thomas knew this bird. It had lived on the property for years and had become a vital part of the ecosystem.

"Siobhan's working on a connection. It's the main thing I wanted to talk about. When she sends me the signal, I'll interrogate him from here. You can sit in on it if you'd like."

"From here."

"My office in the suite. Yes," Banger said as the owl made another pass, taking it closer to the winery. Thomas guessed the bird had a better shot at finding a mouse closer to the building thanks to the cold. "I know you trust me to do what I have to, but I thought it might ease your mind to see it for yourself."

The owl adjusted its wing feathers, threw out its legs, and grabbed a mouse with ease. It landed in an area behind the winery and appeared thrilled with itself as it dove into the meal with gusto. Thomas envied the bird. No matter how much he did with his life, he would never know the freedom of flying and the joy of living so basically. He appreciated the perspective check.

When did his life become so complicated? He couldn't blame

Kick for it. Thomas had been frustrated with his life long before her.

"What do you know already?"

Banger raised his hands over his head and stretched. "Johnson, Young Jonn, and the bartender all worked together on a crew last summer. As you might guess, no one liked Graham Jr."

"Makes sense. Anything else?"

They turned to make their way across the field, closer to the château. "How about the tattoos go back to this particular crew?"

"This is interesting. The attack on Kick's squawk box."

"Most likely goes back to these men. I want to ask him about why they have them. I'm sure it wasn't because of a fun club thing."

"Yeah." Thomas stuffed his hands in his pockets. "I'd like to know too." On the one hand, Thomas was grateful for Banger's progress. On the other, he hated how dark Kick's circumstances were becoming. He ran his fingers through his hair and searched for the owl, but the bird had gone.

"She's vulnerable right now," Banger said, staring in the same direction.

"How so? And why are you telling me? You were crystal clear about cutting my ties last night."

Banger sniffed. "Maybe I felt bad about the Vivienne thing. I kept information from you. This time I think you should stay fully informed." He stepped away from the fence and continued on their path across the field.

The air had warmed enough that it stopped biting Thomas's nose when he breathed. His body grew antsy, and he longed to run even if it had to be a small one. He was about to tell Banger he'd meet him in the office when he realized Banger hadn't answered his first question.

"You haven't explained why Kick's vulnerable." Thomas froze in place and waited for his friend to continue. He dreaded the answer if it was worse than what Joe had told him.

"My team has intercepted multiple death threats on her specifically, but nasty shit is said about all of them. Every time she's harassed, with an article or the protesters and such, the crazies who buy into it come out."

Thomas's gaze fell to the ground as his shoulders slumped. "How many threats are we talking about?"

"At least a dozen."

He spun around. "I left to protect her. Who is her biggest threat? Them or me?"

Banger chuckled—actually chuckled while Thomas freaked out—and turned his head up to the sky. "That's not even the weirdest part of these past few weeks." He stopped beside Thomas and dropped his voice. "The overlap I mentioned? Turns out the bartender's phone records show a couple of calls to a number in Oxford."

Thomas swallowed hard. "England?"

"Not the one in North Carolina, brother." Banger turned in a circle as he spoke.

Thomas's hands wrapped around his neck. Friend or not, if Banger was messing with him, they were throwing down. "You've already told me you suspect Nigel in Presley's accident. Are you implying he also wanted to kidnap my girlfriend?"

"I thought she wasn't your girlfriend anymore."

Thomas growled again as the knot in his stomach grew bigger. "Slip of the tongue. I'm upset. What are you getting at?"

"There's a lot of work to do yet. I just don't like what I keep finding."

"When does your work lead to good news?" Thomas muttered.

"When I can simply go ahead and take out the bad guys. Spread a bit of chaos among the demons of the world, so to speak. I'm afraid the baddies won't be strangers this time."

Thomas shook his head and heard his neck pop. This didn't make sense. "Kick's problems started before our friendship. Plus the nut jobs who keep stirring the shit around her have nothing to do with my research."

"You might be surprised. This Graham fellow—I mean, the dad—is wily. He's as connected as they come. Family goes back to Oakville from before the Revolution. Like yours does in Virginia."

Thomas couldn't follow the logic. Moreover, he couldn't stand the thought of not being able to help Kick. "It's like you're telling me two plus two equals five."

"Then let me work on the math." Banger clapped him on the shoulder. "As I said before, I only want to keep you informed."

"What should we do?"

"Siobhan's trying to convince Kick of the benefits of a qualified bodyguard."

Thomas broke into a nervous laugh. "Lots of luck there. At Christmas, no less."

"It's the best option we have right now."

Thomas couldn't take much more. Not in the mood for self-analysis, he shoved his stomach knot down, gave it a mental stomp, and said, "I have to go think. Meet you back in the suite?"

"Sure. Siobhan should ping me any moment." Banger took off for the château at a quick clip.

Empty of mental capacity for more worry, Thomas took off running across the ridge and over the fields, going down to the river. He ran as fast as his legs would allow.

Thomas entered Banger's suite and immediately heard the man on the phone. He popped his head into the office doorway to check in and see if he had time for a shower.

Banger rolled his hand for Thomas to come in as he spoke. "Hold on, Von, he's back. Turn the camera on now."

So much for washing off his run. Thomas removed his running jacket and set it, along with his gloves and hat, on the credenza before taking a seat. Banger had pulled a chair behind his desk, next to his own. A man's image filled the center of the laptop screen, already beaten significantly. He sat in a small, sparse room that looked like it was on a ship.

The women had been right about the man who attacked Kick. He was a wolfish son of a bitch. Dark hair in need of cutting seemed to cover him everywhere. The man must not have owned a razor or scissors. Thomas couldn't quite place his age but guessed at under thirty.

"Wake him up."

Thomas did a double take at Banger's words and realized the man's eyes had been closed as his head hung to the side. Long bangs had obscured them.

A young man, Thomas assumed he worked for Banger's company, stepped into view. He jostled the tied man, making him start.

"Hello there, Taylor."

Taylor jumped as much as one can while tied to a chair. He did his best to twist around, looking for the source of the voice. "Who are you?"

"I'm no one, Taylor. At the moment, I'm simply a camera placed six feet away. I could be your savior or your destroyer. Your future depends on how you answer my questions. Understand?"

Taylor's head swung back down.

"Do. You. Understand?" Banger reiterated in a sharp tone.

"Yes." By the way he dragged out the word, Thomas clued in that the man had probably been drugged.

"Good." Banger checked his notes. "My friends tell me you confessed to attempting to kidnap my friend, Kick McKenna. Smart choice, fessing up. It saved you some pain."

Taylor's head snapped up, and Thomas saw exactly how much pain the man had already been put through. *Christ*, it had been so long since he'd been in a battle mindset Thomas second-guessed whether he should've been there. He'd gone soft since he'd become a scientist.

Then Taylor said, "Kick" and laughed. It was lascivious and menacing. Thomas's blood pressure spiked in anger, and he suddenly longed to be on the boat.

"Yeah, my manager hired me to take her. Said I could do whatever I wanted, as long as she was delivered to the address alive and mostly unharmed. Paid well too."

Mostly? Thomas growled and Banger placed a hand on Thomas's shoulder, reminding him to keep his shit solid.

Banger spoke into the mic. "This was your manager at Graham Construction?" After Taylor nodded his affirmation, he checked his notes again and continued. "This guy is nothing to the McKennas. Started pouring concrete and moved into drywall five years ago. He's nothing. Who's behind your boss, Taylor? Who wants Kick harmed?"

Taylor shrugged, then whimpered. "I… I can guess is all. We do odd jobs all the time. Sometimes they're for the big boss. Other times they're for his shit kid."

"By big boss, do you mean Big Jonn Graham?"

"Sometimes." Taylor coughed, then asked for water. His lips were cracked beyond being chapped.

"Soon." The team member with Taylor told him. "You're doing great. It's almost over."

Taylor's responding smile almost looked angelic, encouraged. He licked his lips and continued. "Most jobs come through the foreman. Some through the project manager. A few come from Mr. G. I learned fast to stop asking though."

Was everyone in this company corrupt?

Banger inhaled and chuckled. "I bet you did. You listen though, don't you?"

Taylor answered with another smile. This one was filled with pride. Thomas shook his head at the waste.

He wrote *ask him why?* on a nearby pad of paper. He slid the note to Banger.

"So, you don't know who wants Kick harmed. Do you know *why* someone wanted her kidnapped?"

"Like I said, dude, I don't ask."

"What did you hear?" Banger questioned.

Taylor's voice became agitated. "My driver—Wade from my crew— said we had to take the bitch to the address in the warehouse district, keep her drugged until our relief came. He figured they'd either let her go after the weekend or traffic her. I thought she was too old to traffic. Figured she'd be toasted for good."

Thomas couldn't take it anymore. He stood and paced the office, away from the screen. He hated what they were doing but hated this kid more.

"Hit him," Banger said flatly.

Thomas heard the dull thuds and smacks, along with the corresponding grunts and cries, as Banger's associate carried out his orders.

"Mind your words when speaking about the lady, Taylor." Banger finally spoke again. "In fact, how about you don't mention Ms. McKenna at all?"

A tinny groan flowed out of the laptop speakers. "Y… mfph… uk… mfkr."

"What?" Banger asked innocently.

Thomas walked back behind the desk and stood off to the side. He'd never taken pleasure in this kind of work, and he didn't know what to think of the way his friend obviously did.

"Clean off his face and give him some water."

The associate did as directed, then told Taylor to repeat himself.

"You should grab Young Jonn. He's a little mother fu—" His lips caught around his teeth.

"Tell me all about him, Mr. Johnson."

Banger's invitation seemed to perk the kid back up. Apparently, Jonn Graham Jr. had made plenty of enemies at Graham Construction. No surprise there. Taylor told them how the kid was obsessed with Rachel McKenna and had been for a few years. Thomas remembered back to the first time he'd entered the Perked Cup and saw how the boy leered at her. "Could've told you that," he muttered to himself.

Banger sent him a warning glare to keep his mouth shut.

Then Taylor volunteered information on the tattoos. "My boss came up with the idea. Those of us who do the side hustles have them. Then Young Jonn goes and gets one last summer. Only, he wants it to be like a gang thing, see."

Taylor asked for more water. When the man with him looked into the camera, Banger said, "Go ahead. As long as you talk, Mr. Johnson. You talk, you drink. Capiche?"

The associate held out a cup with a straw.

Banger turned to the side and stretched out his legs as if he were on a friendly business call. "Tell me about John-with-two-n's gang, Taylor."

"Obnoxious, ain't it?" The young man chuckled. "Remember how the big cartel was busted up last spring?"

Banger laced his fingers behind his head. "I've heard of it."

"Well, dipshit—that's what we call Young Jonn behind his back, 'cause if we said it to his face, he'd cry to Papa and get our asses fired, right?—anyway, dipshit wanted to start up a cannabis-selling venture and fill the hole that had opened up."

"But cannabis is legal now," Thomas said. He winced as Banger shot up and slapped the desktop. He'd been loud enough to catch the mic. Fortunately, Taylor didn't seem to notice. Thomas slowly settled down into the chair he had originally been in, hanging his head. Banger had gone out on a limb for him in several ways. The least Thomas could do was to respect the process.

Taylor shook his head and winced again. "The legal stuff is expensive, dude. Licenses take time and cash. Lot of it. Dipshit is cleaning up with a new black market. No taxes, no cartel to dodge. I wanted to do it, but the rest of the crew didn't want the commitment. Hell, I taped the bag to the sink in the coffee shop."

Banger leaned in. "Wait. You mean the Perked Cup?"

Taylor laughed. Pride filled the eye that he could open. "Yep. I taped it up to the sink. Jonn was supposed to take his share, put the bag back, then call in a tip."

"Why the hell would he go to so much trouble?" Banger jotted some notes on his notepad.

"Who knows, dude?" Taylor tried to shrug and groaned in pain. "I figured it had to do with the Rachel girl. Jonn's butt hurt she won't pay him any attention. The bitch has an asshole boyfriend too, so it's not like he's out of her league. He thinks more money will catch her eye. Anyway, her mom owns the place."

"Her mother is Kick McKenna, dumbass. The one you tried to kidnap. Didn't you notice their last names are the same?" Banger asked with an almost smile.

"Oh, right." Taylor inhaled as best he could and let it out. "My head's fuzzy, dude."

Christ. Thomas figured if all the men involved in this were swirled into one being, they might end up with a decent IQ. Might. He wrote down *what's the endgame?* and passed the note to Banger.

His friend read it and mouthed *wait* back to Thomas.

"Any chance you had anything to do with the attack on the Perked Cup's ordering unit?"

"You mean the drive-thru?" Taylor hissed as his face twitched. "Yeah, we did it. Payback for the pot, right? I'm mean, she took all of it. Dipshit only wanted to sacrifice some, not the whole thing."

Banger wrote some more, then leaned close to the mic. "You've done well, Taylor. I appreciate it."

"Thank you."

"Certainly. One more question. Think hard. Does this go back to Young Jonn or his father? See, I still don't understand why the McKennas are being picked on." Banger clicked his tongue and tapped the desktop. "As you know, it's my business to protect them now. Someone—you—try to take Kick at a club right under my nose, it makes me mad. I need to find out who and why."

"I wish I could help you more... mister," Taylor said earnestly.

"Again, appreciate your cooperation. Unfortunately, wishes don't help me either."

"Young Jonn would know. His old man is too hard to get to, but the dipshit would know. He runs his mouth more than me."

Banger laughed as Taylor rambled on more about the youngest Graham. Thomas wished he'd bashed the kid's head in when he had the chance in October. His lawyers were involved now though. Plus the boy was under house arrest. His side would have to stage a kidnapping of their own. One the police would actually notice too.

Thomas stood and rubbed his neck, stretching it from side to side. *Christ*, he needed a shower more than ever now. He had to wash off more than his run. The knot from earlier had returned, too, threatening to make him vomit. He still didn't know who was a greater source of danger for Kick—Jonn Graham, et al., or him, by way of the old man who reigned over the Felidae? Thomas still didn't know what to do.

As he walked out of the office, Banger called out, "Don't go far. We still need to talk."

LOVE IS A BATTLEFIELD

KICK

The Christmas tunes didn't bother me this afternoon. Not much did, in fact. I bounced around the work area, chatting up our customers, convincing myself my heart wasn't broken. Anytime a sentimental song came through the speakers with a longing for a loved one at Christmas time, I thought of the new year. I even had to put off thoughts of *him* every time I made an Americano black. I would get through the holidays first, enjoy the time with my kids, and worry about my heart second. The T-man could wait.

Placing a few drops of a cannabis tincture under my tongue helped. I'd done it as part of the product testing for Hugh's new venture. I had read up on a line that gave caffeine a run for its money when it came to focus. Should I have added it to my regimen without consulting my doctor? Probably not. But I waited two hours after taking my morning pills and was reasonably confident it would help, not hurt, my performance. I made sure there was nothing in the mixture to cause impairment, surprised by how much research was being done on the stuff.

Presently, it was time for Deana to end her shift and collect her grandbabies after school. It felt like old times and gave me another reason to look forward to January. Not much longer until I could reintroduce foods in earnest and begin the ending of my detox protocol.

Deana gave me a hug and air kiss before pouring herself a travel mug to go. With no customers currently waiting, she said, "Can you save some time for me tomorrow?"

"Will lunch work? I plan to do next month's schedule and get ahead of paperwork before I take my time off."

"Sounds perfect."

I studied Deana for a moment, trying to decipher what she wanted. She never made mysterious appointments with me. Her visage gave nothing away though I suspected she planned to bring up Thomas and someone's pride. I gave her my sweetest smile. As long as we discussed how proud he was, I didn't mind. "Have a great evening."

I had switched the holiday playlist to punk Christmas songs— I couldn't take the heartstring-pulling anymore—when the door chime announced a new customer.

"And here's the delinquent star of our recent chamber of commerce meetings." I heard Big Jonn Graham before I turned around and saw him. He always played life that way. He leaned on the counter as if he was getting ready to tell me a secret. "Been wondering if you were hiding."

Considering he found me in my coffeehouse, the man hadn't looked hard or for long. He spoke with his grandiose, old-timey, politician-like accent. I almost laughed but behaved. I knew it for what it was—a harkening back to a certain age when former Yankees, like myself, didn't occupy all the empty farmland around town.

I gave him a half-assed grin and waited to hear his order or what he really wanted. However, Big Jonn simply stared back like he expected me to explain my whereabouts. If he wanted to throw me off-kilter, it worked. Plenty of people were members in name only. Not to mention, after what happened on Halloween, I didn't think I'd see a Graham walk through my doors anytime soon, if ever again.

I held a sharp gaze on him and calmly said, "I've had doctor's appointments. I'll attend meetings after the new year when they're all through." Shit. A shiver of disappointment traveled down my spine. I should've simply said appointments or meetings. Looking weak in front of this man had never been a wise thing, especially now. I didn't blame him for his son's behavior. Hell, my oldest had jumped into a world of trouble in response to Shane's death. In the past, I'd felt empathy for Big Jonn's plight. Not anymore.

He reached out and touched the top of my hand, making me flinch. I mentally slapped myself again, hoping it wasn't noticeable. I knew he caught it by the sad smirk on his face, and I almost missed his next remark.

"I came into y'all's shop, hoping to make a peace offering. I'd like to buy gift cards for my crew. From all the to-go cups dotting our job sites, I can tell they love y'all's coffee," he said, then lowered his voice. "Then our families can put the messiness of our disagreements behind us."

His face looked so sincere I kind of believed him. A part of me desperately wanted this all to be over and ached to believe him. But was he crazy? I mean, come on.

I picked up a new rag and wiped at the counter. "The situation of your son's house arrest makes it a tad hard to drop. The police wouldn't stop the process if I asked them to anyway. Young Jonn broke laws. It'll go a long way if your lawyer allows him to confess to the attack on my shop though. I wouldn't care if he pleads to lesser charges as long as it ends quickly too."

"Attack?" He tsked. "My boy's been a handful since his mama passed, but this?"

"Mr. Graham..." It struck me how a man my age could successfully have me feeling like a mindless girl. Then again, growing up with the hostility in my mother's family, I knew how to spot the buildup of a gaslighting. Downplaying the attacks on me and mine, as if I'd blown things out of proportion in my head, was a classic move. I wouldn't argue the merits of the evidence with him.

"Jonn, I don't think you should be here." I moved my hand toward the under-counter alarm and hovered my finger at the button. He raised his hands in mocked surprise. "Ho there, darlin'. Aren't you jumpy? I'm starting to see where you're coming from now."

"What're you talking about?" I clipped.

"My apologies for prying, and I honestly hope I don't sound rude..." I raised my eyebrows, waiting for him to continue. "I heard about the breakup." He rubbed his stubbly chin. "It's a bad time of year to be alone. Bet it's got you edgy."

Edgy? He had no clue and almost had me laughing again. I smiled as I shook my head, determined to keep him at bay while not wanting to anger him. It wouldn't help my case if I threw another Graham out of my store.

He thumbed through a display of beaded bookmarks Cyndi had for sale by the register. "You and I have a lot in common."

"True, but—"

"Let me take you to dinner. One dinner, darlin'."

I didn't like the way he used the same endearment Thomas had. Big Jonn made it sound condescending instead of endearing.

Before I could turn him down, he continued, "A while ago, I offered to help you get your diner back on its feet."

"Coffeehouse—"

"Sure. Anyway, I can still speak with the editor at the *Oakville Mirror* for you if it helps. We could strategize a plan over Italian."

He patted what I admit was a very fit stomach. "Nothing like great lasagna to let a man think, right?" Big Jonn laughed and winked at me. This man was built as if he worked right alongside his crew members, though I didn't see where he'd have the time with all the schmoozing he did around town. Still, he couldn't hold a candle to Thomas—well, the Thomas who cared. There was more to handsomeness than physical attributes.

I didn't realize he had continued speaking. "...No matter what my son witnessed, the success of our town is still important to me. And... I have to say... you look a little overwhelmed."

I closed my eyes and inhaled. Wiping the counter had lost its therapeutic aspects. "I can appreciate where you're coming from, Jonn—"

"Big Jonn."

"Right. Still, I don't think the Assistant DA would approve of you being here. Young Jonn isn't allowed near the Perked Cup or me, but I can't remember if it applies to his family. I could call..." I reached for my phone, thinking Big Jonn might go quietly if he watched me dial.

"Well, now," he purred and smiled sweetly. "There's nothing to worry about, is there? I'm simply doing some last-minute Christmas shopping and prefer to spend my money locally."

The bell rang again, and a young couple entered. They queued up patiently, waiting their turns to order and laughing at something on his phone. The addition of two potential witnesses relaxed me, and I let out a loud exhale.

"Okay. How many gift cards should I ring up? It's a thoughtful idea, Mr. Graham."

With a sigh, he gave me the number and muttered, "Here I was hoping to start fresh in the spirit of the season. Let the shenanigans become water under the bridge. Maybe talk more about a partnership."

His words were smooth, but *Jaysus*, he made the hairs on my neck stand straight up. "The thing is"—I looked down at my feet

—"from where I stand, my toes are still soaked by your bridge water."

Graham paid for the cards and tucked them in his coat pocket. "Then I'll say an extra prayer for our families. It's our Lord's birthday after all."

"Go right ahead." I hung my head and shook it, relieved to see him finally step away from the counter.

He turned and sauntered out the door, humming "Baby, It's Cold Outside" when it wasn't even playing in the coffeehouse.

My body shook from the pent-up adrenaline. *Breathe, Kick. In for four... hold for four... out for five.* I lifted my head and smiled at the young couple.

"Hey there. What can I get you two?"

As if my adrenal glands hadn't been through the wringer already, the fight or flight response spiked again a while later. Alone in the dining room again, a group of kids approached and rushed through the front door. They wore their hoodies up with sunglasses and bandannas covering their faces. A group of unabombers had descended upon my café, and I was sure this time would be the end. My heart pounded out a dirge as I checked the drive-thru area, making sure Crystal was safely out of sight.

My finger hovered over the emergency button as the kids all dropped their hoods in unison. Next came the bandannas and glasses, and I let out a long exhale. They were some of my high school regulars.

My hand flew to my heart to calm the staccato beats. "Hi guys. Why the hell are you dressed like robbers?"

Each one turned to the next, then back at me. "We didn't think about that," the first boy said with a shrug. "We're in disguise."

"We couldn't be seen coming in here," another added.

I blinked at them as I tucked a curl behind my ear. "Whyever not?"

A third explained, "Yeah. Our parents think you're brain-washing us, but we like studying here. Gabe here"—he pointed at the first boy—"is our tutor. He toots really good. And the school librarian is a bi—"

A fourth one—a girl—jabbed the boy in his side. "Tutors don't toot, dumbass, they tutor."

The boys scrunched his nose. "You make absolutely no sense."

The first boy—Gabe—smiled and said, "She's right."

"Tragic."

The girl jumped back into the conversation. "Anyway... It's easier to study here, Mrs. Mack. My grades tanked after we were grounded from you. Please don't tell anyone we came by. Can we get drinks and stay in the corner if we're quiet?"

Grounded from me? The words wouldn't make sense even though I knew exactly what she meant.

"Of course you can study here. Can't guarantee you won't get in trouble, but I won't say anything. You know I work hard to give you guys a safe place to study."

"Exactly," the second boy said. "We told our parents the same thing, but they think we've already been... what's the word?"

"Indoctrinated," the girl answered.

JaysusMaryandJoseph. Counting breaths wouldn't help this one, so I raised my arms over my head and stretched my back. Time to roll with it. I stood at the register and swung the tablet around. "I assume your numbers are in here. Want to enter them and I'll get your orders going?"

Ha! Take that, Thomas and Siobhan. I had two huge hurdles and handled them myself. Thomas had sent more messages about the protesters, but I knew better than to let myself get strung along. The whole breakup-and-stay-friends thing never flew with me. Like slowly removing a Band-Aid one hair at a time, it not only prolonged the pain, it magnified it.

And Siobhan? She had been bugging me, stressing the need for a bodyguard. When I pressed her for a reason, she gave me vague answers about the investigation from the club. Well, missy, I had proved I didn't need one. The protesters did their worst and it backfired. The people who mattered knew me and my business. Okay, Siobhan had mentioned online death threats, but what woman hasn't experienced horrible behavior on social media? Case in point, my daughter. I shivered with anger at the thought of what she had recently been through. If she wanted to go to Broadway, though, she'd have to toughen her skin too.

Most of my after-school kids paid for their orders with credit cards, so it surprised me when they all placed cash on the counter. I tilted my head in question.

The first boy said, "Our parents track our purchases."

Right. Smart kids. Adjust and shift.

Wasn't that what I was doing too? Again, I'd thought about how my life plan had been heading one way and hit a dead end. Well, I could do some adjusting too. I took away one big lesson from my experience with Thomas: I knew I could move ahead with someone else. In fact, I looked forward to it. But maybe this time next year, after Liam left for college. When I had time for myself.

KICK

THOMAS

"Sorry about blowing the interrogation," Thomas said to Banger. A shower had been exactly what he needed to clear his head and focus.

"Fortunately, our guest was too nervous to notice your faux pas." Banger kept his eyes on his computer screen, his fingers typing away as he spoke. A few more clicks, and he closed the laptop. He sat back and stretched his legs. "Besides, it's my fault. I forgot you've softened since becoming a scientist. I should've expected it."

The bluntness rankled. Thomas wrapped his hand around the back of his own neck. "I wouldn't go that far—"

"Stating a fact, brother. It's best you own it."

Damn. Leave it to Banger to set him straight. Thomas dropped into the chair in front of Banger's desk. "Is it possible to put bodyguards on the McKennas even if Kick won't change her mind?"

"It's more like surveillance, but sure. Consider it done."

Thomas relaxed some and exhaled.

"Where's your head at now?"

Thomas rubbed his freshly shaved jaw. "What's your take on Big Jonn Graham?"

"The papa?" Banger opened his laptop and double-clicked on a file. "Family status has risen and fallen multiple times. The original Jonn was a prominent lawyer-turned-politician. This one sought the almighty dollar, used father's seed money and contacts to start his construction business. No questionable contracts. Nothing out of the ordinary anyway."

Thomas couldn't believe he was innocent with as many corrupt employees as he had. "What about his character? Give me your gut, Banger. It's bailed me out countless times already."

"The man's fifty percent charisma, fifty percent ruthlessness. Behind his Andy Griffith routine is a cutthroat. From what I can tell, family's everything to him."

"Goes the same for just about everybody."

"Don't be so sure," Banger muttered. He stood slowly and waved for Thomas to follow. "I need a drink. Let's go to the sitting room."

Thomas spoke as they moved. "Did the interview give you any new clues whether he's behind the attempts on Kick? She's what matters."

"Interview?" Banger chuckled. "Tell yourself what you have to, brother. Taylor Johnson went on a fishing trip with some of my people. Anyway, we're still watching the son. His motive compounds with each mistake he makes, like interest. My team's working on it though." Banger tilted his head to the side, studying Thomas with that intense, icy stare of his. "I promise, I have her back. No matter what. You can rest easy."

Thomas fell onto the divan as Banger poured two cognacs. "Is this Tess's prized stuff? I thought she planned to sell it." Thomas didn't know how much it was worth, but millions would have been a low-ball number.

"She's selling the wine—"

Before Banger could take his seat, the door flew open with a loud creak. A pile of packages, suitcases, and perfume pushed their way into the main room before Tess did.

"Did you have to say her name? It's like she's *Beetlejuice*," Banger muttered in disgust. Thomas wished he had it in him to put these two together until they hashed out their differences. It's what Kick would have done.

She had her sandy-brown hair in one of those pixie cuts and wore a complete yoga ensemble, including one of those long, drapey cardigans like Kick often did—a real contrast with Ellie too. Tess dropped her accoutrement. "I thought I heard talking. Hello, boys." She looked them both over, saw their drinks, and smiled. "Good idea." As Tess poured herself a drink, she declared, "I'm thrilled we'll have three for Christmas, but Thomas, dear, I thought you would be in the States by now. What about your lovely lady?"

The question made Thomas want to puke.

"Tess...," Banger warned, causing her gaze to flash between the two men. Her eyes drew down in understanding and sympathy. "No? Oh, my dear, Thomas. You didn't send her away, did you?"

Almost at his limit of emotion, Thomas took a long pull of the spirit to steady himself. "It was for her own good."

"*Pourquoi*? She's wonderful for you." She downed her liqueur in one shot and turned to Banger. "Did you not see how much he brightened around Kick?"

Banger shrugged sheepishly and shifted his head from side to side.

Tess took a seat across from Thomas on the divan and reached for his hands. She cast a disappointed glare at him, then said, "Do you even know you love her?"

"I..." Thomas's face warmed. "Well..."

Tess let her head hang for a moment. When she looked back

up, her visage was both faraway and sorrowful. "Don't let this place stand in the way of her." She jostled their hands as if it helped her think. "When you treat love like glass, you'll either put it away in a storage case or break it. With the first, you turn a useful vessel into a wasted work of art. With the other… well, it's destroyed, isn't it? Neither help anyone." Tess's brows drew together as she turned her attention to Banger. "Did *you* do this?"

Banger threw his hands up. "Why am I always the bad guy in your scenarios?"

"I *know* you."

He took a drink and rubbed his face. "Not anymore, you don't."

Tess pivoted back to Thomas, tipped her head, and sighed. "Fix this."

Thomas let his head fall. "What about my vows to the Felidae? What if I put her in danger because of it?"

"Fuck them," Tess declared with a certainty that had Thomas's head snapping up and his eyes popping wide. He'd never heard defiance from her. Banger, of course. All the time. Did this animosity run in their blood? Thomas turned to his friend and found him smiling, like he was proud of Tess. It must be genetic.

"Banger and I will protect you two. You deserve happiness."

When had happiness ever been a goal for him? The answer was simple—never. Thomas did his best with his unique life to make a difference. He didn't ask for more.

"Won't we?" Tess had turned her attention back to Banger, who lifted a shoulder.

After a sharp, Gallic growl from Tess, he added, "Yes. Okay?" He pointed at Thomas. "He knows this."

Thomas wrinkled his nose. *Did he?*

"Don't you?"

"I…" He sighed.

Banger asked, "What's going on in your head?"

"It's swimming with what's right and what's wrong." Outside, the golden hour had arrived, reminding him dinner would be ready soon. Thomas wondered if Alaric would eat with them tonight. With their business finished, *Grand-père* had spent the day with the winemaker. It struck Thomas that Alaric pursued passions outside the Felidae. Maybe he could follow the old man's example and get away with it. If they were all together, should he say something?

Banger broke into his thoughts. "When someone makes a tactical error, it's best to admit it, then correct it as soon as possible. Pussy-footing around with it prolongs the fallout."

"I thought you wanted me to leave Kick alone."

"Thomas…" Banger scratched at his head and sat up. "It's written all over your face. You miss her. You hurt her. It's tearing you up. I don't think it's only the guilt eating you either. You cut a hole in your own heart."

"What do I do?"

Tess tapped his knee like she was scolding a nephew or little brother. "Figure out what you want. Then proceed accordingly until you get it."

Thomas turned to Banger for clarification. He shrugged and said, "What she said." Then he clasped his hand around his neck and sighed. "Things are about to get interesting."

"Say nothing to Alaric or any other Felidae—especially Ellie," Tess warned.

"She's right," Banger added. "Don't mention what you know about Vivienne either. As far as I'm concerned, it's a 'better to ask forgiveness than permission' situation. Alaric will never change his mind about protecting the Society, so nothing good will come from confronting him on any of this. With him, stick to the lab and Toni. Nothing else."

Thomas could see their points, but had they just formed a faction? If so, how many were there? His head swam with questions. One of the biggest blurted from his heart through his mouth. "What if I've burned this bridge?"

With wisdom too old and refined for her youthful features, Tess soothed him. "You won't know until you find out, will you?" She stood and walked over to the bar. As she poured more cognac for each of them, she said, "You might have to be patient, persistent too."

Banger nodded along with Tess's words, and Thomas wondered where his friend's optimism had come from. He reluctantly asked, "Why the change of heart, man?"

"Tess. She has me thinking. You have changed a lot since you met Kick. For the better too."

Thomas leaned forward and placed his elbows on his knees. If the three of them were about to form their own conspiracy, he might as well bring them in on everything. He allowed himself to voice what had been quietly niggling in the back of his mind for weeks.

"My aura is back."

Tess took a sip of her cognac and lifted an eyebrow. She handed a glass to Banger, who took a long swallow.

He said, "I never knew you had the ability."

Tess passed the last glass to Thomas. The spicy warmth settled his resolve. "It had faded by the time we met. I figured it was long gone."

Banger and Tess let their heads bob in understanding.

Thomas took another pull from the tumbler, readying himself to share what was really on his mind. "I think I've glimpsed a glow coming from Kick." He smiled at the memory. "It was a warm light. Not too bright. Also, I think she tries to hide it."

Banger waved his glass and sat forward. "Well fuck, brother. Why didn't you lead with *that*?"

2 5

MISSING

KICK

My neck popped as I rolled it while sitting in a deceptively sturdy rocking chair. The things looked to be at least one hundred years old and lacked the loving care usually given to an antique. I breathed in fresh sea air mixed with fresh-cut grass from the rolling fields before me as a curl stubbornly plastered itself to my cheek. When I rolled my shoulders, they immediately relaxed, allowing me to settle into the woven bark seat. For a dream, this place impressed me. I hoped I could come back here again.

The low whine of another rocker caught my attention. I tucked the wayward curl once more and turned. My eyes watered at the sight of my dad. "This is where you grew up, isn't it? I had no idea how I knew this piece of family history. I'd only visited Ireland with Shane, and we stayed around Dublin, visiting his side."

He sighed in the stoic way I missed so much. "Minus the heartbreak and fighting, aye."

"I thought you lived in a city."

"As an older lad, we moved." He stopped rocking and leaned toward me. "What's on your mind, Katie girl?"

My gaze traveled around the worn-out porch. Normally, a building this damp and unkept would have my mold allergy on high alert, but my lungs never protested. I breathed in deep and smiled. "I want peace, Daddy."

He reached for my hand and squeezed it.

"Everything's fallen apart since you died."

"You said the same thing after Shane, and you did fine. In fact, you flourished. You learned how to stand on your own."

Disappointed with myself, I looked at my lap. "I had you to rely on." I thought about how much my little community—from my friends to my loyal customers—encouraged me and didn't understand why their support wasn't enough.

He pressed my knuckles to his cheek, showing more affection in these few minutes than he did when living. A hug from my father had been rare—hell, anyone in my family. "You miss your man."

"No." Dad used to have a sixth sense about my thoughts—it's where I inherited the same understanding about my kids—but he was wrong this time. I inhaled deeper, feeling like it was the first chance my chest had to relax all month. "Shane and I made our own peace. I've moved on."

"I mean your new man," he said with a melancholy chuckle.

"Oh." I scrunched my nose and flicked away another loose curl clinging to the breeze. "You know about him?"

"I do. All of it."

Despite being a grown woman, I blushed at the thought of my father knowing all about Thomas. Dad's chuckle grew uncomfortable too, as a deep pink crawled up his neck, certainly matching my own.

He sniffed and rubbed his nose. "Give him another chance, Katie."

"But—"

Dad's reason surprised me. "Look how quickly you bounced back. Where do you think it came from? It's not from the newspaper articles or the sales you're running at the café."

JaysusMaryandJoseph. Did he see everything?

"I would've agreed a few weeks ago, Dad." I touched my sweater over my heart. "The ache, here, says otherwise now."

My father scooted his chair closer and tapped my knee. "Listen to him. That's all I ask. Listen."

I had a looming sense my father had spoken his peace and was prepared to go. I couldn't let him leave without saying my own. Thomas Harrison didn't matter at that moment, Mickey Allen did. "I'm sorry my promise isn't working, Dad. I can't make her happy." To keep a threatening tear from escaping, I stared at a flock of sheep in the distance.

His chuckle grew to a laugh before dissolving. "Aw lass... I couldn't either, so how can you? In my heart, I knew I asked the impossible. I should apologize myself. It made me feel better in the moment, but it wasn't fair." He lifted his cap and ran a hand over his brown waves before setting it back. "No, she's a grown woman who is so committed to her misery the whole concept of happiness scares her. Never mind her. I want you to make yourself happy, Katie. No one else will do it for you. Trust me."

The tear escaped as I nodded, seeking understanding and acceptance. "She's in Michigan with Bert. You think she'll be happy?"

"Does it matter? The point, Katie dearest, is she's grown. It's not your responsibility to puzzle it out. I should never have tasked you with the impossible." He scratched at his nose again. "I'll tell you this much, happiness could slap your mother in the face, and I'm not sure she would recognize it. Leave it, lass."

"Okay, Daddy."

With those words, my alarm went off. There would be no chance to say goodbye or receive the hug I craved. I fought waking, hoping I could finagle a proper send-off, but it was futile.

I finally rose and padded into my bathroom to start the day. It didn't mean I was ready to call Thomas though. Back in reality, the muscle aches and tightness from physical exhaustion lingered. I craved "me time" so I could recover and prepare for whatever came in the new year. I hoped the mountain trip would help.

Before I left the sanctuary of my bedroom, I made a promise to my father to find the cottage where we met... and soon.

I sat in my office, watching a kaleidoscope of colors dance on the ceiling and walls. While submitting myself to yet another Deana lunchtime lecture about you-know-who, a package arrived from France. Proof of how far off the deep end my mind had wondered, I thought it was a new french press I had purchased and ripped the box open. Inside were a dozen glass, Celtic-styled butterflies. A note simply read For your office window. My confused frown over this new collection had been met by a smug grin from my dear friend. "Did you know about this?" Dee simply shrugged and bused our table.

Of course, the newly acquired rainbow made it hard to read my monitor, but my brain wouldn't focus either.

"Know how I knew you were back here?" Cyndi asked as she strutted into my office.

"It's where I work?"

"Ha. You're hit-or-miss lately." Oh, true. She dropped into a club chair. "No, chica. Barbra Streisand's 'Jingle Bells' is playing. You're the only person I know who still keeps it in a queue." It was my second-favorite Christmas song, though I didn't see why we had to limit it to holiday listening since the lyrics were about winter fun. I had also dropped the hammer on all the heavy-duty emotional tunes when Deana played "The Christmas Shoes" song.

"How are you holding up?" Cyndi kicked back and noticed the ceiling colors. Pointing up, she said, "Did the kids do this?"

"Nope. We're taking our presents to the mountains." I tipped my head toward the box sitting on the credenza.

Cyndi rifled through it and held up the note. "Thomas?"

I let out a confused and frustrated sigh instead of an answer.

"Oh, honey." She came back to the chair and settled on the edge. "That's why I wanted to check on you before we both leave town. What do you think?"

"They're handblown. And not flowers."

Cyndi sat back, crossing her legs. Her foot swung in time to the frantic beat. "He's never been a typical man. Are you going to call him?"

I blew a curl off my forehead and tucked it behind my ear. "In the new year, I think. I need time to rest and recover before I do it. Besides, a new collection—as pretty as it may be—isn't enough of a grovel. Can you make him get on his knees, Cyn?"

She tapped her chin and grinned. "From the looks of his gift, I'd say he's about to all on his own. But don't you think you deserve someone who's drama-free?"

I shrugged. "He doesn't have a psycho ex. That's a rarity at our age. Plus he's been a trooper about my family baggage."

"True." Cyndi recrossed her legs, this time bopping her toe to Tom Petty and the Heartbreakers. "I want it clarified that while I'm super disappointed in the professor's behavior, I'm so proud of you for standing your ground. If you want to try something new, I'll be happy to set you up or help you with a dating app."

I exhaled and smiled, happy to have a release from Deana's guilt trips. "Thank you, roomie. I know I'm ready emotionally. I just don't know if I'm ready for the dating game physically right now."

"Either way, I've got your back." Cyndi bent over the tote bag she'd brought with her and pulled out three packages. "You received your present early with the butterfly necklace, but these are for the kiddos." She set them on my desk. I couldn't wait to see what unique thing she'd come up with for them. "Maybe next year we could go away together."

If I could arrange for Bobby to head up north again, that could be fun. Before I could answer, the sound of someone clearing their throat caught our attention.

"Excuse me, ladies."

The familiar baritone made my body yearn for him again. His soft voice soothed my nerves in a way liquor wished it could. I wanted to hate him for it, but couldn't.

Great. I knew then I wasn't ready to make any decisions about us. As long as I put it off, our future wouldn't be finished. But the universe delighted in throwing me curve balls before I was ready for them. Cyndi jumped up like she'd been poked in the ass. She leaned across my desk to give me a kiss on the cheek.

"Merry Christmas, chica." Before she pulled away, she added in a whisper, "Give him hell."

Cyndi scurried away as I braced to face Thomas.

ALL I WANT FOR CHRISTMAS
IS YOU

THOMAS

Thomas's heart pounded a hard beat as he stood in the doorway to Kick's office. It didn't matter if Deana's face had lit up when she laid her eyes on him. Despite the buzz of activity, she had stopped working and run around the counter to hug him. "I knew you would come to your senses," she had said in his ear.

Word must have traveled about the coffeehouse's owner because some customers frowned as he had crossed the dining room. Then Cyndi passed by and muttered, "I suggest dropping to your knees now and waddling on over."

His eyebrows ticked up in question, then he saw, really saw Kick's drawn face. Pretty as always, anyone else might have missed it. His regrets hit him full force.

Thomas took a tentative step into the office, but Kick's words stopped his small progress.

"I've been doing well. I mean since you left."

"I know. You've been great. I saw the exposé on you and the

café. Your honesty about the flare was inspiring. Bet it helps many women who read it." *Christ*, how he wanted to hold Kick and tell her with his body how proud he was of her.

Kick muttered something like, "Blast him and his voice."

"What?" He took another step forward.

She folded her arms across her chest. "Thomas, why are you here?"

"Maybe I'm not well. Maybe I need you to save me."

"How?"

Dammit all. What didn't she do for him? Thomas ran his hand through his hair. "By listening. Making me laugh. Showing me the world from your point of view." He tipped his head back and closed his eyes. He had to take a chance and trust her with the locked parts of his heart. "By letting me bury myself in you. Lose myself as I wrap my arms around your body."

"Well, hell." Kick planted her hands on her hips. "You're playing dirty."

"I know. Told you that you have a hero complex too." Thomas felt the corner of his mouth twitch. Even now, he couldn't help but tease her. He lived for their banter.

Then the first tear fell. "Do you know how much you hurt me?" Kick pointed to the butterflies she'd already set up on the windowsill where he'd imagined them. "Did you actually *want* to do something special for me, or are they a part of your game too?" She walked toward the window, staring up at the little glass pieces. "You more or less told me we were a game the night you left. Well, I wasn't playing, Thomas. I won't be anyone's joke either."

The moment he had been bracing for had arrived. It was as bad as he'd feared. Then again, he'd known exactly what he was doing to get the maximum effect. It was time to fess up. "It wasn't a game or a joke. I said what I did so you wouldn't fight me, and I needed you to let me leave. But you were, and *are*, real. I had to go because of how real you are."

"To protect me," she clipped with an icy tone.

Thomas's spine stiffened. He took another step forward. "Damn straight."

Kick held out her hands to keep Thomas from coming closer. "Then why are you here now? As far as I can tell, nothing's changed."

"I was wrong."

She stared up at the window. Thomas had the impression she was purposely trying to keep her gaze off of him. "I'm tired, Thomas. I need time to think. That's why I haven't returned your calls."

He sighed heavily, afraid he might have been too effective when he left her. "I know. I'm sorry. As soon as I realized how wrong I'd been, I had to see you. It couldn't wait."

When Kick finally turned toward Thomas, her face was wet and her nose had pinked. He wanted to stomp on his own heart the way he'd obviously done to hers. He reached for her.

"No, no, baby. Please don't cry."

"Don't." Kick gave him a wide berth and sat on the edge of a club chair, sitting with her spine tall and shoulders back with pride. "I won't tighten my emotions for other people's comfort anymore. Hell, you're the one who told me it takes strength to be vulnerable. These are tears of strength. Deal with it."

"I hate being the reason for them though." Thomas fell to his knees in front of her, brushing the tears off her cheeks with his thumbs. "What can I do to make it better? How can I make this up?"

Kick's breath hitched as she sniffed and dabbed at her face with the neck of her T-shirt. "First tell me what happened at the gala. From what I can tell, there's a disconnect between what I experienced and the truth. I need the whole truth if we're going to move forward."

"Well, I thought—"

"Stop." She raised her hand to go with the directive.

"Thoughts are judgments and all I saw back then. Tell me how you *felt*. I promise to not contradict or condemn you."

Thomas sighed, resolved. "I was angry about being summoned to Bordeaux right before finals."

"You didn't have an option to finish the semester?" Kick's brows drew together, and Thomas watched her try to make sense of the situation. How could Thomas explain it though? He couldn't. Not yet. Her commitment had to come first.

"I didn't, but I can't say more. Not yet. I'm so sorry. Which leads me to now. Like then, I'm still afraid you'll tell me to go to hell."

"Hold on. What?" Kick's brow furrowed. "You make it sound like it's a given."

"Sometimes I *feel* like it is. Definitely did then."

"You doubt me?" She looked up at the ceiling. The angle of the sun had changed, and the butterflies no longer made their prismatic display. Kick turned back, and her eyes widened as if inspired by a thought. "This is about your secret, isn't it? It's about what happens in Bordeaux, and this is separate from teaching at Lord."

He inhaled audibly, on the verge of crossing his point of no return. "Yeah."

"The truth wouldn't send me away, Thomas, but secrets will. I might be shocked and angry, but I know who you are on the inside. At least I thought I did."

The tension wouldn't leave Thomas's shoulders, and he rubbed at them. He finally sat in the other club chair, pulling it as close to Kick's as he could get it. "I don't... can't say. Yet."

"I should warn you, I'm close to figuring it out."

He laughed at her preposterous assertion. "What makes you think so?"

"My da— Ah, intuition." Kick touched her heart. "Here. Liam and I both told you how I figure things out. Your secret is so close I can sense it." Her smile was a warning and a promise.

Somehow it eased Thomas's muscles. Her voice softened. "I'm not worried, but I am concerned for you. It's better if you would trust me and just leap."

Thomas's heart deflated again. Trust wasn't his issue. He knew Kick would keep the secret. His gut told him one thing at a time, and the first thing was winning her back.

"I also hate myself for the temporary comment during our fight. I did plan to turn my work over to someone else. It wouldn't bother me to do it, if it were in the right hands. You are not my research." He reached over and cupped Kick's cheek. "I can't walk away from you though. You've awakened a part of my heart that I thought had died."

"I could say the same thing about mine."

Thomas shook his head. "You weren't dead. You were too busy to grieve."

"You hit the nail on the head, though, didn't you?"

"I don't understand."

"We've bypassed all the usual dating steps. Our only official date ended up with me glutened. We're busy, don't you see? At the same time, it's also deep—maybe too deep." Kick spoke with her chin down as if she were thinking aloud. She looked up with resolve in her eyes, turning him on. "I told you I'm struggling with the casual thing, but you need it, don't you?"

"Well—" He absolutely didn't. Not anymore.

"It's okay." She nodded, more to herself than to him. "We both know lifetime vows are a joke to the one who gets left behind." Kick leaned into the chair arm, setting off her breasts perfectly. Thomas seriously considered kicking himself in the ass. She continued, "Today's all we have, so I'll only ask you for the moments we can get. That and no lies."

"You know you've brought the light back to my life, right?"

She smiled shyly. "I used to think so."

Thomas ran his hand through his hair and declared the absolute truth. "You've never been disposable to me." She was breaking his heart. "I don't need dates either. They'd be nice, but our outside commitments haven't changed." He took her hands and raised each one to his lips. "It would be my honor if you'd let me back into your heart the way you still occupy mine. I promise we'll figure out the rest later." He'd make damn sure Banger and Tess held up their promises too. "Tell me what else you need."

"Will you stop with the loquaciousness?" Kick smiled widely and slugged him in the bicep. "I needed a good grovel to make up for your blindsiding." She tilted her head from side to side. "You've come close."

Thomas moved back to his knees and between her legs. Eye to eye, he paused, wanting to get lost in them. Hell, he was a goner. "How's this?"

"It could work, especially since you didn't send me any flowers."

Thomas narrowed his gaze, letting her see his disdain, hoping she'd see everything now. "Flowers are for cheaters who only want to look like they're sorry."

"Right?"

"Now what?"

Kick moved forward and gave Thomas an eyeful of her cleavage, fritzing out his brain. She'd be the death of him. She tapped her lips. *Yes, ma'am.* Thomas moved over her, pressing her back into the chair and kissed her with all he had—his hopes and promises. Kick moaned and squirmed under him, giving back as much as she took. Then she tapped on his shoulder.

Thomas lifted his head and looked into Kick's eyes. Hers traveled to the camera in the corner on the ceiling. "It's on?" he asked.

"Always."

Christ. He sat back on his heels, both hands gripping the edge of the chair. "Think Deana's been watching?"

Kick giggled. "I bet she had a part-timer go buy popcorn."

He hung his head. "I need you so badly."

Kick ran her hand through his hair, stopping to cup his jaw as her thumb caressed the cleft in his chin. He kept his eyes shut and relished the moment. He thought of the time she'd done it in the parking garage, speaking her truth with the help of a drug. With the clearest of minds, Thomas said, "Let me give you the extraordinary. I'm trying to figure out how to do it."

"And I'm the last person to ask for perfection."

The intercom broke their spell, and Deana said in a quiet tone, "Sorry to bother you, Kick. The boys are here."

"Why is she whispering?" Thomas asked.

"Oh, she definitely saw us. She's probably corralling them in the dining room for our sakes." Kick grinned broadly—dazzling him—then bit her lip.

He kissed her again and asked, "What's up with the boys?"

"They're leaving Dylan's Beemer for Rachel and me to take to the mountains. His car does better in the snow than either of ours. I also have stuff to put in Liam's Jeep."

Thomas growled. "Why are y'all driving up separately?"

"Rachel is finishing up an incomplete this afternoon. We'll be fine. I'm the best driver on snowy roads anyway. Remember I grew up in the Midwest?"

He stood and offered a hand to Kick. When she was on her feet, he pulled her into a tight embrace, hugging her with his whole body. "You've given me the best present today."

She narrowed her eyes in a warning before exhaling and relaxing. "As long as you tell me everything. Soon."

"I will."

AFTER HELPING LOAD THE CARS, HAPPILY APOLOGIZING HIS ASS OFF to the boys and enduring another round of threats from Dylan, Thomas settled in at the bar for a quick coffee and snack. He'd been drained when he entered the coffeehouse. Now he was practically dead on his feet, and he still had to drive to Virginia.

Before he could make his last ask of Kick, her friend Charley walked in. She greeted him politely, making him wonder if Charley had been out of the loop on their fight. Since they had made up, he wouldn't call it a breakup. Something struck Thomas as she stepped up to the register to place her order with Kick. The back of his neck itched and his eyes burned, like his mind fought hard to place where he knew Charley. This wasn't about Thanksgiving dinner either. Things like this occasionally happened to the Felidae members and others like them. When a person meets so many people in a lifetime, they're bound to run into doppelgängers of old friends. Sometimes it turned out they were the descendants of these people. Such was Thomas's sensation now. If he hadn't been eager to finish up with Kick, he would have casually worked up a conversation with Charley about her history. It wasn't hard to do when you ran a genetics lab. Instead, he let the women catch up for a few minutes while he searched his memory for old friends of Mexican or Spanish descent. Unfortunately for this task, he'd had many. He was still going through names as Charley passed. She placed a hand on his shoulder and said, "Merry Christmas, if you celebrate."

"Thank you. I do," he said, tipping his head. "Same to you. Do you have plans?"

"My brother is finally coming into town. Can't wait."

"Sounds wonderful."

Charley had been at the end of the line, so Kick made her way over to Thomas once her friend had left. "Why do I feel bad that Rachel's on her way up from campus?"

"There's no need to be conflicted." Thomas squeezed her hand. "I have to leave soon." He kissed her knuckles, not caring if any of the customers saw it. "Sure wish I could bring y'all with me. We need time together."

Kick leaned onto her elbows, leaving them eye to eye again. Thomas reveled in having her full attention on him. "I feel the same, but we wouldn't get much time alone in either of our scenarios. We have obligations, Professor."

"What about New Year's? Could you take another long weekend so soon?"

"With you?" Kick winked, then smirked. "Deana would move heaven and earth to make it work. Yeah." She nodded briskly. "I might not get a day off in January, but I'll make it happen."

"I'll be back on the morning of the thirtieth. Think you can come over around noon?"

Kick's eyes rose, and he practically saw her working out the schedule in her mind. "It should work."

"And stay through the first?"

Her grin turned into a wide smile. "I like this plan, Mr. Harrison. I'll see if Liam and the dog can stay with Dylan. He could use the company too."

"Good. I can travel safely, knowing we have time tucked away for ourselves." Thomas kissed her nose. "Then we can figure out how to make all this into something looking more normal."

Kick's lips parted with excitement. "You mean like a regular couple?"

He returned her earlier wink. "Exactly."

HAVE YOURSELF A MERRY LITTLE CHRISTMAS

KICK

*O*ur quiet family trip to the mountains took a rocky turn on day two. After a late arrival and a morning of cross-country skiing, our nerves were as sore as our muscles. The boys had to share a room, which should've been no big deal for three nights.

However, little brothers forever remained little brothers when the big one was in a bad mood. With Dylan and Suzy officially over, I thought getting him away from the condo where they lived would do him some good. Instead, he'd been acting like a rabid wolf and Liam was a fresh ankle. After a howl, a scream, and a hard crash, I yanked their door open to find them wrestling on the floor in their skivvies.

"Boys!" After they ignored me, I took off my shoe and threw it at the wall where it bounced off and landed smack in the middle of them. You don't spend twenty years with a professional football player and not learn how to throw awkwardly shaped objects. I had a particular talent for short passes.

The boys sprang apart like they'd been electrocuted. I removed the other shoe. "There's one more here for whoever speaks out of turn. Dylan... you want to begin?" Despite his terrible temper, he was my go-to because I could usually make him see reason quickly.

"Sorry, Ma. I just need space," he huffed, raking his hands through his hair.

"And a fucking punching bag." My second shoe bounced off Liam's head. "Ow!" I had warned him.

I squeezed my eyes shut, quickly thinking about the correct way to mitigate. "You know, there's a reason I never became a judge, right?"

"We know," they said in unison. Yeah, it had often been the opening words to a long rant about kids expecting mothers to be cops, lawyers, and judges and the impossibility of it all.

"You two separate. Liam, join me in the living room. You can help me figure out why my laptop won't sign on to the Wi-Fi. Dylan, you have an hour in here, then I want your help cooking." Both boys grumbled and rose to their feet.

I continued. "As for sleeping, the last one up has the option of using the second bed in here or the sofa in the game room. Keep in mind, I won't enforce quiet hours once the rest of us wake in the morning."

"Gotcha," Dylan said.

"Sure, fam."

After signaling for Liam to follow me, I turned back to Dylan. "You know, son, Lee might have a point about the punching bag. There's a gym downstairs. And an indoor pool. Maybe you should try out the facilities, burn off some of the anger."

Dylan dropped his head, pinched the bridge of his nose, and broke my heart. "Sure. Sounds good," he whispered.

I set a hand on his shoulder. "Please don't sneak out though. I need your help later. Give me a heads-up before you leave."

"Gotcha," he repeated.

I turned back to Liam, jumped up slightly, and grabbed him by the earlobe—not the easiest thing when he was nearly a foot taller than me.

"God, fam." He fussed. "What the hell?"

"A young man acts like he's five. He gets treated like he's five."

"But he started—"

"Keep talking. You'll dig a deeper hole." I let go and took him with me into the kitchen where we unloaded the groceries I'd purchased.

"Dylan's in the middle of his first big breakup, Liam," I said. "Your sister is too. The least you and I can do is to be a soft place for them to land." I tapped him on the temple. "Use your noggin. If they snap at you, it doesn't mean you have to snap back. It's usually best to leave the room and give them a minute to decompress."

He whined, "This is going to be a long four days."

A WHILE LATER, LOUD MUSIC BEGAN BOOMING FROM RACHEL'S room, playing the same song over and over, and it wasn't Christmas-y. Initially it amused me to see the way the boys' eyes went wide at certain lyrics from Lily Allen's "Not Fair." By the fifth go-around, I actually winced and my sons grew ornery.

Dylan stood next to me in the kitchen, slicing sweet potatoes, while I prepped the chicken. Liam chopped broccoli at the table. The boys had taken up growling when the song would start over. At least they agreed on something. When the song rolled over a sixth time, Dylan dropped his knife with a sharp wrist flick and took a hard step toward Rachel's room. I reached for his arm, stopping him.

"Let me speak to her."

Dylan turned to me with fire in his expression, then exhaled and slumped his shoulders. "Yeah, okay." He resumed his potato job.

The knob on Rachel's door didn't budge, so I banged on it. Hard. "Rachel! You don't get to lock your mother out of a room in her own house. I don't care how old you are."

The music stopped, *thank Jaysus.* Feet padded across the room. A click sounded, and it opened. "This is a rental."

"I'm footing the bill."

"Right. Sorry." She scratched her nose. "I was thinking."

"Your brothers and I noticed. We need to talk."

She tilted her head, looking truly puzzled. "What about?"

I moved into her room, shut the door, and sat on the ski-themed bed. "Snow, you're not the only one of us who's upset about a breakup."

She waved her hand. "I'm fine—"

"You've played "Not Fair" almost six times in a row." I laughed, remembering the uncomfortable grimaces on the boys' faces. "It doesn't take a degree in psychology to figure out the song's appeal." I lowered my voice and tried not to giggle. "Your usually thick-headed brothers figured it out, and they're kind of freaked out."

"Oh." Her eyebrows lifted. "Oh! Shit… but… don't you think they know I'm not a virgin?"

"Of course they know. They also try very hard to not think about it."

She sat up indignantly. "How is this my problem?"

I sighed, exhausted from the drive and my own emotional roller coaster. "If Dylan were blissfully happy, I might tell him to get over it. Right now you're both on edge. Can we all try to keep our problems in Oakville though? I want us to have fun with each other. Okay, sweetie?"

Rachel almost shrugged, but it dissolved into shakes. "He gave her the present I had asked for. You know what that means? Cody gave that bitch *my* present!"

I tucked a curl behind my ear. "How do you know this?"

Rachel's phone seemed to appear out of thin air. She held it out for me. "She posted it on the Gram."

"Oh." I let my head drop into my hand. Then I grabbed her phone and abruptly stood.

"What are you doing?" Rachel reached for me, but motherly indignance must have sped up my reflexes.

"Blocking them." I worked quickly while Rachel objected. "If you're going to pursue this Broadway thing"—I blocked the girl—"you're going to need social media to advance your career." I found Cody easily enough. His new girl had tagged him. "But you need to learn how to be the boss of your accounts. Don't let anyone get it over on you because of some stupid Gram tag." A few taps and Cody was gone too. I handed the phone back over. "Sweetheart, I know you can undo this later, but please don't. I also know you understand the illusion all this crap is. Curate it so it makes you happy, not sad." I tipped my chin back at her feed. "It should be filled with pretty inspiration images, not stupid taunts."

"Yeah." Rachel blew out a long breath. "I guess so." She brought the phone to her face and yelled, "I Marie Kondo'd you, *bitch!*"

We both laughed and hugged. "There's my girl." I gestured for her to follow me.

My phone buzzed with a text alert from Thomas. They had been arriving at regular intervals since we made up. In need of a distraction, I swiped the phone awake and found a link to a song. I told Rachel to help her brothers in the kitchen and I would join them in a few minutes. After closing the door to the owner's suite, I opened the attachment.

Using the endearment "baby" made Al Green's "I'm So Tired of Being Alone" feel like it was written for me. Thomas tugged hard at my heartstrings with it. His attention pointed to an honest penance, as he'd been pouring his heart out through song lyrics. It was like he'd given himself permission to feel. The songs were my favorite present so far. I sent a message back.

ME

Wow! Putting it all out there. I needed it.
Thank you.

I added an attachment: Pink Martini's "Dream a Little Dream."

ME

Hope your holiday is going well.

The ping back arrived immediately.

THOMAS

Tomorrow will be rough.

ME

I'm sorry. It's been emotion-central here, too.

THOMAS

The 30th will be our refuge.

ME

Can't wait to breathe you in.

THOMAS

You kill me. I'll dream of you. Do the same, baby.

ME

With pleasure.

I left the room and joined my kids in the kitchen for a little chat. "Listen up, crew. Half of us are happy, and half of us are hurting. Can we all make a promise to tread lightly?"

"Guess so."

"Sure, fam."

"Yes, Mama."

"Thank you. Now, how about we also promise only to play

Christmas music? At least until the twenty-sixth. I especially don't want to hear any sad songs or breakup songs. We'll save them for when we get back to Oakville."

"Aren't there sad Christmas songs though?" Liam asked.

"Not this year," I answered. "If one comes up, skip it. Remember our theme for this holiday?"

In unison, they said, "To have ourselves a merry little Christmas," in a drone I'd expect from little kids, not my grown ones.

"Jaysus. There's an enormous chasm between *Elf* enthusiasm and you three." They each chuckled, making me think there might be hope for our trip.

I gripped Rachel's and Dylan's hands, looked them in their eyes, and said, "This will probably be our last holiday together as our foursome." Squeezing the hand to my left and my right, I continued, "It might not feel like it right now, but you will add new loved ones to our table. Littles might even show up if we're so blessed." I caught Rachel's vigorous head shake out of the corner of my eye, but the center of my focus was Dylan. "In the right time."

Liam grinned but stayed quiet. The other two almost seemed amused too.

"I'm not only talking about Thomas." I bumped shoulders with Dylan. "You already moved out." My head tipped to Rachel and Liam in turn. "My empty nest days are right around the corner, regardless. You may not appreciate the brevity of it, but I do."

Rachel asked, "But we can always come back home, right?"

"My house is always open to you guys. I'm not sure if I'll stay in our big house though."

A cloud of fear and sadness descended upon the room. I tapped the table. "Hey now, these are good changes, not bad. You're supposed to grow up and have your own lives."

I took a deep breath and addressed the elephant in the room. "Dylan and Rachel, it turns out your relationships were practice ones. You've both learned important lessons at a young age. I, for one, can't wait to meet the people you're meant to be with."

A micro-smile reached Rachel's face. Neither of the kids was ready for an official move-on pep talk, so I didn't dare go any further. Dylan looked to be near tears.

"All done with the motherly sermon," I told the younger two. "I need to speak with your brother now."

"What should I do?" Rachel asked.

Liam saved the day when he said, "Want to help me with a song?"

"I guess." I glared at my daughter, warning her to listen to my words and enjoy her little brother. They went down the hall to the media room.

I turned to Dylan. "Doing any better?"

"The workout helped a lot. Thanks for the idea." I couldn't believe he still had energy to burn after our cross-country skiing outing earlier, but there was a major, physical difference between us. Dylan walked over to the fridge, pulled out a soda, and popped the top. "Teach me how to be strong, like you were after Dad died."

"I don't remember being strong, lad." Dylan drank from the can, then returned to his chair at the table. I rubbed his shoulder, remembering those horrible early days. "You can start by learning the difference between strength and resilience, like I did. Focus on strength and it's easy to go cold, to numb out. Resilience though? It acknowledges the pain, feels it all, and moves forward anyway."

Dylan sighed. "I want to get back to normal me."

I grabbed his chin as I inhaled deep, preparing for a hard truth. "This *is* your normal now, lad. *This* you loves deeply. You can move ahead with the knowledge and believe one day the right person will be at your side, loving you and being loved in return. It'll be beautiful, son."

"It's embarrassing. Aside from my wrecked heart, the

investors look at all areas of my life to see if I'm a stable risk. How am I supposed to build a successful startup when I can't make one person happy?"

"I think the word you're looking for is humbling, not embarrassing. And let me tell you, there's no better leader than a humble one. That person understands forgiveness. Service too."

"So what do I do?"

I wished I had something strong to drink, but I hadn't touched any alcohol after the attack. "Here's what I did: I set the alarm every day, no matter what. Each morning, I woke up shocked to find myself alone and was afraid I wouldn't get out of bed if I didn't have to turn it off."

Tears threatened as I found myself back in that headspace. I blinked several times to keep them at bay. "My toothbrush still worked, so I used it—even if it looked lonely in the cup."

I reached for Dylan's soda and took a sip. "The point is, I took tiny steps to get through the day. Then one morning, I woke and noticed the sun filtering through the drapes and thanked heaven for it. At the time, it felt like for-fecking-ever to get there. Now it's a memory of the lowest low, mixed with the highs of you kids and life-changing lessons."

"Can't wait," he scoffed.

"You'll get there. I promise." Still not sure if he believed me, I stood and leaned against the counter. The smooth chill helped take the edge off my sad memories. "Do you know where Suzy is now?"

He clipped out acerbically, "In Greensboro with her precious parents. She's moving her stuff into Mai's apartment on the thirtieth."

"Will you be there?"

"I won't lift a thing. It's on her to get a crew, but I will make sure she goes."

"That's the day Liam and Koosh are coming over."

"It's fine. She'll be done by noon. Dum and I have already

ordered the replacement stuff—mainly a new television and couch. We'll be ready by the time Dimp and the dog show up."

"Dylan…" I swear, these kids were born to get on my nerves. Here I'd been pouring my heart out too. Still, I laughed before schooling my face into motherly disappointment. "Don't call your brother Dimp. I feel bad enough abandoning him for New Year's Eve."

"You serious? Mom, stop." He paused so long I didn't think he had more to add. "When Dad was alive, didn't you guys do it big every New Year's Eve?"

I smiled at the memory. "Yes, usually. I haven't thought about it in ages."

"I remember. You'd both dress up in fancy clothes. Granddad and Grandma kept us. Or didn't we have a couple of neighborhood girls one year? Yeah. They were nice to us. Nicer than Gran anyway. Do you want pretty boy hanging out with Gran by himself?"

We shuddered in unison at the thought.

"God no. She'll still be out of town anyway, and he's eighteen. I mean, I trust him not to burn down the house. But I don't want him to feel like he's cramping my style. I still want him to feel special too."

Dylan raised his hands like he couldn't take any more. "Chill. Please." He put his arm around my shoulder and squeezed. "Have you considered the possibility that Liam's dicking around with school and college decisions because he's afraid of leaving you alone?"

"Uh…" *Hell, really?* Had I missed another thing? I thought Liam was the kid I didn't have to worry about, other than how his college prep test went.

Dylan smirked at me. "Didn't think so. In pretty boy's mind, if he dinks around at community college, he won't have the guilt of going away. With Thomas around, he has permission to figure out what he actually wants to do with his life."

My spine straightened. "What does Thomas have to do with anything? I'd never hold you kids back."

"Sure. Doesn't mean we wouldn't feel bad about leaving you alone though."

"We?"

"Yeah. We don't want to see you alone. Something from a psych class has stuck with me. What was it exactly?" He snapped his fingers. "Oh right. 'Nothing is a bigger burden on children than the unlived life of a parent.' Was it Freud?"

"Seriously doubt it," I murmured through my shock and guilt.

He snapped again. "No, Jung. Definitely Jung."

I dropped my head into my hands. "Kill me now. Should I write checks to all three of you or make one big one you can divvy up?"

"For what?"

"Therapy. All this time I thought focusing on you three would fill in the gap your father left. Now you tell me I've screwed you up anyway."

"No. Shit. That's not what I mean." He patted my head and chuckled. "Look at our extended family. You were doomed to fuck us up with or without Dad."

I groaned and fussed with the curls hanging in my face.

Dylan's laugh grew. At least I'd cheered him up. "I'm kidding. All in all, I'd say we're fairly functional. It's quite an achievement." He bumped my shoulder. "Well done."

"Are you serious?" I looked up, hopeful yet cognizant of his penchant for messing with me.

Still, I was stunned. Dylan had chosen a university close to home, but it was one of the best in the country for his major. I thought staying nearby had been as much for him as for me. It had been so close to Shane's death that I didn't think any of us were ready to lose another family member. Had I been wrong? Had I kept him from living his true dream? It hit me hard how we hadn't talked enough about the important stuff.

Over the years, I noticed a common trait among kids whose parents had chronic health problems. While the parent often went out of their way to pretend everything was hunky-dory so their kid could have a "normal" life, the child also kept problems from the sick parent to lighten the parent's daily burden. *Shit.*

As usual, Dylan paid no mind to my tune out and continued on about his plans for Liam. "He can help us get the condo back in shape the first night. Then we're having a guy's poker night on the thirty-first. There's a chair with Liam's name on it. PB will be fine. I'll make sure he has fun."

"PB?"

Dylan tossed his mischievous side-eye my way. "You don't like Dimp, so I'll try out Pretty Boy."

"Seriously?" Honestly, my kids could exasperate me so easily.

"It has a ring." Dylan kept his eye on me, challenging me to yell the smirk off his face.

"The boy has always been insanely gorgeous," I quietly admitted.

"I know, right?"

"It's the dimple."

"The curls too." It was good to see a spark of mischief in Dylan's silver eyes. The corner of his mouth twitched.

"He'll beat you up one of these days though. I hope I'm there to video it."

He puffed his chest out as if he were invincible. "Bring it, Mom. Bring it *on.*" After what he'd just told me, it lifted my spirit to see evidence that he wasn't completely crushed. Dylan would move past the pain of both Suzy's betrayal and their breakup with the efficiency that came from being young.

Something he said earlier gave me pause. I pulled away and gave him a stern look. "Hey, you're not going to make Koosh stay in the house all day, are you? Her bladder can't hold it in forever."

"I'll put PB on Macushla duty. It'll be his hotel fee."

"Way to make him feel like an honored guest. Glad I raised you right."

He squeezed me again and added a couple of pats for good measure. In a surprisingly accurate imitation of my late father-in-law's accent, he said, "But you've done just grand, me darlin' mudder. A grand job indeed."

I wondered how long it would take to know if Dylan was right.

MERRY CHRISTMAS, BABY

KICK

My bladder woke me Christmas morning before dawn. I had decided it would be a good time to reintroduce caffeinated coffee. The genuine stuff. A present to myself for working hard and not giving up despite the setbacks. "My precious," I said in a Golem voice as I watched the water flow through the paper filter into the carafe.

The condo's main living area faced east. There was something about watching the sunrise from the top of a mountain on Christmas morning. It called to me. With my coffee in hand, wrapped in a thick fleece blanket, warm slippers on my feet, I slid the patio door open and slipped into a deck chair, closing myself up tightly to ward off the chill.

Memories of the magic of Christmases past flooded in. Of the time when babies and small children were the stars of the holiday. Each child had taken a turn bounding into our bedroom to wake us up for presents. One did it at three in the morning. I searched my visual memory bank for a face on said menace and glimpsed long, black ringlets bouncing on my side of the bed, yelling, "Waffles, Mama. Izz Kwiss-miss. Make waffles." Rachel—the little imp. Liam had been a newborn, and after only three hours of sleep, I snapped back at her, making her cry on Christmas morning.

There lay the reason I tended to lose those memories—they were intricately bound to the pain of undiagnosed illness, misunderstandings, and the false accusation of being lazy. When it came to the kids' childhood moments, my brain couldn't recall a sweet memory without an ugly one popping up alongside it. It was a major part of the reason I'd clung to the adage of living in the moment. The only problem with the plan was how quickly children grew.

I had done my utmost to keep my illness from ruining their childhood. Still, instead of enjoying what was supposed to be my best years—the magical time as a young parent—I was often robbed of the joy. I wiped away a tear as the sky changed as quickly as my kids had grown.

Blink and the horizon was red.

Blink again, it turned pink.

Another blink and there came the orange.

Tip the mug, swallow some liquid energy, and the sky had turned to yellow.

So be it.

It was time to make peace with the madness of the past. Christmas breakfast before dawn had become a leisurely brunch at eleven. Nothing was wrong or right about any of it, it simply reflected the state of our family. Plenty of people had shitty holidays. I decided against lingering in self-pity and regret and dissected the beautiful memories from the diseased ones. If my body was doing better, it was high time I whipped my mind into shape, starting with the holidays.

It didn't take long before thoughts turned toward what the future would be like. I couldn't believe I'd almost become a grandmother already. I wouldn't have freaked personally. Plenty of my girlfriends had grandchildren. I knew Dylan wasn't ready yet. None of my kids were. I wondered how Thomas would've reacted to the hypothetical. I took another sip from my mug and envisioned him with us next Christmas. Would it happen? Would we travel to Virginia with him? To Bordeaux? I couldn't take the speculation any longer and sent a text in case he was up. My phone rang almost immediately.

"Merry Christmas," I whispered upon accepting the call.

"Are the kids still asleep?"

"Yes. But I am outside. I don't know why I'm whispering."

"I like it. It makes me feel like you're in bed with me."

"Shit. You weren't up. I'm sorry."

"I'm still in bed, but I've been awake for a while. Don't apologize."

I grew concerned by his words and asked, "Is everything okay with your family? In Bordeaux?"

The low laugh rumbled through the phone, laced with a morning rasp. Hearing the sound was another gift. I chided myself for feeling too much, too fast. I had promised Thomas one day at a time, and I'd meant it.

"It's all of it, baby. What has you roused so early?"

"I usually am. The opportunity to see the sunrise from the top of a mountain was something I didn't want to miss."

"Mm. You're facing east then?" he rasped some more.

"The balcony is. We have views on three sides, which spread for miles. It's so beautiful up here. I could stay forever."

"We'll have to go back together. I love the mountains. In fact, I think I'll get up now and go for a hike before we leave for the nursing home. Thanks for the idea. I've been laying here wondering how to fix things I have no control over and kicking myself for wallowing in self-pity."

"I did the same thing. I sat on the porch thinking I'd find

peace and ended up in a pity party. After chastising myself, I remembered this must be a tough day for you too."

"A party for two then?"

"No. Sorry. I've always cleared away the ugliness in my head by placing my focus somewhere else. I honestly wanted to make sure you were okay."

"I know. It was only a tease. And stop apologizing. We both have more problems than Cracker Barrel has biscuits." There was a rustle in the background, like sheets shifting. "Your call will be my favorite gift this year. It's helped more than you know."

"Your chuckle is mine."

"You like my morning voice?"

"Very much. It's my new drug, and I'd gladly get addicted." He rewarded me with another demonstration of his low belly rumble. "I never thanked you for the butterflies."

"You were distracted."

I laughed into the phone. "That's one way to describe it. Seriously, were they handmade?"

"Yep. A glass blower in the village by the vineyard has a big one in the front window. I asked him if he did smaller ones in various stages of flight."

"You commissioned them?" I didn't know what else to say. Until this moment, I thought Thomas's first set of messages had been about appeasing his guilt. I didn't think he had an actual change of heart until right before he'd left France. It sounded like I was wrong. My breath caught, making my words come out breathy. "I love them."

"You're welcome. Don't get too flustered though. You have more gifts coming."

"I do?"

"Absolutely. When you come over on the thirtieth. Expect to be wooed."

"Wow." I was filled with a childlike wonder, thinking about

what he had planned. "It's a good thing I didn't send your present back."

"You didn't?" He sounded almost smug about it.

"No. I ordered it before the gala, but I've been too swamped to deal with the postal service. So you're one lucky fella."

Thomas inhaled and let out a long "hmmm" over the line. "No kidding."

Our conversation lulled, and I saw two predator birds catch a vertical draft, their wings outstretched as they circled each other and let the current lift them. It looked like such a peaceful gift to be able to let go and give the wind control. Then it occurred to me they were probably on the hunt for breakfast. A breeze snuck around the sides of the balcony and caught my breath from the iciness.

"I should go in. I'm getting chilly."

"What are you doing the rest of the day?"

"Shower, dress in holiday yoga gear..." Thomas laughed. Oh, to make him laugh all the time. It lit me up to hear it. I continued, "A light snack until the kids wake. A brunch casserole is cooking in the Crockpot. Between now and then, I'll read. That'll be another gift for me. One of my favorite authors released a Christmas novella for her motorcycle club series. I can't wait to dig in."

His chuckle deepened. "Christmas at a motorcycle club?"

"Why not?" I laughed too, making sure I kept the noise down. "Honestly, I'm tired from skiing and looking forward to vegging out. You should go so you can hike."

"Can I call you later? Our lunch with Ken will be hard for all of us. Your voice lifts my spirits." Thomas's tone dropped and grew serious. "Damn, baby. When I walk through the rooms of my house here—both the newer areas and the original ones—I wonder what your reaction would be to them."

"Oh." I imagined him telling the historical significance of each cubby and corner. "I would love all of it. You know, I might take a nap later, but I'll have the phone nearby. Please call anytime."

"Alright. Bye, baby. Thanks for thinking of me."

"Merry Christmas, sweetheart."

MY KIDS SURPRISED ME BY WAKING UP EARLY. RACHEL TURNED ON an old ceramic tree I'd inherited from my grandmother. It sat on a table in front of a picture window overlooking a ski trail. The presents had been stacked under the table. When I had packed it, my only concern had been for its cuteness and convenience, so it was a joyous gift to feel the history and memories the little tree represented. I felt the warmth of the family members I had loved my whole life as I made new memories with my kids.

As usual, they had unwrapped their gifts in no time.

My favorite present from them was a photo. They had re-created a Santa picture from when they were one, four, and seven. Stranger shy, Liam screamed the entire time on Santa's lap while Dylan frowned at me for not helping his baby brother. Rachel's fake smile, head toward the camera and gaze out of the corner of her eyes, gave away her own nervousness. It's so classically awful it always made me laugh. Their grown-up version, with Liam faking the same scream, was a hilarious surprise.

"You guys know me so well. Thank you." Their grins and pride in pulling off a group present made my heart swell. There might not be silly family movies and magical presents anymore, but this day with our little unit would be a treasure. My last gift to them was ultimately a gift to me—new snowboards for each. Within an hour, they were fed, dressed, and off for an afternoon on the slopes. And I took my nap.

THE PHONE RANG WHILE I READ A BOOK AND LISTENED TO MUSIC, comfortably tucked into the love seat in the living room. "Hey,

Thomas." What the hell was with my voice? It had a wispy Marilyn Monroe vibe.

"Hi, baby," he muttered, adding in a sad sigh.

"That bad?"

"I'm toast. Guess I don't do emotions so well."

"No kidding?" I bit my lip, wanting to take back my go-to sarcasm. I tried to lighten it by adding a giggle. "I hadn't noticed."

He sighed again into the phone, his anguish crystal clear.

"Sorry, sweetheart. I didn't mean to make light of it. Do you want to talk about it?"

"Not really. It won't change anything. Toni's living the nightmare. I'm left watching it happen while trying to support her."

"But I want to help you while you help your family."

"Alright. Tell me what y'all are doing right now." I should've guessed Thomas would deflect. I wished I could tell whether it was to distract himself or me. Was this about emotional overload or more of Thomas's secrets? Then again, maybe he simply didn't feel comfortable talking about other people's business. I respected that, especially since mine seemed to be plastered all over town lately.

When I considered the ridiculousness of what I had been doing, a belly laugh erupted from me. "I've been listening to 'Have Yourself a Merry Little Christmas' for the past two hours. And reading."

"One song?"

My chuckle continued. "No. It's Liam's idea of a gag present. It's my favorite Christmas song, and I made it the theme of this year's celebration since we only have the four of us. Mr. Smarty-Pants hunted for every version of the song he could find. I'm required to listen to it this afternoon so I'll finally get it out of my system."

"Sounds like torture."

"It's fine." I shifted and shook out the back of my hair. "The ones I don't like, I remove. It's been fun comparing them. I have definite opinions about each version."

"There's a surprise. You have opinions about everything."

My eyebrows furrowed as insecurity took over. "Is that a bad thing?"

Thomas's tone returned to its soothing purr. "Not to me." I heard a ruffle of material that was lower than a squeak and softer than a creak. I guessed he was in a leather chair.

"Where are you right now?"

"In the library. It's relaxing in here, looking out at the stables and woods. Joe's upstairs napping after working with the horses. So there's more privacy here than in my rooms right now."

"Wait. You have horses?"

"It's Joe's business, but our family has bred them for generations. He's pared it back from what it used to be. Most of our current horses are boarders."

I sighed in approval and fished for an invitation. "I had no idea. I'd love to ride one sometime."

"Sure. Didn't know you could."

"It's been a while. I ran out of time for it in college."

I sensed his mood turning dark again and heard the longing when he remarked, "I wish you could drive up here now."

My heart broke for Thomas's circumstances at the same time it lifted me to know how much I mattered. "Any chance you could come home?"

I heard another sound like material rubbing on leather. "There's still three big meetings to attend regarding the running of the estate, then a delivery to oversee at my farmhouse. It won't be ready until the thirtieth, and I'm driving down with it first thing in the morning."

"Interesting… What is it?"

His voice lifted, and I could see a smile on his lips in my mind. "A surprise."

I played along and flirted back, hoping to encourage a better mood. "Ooh. I like the sound of this. When do I get to see it?"

"It'll be ready when you arrive. You're planning to spend the night, right?"

"Yes. We're set with the boys."

"Excellent." He grew quiet again. I reminded myself my new beau was a brooder.

"I don't like this gloomy tone, especially not today. No one should be sad at Christmas. What can I do?"

"What if we sexy-Zoomed?"

"No." I laughed at his request. This man and his middle school mind. "As part of your penance, you get the goods in real life or not at all. The Wi-Fi here is sketchy anyway. It would probably end up looking like a trailer for a horror movie."

He clicked his tongue and sighed in a way I knew chastised my joke. Then he paused so long I thought the call had dropped. Finally Thomas demanded in the raspy rumble I adored, "Tell me what you want me to do when you come to me."

"I'd like to see your surprise and then play it by ear. I can't wait to hang out."

"Kick...," he growled.

"What? Oh." I giggled, cottoning on to his meaning. "Well, of course I want to do *that*."

"Tell. Me. What. You. Like."

I reached for my glass of water to quench a sudden dryness. "All of it, I guess."

"Everyone has preferences, Kick. Tell me yours now so it won't take so long to puzzle out. Then I'll spend the next few days dreaming about doing those things to you."

My knees would've folded if I hadn't already been sitting. I racked my brain to find honest, sexy, and seductive words. I hated being hopelessly out of practice. "It's been so long—"

"Kick..."

My breath disappeared, and I blurted, "You know how people talk about the pleasure of pain?"

"Yes."

"It doesn't work that way for me. Pain is and forever will be only pain. I've spent too much time living in—and with—it for it to be sensual."

"Alright. Go on," he drawled.

"With what?"

"What do you mean? Make me picture it."

"Seriously?" I sucked at phone sex. He laughed at my reaction. "Fine," I said defiantly, grateful he couldn't see my good old Celtic blush. "Biting is pain. Pulling is pain. Pinching is pain. I don't know."

"What brings you the greatest bliss?" Before I knew what was happening, Thomas pulled deep truths from me.

A memory from the early days of my treatments came to mind. "A while ago, I tried all the massage techniques out there, especially the aggressive type." I chuckled lightly. "I thought I needed to live by the scripture, 'I beat my body and make it my slave.' Only it didn't work."

"Did anything work?"

I would have told everything to his liquid-smooth voice. The sound brought back images of lying in his bed the morning after we'd been together.

The western sun rays penetrated my eyes, making me sink into the sofa for refuge until they passed. I focused on the light particles dancing overhead as I explained, "I tried this popular Rolfing expert. When she walked into the room, she declared I needed something different. She called it light-touch. Thomas, I relaxed like I couldn't remember ever having done before."

"Fascinating."

"Apparently, my body tightened in a protective response to rough contact. Her light strokes allowed blood to flow into my muscles because they released the tension—like a physical sigh. That's what I want."

"A physical sigh?"

"Yes."

"Hmm."

"Now what are you thinking?"

"I'm thinking about how I'm going to make you physically sigh."

I literally sighed in pleasure over the phone. Thomas's sexy burr meant I'd achieved my goal to lighten his spirits. "Am I helping your mood?"

"I need to go up to my room," he muttered. "You?"

"It's plenty warm in here. Did I say enough?"

"You're killing me."

"Sorry. Too much?"

"Stop apologizing. It's perfect. I knew the answer to my question would get heated, but I didn't expect to be this bothered. When you're back in my bed, I'll have to figure out what it will take to keep you there."

"You already know the answer."

I watched the light particles some more as I waited for Thomas.

"Working on it, baby."

"I know."

"Thank you once again for your honesty and vulnerability. I'm not worthy of it, but you're teaching me how to do better."

Again, the man threw Kryptonite words at me, turning me into a lusty mush ball. "I swear, if the kids weren't here, I'd hop in my car."

"My turn to apologize now. If honesty is what you need, I actually miss them too. I loved Thanksgiving, Kick. All of it."

"Keep letting me in and you can have it."

Thomas shifted again. This time I heard the creaking of floorboards. "I'll figure out a way. I promise."

I stood, too, and watched out the picture window. I loved his new determined inflection. Thrilling to think it was for me. "You know, I'm beginning to believe you. The kids are due back soon though."

"Nice hint." He chuckled again, and it pleased me to hear him continue to do it. "Will you think of me throughout the day?"

I laughed at the challenge. "Yes, and your smooth, sexy accent too. It might make me miss you more."

"Think of me imagining you."

Careful, Kick, you're about to leap off the cliff. Defensiveness seeped into my thoughts as fear of his other side unfairly crept in. I'd been burned harder than I had admitted, but he deserved his chance at forgiveness too.

"Since you ask nicely, I will."

"Yours is the only face I see when I close my eyes lately."

"Careful, Thomas. We're keeping it casual and in the present, right?"

"Yes," he drawled. "We are."

"I don't want to scare you anymore."

"Don't worry about me."

"Thomas, what you said a second ago… Do you mean you've… pleasured yourself… thinking about me?"

He cleared his throat and teased. "I do believe I have, Kick."

A wide grin spread across my face, and I made an unladylike —definitely not sexy—sound. "Awesome." Pride tickled my insecure inner girl.

"Did you just chortle?"

"Is that what that was?"

"You're proud of yourself."

"Maybe? It's a new concept for me."

"Kick…" The liquid honey way he drew out my name almost set off an orgasm. The man should've been in radio. Before Thomas could finish his thought, another muffled voice traveled through the phone.

"Be right there, Joe." He turned his attention back to me. "Been summoned, baby."

"I hope my kids stay as close as you three. Your parents would be proud."

"Thanks. We haven't always been, but we're working on it." Thomas's words caught, and he cleared his throat. "Knowing y'all, the McKenna kids will always get along."

I scoffed. "Hell, I've already broken up a fight between the boys and negotiated the oddest of music compromises between the boys and Rachel."

"Tell me all about it when I see you," he said, laughing. Then his tone turned serious again. "Thanks for cheering me up."

"I'm so glad it worked."

"You know it did. I'll be pestered about my perma-grin, but it's worth it. Have yourself a merry little Christmas, baby."

"You too, Thomas," I whispered. I wished I could keep him on the line forever.

DELIRIOUS

KICK

I parked in the circular drive at Thomas's farmhouse, pulled my suitcase and some bags from the trunk, and followed the path to the side door. My feet practically floated above the pavers. In a few seconds, those weeks apart would be nothing more than a memory. I worked hard to stay in the moment and cherish the good without expectations for more.

Thankfully, Deana had been a godsend when I told her about taking more time off. "Are you kidding me?" she had said. "Go get yourself some of his man-meat right now, shug." Of course, Thomas had still been in Virginia. So she volunteered to cover everything over New Year's with the promise that I feast myself on "the professor's prime rib until you can't walk straight." Calling her Thomas's biggest fan would be an understatement. As a thank-you to Dee and the staff, I declared New Year's Eve and Day additional vacation days. We all deserved it.

Thomas opened the door as my foot hit the steps on the small porch. When he pulled me into his arms, it felt like home.

Without ever completely letting me go, he deftly discarded my bags and walked us into the kitchen before hanging on some more.

I could've spent the next three days right there, doing nothing else. Okay, maybe not, but his presence, his woodsy scent, and his heartbeat had enough power to sustain me. The rest added up to dessert—the best kind.

Thomas tucked his nose in my hair and inhaled deeply. It was pulled loosely into a scrunchy, and several pieces had fallen out in front. He peppered light kisses down my neck, back up, and along my jaw, warming me up. It didn't help that I had worn my heavy winter jacket. Straight-line winds had dramatically announced a cold front in the morning. Right then, one gust shook the kitchen window, but my ski-weight coat made me sweat.

"Thomas?"

"Hmm?"

"I'm getting hot."

"God, baby, me too."

I laughed at him, off in his own lustful world. "Can I have a moment to take off my coat?"

He paused his veneration long enough for me to slip out of it and hang it in the mudroom. I turned around to find him staring at me. The butterflies in my stomach took flight, only they were not the kind to fly because of anxiety. These were the good kind, the happy kind, like being a teenager with my first lover again.

"Well? What?"

A warm smile filled his face as he extended his hand. "Come."

I glided with him as if caught in a trance, around the kitchen island, to find he'd been in the middle of preparing our meal. "You were fixing lunch. What can I do to help?"

He moved toward me and said, "Just this." Then he leaned down and kissed me with all the emotions we'd built up through the numerous texts and phone calls over the past week. The softness of Thomas's lips, his tongue, and his citrusy, sandalwood, *him* turned me to liquid by the time we came up for breath.

I placed my hand on his cheek and said, "You can kiss me anytime. Now what?"

"Sit. Let me serve you."

The idea excited me, but I was too familiar with the consequences of throwing culinary caution to the wind and didn't want our time together to end after another awkward start. Sure, he'd managed successful takeout and the sous-chef time at Thanksgiving, but they weren't home cooking. Most people didn't understand the details and substitutions of eating my way. It seemed cruel to expect him to have it down already.

"Are you positive you don't want help?"

He kissed my temple and eased my concerns. "The soup and flatbread are from the gluten-free restaurant in Durham. Bacon crumbles are uncured. Hard-boiled eggs and nuts are organic. Rachel gave me the recipe for your salad dressing—which is fantastic, by the way. Now let me finish chopping the lettuce."

"Okay, okay." I raised my hands in surrender. "How about I get the plates and silverware?"

"Fabulous… after you read this." He wiped his hands on a towel, then handed me an envelope sitting on the island.

I looked at Thomas curiously, finding no clues as to the contents in his expression. I removed the papers, unfolding them.

"Medical papers. Yours?" My eyes lifted but only found his back. He'd washed his hands and was chopping up cucumbers. "What's this about?"

He looked over his shoulder. "You haven't been with anyone in years—except for me, of course." I blushed at the statement, feeling like an amateur even though I could have numbered off countless reasons why I'd lived my life the way I did. I also knew Thomas didn't intend for me to defend myself. He continued, "This is proof I'm clean too." He padded over and kissed my temple. "I can't remember the last time I didn't use a condom, and I haven't been as active as you think I have. Anyway, would it be alright to ditch the barrier? Just us?"

"But this means we would be exclusive and a bit more than casual."

"It better. Are you planning on seeing anyone else?" Thomas's face flashed with something like jealousy.

"No." I tucked one of those curls behind my ear. "Jaysus, I had to rework my schedule to be with you. When would I get time for another?" My voice quieted when he growled and I realized my blunder. "That's not what I mean… I don't want anyone else," I confessed. "I promise. I thought you wanted us to wait on making any big decisions."

Thomas tipped his head toward the papers. "This is what I want."

I slid my arms around him to let him know how much his declaration meant, and he kissed me again. "It's settled then?"

I nodded, too moved for words.

"Good. Now, would you set our places?" He pointed to the cabinet above the dishwasher and the drawer next to it.

I spotted a napkin holder nearby and set plates for two on the far end of the island. I poured myself a glass of water and moved closer to Thomas to watch him work. I hopped up on the counter, intending to chat with him and sip my drink. I sat with my hands on the edge, my head hanging down as I stretched my neck, working out kinks from nerves and the previous long days. Whether for good reasons or bad, any form of jitters had a way of locking up my neck muscles. I was forever taking moments to stretch this or that limb to keep pain at bay.

The chopping sound stopped, and I looked up to see Thomas staring at me, his eyes dark and heated. I raised my eyebrows in inquiry.

"What are you doing?" he asked, almost sounding incredulous.

A blush bloomed across my face and chest as I looked around. "I didn't feel like moving a stool over here. I-I hopped up on the counter to be close to you and to speak with you while you work. I—"

He took a step toward me like a predatory animal. "Not what I meant. You don't know, do you?"

"What?"

"I caught your movements out of the corner of my eye, turned around, and you were writhing like a cat on a sunny patio. Then the way you bent over—Kick, I can practically see down to your navel. It's like personal porn. You really don't know?"

Suddenly parched, I took a sip of water and shook my head.

He stepped into me and slid his hands, open-fingered, into my hair at the base of my skull. Pulling my mouth to his, he took my lips with a wonderful, claiming force.

He remembered not to tangle his hand in my curls. He listened and touched my hair the way I liked it. He gave me his respect and vulnerability when he took what only I could give him. This might be heaven.

"You're wearing the sweater I asked you to and a skirt. Your hair... it looks exactly how I pictured it. Don't know if I can finish making lunch. I had planned to make sure you had enough energy for later, but... would you mind if later is now?" As I answered with a shake of my head and a devilish grin, Thomas fingered the bow at the waist of my wrap sweater. "May I?"

My head buzzed with desire for this man. When our eyes met, cohesive thoughts flew out the window. All I knew was lust and heat. I nodded, barely cognizant of the meaning of the gesture. He gently pulled my glasses off and set them out of the way. Then he tugged on the bow, watching it easily slide open. The two sweater halves fell away, revealing a lavender satin bra, chosen for the way it showcased my cleavage. My lids fell to half-mast, overwhelmed by the knowledge Thomas would soon see all of me. This wouldn't be like our first time in near pitch-black.

On a sharp inhale, he gently ran his fingertips down my neck, pausing at my collarbone, then continuing down the valley between my breasts. The lightness in his touch caused me to sway as if he were playing an instrument.

"What are you thinking?"

I kept my eyes closed and smiled. "The song 'Delirious' started playing in my head. I guess I was dancing to it as you touched me."

"Do you do that a lot?"

"Walk around with a personal soundtrack in my mind? All the time."

He laughed and resumed delicately stroking the edges of my bra cups. "Is this what you want? From our phone call?"

"You remembered."

"Have thought about little else. Is this what you meant?"

I flashed him my sassy grin again and answered, "It's a start."

He undid the front fastener, and the cups fell away. His hands swept over each breast and held the weight of them from underneath. We both gasped at his touch.

"This is even better." I breathed, watching his response, pleased when his head bowed in appreciation. My skin prickled with the need to be touched everywhere.

Thomas nuzzled into my cleavage, startling me when he inhaled audibly and moaned in delight. Who knew breasts actually heaved? I'd read about it, often mocking words. I chuckled in embarrassment, realizing what I'd done. Then he licked down the center and under my left side, eliciting a moan from me, and all thoughts of foolishness vanished.

"This is the *best* start." I ran my hands along his biceps, getting the feel of my own new landscape.

"Christ, the way you respond to me—"

"Shut up," I countered.

Thomas's smile pressed into my skin as he repeated his ministrations on my right breast. His tongue continued laving the areola, then flicked rapidly over my nipple. My head dropped back as my toes curled. I leaned forward, propping myself with my hands near my hips. It wasn't a conscious move, but it had the effect of shoving my nipple even farther into his mouth. I shifted on the counter as my body came alive from his sucks and flicks. I was wet and coming undone. Thomas unlocked my body with his touch, and I couldn't wait to fly.

He released me with a small pop and took a step back. "Damn," he said, his eyes glazed as if he were in a trance. "I imagined you upstairs again, but I need more now." He took hold of my ankle, sliding down the zipper on my boot before removing it, then the other.

He picked up one of the hard-boiled egg halves and said, "You'll need energy. Eat." I closed my lips and held the egg with my tongue while sucking his fingers as they slid out, then chewed the egg, a slight grin on my face.

Thomas tsked. "Minx." He put the salad bowl in the refrigerator and moved back to me. Taking hold of my hand, he eased me off the counter in front of him and spun me around. The sweater slid off my shoulders, then my bra, leaving only my butterfly necklace and my skirt on, but I could tell where this was going.

Instead of spinning me again, he pulled me against his body with one hand wrapped around my waist. My back melded to his front. His other hand ran up my neck, causing my head to tip and give him easier access as he kissed and sucked, traveling down one side, shifting my jaw, and back up behind my ear.

"It pleases me how much you respond," he whispered. "What if I add more?"

Thomas bent enough to gather my skirt with his free hand and explored my thighs with his fingertips while the other hand moved up from my waist to my breasts once again. He paused long enough to say, "I promise not to pinch, but you said massage was good, right?"

I answered with a long moan and a slight buckle of my knees because his fingers found the apex of my thighs at the same time he spoke. "That's it, baby. *This* is a proper start."

Thomas kicked open a lower cabinet door, lifted my knee and placed it on the shelf edge. Then his fingers slid up into me, and we both purred. On an upstroke, I jolted as if sparked and bucked up on his erection. He stopped his movements and, through heavy breaths, said, "Damn, lady. If we don't move upstairs, we're both going to come in this kitchen."

"Would it be so bad?" I asked, my tone wispy.

"Yes. Said I dream of you in my bed. It's happening. But…" His fingers traveled back up to my neck. "Before we head up, I want to"—he unclasped the necklace and placed it on the counter—"find something." He unzipped my skirt and let it fall to the floor. His hand immediately moved to my right hip where I had a Celtic butterfly tattoo in the same design as the necklace. They were identical to the one on my jean jacket, only much smaller. "There it is," he declared.

I bit my lip to keep from laughing. "Been wondering, have you?"

"Didn't get to see it in the dark before." Rubbing circles over it with his thumb, then tracing the lines of the interlaced design. "Don't hide it anymore." He bent and kissed it. "I'm getting you a bikini to show it off. My butterfly."

Hell, I hadn't worn a two-piece in, maybe ever, but Thomas made me feel like I could do anything. Knowing he understood how the art symbolized the way events can change us so fully we become completely different people—like a new species—meant the world too.

He cupped my ankles, sending a shiver up my spine, and ran his hands up my legs, under my ass—in a similar way he'd done with my breasts.

"You're stunning, Kick," he said low and reverently.

What a humbling thing to hear. After years of working out and yoga practice, I knew how to maximize my posture to appear as svelte as possible. Add in extremely clean eating, and I knew my skin looked good for my age. It was still hard to believe his words. The exact number of pounds I'd yet to lose to make the desired BMI raced through my mind.

I chased the doubt away by turning my attention back to Thomas. I spun around and smiled. "I appear to be at a disadvantage."

"How so?" His grin said he knew my meaning but teased anyway. "You hold all the cards, baby."

I moved my finger up and down. "Still… you're still fully dressed."

He shrugged his shoulders. "It makes me want to worship you more." His grin grew as his eyebrow arched. "My feet are bare."

I crossed my arms to feign prickliness. It only managed to prop up my breasts, making his eyes blink as they stared.

"They are handsome feet, but you should, you know. Tit-for-tat."

"Since you have all the tit—" He tweaked one of my nipples and I flinched. "Dammit. Sorry."

"It's okay," I said, moved by how much my comments about pain were part of his plans.

"And you have the tat—"

"Fine. I'll do it." I cut him off and unbuttoned his top button on one of the plaids I'd bought him while he backed us out of the kitchen. His shirt finally came off in the upstairs hallway, thanks to being out of practice with cuffs and his continuous chuckles. Thomas Harrison turned out to be very ticklish.

I paused to appreciate his body. My eyes couldn't get enough. He was blessed with a lean build, defined waist and shoulders. Athletic without being overly bulky. My hand glided up his chiseled abs and across a deep scar on his left bicep. The muscle underneath flexed as I traced it with my finger. "I didn't notice this before. What happened?" Of course, it had been a crazy day and dark night when we were first together. Then again, the man had a way of distracting me.

He gritted out, "A fight." He seemed embarrassed by it. I

bowed my head, acknowledging his discomfort, and leaned in to kiss it, trying to communicate that it didn't matter. It didn't look like any kind of fight scar I'd ever seen. There were too many jagged lines. But it wasn't like I hung out with dangerous men either.

"Perfect." The word escaped my lips, and I blushed when Thomas's eyebrow lifted, first in confusion, then amusement. I walked around him, keeping my fingertips in constant contact with his toned skin, and explained, "You've been bulkier. In the past."

"True." He sounded surprised by my comment. "Had more free time a while back and competed occasionally. How'd you know?"

"You remind me of a professional athlete in the off-season."

"Sounds bad," he nervously murmured.

"Not at all." I brushed my hands across his back muscles as I spoke. "You're fit. Strong. Beautiful. It's a warrior's build. It's beautiful, if you don't mind the descriptive."

He chuckled. "From you? It's giving me a big head."

"Stop. Never." I laughed at him and placed my hands on his pecs, brushing his nipples with my thumbs. Then I leaned in and flicked them with my tongue, receiving a deep sigh in response. "You're going to be fun to play with too."

"Dammit." He swooped me up into his arms and carried me down the hall into his bedroom, then let me shut the door with my feet while I giggled. The Virginia boy in him read loud and clear in his sanctum. A handmade early-American—not the cheap, seventies chain-store kind—four-poster bed with a navy quilt anchored the center of the wall to the left of the door. Farther down, in front of a window, he had a seating area. I made out the small paintings of what looked like an eighteenth-century boy and girl sitting on the side table. A huge, braided rug covered the hardwood floors and framed the bed. I didn't remember it being there in October and wondered if he bought it to keep the bed from skipping across the room again.

He placed me on my feet and aggressively kissed me, sweeping his tongue into my mouth as I fumbled with the top button on his jeans. He took over, and since they were button-fly jeans, opened the two sides with a well-practiced flick of his wrist. They dropped to the floor, and he smoothly stepped out of them. *Jaysus.* The man had been deliciously commando this whole time. I ran my tongue over my bottom lip at the sight of his stunning, erect penis.

Our gazes met and held. Over the past weeks, moments from my drugged stupor had been trickling back to me. The biggest chunk of returned memory revolved around what happened in the garage. I figured it had to do with my feeling safe in Thomas's care. Now he stood before me and looked ready to give me all the things I had demanded of him then. Like he wanted extraordinary too.

While my heart rejoiced, my head jumped in the way with words like *This shouldn't be*. I couldn't pretend casual would ever be enough. I wanted more. I wanted all the tomorrows. With him. But how many more did he have compared to me? This beautiful man finally stood before me without walls, perfectly comfortable in his own skin in a way I only dreamed of. His deep stare took me in and made my heart sink. He deserved better. The most handsome smile spread across his face. I turned toward the door. And ran.

30

ARMS OF A WOMAN

THOMAS

Seeing Kick standing in his bedroom, ready to be his, overwhelmed Thomas as a gasp escaped his throat. Yeah, he'd made the right decision. She was worth the extra whatever it took to protect her. He would hide her to keep her safe if he had to.

Any amount of time with her would be precious. His body vibrated at the thought of spending more time together, so much so his cock danced on its own. More than anything, he wanted to jump off the cliff with her, like she'd spoken of in the parking garage. He smiled in anticipation as Kick's eyelids descended, perusing his body with lust. Thomas straightened to his full height, fists on his hips, and gave her a show. He couldn't help it.

In a blink, she turned and bolted. Her spunk thrilled him, and it excited him even more to learn she liked a little naughty in her play. Thomas laughed as he chased her. His hands wrapped around her waist in three steps.

"Nothing like a good game of chase." He set Kick down and

spun her around, but the newfound terror in her eyes told him she wasn't playing. Her visage shocked him out of his glee-filled stupor. Fortunately, they were close to the bed, and it caught him behind the knees before he fell on his ass. Thomas kept his hands around Kick so she wouldn't get away as he realized she was desperate to do so. She had the wild look of a prey animal about to be killed when he had been expecting a sultry seductress. Then her tears welled up, breaking his heart. He reached for a curl to tuck behind her ear and pulled her between his knees.

"Please. What could possibly be wrong? Is the guilt back? There's no—"

"I-I... I'm no match. Shit." She exhaled hard and met his eyes. "I want to be what I was the last time I stood in front of a man for the first time. I didn't know how perfect I was then."

"Some things don't change." He sighed, gently brushing away the tear with his thumb.

Her shoulders fell. "I'm serious. Everything's changed. It's one thing to go through it with someone who remembers the days before, but you only get the after. My body's been through hell since then."

Thomas couldn't believe his ears. He stared at her, shocked, trying hard to school his features.

"Come on," she pleaded. "I'm sure none of the women you've been with were as scarred and sagging as I am." Kick put her hands on his shoulders. "You're in your prime and deserve a woman who's in the same place. I might look younger than my age now, but it's a race against time. From here on, the best I can hope for is a compliment ending with the words *for your age*."

Thomas's whole body acknowledged the mood change as he sighed. He brought his other hand to Kick's cheek. He wanted to be offended by her lack of faith in him but thought better of it when he realized she shared her feelings about *her* perceived inadequacies, not his.

"Kick..." Thomas set his hands at her waist but didn't let

himself caress her or move at all. He simply craved the contact. "You're the blessing I didn't dare ask for. No other woman has been that for me. I want you for you, not for anything you can do for me. And I don't see flaws. I only see a tempting wonderland I want to explore."

At his words, Kick shook her head sadly. "The thing is, I adore you. I could love you. Hell, I probably love you already. Sorry for throwing it out there, but it's my truth and you probably should know it." She sighed. "To me, it means your happiness is more important than the love I feel. You may not think you want a family now, but what about a month from now? A year? You could still be reeling from the death of your wife."

Thomas let his head drop while he figured out his answer. "How can I explain this?" He lifted his chin and allowed himself to stroke her forearms lightly. It let him find the honesty he'd held inside for as long as he could remember but never confessed. "Your infertility was one of the things that attracted me to you in the beginning." Kick opened her mouth, and he raised a finger. "Hear me out. Alicia died having our daughter. After the funeral, I made a vow never to impregnate another woman. Ever. My head knows I didn't kill her, but my heart still struggles with acceptance."

She nearly collapsed into him. "Jaysus, Thomas. I'm such an idiot. And the child?"

He swallowed and sat back. "She's dead too."

Kick's groan sounded like a lament, so he changed the topic immediately. Nothing was going to ruin this day, his day, *their* day. Especially not his past heartaches.

"After how hard we fought to get here, tell me why you still thought I wouldn't want you?"

"I don't know." Kick kept her head down.

"Can I tell you another secret?" Thomas asked, then settled her into his lap. His cock twitched, begging for attention, but it could wait. It knew how to wait.

"You can tell me anything."

He let out a cleansing breath and mentally jumped. "About the other thing you said—I'm relieved you might have fallen for me."

"Why?"

Thomas studied Kick as he caressed her cheek. Her stunning green eyes still held a shimmer like diamonds. How could she doubt herself? "The truth is, I already know I love you."

Her hands rose to her mouth and shook. Thomas gently massaged the back of her neck. *"Je t'adore aussi."*

She clicked her tongue. "Sure but—"

"I. Love. You. I have since the first night, when I drove you home. Hell, you grabbed my heart by the way you walked across the parking lot in your cowboy boots and short shorts."

Thomas's fingers slid down Kick's arms as he let his words sink in. He gently brushed the curls off her shoulder and kissed her there. "I have an idea." He gestured for her to stand facing him. "Present yourself like the gift you are." He pointed at her, adding in his professor's face. "Mean it too. Be the woman I love, Kathleen Allen McKenna."

She answered with a tight nod and a lift to the corner of her mouth. Then she uncrossed her arms, revealing her beautiful body. She let her shoulders fall back and held her head high. Kick did him in. How could she ever doubt herself?

"Believe in this confident, enchanting woman. It's how I've always seen you anyway." He reached out and let his fingertips travel over Kick's body again, this time for her benefit.

She swallowed hard as her eyes tracked his movements. "Ev-everyone says I'm a badass, but at my core, I'm afraid I'll end up disappointing you."

Thomas wanted to kick his own ass. This had to be about their breakup. "I'm such a fool. Don't ever listen to a negative word I say, especially if it's regarding you."

"But—"

Thomas palmed her breasts, her belly, her mound, anywhere

his reach would allow. "I know who you are and what you are, baby. Possibly more than you do. You'll let me love you now for it."

Thomas pulled her mouth to his, licking at her lips, asking her permission to let him in. Kick settled into him as her mouth opened and her tongue danced with his.

Thomas lay back on his bed, stretching Kick out on top of him. He breathed deeply, enjoying the vanilla-and-lavender scent surrounding her, grateful he had her back so quickly. With him, where she belonged. His hands floated along her sides, then back up and under the swell of her breasts. Kick's body responded in kind as she slowly writhed against him. He shifted to the center of the bed and turned to his side.

"I want to savor you this time. We can do quickies later. A lot of quickies." He tilted his head to the side to catch her eyes. "Do you trust me?"

Kick gave him the confident, radiant smile he lived for. "Definitely."

"Let me take my time and take care of you."

"Please."

Thomas stretched her right arm over her head and placed it under the bottom of the headboard. "Don't let go until I say so."

"Again?" She teased as she laughed. "This is your thing, eh?"

"You're my thing." Thomas shifted and removed a feather from his nightstand. He quickly opened his playlist on the Angel system. He would've changed tack if Kick hadn't had a sweet smile on her face.

Her breathy voice went straight to his cock. "I'm starting to believe you."

He paused, keeping the feather behind his back. "Starting to? Then you'll stay right here until you absolutely believe me. Now hush." He shifted alongside Kick. "I have a surprise."

"Thomas...," she drew out in a warning tone.

"Time to feel, Kick. Let my actions tell you how much you

mean to me." His gaze traveled along her stretched-out body as he took in the visual feast that was her curves. Having her like this with only occasional flashes of lightning before hadn't done her body justice. Turned out, she wasn't an elf queen after all. From here on out, Thomas would think of her as his goddess. He planned to worship her, didn't he? He decided they would stay naked all weekend. A devilish grin spread across his face as he prepared to make her come until she cried for mercy. "Eyes open or closed. It doesn't matter. Just tell me what you like."

31

IT HAD TO BE YOU

KICK

I let my lids fall, shutting down one of my senses to heighten the others. My heart jumped when "It Had to Be You" started playing. Thomas had remembered my love for Cole Porter. Who doesn't fall for a guy who listens?

He placed a soft kiss on the spot behind my ear, like it was an On button to my pussy, revving my motor and making me hum. I thought he'd pick up where we left off downstairs, but a tickling sensation moved over the spots he kissed, and a smile spread across my face.

"A feather? The light touch."

"Like it?"

I muttered incoherently, caught in a blissful haze, before managing a raspy, "Very much, thank you."

He chuckled in his deep, dreamy baritone, now heavier with lust. "So polite. What will it take to make you feisty again?"

I sighed at the reminder of my pent-up need. "Teasing. Get to business, buster." I bit my lip as the feather found a ticklish spot.

"There she is. How's this?" After spending some time running it underneath my breasts, he let the feather circle my nipples. Goose bumps traveled over my skin, and I forgot all about my foolish insecurities.

"It's incredible." I opened my eyes and caught his playful wink as he decided where to go next. The headiness of watching him did more to turn me on than a lack of sight had. Wetness gathered between my legs as I scissored my feet and the pressure began to build.

He dropped his lips to my breast again and flicked his tongue over the tip of my nipple. Is it possible to become audibly insane? I knew I made no sense. I almost came from that alone.

"You have gorgeous tits, baby."

In my brain-shorting euphoria, I blurted out, "I wished they were functional again. For you."

"What?" Thomas stilled, looking at me with a questioning curiosity.

"I wish I could give you the... taste of them."

Thomas tipped his head back. "You're trying to slay me." He stretched over me and slid his fingers between my folds, then dipped them into me, rotating two fingers to make sure I was ready. His eyes moved down to look at his hand, then back to my face. "How wet you are for me. I'm stunned."

His fingertip grazed the scars occupying the area formerly known as my G-spot, and I bucked into him, panting and gripping his fingers as they slid out. The area had changed, but it wasn't dead. When body parts rearrange and mishaps settle in for the long-term, nerves have a way of finding new life in different places.

The feather took a path down my sides, which were only mildly ticklish, and circled my belly. Thomas paused and peppered light, reverent kisses over my scars. He nuzzled below my navel, saying, "This is sacred and beautiful." Then he kissed and nipped at my stomach, claiming me as his woman. And he was my man. It reminded me I was more than a mother of three. His tongue circled my navel, and I swear my body jolted from an electrical hum.

"How the hell do you do that?"

Thomas responded with a happy, teasing chuckle from his throat. He shifted to his knees between my legs and ran his hands along my thighs. The feather strokes were quick here and kept true to his other light touches. Each upstroke went higher until it danced over my core, his fingers following, grazing the already sensitive folds eager for him.

He paused, and I peered down the length of my body at him to see what caused him to stop. The sight of him between my legs, his head bent, caused me to roll my hips, edging again. He blew on my clit and murmured, "Like one of my orchids."

"Please—" My pants increased when he flicked his tongue over my clit. I vaguely recalled the music changing to one of my favorite Norah Jones songs as I let my mind float away. I was swept up in the sensations, the romantic melody, and his earthy scent on the sheets. The singer was right about how all along I'd been waiting for this man to turn me on. When his fingers twisted and massaged my already sensitive inner walls, I began the climb to release.

"So damn responsive," Thomas praised, rubbing his stubbly chin along the sensitive flesh of my inner thighs. "Such a vixen." He returned his mouth to my clit and continued sucking and twisting his fingers, hitting all the nerves in my pussy he could find.

My back arched as my walls clenched and released around his fingers until there was a sensation of riding on the top of a tsunami of pleasure, waiting for the wave to crash over and through me, praying I had the strength to ride it out. It started in my toes and made its way up my legs until it shattered my core.

A lifetime existed in this moment, hoping it never ended. I growled as I twisted with delight—the tsunami taking my whole body along for the ride. I grew louder with each crest and briefly wondered if the French were right about death by orgasm. At least it'd be glorious. And there was no end to this pleasure. "Okay… okay," I pleaded.

"More," Thomas insisted, lightening his touch on now too-sensitive tissue.

As if truly electrified, several more rippled through me while triumph filled his features. As his fingers danced across my skin, I surrendered and moaned with each new touch.

He bent over me, kissed the tip of my ear, and said, "Now we can go together."

Out of breath, I gasped, "More?"

He chuckled. "With you? Always."

I continued to pant. "I don't know yet."

"Let's try something." Thomas turned me to my side and curled behind me. He lifted my top leg and pulled me onto him with a victorious purr of his own. I pushed back and felt his chest rumble in pleasure. "Nice and easy," he encouraged, rocking slowly into me.

He reached around me. One hand went underneath, squeezing my breast while the other crossed my hip and vibrated my clit. To my surprise, it worked. My body reawakened, and I craved more, hoping it would never stop. He pulled out as I squeezed, then slammed in hard. The friction from the angle set me off again as I cried out his name.

"Yes, baby. With me." He slammed up another time and pinched my nipple and that was it. I threw my head back, overwhelmed by the fervor of climaxing again. This one felt different from the first. It washed over and in me, filling my soul the way Thomas filled my body.

He nosed my hair away from my neck and placed deep kisses on my shoulder. He grunted, "This is me loving you. This. Is. Love." Then he lost himself to his own orgasm.

Somehow we did it. We'd jumped. He wouldn't be my friend

and sometime lover, but my new love. Right then the music changed to Tony Bennett's version of "Fly Me to the Moon," such a perfect description of what we'd done and of what I hoped we could be.

Breathless, Thomas stilled and squeezed me, humming into my neck. We extended our orgasmic fog with quick pulses for as long as possible. I sang quietly to the song as I reached behind me and caressed his strong jaw. I turned to face him and swore his blissed-out face made him glow like an angel. My fingers tingled with a pleasant, warm buzz as they continued tracing his cheeks. Touching him did that for me. I thought he was falling asleep, but his mouth lifted into a wide grin as I sang the last words of the song, "I… love… you."

When he opened his eyes, dark with lust, I saw the love Thomas had professed in them. His breathing slowed while small beads of sweat escaped from his hairline. He looked exactly like my future.

3 2

PRAISE YOU

THOMAS

*D*espite their deliberately slow lovemaking, he was spent, physically and emotionally. This had been what he'd missed for as long as he could remember. In his dreams, he'd hoped their chemistry equated with magic, but the reality shot it to the moon. In his contented state, with a remarkable woman wrapped around him, Thomas dozed.

He jolted awake during one of those falling dreams. Kick still lay alongside him, resting her head in her hand, stroking the feather up and down his stomach.

"How long was I out?"

"Only ten minutes." She bent and kissed his chest, then his jaw. He turned his head to meet her lips. It wouldn't take long for him to go again, but knowing how long it had been for Kick, Thomas didn't want to hurt her. Besides, he still had to feed her. But first he had questions.

"That was amazing. Primal." Kick turned her beautiful hazel eyes to him. "I swear, I thought the earth quaked." She giggled and absently ran her fingernails over his pecs. "Did you know you look angelic when you come?"

"Ah, no?"

She looked back up and gave him a shy smile. "I believe you now, Thomas."

"Thank God. If that was your version of a fuck-buddy romp, I don't think I'd survive more."

She swatted Thomas on the shoulder as he laughed hard, then watched her face growing serious.

In a quiet voice, she said, "I thought I could be fuck buddies with you, but I never could."

He lifted her free hand and kissed it. "We're not." He sat upright and said, "Before we move on to the next thing, tell me about your freak-out. Let's put it permanently behind us."

"Oh." A deep blush spread across Kick's chest as her shoulders fell. She stretched her hands in Thomas's direction. "Well... look at you."

"Alright." He hopped out of bed and stood before her. Planting his hands on his hips, he looked down at himself and shrugged.

"Thomas... you're perfect."

"Thank you. Still don't see a problem." Kick's frustrated growl delighted him, though he knew it shouldn't.

She rose to her knees and faced off with him. Thomas's cock woke back up at the sight. "Not only am I *not* perfect, I'm a physical mess."

His brow drew up in honest confusion. "Where?"

She held her breasts, and he almost groaned. "My boobs are asymmetrical."

Thomas grabbed his balls. "So is my nut sac." He tilted his head to the side. "Are you going to leave me now?"

"Of course not." Kick's words encouraged him, but her frown didn't.

Thomas held up a finger, then bolted for the closet. This conversation—and what he had planned next—called for robes.

He grabbed his summer and winter ones, ran back to the bed, and placed the thick one around Kick's shoulders. He slipped into the lightweight robe and sat on the bed next to her. His gaze tipped to his semihard cock.

"Isn't the evidence of what you do to me enough to prove there's nothing to worry about?"

She leaned into his shoulder as she stared out the window and answered, "The way you turned cold when you broke up with me... Are you sure it had nothing to do with disappointment in me?"

Thomas raked his hands through his hair. "I'm an asshole." He reached around Kick and pulled her tight to him. "It was all about this thing I've been struggling with. You've only ever been a miracle."

"The thing with your research and Bordeaux?"

"Yes." After the weekend, he would definitely call Alaric. He didn't agree with everything Banger and Tess had directed. Once he informed *Grand-père* of his plans—not ask—he would come clean with Kick. He kissed her temple and said, "No more fears about me leaving, alright?"

"I'm still getting used to this, but okay." She tipped her head back and smiled. "You make me feel good enough. I can go from there."

Thomas smacked her thigh. "Damn. I'm aiming for perfect." He jumped up and lifted a finger. "Hold on a sec." He disappeared back into his closet to the wrapped boxes he'd left there. He grabbed a big one and left another small one.

He pulled one chair close to the bed and sat across from Kick. "When I knew I needed you back, I called Deana to see if I still had a shot." Thomas hung his head and chuckled. "She told me she knew exactly what you wanted." He presented the large box to her and sheepishly grinned. "This."

She carefully undid the bow and ran her finger through the taped seams, trying not to rip the pretty paper. She opened the box and laughed as she lifted a Lord University letterman-style jacket. Kick turned it around and saw the "Harrison" across the back. "Aww." She held it to her chest. "I told Dee I missed the days when a boy would give a girl his varsity jacket to ask her to go steady."

He nodded. "She told me about your talk. Took a bit of work to pull it off so quickly. Fortunately, I did a favor for a coach last year. He hooked me up." He rubbed his chin. "Would you really wear it?"

Kick tipped her head back in an angelic laugh. "You bet your ass."

Thomas felt his smile stretch across his face. *Christ*, he was a goner. Soon he'd get to the tricky part when he gave Kick the small package. But it had to wait. Thomas had a special moment in mind to give it to her. "Happy New Year's Eve-Eve." He kissed her deeply and declared, "We need to eat."

"Yes, we do. After I clean up." Kick stood, smiled when she caught Thomas staring at her fabulous ass, and sashayed into the bathroom. The confident vixen had returned. His first goal had been accomplished.

AFTER THEY FILLED UP ON FOOD, KICK REACHED INTO ONE OF THE shopping bags she had brought and pulled out a present for Thomas. She removed his place setting and set the box on the island.

"Happy New Year's Eve-Eve, sweetheart. This is your first present."

He lifted an eyebrow and smirked. "The first?"

"The other one was too heavy. I barely heaved it into my trunk and couldn't get the right leverage on it to take it out."

Kick fidgeted from foot to foot, piquing Thomas's curiosity. He ripped into the paper with gusto. On the counter sat a polished hickory box, a work of art on its own. He lifted the lid and found a Shinola Runwell Chronograph watch with a blue face and a dark brown band.

"It's gorgeous, baby." He held it up and examined it from every angle.

"It reminded me of your eyes," she said shyly. "I also wanted to give you something from Detroit—my original hometown."

"I remember," he whispered as he smiled down at her. Sometime soon he'd plan a trip there so Kick could show him all her favorite places.

These moments of proof of Kick's feelings before this weekend let Thomas know he'd done the right thing in fighting for her. Making her a priority the first time had been an emotional decision done out of fear. This time he let himself jump with the clearest of intentions and would do whatever it took to keep Kick happy as well as safe. He couldn't wait to give her the last present.

He kissed her on the cheek and clipped the watch around his wrist. "It'll track our time together." Funny, Thomas had been planning to buy a watch to wean himself off his phone.

She answered with a slight nod. "So, how are we supposed to get your other present? The wind is still strong, and the temperature is dropping."

"I'll bring it in after we dress. I still have two surprises to show you while there's daylight, and we'll have to leave the house for them."

They dressed quickly, as Thomas's interest in his other present grew.

Once outside, she popped the lid to reveal another, much larger, box from Shinola. He carried it into the house.

"Before you set it down," she said, "let's take it into your music room. That's a hint, by the way."

"Music, huh?" Thomas raised his eyebrows out of curiosity and took it into the downstairs office. The room was large enough to have one wall devoted to his instruments. An adjacent cabinet was command central for the Angel network, along with various components for amateur recording and mixing. He gingerly set the box down, snapped apart the tape from Kick's repacking job, and stared at what sat before him.

"Well, pull it out," she coaxed, antsy like a child.

He carefully extracted a Runwell turntable, speechless. Thomas wasn't a sucker for toys. In fact, he was picky about which new gadgets he indulged in. This piece was a work of art. When he looked at Kick, her tongue worried the inside of her cheek and her brow furrowed.

"Is it stupid?"

He whispered in awe, "It's amazing." Thomas cleared his throat. "Banger's going to be jealous as hell. He has the toy addiction."

"I liked the retro feel of the wood trim." She chuckled and said, "Liam saw it and thought he'd stumbled upon one of his presents. The poor boy almost had a coronary, which rebounded when I told him it was for you."

Thomas rested it on the coffee table since it would need to wait until he could clear a spot for it. It would make a fabulous focal point in the room. He stood and held his arms out. When Kick stepped into them, he engulfed her in a bear hug, lifting her off her toes, then set her down and nuzzled her neck.

"Your thoughtfulness and desire to see me happy humbles me, but having you here is the best present. It's what I've wanted most."

She stretched her chin and kissed a spot underneath his jaw. "I agree."

Thomas became distracted and held her for a few minutes until the clock over the door caught his attention. "Shit. It's getting late. He's going to be mad." He pulled Kick into the mudroom.

"Who's going to be mad?"

"One of your surprises."

"My surprise is a *he*?"

"Come on." Thomas held Kick's new coat out, then zipped her in it. "You'll see. Wear your hood up."

He wore an oilskin duster and matching hat.

"A drover coat?" she laughed. "Are we exploring the outback?"

"Sort of. It comes in handy on days like this."

"Do you have chaps to go with it?"

"Actually, yes." He ushered her out to the kitchen garden and down the back path.

"Hold on… Are you saying you've been to the Outback?"

Thomas shrugged. "Maybe."

She raised her hands. "How the hell many things have you done?"

He arched an eyebrow, mocking her, and answered in a falsetto, "A few."

Then he wrapped an arm around her as they walked the trail past the barn and around the west side of the pond. Grateful it was wide enough for them to travel side by side, he savored this new reality, aware it could end too soon.

"How long do you think an orgasm can last?" Kick's question saved him from falling into a thought funk. Her giggle piqued his curiosity. Her curls' attempts to burst from her hood were also a welcomed distraction.

"Want to run some experiments?"

She bumped Thomas's shoulder. "No, Professor. It feels…" She sighed and said in a rush, "It feels like aftershocks keep running through me. I don't remember this happening before. Then again, I can't remember the last time I had sex in the daytime either."

"No kidding?"

She twisted her lips in thought. "Yup, can't remember. The loud thing was pretty amazing too. I mean, with no one around it just… seemed to explode, but still."

Thomas crooked his elbow and pulled her into his chest with

a resonant growl. "You have no idea." A few silent minutes later after he replayed their romp on a loop in his mind, he said, "What was it you said to me the morning we met? You purr... you growl... but you don't prowl. Baby, you should've mentioned the roaring. I would have dropped to my knees on the spot." He thoroughly enjoyed watching Kick turn a delightful shade of pink.

She slugged him on the shoulder. "Don't remind me. It's embarrassing."

"No, darlin'. It's hot as hell. You should roar for me every day."

"I would love to." She sighed.

"Why do I hear a *but* in there?"

"Not a *but*." She slowed and shrugged. "We haven't talked about what happens after this. Will we still struggle to schedule our time together?"

"Come over here." This would be the perfect time to give Kick her last gift. He walked her to an old, southern live oak tree sitting about fifty yards from the path. The trunk was wide enough to provide full shade and shelter. This was the center of the original plantation. Now, it marked the four corners of the divided land. The view from here was incredible. Situated on a small clearing on top of a hill, they had sight lines to Thomas's house in one direction and the farms in the other three.

Thomas was certain this tree was an offspring of the grand live oak in the center of town. At this point, it was an elderly "lady" in its own right. *She* had obviously been around when the original settlers broke ground. Based on the number of initials carved into the tree, this had been a favorite spot for many lovers. Some carvings looked to be over a hundred years old.

"How do I picture us from now on?" He entwined their fingers, Kick's sweet face consumed his thoughts, and the words came from the place in his soul she'd unlocked.

"Let me be your Atlas, darlin'. Let me hold you up as you direct your world. I'd say loved ones, but it's obvious how you adopt strangers who walk into your life and make them your own." Thomas laughed and shook his head, having a hard time believing this could be true. "Counting myself grateful to be a stray."

Tears welled up in her eyes as they laughed together.

"Let me support you so all those who rely on you can continue their orbit around you."

Kick sighed and looked around. She tucked some errant hairs into her hood.

Thomas jostled her hands. "What?"

"I love this."

"I still hear a *but*."

She shook her head. "As much as I love warm and attentive Thomas, I still have burns from your hot-and-cold routine. How do I know it's really gone so quickly?"

"Ah." She gutted him. Thomas pulled Kick close and leaned his forehead against hers. "It hasn't been fast for me, though you're right about the back and forth. It's a battle I've been waging inside myself since we met. I'm used to being alone, Kick. The icy part of me is a protective measure. I can't promise I'll never revert to it since this is new for me too. I can promise I've thought hard about what I want, and you're it. Can you call me on my bullshit if I do shut down? Can you see my request as proof I've changed?"

"I can do that." Kick wrapped her arms around his waist and tipped her head back to speak. "And what do you want from me?"

"From you?" He reached into his coat pocket and pulled out the last present. "How about this for a start?"

Kick carefully unwrapped the box like she'd done with the first one. She opened the lid and lifted the bracelet within. "Oh, Thomas," she gasped. "It's stunning. Truly. Are these... This is your birthstone, isn't it?"

He nodded. "With yours." Her reaction thrilled him, but he wondered how she would take the meaning of it.

"Wow." She clicked her cheek and observed, "You know, this

roping design between the gems reminds me of the old hand-fasting traditions. It's beautiful."

Thomas laughed at his short-sightedness and should've known she'd see it. "It is." The jeweler had created a braided effect from rose gold, wrapping around fire opals and moonstones. "When Deana told me you needed a commitment, I knew I did too."

He clasped the ropelike bracelet around her wrist. "I'm a modern scientist, but the old ways have always held a special appeal." *My ways*, he meant.

Kick cocked her head to the side. "What exactly are you saying?"

Here was his chance. Either way, Thomas knew he would jump off one hell of a cliff when he eventually let the cat out of the bag. If he *knew* she loved him deeply already, it would make the leap easier. "Deana mentioned a class ring, but I don't have anything like that to give you." Thomas fingered the bracelet. "Can you consider this an ask for tomorrow—like a mature version of a class ring?"

"Are you asking me to go steady, Thomas?"

"Grown-up going steady? Sure." He grinned before bringing Kick's fingers to his lips and kissing them. "I wanted to give you something so you knew I'd changed. I want more than a casual arrangement with you." Kick beamed and Thomas kissed her nose. "We suck at casual."

"Word." Kick's shoulders bounced as she laughed.

As a rule, Thomas never ruminated on what he wanted. He had goals. He helped others. That was it. After speaking with Deana, one word announced itself like a speaker blasting in his head, telling him to grab ahold before it slipped away—*home*. "Without my noticing—or it could've been by design, I don't know—life had become a dark and cold, postfamilial existence." He pushed Kick's hood back and slid his hands to the back of her neck, running his thumbs along her jawline. "Would you be my home for now? Wherever you are, I want to be with y'all. With you and your amazing kids. One day at a time? We can figure out the details as we go."

"You know, you're more than an adopted stranger." Kick placed her hand on Thomas's chest. "If you're saying what I think you are, you've become my heart too." Her fingers traced up to his shoulders. "It's funny how you mentioned Atlas. I've noticed a melancholy about you, like you carry a great weight around. But every so often, I see your weight lift. Sweetheart, if I can ease those burdens at all, I promise I'll do what I can. If it's an opinion, my talents, or my body you need, I would be honored to be the soft place where you rest." She lifted her wrist. "I'll gladly wear this as long as you're through with thinking temporarily. I don't need big promises, but I don't want to make this jump with you if you already plan to leave."

Thomas remembered how angry Kick had become with the things he'd said after the gala. He stroked her cheek and tucked a curl behind her ear. "There's no expiration date for me. It's just… I thought this might seem fast. It was inappropriate to ask for a commitment when I don't even know if you want one. One day at a time seems fair though. Don't you think?"

She unbuttoned his big coat and snuggled inside as the wind practically whipped the flaps back together. "Silly man. So we're going steady grown-up style?"

"Exactly." Since they were making vows of a sort, he asked, "What do you want from me?" He listened to Kick breathe while he waited on her answer. Thomas marveled at how quickly their heartbeats synced.

"I've had champions before—men who emotionally tucked me behind their bodies and kept me out of the line of fire psychologically. It was necessary then, but not anymore. I want you to walk with me. When needed, you can stand against my back as we fight like hell together." A fierce, challenging gaze gave way to the familiar signs of insecurity as she worried her cheek.

"My butterfly." He brushed back the curls on her face.

"You do get it." She stretched up and kissed Thomas under what would henceforth be their oak tree. "Thank you for this."

"Anything for you." Feelings this deep had eluded him for so long Thomas couldn't remember the last time his heart had been filled with such gratitude. He knew Kick had come to his house with casual intentions. He had hoped he could convince her of more, even the smallest of commitments before their weekend ended. To find out they were of the same mind so quickly was a gift. He led her back to the path with their hands linked and checked the time on his new watch. "Good, I can still get his exercise time in."

"Whose?"

"Patience, baby. We're almost there."

I'M FEELING GOOD

KICK

We emerged from the woods facing a large working stable. "We're not on your property anymore."

"No, but all this was a plantation back in the day. My place was what some would call the second house while this would be the big house."

As Thomas finished speaking, a large Georgian-style home came into view down a lane to my left. "And your brother lives here now?"

"Wh-why would you… No. Joe won't leave Virginia." He lifted his chin and pointed at the stable. "I want you to meet Ed. In the stable."

We turned a corner and faced the center aisle of an upscale barn. The heavy wooden support beams and design let me know it was old but had been recently renovated. It had what looked like all the modern trappings of an equestrian complex. Box stalls lined both sides. Thomas strode ahead as if pulled by a magnet.

After hearing the same whinny for the third time, I realized the horse called out to him.

"Coming, buddy. Keep your shoes on." He stopped in front of a box, and a gorgeous black horse stuck his head out and knocked Thomas hard on the shoulder. "Sorry about being late. I was distracted." He rubbed the horse's muzzle and chin like he was on autopilot, then his hand moved up to scratch his ears. "There's someone here to meet you, Ed."

I sidled next to him and waved at the horse like an idiot.

"Kick, meet Eddie. My horse. He's the reason I had to wait to come back. The stable wasn't ready for him until this morning."

I stepped closer to Eddie and let him smell me, making our introductions. He quickly couldn't get enough of my hair and nipped at the curls. "He doesn't seem skittish at all."

"Nah." Thomas pet him some more. "He's a brave fellow, but I'll warn you, he's a lot like his namesake."

I lifted my eyebrows in inquiry, "Which would be…"

"His full name is Edward Teach… Harrison."

"You named your horse after the pirate Black Beard?" I burst into a laugh, then reined it in, in case loud noises startled the animal or one of the others.

Thomas lifted an eyebrow and flashed me a rakish grin. "For a good reason."

Ed began to bump my hand, so I pet his chin, noting the wisps of longish black hair hanging from it and smiled. His coat was inky black with a small, thin star on his forehead. Eddie's mane and chin "beard" were tipped with auburn, creating an ombre effect. I knew women who paid good money for hair with the same look. Add in his dark chocolate eyes and long lashes, and Eddie was one hell of a handsome guy. "He has the beard, but he's way too pretty for a pirate." Then the horse bit my hair and pulled. "Ow!" I immediately grabbed my head. Maybe looks were deceiving.

"Enough. That's hair, not hay." He turned to me with an

apologetic pout. "Sorry, baby. He proved my point though. This fella takes what he wants." Thomas slipped Eddie's bridle off its hook, unlatched the door, and stepped inside. "Time to stretch those legs, big guy."

He leaned over the door and said, "Don't worry, we're not riding today. He's still antsy from the drive and new digs. We're just going to burn off his piss and vinegar in the ring."

"Okay. Are there treats for him somewhere? What if I brought him one?"

"Good idea. Ed's into carrots." Thomas tipped his head. "The office is behind us on the left. Look for a woman with long silver hair, named Betsy. She can find one. Or one of the stable hands."

I never ran into anyone, but I found a tray of carrots and took a large one. Seeing the obvious affection between the horse and his human, I knew Eddie and I needed to become good friends. Bribing him was completely within my moral parameters.

When I turned back to the center aisle, I heard a clip-clopping and saw Thomas and Eddie already at the far end of the barn. They veered left once outside, the late afternoon sun shone golden upon them both, making them look like they were about to star in a Western. The coat made sense now.

I hustled out of the barn and joined them before they disappeared into a building I didn't know. The wind whipped as I crossed the threshold, stealing my breath.

"Isn't there a manège around here?" I called out over the howling sound.

"Yes, but he prefers the outdoors. Ed grew up wild."

Thomas exercised his horse while I leaned on the fence and watched. A petite but solid woman with a swagger as big as John Wayne's and a silver ponytail waving behind her approached me. "Are you a friend of the professor's?"

"I am." I held out my hand. "Kick McKenna. Are you Betsy?" The wrinkles around her eyes and her hair gave the initial impression of being much older than me. On closer inspection, I guessed her age at no more than five years my senior. Her whiskey-colored irises sparkled with the joy of someone who had spent their life doing what they loved.

"I am. Did he mention me?" She seemed a tad smitten, and I couldn't blame her.

"Only your name, but you have the look of someone who runs the place."

Betsy's laugh was loud, rough, and warm. "I like you. My husband says he pays the bills and I do everything else." She dipped her head toward the center of the arena. "Our new boarder is quite the looker." At first I thought she referred to Thomas and considered her brazen for mentioning her husband, then immediately ogling my man. *Mine. Shit.* A pleasant shiver traveled up my spine as I realized I could make the claim now.

"Oh, you mean Eddie? He is gorgeous. I just met him."

We watched them work for several minutes. The deep, gold light kissed Thomas's skin and added to his cowboy effect. The light bounced off Eddie's shiny coat as he circled Thomas, and I pulled out my phone to take pictures. Seeing Thomas work comfortably with his horse and Eddie's trust in him stirred my libido. Theirs was a rugged, primal connection to the past, more real than any of the folksy traditions I grew up practicing. I wanted him. Again.

Jaysus, when did I become wanton? I stopped clicking and checked the time. About four hours ago, I guessed. I crossed my arms on the rail and set my chin on them, watching their magic unfold.

The duster shifted around Thomas's body, egged on by a petulant wind, making him look like a wizard performing magic tricks. Eddie's attention focused solely on his human stunned me. I knew from experience the horse was right—Thomas inspired trust from those who held his loyalty and his love. It was an honor to possess it. My desire to please the man matched the animal's.

I murmured, "The way his mane and tail flow in the wind, he reminds me of the Corolla horses." Perhaps it was the influence of Thomas's earlier comment about Ed being a little wild. I thought it meant his initial owners didn't take good care of him.

Bonnie turned her face to me, puzzled. "Well, he is. The professor adopted him from the Wild Horse Fund. Didn't you know?"

I shook my head, amazed at yet another golden nugget of insight into this amazing man. *My* amazing man. "It's been a fun surprise." Who was this man who I suspected had been a soldier, considering his knowledge of weaponry and the way he carried himself. I decided to ask him about it soon. Along the way, he'd had and lost a family, became a scientist, an expert dancer, a renovator, played guitar, and now was an equestrian? The last part might have to do with his family's business, but when did he have time for the Wild Horse Fund? At the gala, he'd mentioned real estate people who worked for him. Again, it could relate to something he'd inherited. As I did the math though, the answers didn't compute. It buzzed in the back of my mind for the rest of the day. I needed to ask Thomas about it but was afraid he'd change the subject, like he did any time I asked him about what was in Bordeaux.

As my Gran used to say, "Careful what you wish for, Katie darling."

"Best... view... ever... Don't... want it... to end."

We had put on a movie after a simple dinner. However, Thomas's naked weekend plans made it impossible to hang out together and watch *New Year's Eve* to the end. It didn't take long before we were thoroughly aroused again. Thomas planted himself squarely on the center cushion of his sofa and pulled me onto his lap. From just a straddle, he moved my hips up and down, my sensitive clit once again ignited by the velvety friction of his cock. My head fell back as I gave in to the sensation, and he entered me. This wasn't like the slow and delicious time we'd spent in the afternoon. This was a no-holds-barred, libidinous screw from the bottom. My job was to hold on and enjoy the ride.

"This… right here… It's heaven." Thomas purred as my breasts bounced against his face, my core ready to explode.

"Same," I gasped.

He lifted my breasts closer to his face, fingers massaging, kisses hectic. "I love your tits."

My head buzzed from the fluidity of our movements, his tongue on my skin, the scent of Thomas's woody aftershave, the sheen of perspiration developing across his forehead, and the intensity of his piercing stare. I didn't dare to look away from the unsaid words he communicated.

"Please, Thomas." The pressure became too much.

With an obliging hum, he lowered his hands, one circling my clit, the other clamped to my hip as he drove us home with more force than I thought possible. The waves came fast and took me over the edge. I screamed my ecstasy and brought him along with a "shit, yes" of his own.

When we fell back to earth, I collapsed into his neck, nipping at my favorite spot under his jaw. My vocabulary had taken a hiatus. As it eventually returned, the only sentence I managed burst out of me as a gasp.

"I really, really love your penis."

A delicious rumble came from Thomas's chest, reaching to the depths of my core. "You want to high-five, or something?"

"Maybe." I laughed and let my forehead fall to his. "You're very good at this."

"Baby, you've got me. You don't have to stroke my ego."

"Well… I might be orgasm drunk."

"Mmm. Good. Let's keep you this way." He brushed his fingers across my back as our breathing matched and slowed. This was more than satisfaction, more than love. We were worshipping each other. I hoped he felt the same. Our coming together honored our past lives along with our present and future. Whether on a bed, a sofa, or the grass, I believed whenever we made love, that place would be an altar of thanksgiving.

Something had shifted earlier when we made a commitment under the tree. If we had been casually dating, my heart would've remained shielded to a degree. I knew I wouldn't have entered this space so freely. Our commitment changed us fundamentally, making our expression of love visceral and celebratory.

"What are you thinking?" he murmured into my ear. "Your smile's infectious."

"This isn't what I expected. I didn't allow myself to hope for so much, Thomas."

"Feel the same, baby." He shifted us back down to the blanket on the cushions and covered us with a second one. Thomas brushed a curl off my face and studied me intently as he listened.

"I love your home too."

"You make it a home." He held my braceleted wrist and kissed it. "Let me show you the estate as soon as we can get away."

"Ooh. Can't wait." My eyes were half-lidded, enjoying the sensations of his light kisses and touches along my skin. I didn't know what I craved more, the physical sensations or listening to Thomas finally open up. It seemed like he might be on the verge of telling me everything, but I didn't dare push. I kept up the easier questions, the ones still letting me see inside his heart. "You like old houses?"

"I do. This one's about the same age as the one in Virginia but only because our original house burned in the mid-eighteen hundreds. The estate itself goes back to the seventeenth century."

"All this time in your family?" When he nodded, I added, "So, you're a Son of the American Revolution. How cool is that?"

Thomas dropped my wrist and shrugged as the darkness I thought he'd vanquished from his face reappeared. When it cleared, he seemed distant. It unsettled me. Hell, had I pushed too far? If so, I wasn't sure what I'd said.

"It's all ridiculous."

"Don't you keep the heritage designation though? You mentioned how part of the house is a museum."

"Sure, for educational purposes. It's mostly for locals and schoolchildren."

I reached up to caress his cheek. Even if Thomas thought little of himself and his family, they fascinated me. "My heritage feels like it's someplace else." I thought about it for a minute and giggled. "Though you know what the family in Ireland calls us?"

"Uh-uh. What?"

"The Americans. For the longest time, it made me mad. Then I realized they were right. You feel more authentic, I guess."

"You were born here. Raised here. Y'all are as American as me." Thomas kissed my temple and stood, leaving me chilly despite the plush. "Getting water. Want one?"

"Yes, please." He'd given me one helluva ride.

I rolled onto my stomach, propped on my forearms, and watched him retreat to the kitchen. The light from the refrigerator put his perfect ass in silhouette. Movement as his muscles did the simplest task, hypnotized me. When he bumped the door closed and returned, strong thighs walked with purpose as he carried our glasses. Shredded abs and shoulders remained tall and set back and held an air of pride I hadn't seen in him before. Thomas padded into the den like a lover providing for his beloved. The knowledge empowered me.

He sat on the edge of the cushion and handed me a glass. I took a sip and moved to sit up. "Wait, baby. Stay there." He set our waters on the coffee table, next to my glasses. Then he glided his hands along my back. The chill from his fingers set gentle goose bumps loose, but the slight temperature drop felt great. Thomas leaned over me and purred into my ear. "Your back is exquisite." My mind jumped to a sarcastic snip about back fat, and I shook my head, rebuking the stubborn, self-deprecating thoughts.

His hands moved to my ass with light sweeps, barely touching my skin. "How's this?"

A warmth formed in my core, but it wasn't from another orgasm build. This type of change had been forming recently, along with a pleasant buzz, right before my skin glowed. I dropped my head into my hands and willed it to stay away. Until I met with an aura reader, I couldn't let anyone know about this. What would Thomas think of it? He was a scientist, for feck's sake. There was no way he'd accept my woo-woo aura even if it did make me feel better. I guess I still had a secret too.

"Get out of your head, baby. I feel you going far away."

"Don't worry, sweets. It's all good." Thomas tickled my sides and broke the hum. I wiggled away before giving him a playful stink eye even though I wanted to thank him. "You..."

A cheesy grin flashed across his face. "Me?"

"Yes, you." I waved my hands in front of his body. "You hypnotize me from behind with your ass divots, then you do the same on the way back with your V-shaped muscle things. Do you know they make me forget my name?" I arched my brow. "You've made me wanton."

He pulled me against him as he barked a quick laugh. "Sounds good to me, as long as you keep making those sexy-as-hell noises. My plan is working."

The movie ended and Thomas's music came on. We finished our waters and snuggled back into the blankets while listening to Nina Simone's "I'm Feeling Good."

Another deep sound of approval came from Thomas. "No better song for right now." We stayed in this lovers'-pillow-talk haze until the song ended.

Then he jostled my shoulders and asked, "I have ass divots?"

"You know you do." I sighed. "We used to call them dancer's dents, and yours are spectacular."

All silliness left his face as he pulled me into him. "Remember the first time you came here, when you made the smoothies?"

"Sure."

"You hypnotized me then, you minx. I heard you singing as I came down the stairs with my suitcase. Then I saw you dancing in your yoga pants and was gobsmacked. I stood there, staring like a creeper. Talk about forgetting my name. I almost forgot about my commitments and begged you to let me fuck you for days. Weeks."

"No kidding?" My jaw dropped at his confession. I bit my lip, recalling how he came up behind me and led us around the kitchen in a dance. I was too afraid to do more than enjoy the surprise. Too guilt-ridden over falling for someone new. "Neither of us were ready then."

"True. You had me mesmerized all the way to the airport though."

I tipped my head back and laughed. "Aww. I love this side of you. You know, your sweetness is as hot as your body."

"No, darlin'. Yours is."

I drifted off in Thomas's arms, listening to the rest of his playlist. The sound of his own melodic heartbeat and his masculine scent were the last things I noted, along with the feeling of rightness in my world.

A MEEK DAWN HAD BROKEN AS GRAY LIGHT CLUNG TO THE remnants of nighttime, reluctant to leave its dark embrace. My gaze lifted to Thomas on a horse, in an old-fashioned coat, with tall riding boots and what I could swear were authentic breeches —not modern equestrian gear either. His jaw set and his brow narrowed as his eyes continuously scanned the scene. He looked younger, barely a man.

He seemed to be heading to a Revolutionary War reenactment, and I wondered if this was another of his many hobbies. How many hobbies could a man in his midthirties balance?

I didn't understand why Thomas wore his inky black hair long and queued.

A chilly mist surrounded us and my arms. Higher areas of the landscape twinkled from beams of young sunlight touching the frost, morphing the dark foliage into a bright silver. Thomas's breath puffed steam on his exhales.

His horse huffed steam puffs too, antsy to be on the move, and I wondered where they were going. I turned as a muffled sound startled me. A company of men appeared out of nowhere. Most of them were behind Thomas, waiting on a muddy road. They were close enough to smell the wet dirt and sweat, but I couldn't hear any words aside from grunts or murmurs.

The keen sense of an emotionally charged atmosphere overwhelmed my reason. Thomas and the men exuded an anxious anticipation. Some vibrated with fear. The worst, to me, were the few who seemed genuinely happy, almost aroused. A shiver slithered over my skin.

Recognizing a lucid dream, I tried futilely to wake myself up. I couldn't move beyond twisting my torso as my feet stayed glued to the ground. I couldn't speak to anyone either. Panicked butterflies took flight in my stomach. Two more men on horses pulled up to Thomas and stopped short in front of me. My hands flew up to my face out of fear the animals would trample or bite me. This was too real. Again, I tried to call out, but no words left my throat.

The three riders led a march, their horses trotting in unison. Men in single file passed on both sides of me within a hairbreadth. Heavens, they smelled. I didn't think any of them had brushed their teeth ever. Their puff-of-steam breaths were deadly.

Before I knew what was happening or what I should do about it, shots filled my ears. It sounded different from anything I'd heard before, but I knew it was a type of gunfire. My ears wanted to burst from the reverb, and I slapped my hands over them to muffle the noise. The movement caused a soldier to knock into my elbow, twisting me to the right. On the other side, another man bumped me again and twisted me to the left. It continued with each passing man, turning me into a human pendulum. The perception of falling overtook me, and I begged to be set free from the horrible sense of fear.

It was common for me to have a terrible time waking from lucid dreaming. My head was partially relieved as I woke but also confused about my location. I was in a big, comfy bed, and someone shook me gently.

It was Thomas. My Thomas.

We were in his bed, in his bedroom. Rays of new sunlight mixed with the gray, predawn light in his room, like it had in the dreamscape. I grabbed my head and bolted to sitting.

"You're not a Son of the American Revolution," I declared, half-awake and raking my fingers through my hair. "You're a *veteran.*"

Considering the light in the bedroom matched the light in my dream, my head stayed trapped in the fog between both, but the oddest thing came to me as clear as the sun. Thomas hadn't dismissed me for saying something so preposterous. He hadn't reassured me or lifted his eyebrow in his mischievous way to tease me. His face filled with terror, like he'd been caught. He sighed and closed his eyes in resignation as he bowed his head.

From under the covers, I jumped to the corner of the bed, despite my lack of clothes. I scrambled to my knees, crouching in a protective ball. I wasn't steady enough to run away, but I needed distance. From him and the clear look of guilt on his face. A chill ran through me, the shiver rattling my bones. It wasn't from the cool morning air against my naked skin. It was the recognition of truth I saw all over him.

What did Liam say I had? A secret radar? The murky soup of

dreamland wore off, and I knew, somehow, I'd discovered Thomas's deepest, darkest secret. Here was the shadow behind his eyes. Here was his fear. The math of his life hadn't added up because the sum was unthinkable for a normal person. Take away what everyone thought was impossible, and it made sense.

"JaysusMaryandJoseph! Am I right?"

Thomas dropped his head as if the vertebrae in his neck had disappeared.

He had to be hundreds of years old.

How does something like that happen?

To be continued...

Thank you for taking this wild ride with Kick and Thomas. To read the blockbuster finale of their journey, *Kick Home*, scan the QR code below for ordering information.

FOLLOW KALLYN

You can find Kallyn here:
   Website: kallynjones.com
   Facebook: KallynJonesAuthor
   Instagram: KallynJonesWriteNow

If you have a minute to review *Kick Back* at your retailer and/or favorite review site, it would make my day. Book reviews (even short ones) are the best way to spread the word about Kick and Thomas to other readers like you.

Listen to the *Kick Back Tunes* playlist on Spotify! You can find the link to it on my website.

ACKNOWLEDGMENTS

- To my fabulous editors Jenny, Lisa, and D.A. There is nothing better than making you laugh and giving you a real word that's new to you. I can't think about what a mess my story was before your amazing minds touched it.
- To the vibrant writing community in the Triangle. Thank you for your inspiration and support. Hugs and squeezes to Laura, Annie, Jennifer, Renae, Sheon, Jamie, Patti, Beth, Jeanne, Stuart, Crista, Jake, Nancy, and Barbara. Writer friends are the best.
- To my friends and family who have been so supportive during this new venture of mine. Special kisses go to Mom, Linda, Joye, and Shannon. Thank you for trying to hawk my grown-up fairytale wherever you go!
- Finally, to my beloved men, W, C, N, and J. Y'all may be messy as hell, but I can't imagine life without you. I'm forever grateful for you love and support.

ABOUT THE AUTHOR

Kallyn Jones returned to her roots as an author after a successful career as a brand specialist. She writes about sexy, down-to-earth characters and the complicated families they make along the way. She delights in placing heroes and heroines in unusual places. She believes the happily-ever-afters that are fought for the hardest are also the sweetest.

An autoimmune warrior for most of her life, she's also a mom to an autoimmune kid. She champions those who often find themselves flat on their backs for days or weeks at a time, through no fault of their own. The Southern Oaks series is dedicated to them.

Kallyn lives in her adopted hometown of Raleigh, North Carolina with her own hero, their three sons, and a princess dog. In her spare time, she enjoys trail walking, digital painting, and testing new recipes that fit her dietary regimen. She's proud to say her fellas usually love these experimental dishes. Usually.

www.kallynjones.com

9 781737 709794